Rose's Redemption

To Jill,
Enjoy! Blessings!
Donna L H Smith

Rose's Redemption

Donna L.H. Smith

© 2018 Donna L.H. Smith

All rights reserved. No part of this publication may be reproduced, stored in a retrieval system, or transmitted in any form or by any means—electronic, mechanical, photo-copying, recording, or otherwise—without the prior written permission of the publisher. The only exception is brief quotations in printed reviews. For information address Hartline Literary Agency, 123 Queenston Drive; Pittsburgh, Pennsylvania 15235.

The characters and events in this book are fictional, and any resemblance to actual persons or events is coincidental or is a fictionalized account of true events.

Scripture quotations from The Authorized (King James) Version.
Public Domain.

ISBN: 9781728604268

*How do I thank the Living God who loves me
so much that he's given me
the grace to continue this work?
I dedicate this story to my precious Savior, Jesus Christ.
As always, I give you the glory.*

"Once again author Donna Smith has captured us and transported us to the old west. Her ability to weave a compelling story, populated with lovable characters is one of her strongest gifts. She's definitely an author to put on your must-read list."

– Edie Melson, Award-winning author
& Director of the Blue Ridge Mountains
Christian Writers Conference

Table of Contents

Chapter One 1
Chapter Two 6
Chapter Three 11
Chapter Four 16
Chapter Five 21
Chapter Six 26
Chapter Seven 30
Chapter Eight 35
Chapter Nine 40
Chapter Ten 47
Chapter Eleven 52
Chapter Twelve 57
Chapter Thirteen 61
Chapter Fourteen 66
Chapter Fifteen 71
Chapter Sixteen 77
Chapter Seventeen 81
Chapter Eighteen 85
Chapter Nineteen 90
Chapter Twenty 95
Chapter Twenty-One 104
Chapter Twenty-Two 107
Chapter Twenty-Three 112
Chapter Twenty-Four 116

Chapter Twenty-Five 121
Chapter Twenty-Six 125
Chapter Twenty-Seven 130
Chapter Twenty-Eight 135
Chapter Twenty-Nine 140
Chapter Thirty 147
Chapter Thirty-One 152
Chapter Thirty-Two 157
Chapter Thirty-Three 163
Chapter Thirty-Four 169
Chapter Thirty-Five 175
Chapter Thirty-Six 182
Chapter Thirty-Seven 187
Chapter Thirty-Eight 194
Chapter Thirty-Nine 200
Chapter Forty 207
Chapter Forty-One 216
Chapter Forty-Two 223
Chapter Forty-Three 228
Chapter Forty-Four 233
Chapter Forty-Five 239
Chapter Forty-Six 244
Chapter Forty-Seven 249
Chapter Forty-Eight 254
Chapter Forty-Nine 259
Chapter Fifty 263
Chapter Fifty-One 268
Chapter Fifty-Two 276
Chapter Fifty-Three 284
Chapter Fifty-Four 290
Chapter Fifty-Five 294
Chapter Fifty-Six 299
Chapter Fifty-Seven 303

Chapter Fifty-Eight 308
Chapter Fifty-Nine................................312
Chapter Sixty 315
Chapter Sixty-One 320
Chapter Sixty-Two 325
Chapter Sixty-Three 330

Acknowledgements 337
About The Author 339

Chapter One

*New Boston, Kansas
Late September 1871*

It can't be him!

Rose Rhodes hoped she was mistaken.

She tripped over a railroad tie as she walked toward The Pioneer Store. If he recognized her, she'd be ruined. She'd have to leave town. This was home, more than anywhere else. The excitement—the exhilaration of building something worthwhile, the camaraderie. She'd made a real friend for the first time in her life—Meghan Gallagher—and escaped the influence of her mother, the Chesapeake Madam.

Jake Thomas left The Pioneer Store and headed her way. She'd covered with makeup the small mole on her cheek and let her hair curl over it. But even though the bonnet partially covered her face, she didn't trust herself to meet his gaze.

He tipped his hat. "Howdy, miss."

She nodded, not realizing she still held her breath until after he'd passed. Exhaling slowly, she finally reached the comfort of the store.

Michael Nieman smiled broadly as she closed the door.

Rose let out another breath. "If you've got number five buttons in white, I'll take ten." She went to the counter and waited while Mr. Nieman looked in the button drawer.

"Here you are, Miss Rhodes. Five cents."

She pulled out a nickel from her reticule.

"How's Doc Allison? I haven't seen him lately." Mr. Nieman placed the buttons on the counter, then counted out ten.

She smiled. "He's fine—just left on one of his 'fishing' trips."

Mr. Nieman humphed. "Does he even know one end of the pole from another?"

Rose giggled. "He likes to think so." She pulled her handbag strings tight.

The storekeeper handed her the small paper bag. "So, he left you in charge? How long have you been working for him now?"

She tilted her head to one side. "About four months."

He nodded. "Ah, yes. That's about how long you've been in town, isn't it?"

Well, eight, if you counted when she went by her real name, Rosalie O'Roarke. She wasn't about to tell him that, though. "Yes. I got here the day after the tornado and went right over to see if I could help. It was wonderful to see how the town pulled together to rebuild." She picked up the sack and turned to leave. "You can hardly tell what buildings were even damaged. The town has recovered well."

"You take care of yourself, Miss Rhodes. Thanks for stopping in."

She smiled and left.

Her light-hearted moment faded when she thought of Jake. He'd beaten her to a pulp earlier this year, then fled town. Now it seemed he was back. *Please, God, don't let him find me.* He'd gotten more violent with her the last few weeks before the beating. The last time, she thought she'd die, but instead, she healed and found a new friend in Meghan Gallagher.

She crossed Main Street near Second, knowing safety was close by. The gunfights that seemed to go on forever finally ceased when James Riley left town. No one knew where he went. He shot the last victim a month ago—a friend of Billy Bailey's—before sneaking out of town. The sheriff searched—but couldn't find him.

As she reached Baldwin's Boardinghouse at First and Pine Streets, she let out a long breath. She was safe.

⌒

Doctor Scott Allison watched Rose leave, observing her through the window near the door. She'd only been working for him a few months, yet she was completely trustworthy. Not only was she a quick study, he was astounded how drastically she'd changed her appearance from dance hall girl to respectable. His mind drifted back six months, when she'd been badly beaten by one of her regular customers. Maybe that caused her to think about changing her life. And she'd done it, with not many people the wiser. Meghan knew, and of course that cowboy of hers. Maybe Olivia Baldwin, the boardinghouse owner, and possibly her cook. Hopefully not many more, for her sake. The more who knew, the more likely it would be that her secret would slip out.

He let out a long breath as he thought of Meghan. How had he truly mistaken his feelings for her? And hers for him? Thinking he loved her, he now knew it was more like a crush. He'd claimed her more as someone to admire and adore, rather than a helpmate, someone to love and who would return his love. His conscience pricked him again as he thought of trying to force her into marrying him before he treated her cowboy. He'd been hurt by her rejection, so desperate. Rose had set him straight by showing him how wrong he was—and she'd threatened to quit unless he released Meghan from her promise. Rose's boldness made him respect her even more. Meghan said she'd forgiven him, yet she kept her distance. He still needed to check in with Wilcox occasionally, although the cowboy was healing well now. What if Wilcox had died? He shuddered to think what might have happened. Meghan would have never been able to trust or forgive him. He packed up his fishing gear.

Could God ever absolve him?

⁓

Jake Thomas entered the Silver Spike and sauntered up to the bar, running a hand through his hair. Where was Rosie? He missed her.

"Hey Sam, where's Rosie O'Rourke? I didn't see her when I got back yesterday. Was it her day off?"

The bartender shot him a puzzled look. "You haven't been around for a while, have you?"

"What difference does that make? Is she here or not?" His blood began to boil.

Sam turned away, picking up a glass he'd washed to wipe dry. "Well, if you'd been here, you'd know she left town right after the twister."

That's right, an early summer tornado had struck New Boston. Jake had high-tailed it up to Kansas City to evade the sheriff after knocking Rosie around, but he'd heard about it.

"Where'd she go?" This was maddening.

Sam shrugged. "No one knows. The girls found her room empty within two days of the storm. With so much chaos, no one missed her."

"She didn't tell anyone where she was going? Not even you?"

"Nope." Sam turned again to place the glass on a shelf. "I couldn't believe it when the girls said she'd gone. She had it good here."

"Is there anyone I could talk to who might know where she went?"

Sam rested his chin on his thumb a moment. "Well, I don't know for sure. After you left town, the Doc took care of her, and I seem to remember he asked the school teacher to help. They might know something."

"So, Doctor Allison is still here? Who's the school teacher?"

"Doc's still here. I think the teacher's name is Miss Gallagher. I believe she's staying at the Baldwin Boardinghouse."

"Thanks, Sam. Give me a whiskey while you're at it, will ya?"

He'd find Rosie if it was the last thing he ever did.

Chapter Two

Scott dismounted when he reached the small stream about ten miles west of New Boston, his favorite place to go. He chuckled at the thought of calling it his "fishing" spot, though sometimes he did catch a few. Mainly, he came to relax and get away from the endless stream of patients and maladies.

Throwing his saddlebags over his shoulder, he reached for the reins to tie around a nearby tree at the stream's edge. He unfastened his pole and his wicker tackle box, which held his lures. He set them on the ground while he loosened his picnic basket, full of canned goods.

This would be a wonderful time away. He set up his tent and straightened out his blanket inside. Now that the gunfights had seemingly ended, he planned on relaxing a few days. Rose could handle anything short of major surgery, and hopefully there would be no more gunshot wounds for a while now that James Riley had left town.

Even though he wasn't much of a camper, he enjoyed being outdoors.

"Is that you, Rose?" Olivia Baldwin called out as she entered the parlor.

"Yes, I'm h-home now." She sat on the couch to catch her breath.

Olivia brought in a tray with tea and muffins. "Are you all right? You look upset."

"Jake's back in town."

"What? Are you sure? You saw him? Was it really him? Where was he? What was he doing? Did you report him to the sheriff?"

Olivia always talked way too much when she got excited or nervous. Rose had learned that early on.

She reached for a cup of tea, her fingers trembling. "He passed right by me. I thought for certain he'd recognize me."

Olivia took a sip of her tea, then placed a hand on Rose's arm a moment. "What are you going to do?"

"Nothing. Just try to stay out of his way." She tasted the brew and let the steam warm her nose.

"Surely the sheriff ought to know he's back. He should be arrested for what he did to you last spring."

"I don't want people knowing who I am. I've changed my life. If anyone discovers me, I'll be either thrown out or forced back into my old life. That's the last thing I want. I love it here." She set the cup back on its saucer.

"Well, you know that I agree with your new life. And you have Meghan, Duncan, and the doctor's support, as well."

At the mention of Scott, heat traveled up Rose's neck. She smiled.

"And how is the doctor? Did he leave on his fishing trip?" Olivia's eyes twinkled, her smile knowing.

"Yes, this afternoon."

"How long will he be gone?" Olivia took a sip of tea.

"About three days. He's been so tired, what with all the shootings... and the large flow of patients since—especially with the town's growth." Rose savored a long draft of tea.

"Thankfully, the gunfights seem to be all over now."

"Yes. I'm grateful, too."

"You have feelings for Doctor Allison, don't you?"

Rose stirred her tea before taking another long drink.

"I thought so. Is he over Meghan yet?"

Rose set her cup down on the table, then folded her hands. "I don't know. I think he's trying. He knows what he did was wrong, and I believe he's trying to put his fondness for her behind him."

"Well, I think you two would be perfect for each other."

"We're so opposite. He's educated, I'm not."

"You're good for him, Rose, and he needs you."

"Yes, he does. But I want him to *love* me. Jake *needed* me. I want to love and be loved."

"*Do* you love him?"

"I think so. Ever since he took care of me last spring, I've had great affection for him beyond what I knew I should. I've never really felt this way before. He was so gentle and kind in not only his doctoring, but how he spoke to me. No man has ever treated me with respect before."

Olivia set her empty cup back on the tray a little harder than normal. The cup rattled in the saucer. "If he hadn't made such a fool of himself over Meghan, I'd like him a lot better."

"Everyone deserves a second chance."

"You're right. But he..."

The front door opened and latched closed. They turned to look. No more time to try to persuade Olivia. She knew Meghan and Duncan didn't usually like to hear her talk about Scott, either. Just her work, but not who she worked with.

"Hello in there." Meghan and Duncan moved into the parlor. Duncan plopped in the wingback. Meghan sat beside Rose.

Rose leaned over to take a closer look at the cowboy. "Duncan, are you all right? You look pale. Did you exhaust yourself? You need to take care of yourself. You'll heal faster."

He smiled sheepishly. "With my nursemaid here..." His head tilted toward Meghan. "It's hard to fatigue myself, but I may have pushed a little too much today." He ran a hand through his hair. A stray lock of his straight nearly black hair flopped into his eyes and he pushed it back.

"He wanted to go to our tree by the creek. It's been weeks. I couldn't deny him." Meghan grabbed a small blanket and spread it over his legs.

"Are we still getting together tomorrow?" Rose continued her private tutoring lessons with Meghan on Saturday mornings. Her friend also taught the de Campo children in the evenings. Their mother, Luisa, felt they should be educated outside the school, since they were Mexicans. She was afraid of prejudice. The children were smart and grasped what they learned quickly.

The de Campos had also come to the boardinghouse the day after the tornado. Their house was demolished, and Luisa's husband had died in the storm. She'd been a great help to Olivia.

Meghan said there were eighteen students in the town's school this year. Ten more from the eight she'd started with. And with the town still growing, more could be expected to join school now that class had started again.

The Catholic church had graciously lent the school a railroad car for the previous spring's one-month school term. At present, the school met in the Catholic church itself, until plans for a school building could be finalized. The town was growing quickly. With the Santa Fe railhead in New Boston, railroad executives expected explosive growth.

Meghan smiled. "Yes, we are, if you're up to it."

"I'll be ready. I love learning." She wanted to put every appearance of being an uneducated former dance hall girl behind her.

Scott gathered up his basket and pole and started toward the stream, whistling as he went. He'd have time to think. These times away always refreshed him. He'd leave town exhausted and return ready to meet whatever medical challenges came his way.

A shadow from a bird in flight fell over him. Probably a crow. He looked up and raised his pole to shield his eyes as he continued walking.

His foot fell. His leg twisted violently. The bone snapped. No! A prairie dog hole, hidden by the high grasses.

Excruciating pain shot through his leg. He curled up and rolled over on his side, needing a better angle to truly examine his leg. He lay there a long time before he could think straight.

No blood. No skin broken. He sighed in relief. Could he set the bone himself?

Looking around, he spotted a white birch tree a few feet away. He dragged himself toward it, every tug of his leg over the rough ground sending agonizing stabs of pain through him. Finally, he reached the tree. He rested his back against the trunk, panting from pain and exertion. Leaning over, bending his knee, he felt his calf, determining where the break was. He needed help. This was his favorite spot because no one ever came by. He was always totally alone, and he liked it that way, except this time.

Again, he wondered—could he set the bone himself? Had he brought any liquor with him? He didn't usually imbibe alcoholic beverages, but he could certainly use some to help kill the pain.

"Why did this have to happen now?"

"God?" He looked around as if God would miraculously show himself. "Can you help me?" He hoped God heard this prayer, even though it seemed God never heard or helped him at all. When did God ever answer his prayer in the affirmative? Well, maybe a couple of times when he was a boy.

Why should he expect God to hear him now?

Chapter Three

Rose sat on the west porch with Luisa and Olivia. It was their nightly custom after dinner, with the dishes done, to sit on the west porch, leaving the north porch to Meghan and Duncan. Rose wondered if she would ever find a man to love her like Duncan loved Meghan. She had feelings for Scott, and it seemed the boardinghouse women could read those feelings as easily as reading a book. He still frustrated her at times, but their working relationship was going very well.

She was now quite experienced at surface suturing and wound cleaning, and she helped him with major surgery, too. He taught her about disease, what little they knew. Exciting new theories regarding unseen organisms were the talk in the most prestigious medical journals, which Scott read enthusiastically. He'd let her look at one of his medical journals once, but she was still only learning to read and write. She'd quickly returned it saying she'd like to borrow it later, after she could comprehend it.

Hearing him talk about medicine thrilled her. Her love and understanding for science and medical treatments grew daily.

"Where are you, Rose? Thinking about Scott?" Olivia's voice interrupted her thoughts.

She smiled. "Yes, I was, actually. I'm so thankful he's letting me work for him. Every day he teaches me something new about medicine. I enjoy it."

Olivia chuckled. "I'd say you love more than that."

Heat traveled up her neck. "Well, I can't deny I'm attracted to him. I'm so grateful in many ways, it's hard not to have some affection for him."

"You think you—marry him—someday?" Luisa chimed in.

Rose rolled her eyes. "I don't know. Right now, I'm just his assistant. I don't know if he has any personal feelings for me or not."

"But you do, for him." Olivia wrapped her hand around Rose's.

Rose gave Olivia's hand a squeeze. "Yes, I do. But I'm cautious with my feelings. It may take time for him to get completely over Meghan. I'm not certain he's ready to look at any other woman yet, even me."

And after Jake's fierce beating, could she ever allow a man to touch her again?

༄

Scott awoke in great pain. He hadn't even realized he'd fallen asleep. Or had he passed out? Although some pain had faded, he knew it was crucial his leg be set. He looked around but saw nothing he could use to anchor his leg. Not even a rock or embedded fallen tree.

Even though the evening wasn't cold, he shivered. He needed to build a fire, to keep warm so he wouldn't go into shock. Sometimes medical knowledge wasn't helpful. He knew what needed to be done, yet he was powerless to do it himself.

What if he died out here?

A slight breeze blew over him, causing another shiver, but was someone—humming? No one ever came out here. The sound moved toward him.

He held his breath. Yes, someone, a short distance away, sang a tune, a melody without words.

"Hello! Anyone out there?" Scott held his breath and waited for an answer.

"Helloooo!" A man. Maybe he'd would be all right.

In the twilight, as the man came closer, the setting sun behind him created a soft golden glow all around him. His hair was white, and it seemed his clothing was different shades of white and tan. His complexion was also light.

"I need help. My leg's broken." Scott hoped the man had access to a buckboard or some other wagon and could get him back to town, where he could tell Rose how to set his leg.

"How did it happen, son?" The man knelt beside him.

"I stepped in a prairie dog hole. I'm a doctor, and I know where the break is."

"Which leg is it?" The man peered closer.

"My right."

"Do you mind if I have a look?" The man's voice soothed his fractured nerves. The tones were melodic. Comforting in a way.

"Are you a doctor?" Should he allow the stranger to examine him? What if the man made the break worse in his clumsy attempts to examine it?

The man smiled knowingly, like he knew something Scott didn't.

"No, but I have knowledge of healing."

"You do?" Scott raised an eyebrow.

"I've learned some things along the way. Will you let me look at it?"

He thought a moment, then nodded. "All right. But be careful."

The man cautiously and gently felt along his leg until he came to the break. Scott hissed at the touch, even though gentle.

"Easy, son. I know it hurts. I'm sorry."

"That's all right. I'm a poor patient." He glanced down, almost embarrassed, then gazed into the man's startling greenish-blue eyes. They were tender and kind. His weathered face made him seem old, yet Scott detected a youthfulness and strength about him. The man looked to be in his sixties. He wore tan loose-fitting pants, almost like what Mexican peons wore. His white flowing shirt seemed like something from the last century. And how did he keep his feet clean in those ancient-looking sandals?

The man nodded. "I understand. But this leg must be set immediately. Are you ready?"

"You'll stay and help me splint it?"

"Of course. I know how to take care of broken bones. I'll stay the night with you, then fetch a wagon in the morning. We'll need to get you back to town."

"Thank you. Let me introduce myself. I'm Doctor Scott—" He cried out as the man jerked his leg.

"I'm Rafe. We'll talk in the morning." The man put his hand on Scott's forehead.

The man's striking eyes were the last thing he remembered.

⁓

Duncan said goodnight, and then Meghan joined Rose and the other women on the west porch.

"Is Duncan all right? Did he overdo it today?" Rose hoped he'd be careful and not hamper his recovery. He'd already been injured once this year—with a slight concussion and wrenched back. After the tornado, Meghan had taken care of him a few days here at the boardinghouse to make sure he didn't further injure himself. Duncan recovered well from that. Meghan took more notice of Duncan after the tornado, even though she'd still allowed both Duncan and Scott to court her for a couple of months afterward—before she finally decided, choosing the cowboy.

"He's fine, though tired." Miraculously, Duncan was alive after being shot in the chest trying to intervene in a gunfight. It was a noble, but senseless thing to do. He nearly died.

Scott had inexcusably tried to force Meghan to marry him. She was duty-bound to set Scott straight. She'd even quit. Soon after, he'd released Meghan. She would never have agreed to return to work if he hadn't. Later, he'd told her he realized he didn't really love Meghan but was infatuated with the idea of her.

Could Scott ever look at her with love in his eyes straight from his heart?

Chapter Four

Scott awoke to sounds of fire crackling just outside the tent. As he tried to rise, pain consumed him.

He rolled to the left and lifted the tent bottom a couple of inches. It was dark, but to the east, threads of pink began to appear on the horizon. The sun would be up soon. He couldn't help wondering about the man who'd come to help. The man turned, knowing he was being watched.

"Just relax, son. You'll be all right. Your leg is set and splinted." He poured a cup from the coffeepot and handed it to Scott.

Bacon sizzled in the skillet. Scott wasn't hungry, but he needed to express his gratitude.

"Thank you for staying with me and helping. What did you say your name was?"

"My name is Raphael, but you can call me Rafe. Suits better in the West."

"Rafe, what brings you out here in the middle of nowhere?"

"You do."

"What do you mean?"

"You're in a pickle, son. I came to help you get back to civilization. You have a very capable assistant who can help you from there. But stuck out here all by yourself... well, you were in a lot of trouble." The man picked up a plate and set the bacon in it. "Here. Eat this. I'll be back shortly to take you to town. I've got to see a man about a wagon."

Scott nearly choked on his coffee. "What do you mean, you came to help me?"

"Just what I said. God wants you to know that he loves you very much. He wants you to pay more attention to how you live your life. Get to know him by heart, not just in your mind. Think about it. I'll be back soon." He turned from Scott.

"Wait—"

Scott blinked. Where'd he go?

⁓

Rose unlocked the medical office door and prepared to handle patients. Since she'd done most of the cleanup work the day before, all she needed to do now was set out bandages, instruments, carbolic acid, and other things needed for the day. With any luck, no patients with serious injuries would come in today. Although she'd helped Scott in many ways with surgery, setting bones, and examinations, she didn't feel confident or experienced enough to handle anything requiring surgery.

A knock at the door. *So, it begins.*

"Come in."

A kind-faced older gentleman dressed in different shades of tan and white entered. "Miss, can you help me? The doc is injured, and we need to get him inside."

"What? Doctor Allison? Scott?" She scurried to the door. "What happened?"

"Let's get him inside first." The man turned away.

Rose followed him out the door to a buckboard. Scott was lying unconscious inside.

"Oh, my goodness!" What had happened? How had this man found him? Scott always went away to be alone.

"Well, miss, he said he stepped in a prairie dog hole. His leg was in desperate need of treatment when I came across him." The man's voice was calming and mild. "Oh, by the way, I'm Raphael, but you can call me Rafe."

Rose swallowed. "I'm so thankful you were there to help."

"I was sent to help him. Let's get him in now."

Wondering what he meant by being sent, but not wanting to ask, she went to one side of the wagon bed, the man at the other. Rose pulled on Scott's left leg. The man kept the broken right leg from hitting the wagon bottom. When they got Scott to a certain point, they reached in, one on each side, and pulled Scott to a sitting position. Then each one put one of Scott's arms around their shoulders and dragged him to the door.

"You best let me take him from here, miss. You'll want to get things ready for him inside. He needs a more professional splint." With that, the man hauled Scott over his shoulder, arms and legs dangling. The man certainly was strong for someone his age.

Rose hurried into the office and set out a fracture box. She went out back and brought in a bag of sand. A fracture box would help stabilize Scott's leg. More than one sandbag would be needed, but she could at least get started.

"Could you put him in his bed, since he'll be there for quite a spell?"

"I'd be glad to, Miss Rose. The bone didn't break through the skin. That's one good thing about it. But the bone was dislocated and needed setting." Rafe's voice soothed and comforted her. But how did he know her name? They hadn't been introduced.

He carefully set Scott down on the exam table. She went to work removing the old splints and getting the leg ready for the fracture box. They'd do that once Scott was placed in bed.

"Is there anything else you need from me, miss?"

Rose looked up a moment. "Could you help me get him to bed now?" She removed the sticks and rags from Scott's leg.

The man nodded, with a smile. "Of course. Anything to help you, my dear."

Scott moaned a few times as he was moved about, but never regained consciousness. He must be in terrible pain. She'd have some pain packets ready for him to drink as soon as he woke up.

Rose could then check to be sure the leg was straight with the help of the sand and angle the pillows to elevate. The sand held the leg straight. The pillows angled the foot upward to keep it from swelling too much.

As they moved back into the main room, the man turned to her. "Need anything else, Miss Rose?"

"How do you know my name?"

He smiled. She blinked, and he was gone. What manner of man was he? She didn't hear the door open or close. No one just disappeared like that.

A moment later, the door opened, and a young man dressed in black pants with a white shirt and black suspenders entered. He was holding up one hand by the other at the wrist. His blond hair was curly and a bit longer than fashion.

"Is the doctor in?"

Rose tied her apron strings and nodded toward the exam table. "Sorry, the doctor has been injured. I'm his assistant. Maybe I can help you?"

The young man came close and showed her a deep cut on the inside of his hand, just underneath the knuckles. "Had accident with—how you say it—mill blade." The man's English was broken, and he had some sort of accent. She wasn't sure what.

Rose examined his hand. "And your name, sir?"

"Bernhard Warkentyne, ma'am. My friends call me Bernie."

"I'm Miss Rhodes. Thank you for coming in. I'll just clean and suture that and you'll be fine. You'll need to change the bandage once it stops bleeding. If you can't do it yourself, come back and I'll be glad to."

Mr. Warkentyne looked skeptical. "Will doctor be all right? I see him—carried in. You sure—you can—able—to help me?"

"I can definitely help you Mister Warkentyne." She set out the supplies needed. She'd closed many wounds by this time, and almost felt like an expert. Sometimes Scott let her stitch up the surface skin from surgeries, after he'd sutured internally.

"The doctor will be fine—eventually." She swallowed. "And yes, I am perfectly qualified to suture your hand. In fact, I stitched the doctor's hand from a cut like yours, just a few months ago. It was my first act as his assistant." She cleaned the wound, then began closing the cut.

Concern melted from his face.

"So you injured your hand on a mill blade? Are you a miller? Where are you from?"

She'd bandage this young man's hand, then check on Scott. Unconscious now, what kind of pain must he be in?

And who was the man who brought Scott home?

Chapter Five

People talked in the next room. Scott recognized Rose's voice. She was talking to someone. He must be back home. It felt like his bed. The older man said he would take him home this morning, but Scott didn't remember anything from the time the man said he had to find a wagon. There was something unusual about that man.

"*Da*, I—build mill. Soon many—farmers come. Some already. Others later. I and others—from Russia. We—Mennonites seek peace. Place to live. English—hard." The man grunted a moment.

"You're doing quite well. The more you speak, the better you'll get." Rose's "patient" voice was friendly, kind, yet efficient. That's one thing Scott liked about her.

"*Spas*—thank you. I—practice. Talk much English."

"That was pretty good. We would say, 'Practice makes perfect.' You'll improve." The scissors made a small noise as she placed them on the table. She must have finished bandaging the man's hand. "There. You'll be fine now."

"Already? That was—quick."

"It doesn't take long, Mister Warkentyne. I wish you luck on your mill."

Scott could almost see the smile on her face as she spoke.

A severe pain jolted up Scott's leg, causing him to groan.

"Thank you for coming in. It seems my other patient is waking up."

"Thank you, Miss Rhodes." The door opened and closed.

"Scott?"

He forced himself to move. Another grunt escaped.

"Rose?" He struggled to sit up.

"Yes, I'm right here. Drink this." He looked up. Was she ever a wonderful sight? He drank her in like a thirst he couldn't quench. She held out a glass.

"What is it?"

"Pain medication."

He drank the foul-tasting stuff, knowing it would take the pain away and help him sleep. "Is my leg all right?"

Rose laid a hand on his shoulder. "It will be. That man, Rafe, and I got you all set up in a fracture box."

"Good job. Thank you. Is Rafe still here?"

"No, he left. We'll talk later."

⁓

As Scott drifted off to sleep, Rose went back to the main room and cleaned up her mess from bandaging Mr. Warkentyne's hand. He said he was Russian. She'd have to ask Meghan where on earth Russia was. Probably somewhere on the other side of the world. Her geography lessons weren't very interesting. She'd have to pay more attention. It would be nice to know where new people were from and visualize it on the map.

She spent time putting the supplies in order, checking and inventorying. Although Scott did all the accounting, she was learning. Meghan had taught her even more about basic mathematics. Rose already knew how to manage money, but learning how numbers related to the medical practice was more challenging. Scott had encouraged her to look over his books and learn how the accounting systems operated.

The door opened.

"Is the doctor here?"

That voice. She caught her breath and whirled around.

Jake.

⌒

"Sorry, miss. I didn't mean to scare you." Jake determined to be respectful and on his best behavior. When he couldn't find Rosie, Trina had offered, but she was nothing like his Rosie girl.

"Can I help you?"

"Is the doctor here? I have a couple of questions for him."

The woman cleared her throat. "Yes, he's here, but he's been seriously injured. He's sleeping now. Is there something I can do for you?"

Jake took a long look at the woman. There was something familiar about her, but he couldn't quite place it. She was a pretty girl, but plain. Young, probably not even twenty. He'd never known Rosie's age, but she was young, too. Experienced, a little jaded, but plucky. And she knew how to give pleasure to a man.

"Well, unless you can tell me how to find Rosalie O'Roarke, you can't help me." He scratched his chin.

The woman paled at the mention of Rosie's name. Maybe she knew something. Was Rosie dead? The barkeep had said she'd left town.

"Are you all right, miss? Sorry to frighten you. I seem to do that. Don't mean to." He stepped closer. She moved a step back.

"Um, what did you say your name was?"

"Miss, my name is Thomas. Jake Thomas. I'm looking for Rosalie O'Roarke because she's my special lady. Life is fine when I'm with her. Not so good when she's not."

The young woman wiped a hand on her apron. "I understand Miss O'Roarke left town."

"That's what I heard, but I can hardly believe it."

"Why not?" There was something familiar about this woman's voice, and her appearance, only he knew he'd never seen her before. The more she talked, the inflections, the tones. He couldn't quite remember. Maybe that blow to the head a couple of months ago... in that bar fight. He'd had some trouble recognizing things like he used to. He had his memories though.

"She was a gal who liked to stay in one place, not traipse around all over the countryside." Jake scratched his head. He needed a bath. Maybe he'd get one.

"I can only say I don't know where she's gone. I—I didn't know her." The woman patted her hair. Someone else he knew also did that. But who?

"All right." He turned to go, then twisted back. "Hey, can you tell me where the schoolteacher is? Does she live at the boardinghouse?"

The woman blinked. "What do you want with her?"

"Like I said, miss. I'm trying to find Rosie O'Roarke, and I'm talking to anyone who might be able to tell me where she is."

The woman didn't answer.

"Thank you for your time, miss."

What was it about that woman that seemed so familiar? It would come to him. In the meantime, he had to find Miss Gallagher.

After Jake left, Rose let out a long breath she didn't realize she'd held. What a nightmare. Jake was not only back in town, he was looking for her. She knew him well enough to know that he was like a leech when he wanted something. He wanted more from her than she could give. And when she wouldn't tolerate certain things, he started hitting her. More and more, until the last time, she'd been in bed several days and couldn't work.

He said she was special to him. He treated her more like a piece of property—but he didn't own her. Evidently, he thought he had some special claim on her. He didn't. How could she get that through his head? It was best to avoid him completely.

It was a wonder he didn't recognize her. Now, he was going to talk to Meghan. Rose looked at the clock on the wall. School was in session right now. Would he go there and disrupt class? Or wait and come to the boardinghouse tonight?

She'd run to the boardinghouse now while Scott slept, pick up some things to stay at the office awhile, to be closer to Scott, although he wouldn't be of any help in an emergency. She didn't want to be near anywhere Jake might be.

Chapter Six

"Are you sure you heard from God? It doesn't make sense."

Rose had never heard Meghan speak in that tone of voice before, especially when speaking to Duncan. She quietly closed the front door to the boardinghouse and crept toward the stairs.

Duncan sounded equally strained. "No, not *sure*, but really believe so. Feels right."

As Rose tiptoed toward the stairs, she glanced over and saw them, face-to-face, hands on hips. They must both have a stubborn streak, and each seemed to bring it out in the other.

A floorboard creaked. Normally, she never noticed it.

"Rose, come here, will you?" Her shoulders tightened as she turned slowly. Two faces looked her way.

"No, please." Rose continued toward the stairs. "Whatever you're talking about, I'm not getting in the middle of it."

A knock on the door made her turn around. As Meghan opened it, Rose caught her breath. Jake.

"Excuse me, but are you Miss Gallagher?"

Meghan opened the door farther and gestured for Jake to enter. Rose gripped the stair railing and climbed quickly. Although she wanted to escape to her room, jump into bed, and pull the covers up over her head, she also wanted to hear what was going on. Would her new identity be exposed? She reached the top of the stairs, turned, and sat down.

"Come in, won't you?" Meghan, always the gracious hostess. "Do you have children in school?" Jake and Meghan evidently moved into the parlor, so Rose couldn't see them, but she could hear the conversation.

Jake cleared his throat. "Uh, no miss, I'm looking for someone. I was told at the doctor's office you might know where Rosalie O'Roarke got to."

Rose closed her eyes tightly. How would Meghan respond?

"Oh, pardon me. This is Mister Duncan Wilcox, my fiancé. And you are...?"

"Name's Thomas. Jake Thomas. Rosie was always my special lady. I heard she left town, but I'm talking to everyone who knows her. I need to find her.'

Meghan coughed. "Um, yes, that's right. Rosie left town...after...she said you attacked her."

"Just forget about that, will you?" Jake's voice rose.

"See here, now. You asked the question. The lady answered. That's all there is to say. Or was there something else?" Duncan's voice had an edge to it.

Jake coughed. His next words were calmer, softer. "Sorry. I didn't mean to rile ya. I'm just looking for Rosie. I want her to be my special lady again. I need her. She's like no other woman."

"You said—you were at the doctor's office? Has he returned?" Meghan sounded skeptical.

"No, miss. He has not, but his assistant was there. Nice lady, she is. She's the one who told me Rosie left town."

"It's true. Rosalie O'Roarke left town just after the tornado in June. No one has seen her since. You can check with the Silver Spike."

"Already did. She cleared out. And didn't tell no one where she was going. I heard you, Miss Gallagher, were her friend. If anyone would know, you would."

Meghan cleared her throat. "She didn't tell me she was leaving, let alone where she was going."

"Now, if that's everything, Mister Thomas, I suggest you look elsewhere." Duncan's voice also softer, but the edge was still there.

Shuffling. They were exiting the parlor. Rose quickly got to her feet and scurried to her room. Her fingers trembled on the knob. Once inside, she locked the door and leaned against it, releasing a long breath.

She was safe, but for how long?

⁕

Jake left the boardinghouse frustrated. Surely Rosie had told someone where she was going. Stomping toward the Silver Spike, he decided to get good and drunk, and see if that new girl, Trina, was interested in entertaining him again. A pretty girl, and young, but she wasn't Rosie. She'd do in a pinch, though.

Where did Rosie go?

As he tramped into the Silver Spike, a couple of wranglers staggered into him on their way out the door. Heat flushed through him.

"Watch where you're going." He swirled around and punched the jaw of one of the cowboys who'd bashed into him. The man fell against his compadre and they tumbled to the floor.

"Who hit me?" The man roared as he lurched up from the floor. Jake was sure he could be heard in the street. Who cared? Should he own up to it? He wasn't angry enough for a brawl, just fuming over Rosie.

Jake glanced at Sam, who shook his head. That meant Sam didn't want a fight. He winked at Sam, then turned to face the man he'd punched.

"Hey, cowboy, sorry about that." He brushed off the man's shoulders and straightened his shirt.

The wrangler swayed, peering at him through slits. "Oh—oh, okay. Sorry to have bothered you. Another time, then?"

Jake gave the guy's shoulders another light brush-off. "Some other time." He noticed the whole room had gone quiet. All eyes were on them. He gave a nervous laugh.

"Show's over, folks."

The two cowboys staggered out. Jake sidled up to the bar.

"Hey, Sam, whiskey, please." Sam poured him a drink, and he downed it quickly. "Leave the bottle, why don't ya?"

The bartender's eyes narrowed. "Now Jake, I don't want you tearin' up my place again."

"Where's Trina?" Jake swallowed his second drink and let the alcohol burn down his throat, though most of the time he didn't notice the scald. Whiskey relaxed him. He let out a breath, inhaled and gulped a third drink.

Soon, he'd find his Rosie girl and take her for his own.

Chapter Seven

After supper, Rose packed her carpetbag with a couple changes of clothes and prepared to head back to Scott's office. Meghan met her at the door.

"Can I walk with you? I need to explain what you heard this afternoon." Meghan smoothed non-existent wrinkles from her skirt, then repeated the action.

"Of course, though it gets dark early. Will Duncan come in a while to escort you home?"

"Uh—no. I'll be all right. I've walked the streets of this town for months, and I've never been accosted yet—except that first day." Meghan grabbed her shawl and led the way out the front door.

Rose picked up her bag and followed. What had happened between the two lovebirds? Maybe that's what Meghan wanted to talk about.

They walked in silence until they turned on to Main Street. Rose wondered if she'd ever share. It must be very difficult.

"Rose, what did you hear this afternoon?"

"Not much. Just that you were questioning whether Duncan actually heard from God."

Meghan nodded. "That's what I thought. He said he's being called to preach—be a minister."

"Really? When did that happen?"

"He says it must be during the time he was in a coma, but it's only an impression. It's not like he heard the voice of God or something. Or if he did, he doesn't remember. I had this picture of what I thought our life together would be like. He'd be a ranch owner, or a prosperous businessman. But a preacher?" Meghan's hands lifted in exasperation.

What could Rose say to her friend? "Well, maybe you two should pray about it for a while. I'm no expert on God, but isn't that what you do? Pray? Have you talked to Olivia about it? She's a wise woman."

"I plan to talk with her later. I guess I'm still a little upset. Of all things God could call him to…"

"But isn't that what God does? Like I said, I don't really know about that, but I have heard stories of people saying they heard from God. Even you."

"Me? Oh, yes. When I felt God wanted me to read to Duncan while he was in a coma."

"There, you see? Couldn't God have spoken something like that to Duncan?"

Meghan let out a long breath. "Yes, I suppose so. It's just not what I expected."

"Life is seldom what we expect. I certainly didn't imagine, as a young girl, I'd be forced into being a dance hall girl, and other things, by my mother at such a young age."

"I know. That was terrible. Have you heard from your mother lately?"

"No, and I'm glad. I don't really want to see her again. She was never much of a mother to me."

"Have you forgiven her?"

"What do you mean?"

"Do you still harbor ill will toward your mother?"

They neared the tracks. Rose stopped. Her friend turned around to face her. "Meghan, you can't be serious."

"I am. Do you hate your mother?"

Rose's blood pulsed through her veins. She was a lady now, addressing another lady, her best friend. She still clenched her fists, then relaxed them.

"I don't know if I hate her, but I can't forget what she did to me."

"But can you let it go?"

"I don't understand."

"Forgiving doesn't mean forgetting. It means to release *your* anguish, pain, anger. Letting it go will free you. That's what forgiveness is. You let it go."

"But—what she did..."

"Yes, it was horrible." Meghan paused. "Um, may I say something, Rose?"

Rose swallowed. Would this be a lecture, like her tutoring sometimes was? A monologue where Meghan talked, and she listened?

"Sure. Say whatever you want. We're friends, aren't we?"

Meghan put her hand on Rose's shoulder. "Rose, you've changed your life on the outside. And that's wonderful. Now, I think, maybe it's time to work on the inside. Forgiveness of your mother, of Jake, is a first step. Jesus says we need to forgive, so he can forgive us."

She remained silent a moment, letting Meghan's little "lecture" sink in. Her friend had a good heart. However, there were many things Rose had never told her. Shameful, hurtful things that would shock the sheltered young woman.

"I don't know if I can."

"Well, sometimes it takes a while for the feelings to heal, but forgiveness is a decision, a very important one. I'll pray that God shows you his love. Would you consider coming to church with us? We could take you to one of the tents, or you could spend the morning under our special tree."

She looked down. "I'll think about it."

Meghan removed her hand from Rose's shoulder as they continued across the tracks. When they reached the medical office, she turned once more to Meghan.

"I promise, I'll think about everything you've said. Thank you for being my friend. I've never had a real friend before. You took a chance on me, and you've taught me so much."

Meghan smiled, and gave her a hug.

"You're a great student, a quick learner. And I venture to say, what I've done for you pales in comparison to what you've done for me."

She knew what Meghan alluded to. When she'd quit being Scott's assistant, until he humbly came back and apologized after releasing Meghan from a promise to marry him. She shuddered to think what might have happened if Scott hadn't gotten some sense into his head and changed his mind.

Scott heard the office door open, then close quietly.

"Rose?" He shifted right toward the bedroom door.

"Yes, I'm back. I thought you might be sleeping, so I tried to be quiet." She came to the door. Her lips were pressed tightly. So very attractive to him, even when she was unhappy.

"Is everything all right?" He pushed himself to a sitting position, leaning back against the wall.

"Why would you think it's not?" She looked away and wouldn't meet his gaze.

He patted the side of the bed. "Come and sit. Tell me what's happened. I thought I heard voices earlier. Did someone come?"

A tear rolled down her cheek. She wiped it away. He'd seen her angry, hurt, compassionate, and amused, but never tearful.

"What's the matter, Rose? You can tell me."

She exhaled slow. Her whole body seemed to deflate. She came around the foot of the bed sat on the edge, very carefully, so as not to cause him pain. He held his leg to keep it from moving.

"Jake Thomas is back in town, and he's looking for me."

Scott jerked forward. A sharp pain ran up his leg. He groaned.

"Are you all right?" Her expression changed from sorrow to concern in an instant.

"I'm fine, I just moved too quickly. Jake Thomas? Isn't he the one..."

"Yes." She looked at the floor.

He reached out and lifted her chin with two fingers. "You should go to the new sheriff. He could help keep an eye out for Jake and make sure he doesn't hurt you again."

She twisted her head away from his touch. "You know I can't do that. No one must know."

He thought a moment. "Surely the sheriff can keep a confidence. He didn't know you from before. He's only met you as you are now."

"Enough of me. How are you feeling?" She placed her cool hand on his warm forehead. It felt good.

"I don't have a fever. It's just this blasted leg, and the aggravation of not being able to do anything for myself." He pounded the bed, then moaned when his leg bounced.

She took his pulse. Her touch sparked something in him. No other woman's touch had done that, not even Meghan's.

"You'll be fine. I'm going to the hotel to get you some supper. I'll be back soon. And I'm staying here tonight, maybe longer. I'll sleep on the cot in the other room."

"Rose?"

How could he convey how important she was to him? The fact that she was here, taking care of him, meant so much. He'd challenged her in her learning, and she was a quick study. She'd defied him over Meghan, and yet, that made him see her with new eyes. He realized he didn't really love Meghan.

"What do you need, Scott?"

"I—I just wanted to say...thank you."

Her smile lit up the room. Yes, it was entirely possible he could fall in love with Rose.

Chapter Eight

"Hel—lo! Anyone here? Doctor Allison?"

The next day, Scott awoke with a start. Someone had slammed the door. He listened a moment but heard nothing. Where was Rose? Who was this? What time was it? He picked up his pocket watch from the end table. It read just after noon. Rose must be at lunch. He'd slept the morning away.

"I—I'm in here, if you want to talk to the doctor." Scott pushed himself up and slid back against the wall, grunting as his leg protested even the slightest movement. He was going to need crutches soon, but he had to be able to stand first.

The man of around forty-five stood in the doorway. A couple of lines wrinkled the forehead on his tanned face. Scott's eyes traveled downward and fixed on the tin star.

The man extended his hand. "I'm Sheriff Stuart Randall. I heard you had an accident, Doc. Is there anything I can do?"

Scott reached up and shook it, then indicated he should sit in the chair next to the bed. The sheriff took him up on the offer.

"Hello, Sheriff Randall. I hope you're here to bring order to this wild railroad town."

"That I am."

"I'm glad to hear that. It's only been a few weeks since all the trouble."

"I heard about that, too. I'm here to make sure that doesn't happen again."

"That makes me feel a lot easier."

"So, Doc, what happened?" He looked at Scott's leg.

"I fell in a prairie dog hole outside town. A stranger brought me in." Scott couldn't help the small smile he was certain crossed his lips as he thought of the old man. "I'm out of commission for a couple weeks until I'm strong enough to stand on crutches."

"Will your assistant be able to handle everything?"

"She's very capable. The only thing she can't do is major surgery."

"What if that were necessary?"

"Well, I guess I'd get out of this bed sooner and find a way to stand up and tell her what to do."

"Don't you think you should send for another doctor, at least temporarily?"

"Only as a last resort." Scott paused a moment. "Listen, Sheriff, I'm sure you're a busy man. Did you come over here just to visit, or is there another reason?"

Randall nodded. "Well, I am here for a couple reasons. There's a man around town, a sort of troublemaker, who's looking for a dance hall girl named Rosalie O'Roarke. Word is you treated her after that man beat her up earlier this year. What can you tell me?"

Scott let out a breath. "Yes, I treated Miss O'Roarke last spring for bruises, cracked ribs, and numerous abrasions. If he'd kept it up, she might have died."

"I heard she left town. Is that true?"

Scott put a hand under his broken leg and gently adjusted its position. Pain shot up to his hip. He winced. "As far as I know. I haven't seen her around since early summer."

Randall leaned forward. "I may as well tell you. Your assistant came to see me this morning. She said you had sent her to ask my help. If you don't tell me the truth, how can I do that?"

Scott blinked. "I didn't know. I've been asleep all morning. I'm glad she went to see you. What did she say?"

Randall leaned back in the chair and scratched the back of his neck. "She said she needed protection from that rascal who beat her earlier this year."

"That's true. He's back in town, and he's been looking for her. She's scared to death. She changed her life after the tornado, and very few know that Rose Rhodes is really Rosalie O'Roarke. But she needs to keep her new identity a secret. The town doesn't know."

"What can you tell me about this—Jake Thomas?"

"I haven't met him. I only know what he did to Rose. According to her, he's mean and brutal. I could tell that from what I saw."

The sheriff stood. "Thanks, Doctor Allison. I can't arrest him until he breaks the law, but I'll certainly keep an eye on him."

"Thank you, Sheriff. I know she'll appreciate it. I do, too."

Scott leaned his head back against the wall a moment and let out a long breath. Hopefully, Rose would be safe now. Blast this broken leg. He needed to be on his feet, not laid up like a helpless cripple.

Rose picked up the tray from the buggy seat. She'd brought Scott beef stew from Olivia. She hurried so it wouldn't cool off too much. Olivia had scooped the stew into a covered dish while it was piping hot.

As she walked slowly to the door, she carefully picked her way. The last thing Scott or she needed, was to trip and drop the tray.

Just as she reached the door, a voice called out from behind her.

"Miss! Hey, miss!"

Oh no. Jake Thomas again. What did he want now?

She stopped just outside the door before turning toward him.

"Thanks, miss." He was holding his left hand up, supporting the elbow with his right. "I need some help."

"Come on in, then. I'll look at it as soon as I get this stew to the doctor."

"He's still laid up, huh?"

"Um, yes. He broke his leg. That will take at least eight weeks to heal."

"So, you're still doin' the doctorin'?"

"Yes."

As they turned to the office door, to her surprise, Jake opened it for her. If he knew who she was, he'd never do that.

She stepped inside and headed toward the bedroom door. "Scott? Um, Doctor Allison, are you awake?"

Scott looked up at her, then sat up against the wall. "Yes, and I'm hungry. Ooooh! I'm catching a whiff of something."

"Olivia made beef stew. It's very tasty." She set the tray down over his lap. "Do you need anything? I have a patient."

"Thank Missus Baldwin for me next time you see her, will you?" He looked at the tray a moment, then into her gaze. "I've got everything I need for the time being."

"Certainly." Rose turned toward the main room. "If you'll hop up on the exam table, I'll be right back."

Scott smiled, then cocked his head to one side. A frown replaced the smile. She'd tried to hide her fear. Evidently not successfully. "Who's here?"

She leaned toward his ear and lowered her voice. "Jake Thomas."

Scott's eyes widened. When he answered, his tone was strong, but it was a whisper. "What's he doing here?"

"He hurt his hand." She put a spoon in the stew. "Let me know if you need anything."

She turned to leave, but he grabbed her wrist, his grip strong, but not harsh. "You be careful. The sheriff was just here. Sorry I slept all morning. Was everything all right?"

She gently released his hand from her wrist, but gave his hand a squeeze, appreciating his concern. "We'll talk later." In a normal voice, she said, "Enjoy your lunch, Doctor Allison."

She certainly wouldn't be able to eat anything, or even think straight until Jake was gone. The sooner she treated his hand and sent him on his way, the better.

Chapter Nine

Her touch was tender, her skin soft. Desire arose in Jake. He pressed it down. She was a nurse, for Pete's sake. An honorable woman. Someone so far above him she'd never look his direction. He wished for Rosie. She always knew how to make him feel good. Why couldn't anyone tell him where she went?

"Ow!" Even though she was careful, the cut from the shattered whiskey bottle was deeper than he thought. Sam, the barkeep, said it would need stitches.

"Sorry, sir." Her voice was so familiar. There was something about the way she said "sorry" that he recognized. He'd never been called "sir" before, though.

Once the cut was clean, she threaded a needle by holding its eye up to the light. The way she held the needle. He'd seen it before, many times. He smiled as the memory came.

Rosie! His Rosie. What was she up to? Why was she posing as a doctor's assistant? She dressed differently than he'd ever seen her before. A lady. He knew otherwise.

Everyone said she'd left town. Yet here she was all along. The doctor had to be in on this. That teacher—she knew, too. And the boardinghouse lady? Jake figured they were all in on the secret.

They were conspiring to keep her away from him. That would change. Now that he knew who she was, he could bide his time and think what to do next. Watch her. See what her game was.

He'd always been able to hide his feelings when he wanted to. As she finished stitching and bandaging his hand, he pulled out a coin.

"Here ya are, miss. Payment for services rendered." He flipped it to her. She missed catching it, and it clattered on the floor.

"Everything all right in there?" The doctor called out from the bedroom. He must still be bedridden. Good. He wouldn't be able to interfere when Jake made his move. But he still needed to plan it out.

"I dropped his money, that's all." Rosie sounded a bit nervous, now that he thought about it. A quiet "All right" came from the bedroom.

Jake took her hand and kissed the back of it. "Charmed, miss." He smiled.

It was Rosie all right. The feel of her soft skin sent shivers of delight through him. He'd have to plan wisely.

∽

Rose's skin crawled. Jake's gaze, when she accidently caught it, seemed to bore right through her. Had he recognized her? Would he have played it cool, as if he hadn't recognized her, or have it out with her right then?

After cleaning up the medical supplies, she moved toward Scott's bedroom.

"How are you feeling?"

He leaned up on an elbow. "I can't wait to get on my feet again. I'm going to need crutches."

She sat in the chair beside him. "How long ago did you break this?" Knowing full well it was only a couple of days.

"I need to get out of this bed! Lying around is driving me insane." He punched the bed with his fist, then groaned.

"You're causing yourself more pain. Being quiet will help you heal faster, not by jostling the bed."

"Easy for you to say. You can walk, be on your feet."

"Scott, I know this is frustrating, but please be patient. You've got a long road ahead of you. If you were advising a patient, what would you say?"

He let out a long breath and lay back against the pillow. "I'd say exactly what you're telling me."

"That's what I thought. You know it will be at least a month before you can manage crutches, and even then, on a limited basis." She rose.

"What are you going to do now?"

"I'm going home for supper. Make sure you eat yours."

"Good. Could you check the mail why you're at it?"

"I did that at lunchtime. There were no new medical journals."

"You read my mind."

"I should know that much about you. I've been working for you four months."

He snorted. "You don't know everything about me."

"I know enough." She giggled. "I'll be back shortly. You rest until then, all right?"

"All right." He nodded and turned his face away.

A bit later, as Rose entered the boardinghouse, she heard Meghan talking to someone in the parlor. She stopped in the doorway, catching Meghan's gaze. Her friend motioned for her to come in.

"Rose, I'd like you to meet Hannah Samuelson. She's new in town. Rose Rhodes is the doctor's assistant." Rose followed Meghan's gaze to a young woman, even younger than she and Meghan. Hannah had hair the color of an overripe peach. Her skin was pale and smooth, with freckles. She wore a simple, blue and white gingham dress with a white full apron over the top. Rose thought she was plain, but her expression was pleasant and sweet.

"Nice to meet you, Miss Samuelson." Rose extended her hand.

"Please, call me Hannah. M-Miss Samuelson is my m-maiden aunt." Hannah's cheeks blushed. "S-spinster aunt. I'd rather not be th-thought of in any way like her." Her chin dipped.

"Hannah it is, then. And you can call me Rose." Rose gestured for her to sit on the settee, then sat at the other end. Meghan sat across from them in one of the wingback chairs. "When's supper?"

Meghan shrugged. "I'm guessing a little while yet."

Rose nodded, then turned back to Hannah. "Where do you come from?"

"O-Ohio."

"That's a long way. What brought you out here?"

"I-I'm going to be a Harvey girl. M-Mister Harvey came to my hometown. He made it sound so glamorous."

"Have you been to the hotel yet?"

"Yes. I met Missus S-Sampson."

Meghan leaned forward in the wingback. "Jewel Sampson? I know her. If you work for her, I'm sure she'll be fair. I have her children in school."

Rose shot her friend a look. She'd heard Meghan talk about how Mrs. Sampson thought her son stupid.

"Supper's ready!" Olivia called from the dining room.

Rose put a hand on Meghan's arm. "Can I talk to you later? It's important."

⌒

Rose hoped what she had to say wouldn't put her friend in a "teacher" mind-set. Tonight, she needed a friend.

"Let's go up to your room. No one usually bothers us there." Meghan turned to climb the stairs.

"You're right, they don't. Maybe it's because they think we're having a tutoring session and they don't want to interrupt."

"Mmmm, possible. Let's take advantage of that."

As they climbed the stairs and entered her room, Rose wondered how best to bring this up. She decided to plunge headlong into it, as she closed the door behind them. Meghan sat at the small desk near the window. Rose sat on the bed.

"Meghan, I'm desperately feared. Sorry, my old language slipped out. I'm scared that Jake will recognize me—if he hasn't already."

Her friend came to sit next to her on the bed, putting her arm around Rose's shoulders, comforting.

"You have every right to be frightened. Did something happen today?"

"He came to the office to get some stitches in his hand. I was certain he recognized me."

"What made you think so? Did he say something?"

"No, but partway through the suturing, he stared at me. From the corner of my eye, I saw an almost startled expression. I acted like I didn't see it."

Meghan was silent a moment. She brought her arm back around and stood to her feet. "Well, you're just going to have to be careful whenever you're around him."

"I already am."

Meghan tipped her head. "Even more so."

Rose let out a long breath and stood to her feet. "Just when I thought things were going so well..."

Meghan gave her a quick hug and left the room.

Should she confront Jake? What difference would it make? Would she have to leave town, just when things were beginning to turn around for her? Her stomach rumbled, but not from hunger. She placed a hand over it and willed it to silence.

Letting it all play out was probably her best option. She'd been tempted at other times in her life to act—and had learned to bide her time, to wait and see what would happen. That seemed to be the best thing to do here. But would things work out the way she hoped?

Jake made his way back to the Silver Spike. He had some serious drinking and thinking to do. He didn't want to get roaring drunk this time, just take the edge off his rage. To think that Rosie was here all along! Different kinds of heat flushed through him. The passion of longing, of desire, and fury, too. But this needed to be handled with great care. He needed a plan to get Rosie back under his control.

A thought came. Wasn't Rosie's mother a brothel owner? Maybe she could help. What did she go by? The Chesapeake Madam.

"Hey, Jake. What'll ya have?" Sam, the bartender, finished wiping up a spot of spilled alcohol on the bar.

"My usual. Whiskey. And leave the bottle." Jake dug into his pockets and pulled out a silver dollar. "Is Trina around?"

"She's upstairs. You may have to wait a little bit. She'll come down when she's ready. I'll let her know you're looking for her."

Jake poured himself a drink. Soon, he'd be in his heavenly place again. Trina was learning, but she'd never be his Rosie girl.

The next morning, Jake dug his knuckles in his eyes to wipe out the sleep. He glanced over to Trina's side of the bed, where she was fast asleep. He noticed an ugly bruise on her upper arm. Did he do that? His head hurt to remember. Well, if he had done it, she was to blame. After all, she wasn't Rosie. He needed to get his girl as soon as possible.

He poured some water into a basin and washed his face and hands, then slipped out of the room as quietly as possible.

Clarity of action always came after a night of partying. He knew exactly how he would get Rosie, but he would need to be patient. First, he'd telegraph Madam Margaret and get her here to New Boston to help Rosie forget her uppity ways.

Rosie could no more be a lady than he could be a gentleman. Although on occasion, he could pretend—if he had to. He liked being a common man, though, with earthly thoughts. No one ever expected much from him that way.

After sending the telegram, he snuck out of town and went to work.

Chapter Ten

"Rose, could you come here a moment, please?" Scott felt like a prisoner in his own bed. He had to at least try to stand, even if only for a few minutes. It was the end of the day. The patients were gone. Rose had done a splendid job of treating their minor wounds.

She came to the bedroom door, not looking him in the eye. Was she tired? It had been a long day. Or was something else the matter?

"What do you need?" She slowly untied her apron strings behind her.

"To get out of this bed! It's been nearly a week now. I need to get up or I'll never regain my strength." He struggled to sit up, then leaned against the wall. Guessing what he wanted, she fluffed a pillow before putting it behind him.

She let out a long breath. "We've been through this. You need your rest—and you know as well as I do that your leg hasn't healed enough. Standing up right now would harm your recovery."

He put a hand to his head. "Please, Rose. Help me. I'll go insane if I can't at least sit up in a chair. Crutches will help me stand."

Rose came to sit beside him in the chair and reached over to lay a hand on his arm. "Is there another way to be up—so you don't have to stay in bed all the time?"

He thought a moment. "I suppose I could get a wheelchair. Patients could use it later. We could loan it."

She beamed. "That's a wonderful idea. Shall I order one? Do we have the money for it?"

He returned her warm smile. "Yes, I believe we can afford it. And order several sets of crutches, too. We'll need those."

"Anything else?" She turned to go back to the main office.

"Rose, is everything all right? Has Jake given you any trouble?"

"No, but I'm very nervous about him. He's certain to see right through me and tell the whole town who I am. Once they find out, they'll make me leave, and everything will have been for nothing."

He grabbed her hand. Soft skin, yet her fingers were so nimble when it came to stitching incisions and cuts. "I may have a broken leg, but I'll fight anyone who tries to run you out of town."

"Scott, can I ask you a question?" Her voice seemed tenuous. What was she afraid to ask? He rubbed the back of her hand with his thumb. Anything he could do to comfort her.

"Of course. You can ask me anything, anytime, unless I'm performing surgery...which of course I'm not right now and won't be for a while."

"Will it upset you to talk about Meghan?"

Talk about going for the jugular.

He swallowed hard and shifted on the bed. "I think we both need to talk about her."

She nodded. "I agree. You first."

He looked down a moment. "What can I do to make it up to her? I'm so ashamed. How could I have ever done that? I sit here day-after-day, wondering what I can do. All I do is think about the last six weeks. Why did I ever think trying to force Meghan into marrying me was the right thing to do? I was raised better than that. I can't even understand myself. I think about it, and I have no explanation, except that I was desperate." He put his head in his hands.

She squeezed his hand before letting it go. He let it drop in his lap. "You weren't thinking straight. The rejection you felt from her choosing Duncan—hurt you deeply. Truly, at that time, you believed you loved her. Yet, what you did was totally out of character for the kind and generous man I know you are."

"But I—"

She put a finger to his lips. Heat flowed through him. Even though her touch was light and gentle, it was as if a torch had seared his lips together. He couldn't speak. All he could think to do was to take her hand in his and place his lips on the back of her hand.

"Rose..." He held her hand to his cheek.

"Hush, Scott. It's all right." They sat quietly a few moments. Peace and contentment filled him whenever Rose was around. She was a wonderful woman. He was so proud of her, and thanked God she was his assistant. How could he have ever thought he'd loved Meghan? But Rose, well, that was certainly possible. One he relished thinking about. He remembered she wanted to talk about Meghan, too.

"You said you wanted to talk about Meghan?"

She gently pulled her hand away from his grasp and folded her hands in her lap. "Yes, I did." The chair creaked as she leaned back in it.

"I—I want to know how you feel about Meghan? Are you still in love with her?"

He thought a moment. "No. And didn't we talk about this once before?"

Her gaze seemed to bore right through him. "Actually, we haven't. Not about what I'm going to say now."

He leaned forward. "I'm listening."

"I appreciate that—thank you." She looked down, then wiped her hands on her apron.

"Is it difficult to talk about?" Why wouldn't she look him in the eye?

"In a way, but I need to know. Did you love her? Do you still have feelings for her? Could anyone else find a place in your heart? Someone like—me—perhaps?" Finally, she looked up. Eyes filled with fear and longing met his.

He stroked her cheek. She caught her breath, and placed her hand over his, drawing his hand to her cheek.

"Scott, I—"

"Hush now. I want to tell you something, and I hope you're listening with your heart, as well as with your ears." He drew her hand from her cheek and held both her hands.

"You are precious to me." His voice came out husky.

He cleared his throat. "Rose, you mean so much to me. You've already found a place in my heart." Keeping one of her hands to himself, he gently touched her cheek with his other hand. "I have great affection for you. I'm so thankful you decided to change your life and work for me. You are such an intelligent and caring woman. But you are also strong and compassionate. That's what makes you such a great nurse."

He pulled her to sit with him on the edge of the bed. "And yes—I could definitely find a deeper place in my heart for you. My great fondness, which I have now, might easily turn to love—if given a chance. How would you feel about that?"

She smiled. "I believe that goes for me, too."

His heart pounded. Even though the sun was setting, suddenly the day seemed brighter. He'd be out of this bed soon, and the potential of a future with Rose began to take shape.

⁓

As Rose locked up the office for the night, a shrill train whistle blew when it pulled into the station. She'd have to wait until the giant steam engine stopped before walking across the tracks. What if the brakes didn't work as she crossed the tracks? Plus, bursts of steam could burn her. It would only be a minute or so, but her stomach growled. She hadn't eaten for hours.

Where would her relationship with Scott lead? Marriage?

Thoughts jumbled around in her mind. She pictured herself in a wedding gown, or at least a simple ivory dress, with a bit of lace and a couple of ruffles, nothing too fancy. White was reserved for virgins. Ivory or even a pale pastel would do for her. She'd never wear white, thanks to Madam.

Could Scott really fall in love with her? She was pretty sure she already loved him. When she'd asked if she could have a place in his heart, the rounded brightness of his eyes as she met his gaze seeped into every nook and cranny in her heart with warmth. Yes, there was hope he might grow to love her. With Scott, she could easily be happy the rest of her life.

Sadness overtook her. Nothing that good had ever happened to her before. Only lust for her body, not love. Certainly not the kind she saw in Meghan and Duncan.

Chapter Eleven

A week later, Scott sat in his wheelchair in the exam room. He rolled bandages, dipped instruments in carbolic acid, and set them out to dry—whatever he could do sitting down. He was thankful the Kansas City medical supply house had one. Rose had ordered three pairs of crutches of different sizes—one for children, one for shorter adults, and the last for taller adults, like him. Things seemed to settle down a bit. Jake hadn't bothered her. Scott had attempted to be a decent patient, not always complaining, like in the beginning. He'd nearly driven her to distraction.

He'd been trying out the crutches a few minutes every day. That turned out well, because a couple of gamblers came in with gunshot wounds. She couldn't have treated them by herself. He hadn't trained her in anything other than general nursing and only allowed her to suture surface cuts.

The door flew open. Sam, the bartender from the Silver Spike, was carrying in one of the girls. He panted from the exertion.

"Doc, help! It's Trina! She's been beaten."

Scott indicated the exam table. "Put her there." Her breath caught as Scott turned to her. The memories of the beating she'd suffered about six months ago came flooding back.

"Miss Rhodes, please bring the supplies."

Time seemed to slow. Memories of being in bed, with Scott and Meghan tending her came to mind.

"Rose!" She blinked, startled from her thoughts, then turned to gather ointments, alcohol, instruments, and bandages. He shouldn't have had to ask her again. She needed to forget the past and concentrate on helping him, now.

Scott wheeled over to the taller crutches and eased himself up from the wheelchair. He slipped the crutches under his armpits and thumped across the room to the exam table.

She moved to his side to assist him and to provide balance in case he tottered. He was beginning to get the hang of using these crutches. They had already wrapped the crossbars with a great deal of padding. It helped a lot. She knew he hated being stuck in a wheelchair all the time. At least now he was on his feet, sort of.

The bartender gently placed the injured young woman on the table. Rose's eyes teared up. She tried to swallow the lump in her throat, but it stuck. She also seemed glued in place, watching as if from a distance. If Jake ever found her... Poor girl.

Scott pointed to the couch on the other side of the room. "You don't have to wait, but if you'd like, you can sit on the couch." He pressed his lips together before speaking. "We'll take good care of her. What happened? Do you know who did this? Has the sheriff been notified?"

"Well, Doc, I can't be sure who did this, but I have an idea. It's probably the same guy that beat up another girl last spring." Sam went over to sit on the couch. "I came straight here. Haven't talked to the sheriff yet. It didn't help before. He can never be in more than one place at a time—and it seems he's never in the place he needs to be."

Scott snorted. "That was the old sheriff. Our new one is quite set on bringing law and order to this town. So, you think Jake Thomas is behind this?"

Sam's eyes widened. "Thomas? Oh, you think he's the one who beat up the O'Roarke girl?"

Snapping out of her temporary paralysis, she began to clean the young woman up and get her ready for treatment. If she kept her mouth shut, maybe it would all go away and be just a nightmare.

"She told me so."

"Really? Whenever I asked her, she always claimed not to know."

"Well, it's probably because she was afraid you wouldn't take her side because you didn't want to lose a customer."

Sam stood quickly. "I can't believe any of my girls would think I'd take a customer's side over them. If they can't work, I don't get customers."

"Maybe it's hard to trust you." Her voice held a bit of an edge. It surprised her.

Sam spluttered. "H-how can you think that? I honor and respect my girls—and pay them well." He took a step toward them.

She softened her tone. "Please sit down, sir. We'll do everything we can to help her. What's her name?"

She began to carefully undress the unconscious young woman, still remembering every blow Jake inflicted on her, until she lost consciousness. What an ordeal. Unfortunate young woman.

Out of the corner of her eye, she noticed the bartender sit down. "Her name is Trina. She's become a favorite of Jake Thomas, since he can't find Rosie O'Roarke."

She shivered. She'd unfastened the top of Trina's fancy dress, and together with Scott, they pulled it down to her waist, her camisole providing modesty.

Rose listened to the finer points of assessing injuries as Scott used this occasion to teach her—and maybe get her mind off the poor girl. "You're already doing a fine job of identifying types of wounds in your training so far, Rose." He pointed to the girl's face. "What do you think caused the injuries to her face?"

The girl's face was a mass of red, ugly welts. Her eyes were swollen and bruised. A trickle of blood flowed from one side of her mouth and her nose. Her cheeks were purple and misshapen.

A tear escaped as she felt Scott's gaze. She was trying to keep her focus on the analysis, knowing it would help her deal with diagnosis and treatment. How could she keep her objectivity?

She swallowed hard. "It looks like someone punched her—all over her face. Hit—everywhere. Bruising and swelling, with minor cuts and scrapes all over."

"Treatment of choice, Nurse?"

"Cleaning the cuts and clearing away the blood. Ice for the swelling. Suturing any deep cuts. And plenty of laudanum. Is that right, Doctor?"

"Yes. Now what else do you see? What about her arms?"

Her gaze swept over the young woman's limbs. Oh, my goodness. What an unlucky young woman.

"They're in the same condition as her face, Doctor. Bruising, minor cuts, none requiring stitching that I see."

"Correct again, Nurse." Scott turned to the bartender. "Sam, we're going to continue examining her. She'll be spending the night here. Why don't you come back in the morning? And go talk to Sheriff Randall. Tell him everything that happened, and what you suspect."

Sam rose and ran his hands through his hair. "I'll go see him, but there's probably nothing he can do. I'll be back about noon tomorrow for her." He put his hand in the pocket of his work apron. "What do I owe you?"

"We'll let you know when you come back for her. And remember—go tell Sheriff Randall about Jake Thomas. You may find him to be a better listener than you think."

Sam nodded and left.

As soon as the door clicked closed, she turned away. A sob racked her. Scott come up behind her, putting his hands on her arms, gently massaging them.

"Oh Scott! What have I done? This poor girl!"

"Shhh. You did nothing. It's that rascal Jake. He's the one responsible for this."

"But she took a beating in my place."

"No, not in your place. If you were still Rosie O'Roarke, he'd have beaten you again when he got into a rage."

"I—I just know what this girl is going through."

"Yes, you do. You'll be able to help her once she begins to improve."

The door slammed.

She gasped.

Jake—again.

What was he doing here?

Chapter Twelve

Rosie rushed behind the doctor. Silly girl. She looked more frightened than a jackrabbit trying to keep its foot out of a trap. It was his Rosie, all right. The way she moved, he could see right through her ridiculous disguise.

The doc hobbled around the end of the table to protect Trina. She lay motionless. Unconscious still. He hadn't hit her that hard, had he?

"Mister Thomas, what are you doing here?"

He stepped forward, but when Rosie caught his gaze, he stared her down. Had to make her nervous, so when he decided to make his move, she'd be under his control.

"How's my girl, Trina?"

Doc limped over on his crutches. Some protection he'd be. He could use that for his advantage. If it came right down to it, he could easily overpower the doctor and take Rosie with him. But Madam Margaret wasn't here yet. He needed to wait. Make Rosie squirm.

How dare she try to be uppity? To pretend to be more than she was? He needed to take his hand to her. She needed a good whipping.

When it was time, he'd take her out to his cabin beyond Florence. His place of refuge. No one knew about it or where it was. It was out in the middle of nowhere but allowed him access to several smaller and larger towns, where he could sell his cattle. Well, he thought of them as his cattle, especially after he changed the brand on them to his own—using an "O" ring iron. It could change any brand from one to another with ease.

Once Rosie settled in her mind that he owned her, he'd be just fine. At some time in the future, maybe he'd marry her, and they'd happy. She was the only one who really knew how to make him feel good. Life was torture without her.

"What are you doing here?" The doc's voice certainly had an edge to it, yet he was professional. Although he didn't lose his temper, his contempt was clear.

He smiled. "Why, Doc, I just came to see how my gal is doing. I heard something happened to her."

The doctor's face turned red. "Are you responsible for this? I'm turning you in to the sheriff."

His smile faded. "What makes you think I did this?" His right hand settled on his holster loop. He hoped he wouldn't have to shoot it out with the doctor—seein' as how the doc didn't have a gun.

Rosie said nothing and refused to meet his gaze. She seemed to shrink, hiding behind the doctor. Surely, she knew he could overpower the doctor with one punch or a hard shove.

The doctor glared at him. "You seem to have a history of beating on women."

"What makes you say that?"

"I heard it directly from another one of your victims."

"And who would that be?"

"Miss Rosalie O'Roarke. She told me last spring."

Rosie seemed to shrink farther back from the doctor. She tried to look busy, but he knew she listened to every word.

He would bide his time. He pulled out a couple of silver dollars. "Here, Doc. This ought to help take care of the girl. I'll be back to see her tomorrow."

"You'll do no such thing!" Rosie stepped forward, and stood halfway behind the doctor, with her hand on the Doc's arm.

He chuckled. "Well now, miss. And who are you to say who I can or cannot see?"

Her bottom lip quivered. Rosie's lip always shook like that when she was scared. Right before he'd give her a good whack.

"Her employer is coming for her tomorrow." She stepped behind the Doc.

The doctor maneuvered his crutches to stand directly in front of Jake. "Mister Thomas, I suggest you leave. Thank you for the payment in advance. Now get out of here."

Jake chuckled as he turned and left. He'd have the last laugh.

The scissors clattered to the floor.

"I'm sorry, Scott." Rose's hands shook.

"It's all right. He's gone now. I'll make sure he won't bother you again. I can't believe the nerve of that man."

"I hate him." She put one hand to her mouth to stifle a sob, while bending over and picking up the scissors with her other hand.

Scott turned to her, reaching out to squeeze her arm a moment before making sure his crutch didn't fall. "I understand, but we've got a patient to take care of here." His touch warmed her inside and out. Comforting. "One thing we must do is learn to control our emotions. We can't get too emotionally involved with either the patients or those around them."

"Yes, Sco—Doctor." She desperately needed more comfort, but that would have to wait. Taking in a deep breath, she exhaled slowly, turning back to the girl on the table, who had yet to regain consciousness. Rose would try to put aside her emotions until after she was off work. It would be hard. Maybe she could talk to Meghan.

When her shift was over, and she'd made sure both Scott and the young woman, Trina, were comfortable, Rose hurried home to eat dinner—and bring supper back for Scott. They talked about overnight care. Since he lived at the office, he would take this first night. He was quite mobile in his wheelchair, and he had his crutches in case Trina needed something in the night, although he'd given the girl a heavy dose of laudanum. She'd sleep through the night. Rose would take the second night, if needed.

She came to the railroad tracks and was just about to cross them when the familiar voice behind her caused her stomach to roil. Even though she hadn't heard that voice in three years, she recognized it. Madam Margaret. Mother. What on earth was she doing here?

"Porter! Take my bags to the saloon, The Rusty Nail. I'm taking it over. It will now be called Madam Margaret's."

"Why, shore, Madam. We'd be happy to make sure yore luggage gets to The Rusty Nail ... uh, Madam Margaret's." Jackson was much more than a porter. How could Madam not know that? Well, she never noticed such things.

"Thank you, Porter. Here's a little something for your trouble."

Rose hurried along, praying Madam wouldn't see her. That's all she needed. Why was she here? Had she found out *she* was living here—or was it a coincidence? Who would have told her?

A sickening feeling at the pit of her stomach gripped her. If Jake had recognized her, maybe he'd sent for Madam, hoping to force Rose to go back to her old life.

Never. Nothing could ever make her do that. Not Jake. Not Madam. Not even the town, if they found out. She would just leave and find another place to live, but she refused to be a dance hall girl ever again.

Chapter Thirteen

After dinner, Rose approached Meghan. She'd helped Olivia with the dishes, and now the boardinghouse owner had retired to her room for the evening. "Do you have a few minutes to talk?"

Meghan nodded. "Sure. Duncan is tending to some business at the ranch, so we can visit. Shall we go up to your room—or mine?"

"My room. We won't be interrupted there." Rose led the way as they climbed the stairs.

Once they entered the room, she closed the door. "Meghan, I'm in a fix."

Her friend sat on the bed near the bedpost, hooking an arm around it. "Did something happen?"

Rose pulled the chair from the desk, turning it to face the bed. The concerned look in her friend's eyes brought some comfort to her. She knew Meghan would understand. Clearing her throat, she hoped to rid it of the clogging fear that had settled there when Jake showed his face in the doctor's office earlier. "You already know about Jake. I'm still terrified about that situation. I keep expecting him to confront me about my past."

"He hasn't, though, has he?"

"No, but I'm afraid he will. However..." She swallowed. "Something else did happen."

Meghan leaned forward. "Is it Scott?"

She looked at the floor. "No. It's my mother."

"Your mother?"

She caught Meghan's gaze. "She's here."

Meghan cocked her head to one side. "In New Boston?"

Her voice came out as a croak. "Yes."

Meghan's eyes widened. "What's she doing here?"

"I have no idea."

Her friend leaned forward. "Does she know you're here?"

"I don't know." She took a handkerchief from her sleeve and twisted it. "I haven't had any contact with her since leaving Baltimore three years ago."

"When did you see her?"

Meghan's voice soothed her shattered nerves. Thank God for a friend like Meghan. Rose could share many things with her—but not everything. She would never share some of the horrible things she'd done for pay. But she could share some of the more important things that were happening now.

"While I was walking home for supper, I was crossing the tracks and heard her voice. She called Jackson a porter." She brought two fingertips to her forehead and shook her head. How could Madam be so condescending to a man of Jackson's station?

Meghan smiled. "And Jackson didn't correct her, did he?"

She let out a breath and brought her hand to her lap. "No, he just took it with all the grace and politeness he always shows."

"So your mother is here in New Boston. Are you going to seek her out and speak to her?"

"I don't want to talk to her." Rose jumped up, wringing her hands. "I have nothing to say. I'm hoping to stay out of her way while trying to find out why she's here. Without her knowing, of course."

Meghan unhooked her arm from the bedpost, then leaned her arm against it. "How are you going to do that?"

"I'm not sure. Do you have any suggestions?"

Her friend sat up straight. "I think it might be best if you do nothing for the present. But if you do encounter her, and she recognizes you... you could talk to her and try to work out the bad feelings you have for her. Maybe God brought her here to help you learn to forgive her."

Rose rolled her eyes. "Please, Meghan. No sermons. We've talked about this before. She ruined me. I can't forget that."

Meghan grabbed her hand, gently, but firmly. "I'm not asking you to forget it. Just forgive her. All that means is that you let it go, within your heart." Her touch calmed Rose, and she sat. "It doesn't excuse her for what she did. It's your heart that will be freed, if you can make the decision to let the pain go."

Rose stood up, nearly knocking the chair against the desk. "I—I can't forget. She ruined my whole life. Stole my innocence. Forced me into a life no one would ever choose."

Meghan knelt before Rose and put a hand on her arm. "I know. What she did was terrible. Do you remember when we talked about this before?"

"Yes, I've been trying to think right as you asked me to, but I'm still hurt by her actions. It's been five years since she forced me into that life." She untwisted and re-twisted her handkerchief. "I want to change—to be different. Respected. Loved. How can I be that with my past always hanging over my head?"

Meghan stood and moved to her side, putting her arm around Rose's shoulders. "You've already changed your life on the outside. I'm so proud of you for doing that. It takes a lot of courage to do what you're doing." She gave Rose a squeeze. "God loves you, Rose. Even though it doesn't seem like it sometimes."

She had no response to that. Meghan gathered her in her arms for a hug. She let out a breath.

"I'll try. That's all I can promise."

Meghan released her but squeezed her arm as she withdrew. "That's a good start."

Rose grasped her friend's hand. "Thank you, Meghan. Is there anything you want to talk about? We've been so busy lately, I feel I haven't visited with you in ages."

Meghan returned to sit on the bed and released a long breath. "It has been a while."

This conversation wasn't over yet. Rose went back to the chair. She wanted to help her friend, if she could, be an encouragement, as Meghan had been for her. She truly valued her friendship with Meghan—the first real friend she'd ever had.

Rose leaned forward. "How are the wedding plans coming?"

Her friend looked down a moment, then lifted sad eyes to meet her gaze. A tear rolled down her cheek. Rose gulped. "Is everything all right between you and Duncan?"

Meghan took a handkerchief out of her sleeve and dabbed her eye. "Yes—and—no."

Rose jumped up and put her arm around her friend's shoulders. "What's happened?"

Meghan whimpered, then sniffed. "It's that blamed call to ministry Duncan believes he has. I'm still struggling with it."

"I'm sorry. Did you get a chance to talk with Olivia about it?"

"Yes."

"What did she say?"

"That it's a woman's place to support her husband in whatever he does, and that God must have something very great in mind to call Duncan to that level of service."

Rose squeezed her hand. "I don't know how God operates any more now than the last time we spoke of this." Her neck stiffened. "You're still together, aren't you? I don't see Duncan around much."

Meghan raised her hanky and blew her nose. "We're still engaged but decided to seek God in our own way for a couple weeks, while he's out at the ranch. School takes up my time here anyway." She wadded her handkerchief into a ball. "I miss him so much, but he said we need this time away from each other—for a short time—so God can speak to us."

Rose frowned. "I don't know that I agree with that. I do know that both you and Duncan hear from God. I'm sure everything will work out." She gave Meghan another hug.

"Thanks, Rose. And thank you for not judging."

Rose stood, bringing Meghan up with her. "Who am I to pass judgment? Now you go and prepare tomorrow's school lessons—not just for your school students, but for me and the de Campos, too."

She pulled Meghan into her arms for one last hug, then released her. True love didn't seem to be enough for Meghan and Duncan. And yet, she hoped it was. She'd be happy just knowing a man loved her for who she was, not her body.

Chapter Fourteen

The next morning, Scott hobbled on crutches to unlock the office door. Clomping over to the coatrack, he pulled an apron from a hook. He loved the feel of the crisp, starched apron, yet it's comfort often made him forget he wore one.

Trina had regained consciousness earlier and decided to walk back to the saloon by herself. She seemed to be in better condition than he'd originally thought. A beating, yes, but her injuries were not serious. Rose's had been far more serious, including cracked ribs and a sprained wrist or arm. He couldn't remember exactly.

The crutches clacked on the floor as he made his way across to the supply table, where he set about gathering the necessities for the day...bandage rolls, instruments, and pain powders. He also needed towels and blankets. Never knowing just what he'd need, he liked to be prepared.

He forgot a moment and stretched up to reach for a towel on the top shelf. Sharp pain shooting up his leg quickly reminded him to shift his weight.

The door opened. He glanced over as Rose bustled in, her mouth turned down. Who'd caused that? What was she worried about?

"We're ready to meet the day."

"Fine." Her voice cut off. She rarely only answered in one word, let alone in a blunt manner, except during that time she took him to task over Meghan.

"Trina is fine, and she went home under her own power. Is everything all right?" He looked around, then clumped over to the front window and looked out. Turning back, he caught her gaze. Something was most assuredly wrong. Not even good news caused a change in her expression.

She let out a long breath, as if she were trying to hold a heavy weight on her shoulders.

"Let's sit, Scott. It looks like you've been on your feet long enough."

He followed her to the couch and sat at one end. She at the other.

She looked down, then met his gaze. Her lovely doe eyes were filled with turmoil. Thunder and lightning rolled from her expression. Had he done something? Or was it that scoundrel?

"Is it Jake? Has he been bothering you?"

She lifted her eyes to the ceiling, then closed them. When they opened, she lowered her chin; regained some control.

"My mother is here."

His eyes narrowed. "In New Boston? Did you see her? Why would she come here?"

She pulled out a handkerchief and started to twist it, something similar he'd seen Meghan do when she was upset about something. He'd encouraged the unusual friendship.

"I've seen her from a distance, but not talked to her."

"Does she know you're living here and that you've changed your life?" He drew closer.

"I don't think so. I haven't talked with her in three years. Not since I left Baltimore."

"But how could it be a coincidence that she's here when you are?"

"I don't think it's by accident."

"Has someone told her?"

"I suppose it's possible."

"Who?"

"I don't know for certain, but if Jake recognized me..."

"What are you going to do?"

Tears formed in her eyes. He scooted over the rest of the distance between them. Leaning over, he wiped away an escaping tear with his thumb. She turned her face into his hand, her cheek cupped in his palm. He loved the feel of her soft skin.

"I don't know. I want to run away where she can never find me."

"What would that solve?" He squeezed her hand. "You mean a lot to me, you know. I don't want you to leave."

"What else can I do? If the town finds out who I am, they'll run me out anyway. I might as well give them a head start." She sniffed.

"I don't like that idea."

She pulled her hand from his. "You know what they'll do. They'll rise up on their self-righteous high horses and force me to leave town."

"Why do you think so?"

She said nothing.

"Has anyone said anything?" He clenched his fist.

She put her head down. A sob escaped. He put his arm around her shoulders a moment, then released her.

"What happened?"

"Madam always told me that's what would happen. She said it had happened to her."

"What did she say?"

"I don't remember her exact words, but she's said it my whole life." She stiffened her back and her chin jutted out. Evidently in imitation of her mother. "'Rosie, ma dearie, ya are what ya are, and ya cain't be nobody else. If ya tried, they'd just run ya out of town, like they did me. You can't change, and they never will.' I want to prove her wrong." Relaxing, she leaned back.

"You've already done that. You're not the same woman you were even six months ago. I'm proud of you, and I'm glad you're working for me."

She laid a hand on his arm a moment. "Thanks, Scott." Straightening her handkerchief, she blew her nose. "That means a lot."

He reached over and put a thumb under her chin. "You're important to me, in so many ways."

"You think I should stay and see what happens?" Her eyes were wide, full of fear and dread.

"Yes, I do. I won't let anyone insult you or force you to leave town." He smiled what he hoped was a smile of encouragement. "Should you talk to her?"

"No. I don't ever want to speak to her again." She pulled away from his touch.

"Why not? Are your feelings that strong?"

She let out a breath. "I've never told you about her, except her name. And yes, I do think I hate her that much."

"What more can you tell me that you think I should know? She's a brothel owner. But she gave birth to you and raised you. Shouldn't that count for something?"

"There's a lot you don't know about me."

"I know all I need."

"You wouldn't want anything more to do with me, if you knew."

"Why? I know what you did for a living. You had to—you were—not able to read or write. What else would I need to know? Women in your position don't have much choice in how to live."

She looked down, then met his gaze. "My own mother forced me into that life."

He cocked his head to one side. "What difference does that make?"

"Doesn't that trouble you?"

He put his hand on her arm. "It angers me that she did that to you. You're not responsible for that. You deserve to live a decent life. So, in that respect, no, it doesn't bother me."

"It bothers me."

"You're a different person now. The old Rosie is gone. It doesn't matter how you got that way. In her place is you, Rose—intelligent, bright, inquisitive, and gifted. A woman who has learned so much in the last few months. You've become indispensable to me, you know. I don't know what I'd do without you."

She really had weaved her way into his heart and life.

Was he beginning to fall in love? What did that even feel like?

Chapter Fifteen

Jake strode into Madam Margaret's saloon. The décor was only slightly different than that of most other saloons he'd been in. If a man had designed the interior, it was usually gaudier, attention-getting. Evidently before she'd arrived, Madam had insisted on a few changes. Where bloodred satin brocade had papered the walls in between bright white chair railing and panel separators, a deep purple paint now colored the panels. Suggestive artwork of lovers in various poses hung—one on each panel. There was no mistaking what sort of place this was.

He had to hand it to Madam Margaret. She seemed to know what a guy like him wanted to see when he entered this tavern. Looking around, then up, he noticed the crystal chandelier. Hmmm. Trying to bring some class to this place. No doubt so she could charge more for everything... from food to the girls.

"Hey Barkeep, where's the Madam? Is she here?" Jake pulled out a silver dollar.

The bartender narrowed his eyes, then looked him up and down. "Do you have business with her?"

"You might say that. I believe she can thank me for getting her here."

"Oh, so you're Jake Thomas?"

"That I am."

"Want a drink?"

"Yeah. Whiskey."

"Sure thing. Be right there." As the bartender turned to grab a bottle, Jake twisted around to take another look at the stage to his right. Madam must be going to employ singers and dancers, too. That would make this a real rip-roarin' place. Somewhere he'd like to settle down with Rosie. If they married, she'd inherit, and he'd eventually wind up in charge here. He smiled to himself. They'd rake in the money. He wouldn't have to rustle steers anymore.

"Here ya go, Mister Thomas. Enjoy." The bartender put a small shot glass nearly filled with whiskey in front of Jake.

He drank it down in one gulp. It would take the edge off in a few minutes. He'd be more relaxed. Then he'd find Madam Margaret.

Later that evening at the boardinghouse, Rose was clearing her dishes away from the supper table when Meghan tapped her on the shoulder.

"Do you have a few minutes to visit?"

Rose carried her dishes to the kitchen. Meghan followed her.

"Can I ask a favor of you? It's for the schoolchildren."

Rose placed her dishes in the sink, nodding to Luisa with a smile, before turning to Meghan.

"Of course. Let's go out on the porch. It's still warm enough. Although I think I'll grab my shawl. The evenings are getting cooler all the time." Rose grasped it and opened the door.

"Good idea. I'll get mine, too."

As they stepped out onto the west porch, the sun was now setting, creating a lavender peach array against the few clouds. They sat down in the wicker chairs.

She turned to Meghan. "What's the favor?"

Meghan smiled. "I had an idea the students would love to know what a nurse does. As part of a general health unit of their science curriculum. You could tell them about your job, describe some of the more interesting people you meet in the office. Also tell them about the wide variety of duties you perform. And—how important nurses are to doctors."

She returned the smile. "I'd love to—but..."

"But what?"

"Are you sure you want *me* to?"

"Why wouldn't I?"

She fidgeted. "When would you like me to do this?" She cleared her throat. "And where is the school meeting these days?"

Meghan cocked her head to one side. "What are you afraid of?"

She couldn't put her fear into words.

Meghan continued. "We meet in the Catholic church with twenty students so far, and we're still growing. We outgrew the railroad car where school was held last year—when we only had eight pupils. Mister Fagin approached the Catholic priest as soon as we knew how many schoolchildren we were going to start with."

She needed to conquer her fear of public speaking. "How are they doing? I remember two of the boys were going to be a challenge for you—to find something they wanted to learn."

"Yes, Tommy Sampson and Jeremy Baker are still struggling to discover that. It's a process of elimination, but we have hope they'll find something soon."

Rose nodded. "When did you want me to come?"

"How about next Tuesday?"

Rose thought a moment, then let out a long breath.

"That will be fine. It will nice to see them. I have a hard time remembering all their names. I don't know how you do it."

Meghan giggled. "Memorization, I assure you."

"Well, you do a wonderful job with them."

"Thank you. But I'm sure you see some of those children in the medical office from time-to-time, don't you?"

"Over the summer, we certainly saw our share of scrapes, scratches, cuts, and a couple broken bones from kids trying to race across the railroad tracks."

"They need a safe place to play." Meghan got an idea. It was written all over her bright expression. "I know. I'm going to ask the railroad to set aside some land for a park."

"That's a terrific idea. But what's in it for Santa Fe? They won't want to pay for it, will they?"

"If they see the advantages for their children, I think they will. It would benefit the whole town."

Rose looked toward the west. The last streaks of light were quickly fading. "I hope the railroad executives will want it." She stood. "Thanks for asking me to come to the school. I'll start thinking about what I want to say. I'll have to practice it a lot."

"You have a few days before next Tuesday." Meghan rose. "So that's it. You're afraid of speaking in public. I understand. You'll be fine, though."

They started toward the door.

"Oh, and would you ask Scott if he would come, too? A different day, of course."

"I'll ask. I'm sure he'll want to come. He'll enjoy it—even though getting around is hard to do."

"How's his leg doing?"

"He can walk around the office on crutches. I think he should still be in the wheelchair until we know how his leg is actually doing."

"When will you check it again?"

"About three weeks."

"That's a long time."

"It takes six to eight weeks for a break like that to heal. It could have been worse. The bone could have broken through the skin, but it didn't. And for that, we are truly grateful."

They reached the front door and went inside, then stepped into the parlor, each one sitting on one end of the couch.

Meghan smoothed out a wrinkle on her skirt. Rose lifted an eyebrow. "Are things all right between you and Duncan now?"

Her friend cleared her throat. "I haven't seen him in a week. They've been on roundup."

Rose leaned over and placed a hand on Meghan's arm and squeezed. "Oh, I didn't know. I've been so busy..."

Meghan smiled a small smile. "You certainly have. I don't know how you do it all. Has Jake given you any trouble lately?"

She leaned back. "I haven't seen him for days, and I hope I never see him again." She looked down. "I think he might know who I am. If he does, he's planning something. I feel it." She turned toward Meghan. "Anyway, back to Duncan. When are you two going to talk? And how are you feeling about his call to ministry? We haven't talked for a while."

Meghan looked down. "I'm not altogether reconciled to it yet. In my wildest dreams, I would never have thought this would happen. I guess I need to get used to the idea."

"Maybe God will change his mind. Or maybe Duncan didn't hear him right in the first place."

Her friend shook her head. "I don't think God changes his mind much. I'm still learning about the Bible, but I remember one verse says, 'he changes not.'"

She humphed. "But haven't I heard in church recently that God relented a few times on decisions he'd already made?"

Meghan tilted her head to one side. "Well, yes, sometimes he does, only for certain situations. Instead of destroying people, he would give them another choice. God's heart is to choose mercy over judgment."

Rose let that sink in. "Is God merciful?"

"That's part of his nature."

"I have some gripes about that."

"One thing to think about. You're still alive and in good health. Yes, you've had a tough life. Goodness knows I can hardly understand why he allowed those things in your life. But if you choose to follow him, he'll show you the way. I just know it."

"I'll think about it. I know he's helped you. I need that, but I haven't seen anything like that in my life yet."

Meghan reached out and touched her arm. "I'm praying for you. I believe God will do something on your behalf soon."

"I hope so." She needed God to help her keep her secrets.

As Meghan left to go upstairs, Rose stayed in the parlor, thinking. Dishes clinked from the kitchen. Luisa and Olivia chatted as they cleaned up. Carlos and Maria were studying in the dining room. Where the others were, she didn't know. Hannah might still be at work at the hotel. Bernhard Warkentyne was probably coming home from the mill, unless he was working late.

The train whistle sounded. In the past week, the train schedule had nearly doubled. There was at least one outgoing and one incoming train everyday now, as opposed to one every other day. A few months ago, only one train a week would arrive or depart.

How quickly things changed in New Boston. She loved this town. The growth astounded her, and yet she loved seeing the town building. It was constructing the future of a people, including her. She prayed the town would never learn her secret.

Chapter Sixteen

The next morning, after breakfast, Rose found the door to Scott's office unlocked, but he was nowhere to be found.

"Scott?" She walked to the closed bedroom door and knocked. "Are you in there?"

No answer. Where was he?

She checked the outhouse in the back, knocking on the door. Seeing no crutches, she returned to the office. When she reached the bedroom door, she decided to throw caution to the wind, and banged on the door.

"Scott! Wake up! I'm coming in."

As she opened the door, he stood on the other side of it. He was using only one crutch, under his left arm. She looked him up and down to make sure he was all right.

"Is something the matter, Rose? Were you worried about me?" As he limped over, the single crutch thumped along with him.

"Are you all right? You didn't answer when I knocked."

Scott ran his free hand through his hair. She loved the way it flopped on his forehead first thing in the morning, before he used hair oil to grease it in place. He smiled.

"Sorry, your first knock must have woken me up." He stood in his pajamas, the right leg split up to just above the knee to accommodate the splints, now that he was out of the fracture box. Handsome. She shook her head. *Don't think about him that way.* He was her employer, and only that, for now. She did hope something would develop. He seemed to be attracted to her. Let nature take its course. First, he needed to heal from this broken leg. And she needed to make sure Jake wouldn't become a problem.

He hobbled over to his wardrobe and picked out a shirt, then tossed it to the bed.

"Would you like me to help you pick your clothes out? Then I can get your breakfast from the hotel kitchen."

"You're a godsend, Rose." He clumped to his bed and sat down slowly, sticking his injured leg straight out in front of him as he eased onto the bed.

She went to his closet and picked out a pair of slacks already slashed up the side seam.

"I'll be back in a little while. Since you seem to have decided to get rid of one crutch, I think you can get dressed by yourself." She shook her head and let out a long breath.

"Thank you for getting several men to help me dress the past few weeks." He smiled.

"It wouldn't have been proper otherwise." Heat traveled up her neck. She looked down to the floor.

He chuckled. "Why, Rose, I believe you're blushing."

Surely her face was beet red. "Whatever do you mean, Doctor?"

He rose from the bed, just as she moved toward the doorway. He stuck out his crutch to block her way. "Just a moment, Nurse."

He came so near, shivers went up her spine. Her shoulders inadvertently shook once. This earthquake inside her must stop.

She slowly moved the crutch out of her way, but as she passed, he drew her to him, and placed a kiss on her cheek.

"I have feelings for you, Rose. And I think you have some for me." He slowly turned her to him. "Admit it."

She placed one hand on his heart, the other on his shoulder. "Yes, Scott, I—I do have feelings for you. But we ... must ... not ..."

He lowered his lips and brushed hers, a tentative, sweet kiss, searching. It was as if his lips were a match that lit a fire within her.

No one had ever done that before. She'd wondered if anyone ever could. As he deepened the kiss, she leaned into him. A soft moan came. Was it from her or him?

She could have stayed like this forever.

"Hello? Anyone here?"

A patient had arrived. He quickly ended the kiss. Swallowing, she turned to enter the main office. She straightened her dress and coifed her hair, hoping her expression didn't give away her feelings.

∽

Jake struck the bar of Madam Margaret's Saloon with his fist.

"What do you mean, she won't see me?" Heat flushed up his neck. He'd been polite with his written note requesting to see her. Surely, she'd want to see him when she discovered he had information regarding Rosie.

The bartender mopped up a small puddle on the bar near Jake.

"She says she don't know you. Right now she's busy. Getting ready for opening night in a week or so."

Jake shook his head. "She'll want to see me when she knows why I want to talk to her."

The bartender turned away and tossed the towel into a bin behind the bar.

"If she won't talk to you, there ain't nothin' you can do about it. I gave her your request. You'll just have to wait and try again later. But, she's a very stubborn woman and doesn't change her mind easily."

Jake scratched the back of his neck. Just last week the bartender acknowledged she knew him. Called him by name. What had changed?

"Will you give her a message from me again?"

The bartender's eyes narrowed. Jake pulled out a silver dollar and with his index finger, slid it to the bartender. "Would this be enough incentive to deliver a short message?"

The bartender picked up the silver dollar and pocketed it in his apron. "Sure. What do you want me to pass along?"

Jake smiled. "Tell her I have information about Rosie—uh, Rosalie. She'll know who I mean."

The bartender cocked his head to one side.

"Okay. I'll tell her. But don't expect her to respond right away. Like I said—"

Jake joined in. "I know. She's busy."

He needed to punch someone. Nobody better provoke him. His self-control dissolved by the second.

Chapter Seventeen

"Keep the cut covered for today, Tommy." Rose's sweet voice filtered into the bedroom from the office. "Tomorrow, unwrap it for an hour or so. Don't get the stitches wet."

Exactly what Scott would have said. He shook his head in amazement. In just a few short months, Rose had completely changed her life, leaving the dance hall behind. She'd become indispensable to him. Not only at work, but personally, too. And that kiss. Heat traveled up his neck at the mere thought of it. How had she felt about it—considering her background? He wanted more, and hoped she felt the same way. But he would never force her. She'd turned her face upward to him as he lowered his. From the first brush of his lips to hers, he was entranced. He'd never felt this way about ... Meghan.

A sigh escaped. How could he have been so stupid? He still felt a need to make amends. If only he could think of something. He'd apologized and released Meghan from her "promise." Later, maybe after she and that cowboy were married, he could think of something appropriate to do.

His leg hurt. He'd been on it too long, the blasted thing. In about three weeks, he and Rose planned to check it. The wait was interminable.

He watched as she walked the patient to the door. When she turned, his breath hitched. She looked radiant. Her beauty shone through the room as bright as the morning sun. He wanted to gather her in his arms and hold her forever. Her eyes narrowed.

"Doctor, I believe you look a little peaked. I think you need to get off your feet."

He nodded. "You're right. Would you help me?"

"Where would you like to go? The couch or your bed?"

"I've had enough of the bed. I don't need to lie down, just sit and give the leg a rest."

She moved to his side and took his arm. He felt like soft clay in the hands of an artist. She could ask for anything, and he'd give it to her.

"Come with me, Doctor Allison. I'll make sure you're comfortable. Are you hungry?"

He smiled. "Starving, but I want to try walking to the hotel restaurant."

"Are you sure you're ready to walk that far? It's only been three weeks."

"I can't just stay here all the time. I'll go insane."

"Well, you rest for another few days, and then we'll see."

"Nurse, you drive a hard bargain."

"Yes, I do. See that you remember that in the future, Doctor."

He put a hand on his heart. "Have mercy on me. I am indebted to you...always."

She giggled, and then gave him a playful slap on the shoulder. "Why, Doctor Allison, if I didn't know better, I'd say you were flirting with me."

"Who, me?" He cocked his head to one side.

"Yes, you." Her cocoa-colored wide-open eyes bored a hole through his heart.

"Why would I do that?" He couldn't help smiling. Then, after a quick glance over his shoulder, even though he knew they were alone, he drew her to him, inhaling the scent of her rose-scented bath salts.

She gasped, then placed a hand on his chest. "Scott, what if a patient walks in?"

But she didn't push him away.

"Let them. I don't care." He leaned in a bit closer.

"What will they think?" Her mouth opened in pretend shock. At least, that's what he thought it was.

"Does it matter so much?"

She looked up at him with love-filled eyes and raised her chin. He lowered his lips gently to meet hers. She released a soft moan. He deepened the kiss. Every nerve in his body tingled. Tiredness and pain drifted away. All he wanted was to lose himself in her embrace, in all of her. His free arm sought the small of her back. Her slender arms entwined around his neck. She smelled of rosewater. How appropriate. He kissed her until he thought he would burst with happiness. She broke off the kiss and stepped back.

His breathing matched hers. Their eyes locked. Then, she put her arm around him and led him to the couch. She assisted while he lowered himself to a sitting position, then helped him swivel until his leg stretched out along the length of the couch.

"You are an amazing woman, Rose."

She smiled. "Thank you, Doctor."

"You smell just like your name."

"I've been using rosewater since I was a girl."

"Do you think we might have a future together?"

She said nothing for a moment and her brow furrowed. He wished he could erase those lines which he felt clouded her expression. What was she thinking right now?

Her eyes closed a moment, then opened and met his gaze. "We might." Her tone was hesitant. He waited.

"We're different, you and I. You're educated. I'm not. You also know my other problems. Until they're resolved, I don't want to jinx our relationship."

He looked at his feet a moment.

She brought several pillows from his bedroom and propped them behind him. He leaned back into them, thankful the tops rested at the back of his neck.

Drowsiness flooded him, and as he succumbed to sleep, he felt the warmth of a light blanket being put over him. Feathery kisses grazed his forehead, then his nose, then finally, his lips.

⌒

In his dream, Rafe came to him. They were out by the creek where he'd broken his leg.

"How are you doing, son? Is the leg healing well?"

"I think it's coming along."

"Good. Be patient with it."

Scott nodded. He couldn't think of anything to say in response.

In the dream, it seemed that Rafe looked at him with more intensity than he'd ever seen before. The intensity seemed to cut through to the depths of his heart, but implanted pure love, no condemnation.

Rose's voice cut through the dream. She shook his shoulder. "Scott, Doctor. You have a patient."

What did his dream mean?

Chapter Eighteen

Scott fumbled with his stethoscope. Unlike his usual confidence. Wilcox sat on the exam table. But this was—awkward. Hopefully, this would be the last time Scott would have to see the cowboy. He'd given permission for Wilcox to ride, even on roundup, and supervise, but not do any actual heavy labor, such as branding, roping, or heavy lifting of any kind.

"How are you feeling, Wilcox?"

"Fine, Doc. Hope you'll agree."

"Unbutton your shirt, please."

Wilcox complied. Scott put his stethoscope to the cowboy's chest and listened. The thump, thump, thump was as regular and steady as the second hand on his watch.

"Let's look at the scar. Do you feel any tightness around it when you stretch or when you inhale?"

Wilcox thought a moment. "Nope."

The short sentences without subjects aggravated Scott. How could he have a decent conversation with the man? Then a thought struck him. Hadn't Rose said Wilcox was going to become a preacher?

"Say, Wilcox, did I hear right? Miss Rhodes told me you were thinking of becoming a preacher."

"Yep."

"I think you're going to have to talk more than one-word sentences if you're going to preach and expect a congregation to listen."

"Uh-huh."

Scott wanted to punch him in the nose. Why couldn't he talk like normal people? He shouldn't be judgmental, but the cowboy had rankled him ever since they'd met—when he'd brought Meghan in after she'd been grazed by a stray bullet her first week in New Boston. She'd courted the cowboy as seriously as she'd courted him. They had been romantic rivals for her affections, but that was all past now. He'd moved on and hoped Meghan and Wilcox had forgiven him. Meghan said she had—but she kept her distance. Last week at The Pioneer Store, she'd hidden at the back of the store, pretending to look at pots and pans an inordinate amount of time. Maybe they felt as awkward around him as he did them.

"Okay, you're discharged from my care. You can do all the heavy labor you need to." Scott cleared his throat, and took his time removing his stethoscope from his ears. He folded it carefully and set it down. Again, he cleared his throat. "Could you answer me one question, a personal one—about your faith?"

Wilcox's neck stiffened, and his chin dipped. "Try to."

Scott looked at the floor a moment, then locked gazes with Wilcox. "Do you believe in angels?"

Wilcox relaxed.

"Oh, yes."

"What can you tell me about them?"

The cowboy rubbed his chin. "What would you like to know?"

"Whatever you can tell me. I know they're in the Bible." Scott folded his stethoscope. "Do you think they come to earth nowadays?"

Wilcox's eyebrows knitted together, his head cocked to one side. "Yep, they come ... in response to prayer, sometimes."

"Really?"

"Yep."

"Have you ever seen one?"

"Nope, not that I know of. Though the Bible says we sometimes entertain angels unaware."

"So it's possible that anyone at any time could see an angel?"

"Yep." Wilcox's eyes narrowed. "Why are you asking all these questions?"

Scott exhaled. "I—I think—I—I might have talked to one."

"Really? When?"

"The day I broke my leg, something strange happened."

Wilcox smiled. A friendly, caring grin. Hmmm. Maybe the cowboy would be a good one to talk to. Scott had not mentioned his encounter with anyone except Rose, not even the Reverend Osborne Street.

Scott swallowed. "I hope you won't think I'm insane." He looked down a moment; then, hard as it was, he looked Wilcox in the eye. "And—uh, I want to officially apologize to you for my behavior a couple months ago. I'm a different man now. At least, I'm trying to be."

The cowboy's beam widened. "All's forgiven, Doc." He extended his hand.

Scott grasped it, impressed with the cowboy's firm, yet welcoming handshake. Could it be possible they might be friends someday?

Wilcox gestured for him to sit. "Care to sit down and tell me about it, Doc?"

Rose listened from the back of the office as she performed inventory. Her back was to them, as Scott revealed his remarkable encounter with Rafe to Duncan. Was the sweet-faced old man who brought Scott home really an angel? Finishing, she put the clipboard down and went to clean the instruments on a table in the exam area. She could still perform her duties while watching and listening to what was going on, without intruding.

"That's the end of it. What do you think, Wilcox?"

Duncan cocked his head to one side. Then his lips curled up. Meghan was fortunate to be engaged to such a considerate man. It seemed Scott was beginning to be a little more like Duncan. The ways he'd cared about her, the fact that he listened with respect when she'd shared about Madam and Jake. Yes, Scott was changing from the driven man who'd tried to blackmail Meghan into marrying him. That day had crushed not only Meghan's heart, but hers, too. She'd already begun to have feelings for him, but he nearly killed them when she overheard him threaten to let Duncan die. Only because Scott had done the right thing, and appeared remorseful, begging her humbly to return to work as his assistant, had she continued to work for him. That kept her feelings alive while she hoped for more, that he'd come to love her for who she was.

"Well, Doc, sounds to me like you had a true angelic encounter. You really got to talk to one. And you were rescued. That's what they do."

Rose finished her cleaning up of instruments and turned toward the conversation.

"I didn't mean to eavesdrop, but I talked to Rafe, too."

Duncan's eyes widened. "You did? When?"

She pulled up a stool and sat near Scott. "When he came here, he asked me to help him bring in Scott—Doctor Allison."

Duncan's expressive eyes seemed wider than usual. "All I can say is—what an amazing story. God must have something really special in mind for you two—to reveal himself to you in that way."

Interesting when Duncan became comfortable with someone— or—was it because he was talking about God? He spoke in full sentences.

"Angels are all around us." Duncan's arm gestured in a wide arc. "We don't usually see them. The Bible says they're messengers. Angels delivered messages to Old Testament prophets and announced the birth of Christ to the shepherds in the countryside.

"They also help protect those who believe in God and God's son. Apostles were freed from prison and angels ministered to Jesus after he was tempted by the devil." He paused a moment. He certainly could preach and teach. She loved hearing him. His words lit a different kind of fire in her heart. Like awakening her to something she hadn't known before.

"Angels can come in all their glory, or as a kindly human being of any age, almost always coming in human form as men. They can appear in whatever form God believes the person they're ministering to will best accept their help and assistance."

Duncan turned to face Scott. "Does that seem to agree with what you felt when you encountered Rafe?"

Scott caught her gaze and his eyes reflected an intensity she hadn't seen before. They seemed to pierce her soul. This was important to him, and therefore, to her.

"I think so. I did question him at the time about his medical knowledge. If he'd been a young man, I probably wouldn't have let him help me at all."

Duncan leaned forward. "Can you describe him?"

A knock at the door interrupted the conversation.

Though reluctant to leave such a vital discussion, she answered it.

Chapter Nineteen

Jake tied his horse to the railing and checked into the Silver Spike. It had been a couple of weeks since he'd been in town. He needed Trina, even though she wasn't as skilled in pleasure as his Rosie girl. He'd done some serious thinking about her while out on the range. People would say he rustled cattle, but in his mind, it was business. He got away with it.

He'd nearly gotten caught a couple of times but managed to hide. Ranch hands hadn't been able to capture him. He chuckled. Stupid cowboys—not enough brains to figure out which way was up.

"Hey, Sam. Is Trina upstairs?"

The barkeep looked up and rolled his eyes. "Yep."

Jake pulled out two silver dollars. "One's for a bottle, and one's for Trina."

"Now, Jake, you know Trina sets her own price. You'll have to pay it if you want to spend time with her." He paused while he put the coin for the bottle in the cash register. "But after what you did last time you were here, I'll bet her price went up." He shoved the other coin back to him.

Jake slammed his fist on the bar. "She'll take what I give her—and like it."

Sam shook his head. "No more shenanigans, Jake. If you rough her up again, I'll kick you out of here so fast—"

Jake leaned forward and grabbed the barkeep by the shirt collar.

"I'd like to see ya try, Sam." He released the man's shirt, then stepped back from the bar. "Don't you worry. She's only a substitute for who I really want."

He turned and strode up the stairs.

⌒

There he stood.

"Miss Rose—are you going to ask me in?"

She opened the door farther. "We—we were just talking about you."

Rafe smiled. It was a warm beam. Goosebumps ran all up and down her arms, shoulders, and neck.

"I have some jawin' to do with ya." Was he really an angel—to talk like that?

Duncan jumped off the exam table, his knees buckling. Scott stood, mouth hanging open, as if he didn't believe his eyes.

Rafe walked past her, then turned and gazed into her eyes. Love poured out. Love so intense and powerful, so pure, she had to look away. Yet, he still addressed her. His voice, kind and soft.

"Close the door, Rose. We don't want to be interrupted now, do we?"

"Yes, sir." She swallowed. The click of the door latch seemed at once loud, yet the sounded faded away. A presence came over her. At first, goosebumps covered her whole body. Soon the chill gave way to a warmth. Like several warm blankets enveloping her, one after the other.

"We were just talking about you—and here you are." Scott limped over to Rafe on one crutch.

Rafe smiled again, this time at Scott.

"Are you an angel?"

The old man didn't answer, but Scott's expression changed—softer and bright.

"Sit down, son. You need to preserve your strength."

Scott hobbled back to the couch. She scurried over to help him.

Rafe turned to Duncan first and whispered something in his ear.

The cowboy began to quietly weep. She'd never seen him do that before—even when he realized he was going to live after being critically wounded. He'd been so weak. It was a miracle he was alive. Had Meghan ever seen him cry?

Rafe reached down and pulled the cowboy to his feet. That seemed to strengthen Duncan, and he wiped his eyes with one fist. Their gazes locked. The old man's expression was the same look of pure love given to both her and Scott.

Time stood still. Her only thought—pure, unfiltered love. Rafe spoke. She couldn't hear what he said. But Duncan did. His countenance brightened considerably.

Duncan sank to his knees again, and then he lay facedown on the floor. He raised his head once, then put it down. Tears ran down his cheeks, but no sound came from his throat.

Silence reigned.

She daren't move. The thick air could only be felt, not seen. A denseness of love—warmth and heaviness. She'd never experienced anything like this before.

The moment seemed to last forever but couldn't have been longer than a couple of seconds.

Rafe turned to her. A jolt sent tremors through her. What would he say? Her heart sank. Would he condemn her?

"Rose, don't be afraid to turn to the Father, and his son, Jesus, anytime you need a brother or a father. He knows you grew up without a pa."

Her eyes misted, blurred to the point where she couldn't see. Truth pierced her heart, but it didn't hurt. Warm love like liquid gold flowed through her from his words. Every word seemed to light a lamp within her soul.

"God is pleased with your decision to change your life. Rely on your friend to give you encouragement and direction."

How did he know about Meghan? Of course. If he was really an angel, God must have told him. She was learning things about God she'd never known before. Even though she'd visited church a few times, and heard the gospel message, she hadn't quite been able to accept it. Would he know that, too?

"Meghan Gallagher is right when she told you that God wants you to receive him in your heart. And if you forgive, your sins will be forgiven. As Jesus forgave the woman caught in adultery in the Bible, he will forgive you, if you—"

A sob escaped her. "If I can forgive Mother and Jake."

He placed a hand on her shoulder. His touch was like a hot liquid being poured on her frozen soul. The love. From the core of her being, she knew she was loved—by God. Her heavenly Father. What was happening to her? Could she really believe God loved her?

"Rose, feeling forgiveness takes time, and it's not easy. In the deepest part of your heart, you know what you need to do. But, know that the Father is pleased that you are trying to change your life. Ask him to help you to do it."

She pulled her handkerchief from her sleeve and blew her nose.

Another stillness overtook the room. It seemed a "holy" atmosphere. Though how she knew that mystified her. Yet that's what it was.

Rafe turned to Scott, got down on his knees—not to worship, but to be on Scott's level.

Scott closed his eyes. Rafe leaned over and whispered into Scott's ear. It seemed that whatever Rafe said to others, she didn't hear.

Scott's eyes filled with tears. One escaped and ran down his cheek. First Duncan. Now Scott. What was said that made both men weep?

Rose bowed her head. The old man's words rolled over in her heart. *"You know what you need to do. Feeling forgiveness takes time."*

Then she heard Scott stir on the couch. She opened her eyes and saw Duncan pulling himself up off the floor.

Scott cleared his throat. "What just happened?"

She looked around.

The old man was nowhere to be seen. The door had not opened or closed.

Chapter Twenty

Scott's skin tingled. Adrenaline spiked through him, leaving him shaky and weak. He looked around. Had Rafe really been here? If so, his visit had set Scott's mind and heart ablaze. He was reminded of the scripture about God being an all-consuming fire. Was that a good thing or not? He didn't know.

Wilcox dragged himself from the floor, wiped his eyes, then slipped out of the office.

Rose's eyes were wide, and her mouth hung in an O shape, her hand at the base of her throat.

Scott pulled himself slowly off the couch, then sat as a heaviness overtook him. He couldn't explain it, and yet he could. Rafe's words thundered through his mind and soul like a herd of stampeding buffalo.

"Son, you've asked forgiveness for a grievous wrong, and that's a good thing. You are being shown mercy."

Scott bowed his head. He knew what Rafe referred to. Would he ever be able to get past the horrible bullying he'd done to Meghan? His throat squeezed. He'd asked forgiveness, and she'd given it, yet she avoided him like he was a leper. He didn't blame her.

His mind repeated the conversation he'd had with her over and over, constantly reminding him of his terrible actions.

How could he have been so cruel?

"Do you want your cowboy to live?"

She'd certainly see the benefit of marrying him in order to save the cowboy's life.

"How can you ask such a question?" She cocked her head to one side in that endearing way he loved.

"Answer it. Do you want the cowboy to live?" He grabbed her arms.

"Of course I do." Her eyes filled with tears. She pulled away.

Meghan sure was a feisty one. Maybe using tenderness would help. Would she respond better to gentleness? He would try that, purposely making his voice gentle.

"Then marry me, and I'll do all I can to save him."

Her mouth dropped open, her misty eyes widened with horror. "You can't be serious!"

Keeping his tone low and even, he stiffened his neck and looked down at her. "Meghan, either you promise to marry me right here and now, or your cowboy will bleed to death."

"You can't do this! You took an oath!"

He reached out for her, but she moved away. He pleaded. "Meg, I'll do anything if you'll marry me. You can have anything you want, just promise to marry me—now."

McMasters pounded on the door. "Doctor! He's breathing hard! You've got to come quick!"

His gaze settled on her lips. This was the moment he'd been waiting for all these months. Now she really would become his wife. He would be married, have a wife, and be a respected man in the community. "Well?"

She grabbed his arms and shook him. "Scott, you have to save him! You have to—now!"

Though not the reaction he had hoped for, he gave her the benefit of the doubt. After all, she was in shock. Although why she hadn't expected he would fight to keep her for himself, once she'd broken it off with him, he had no idea. He couldn't just let her go to that cowboy without some sort of fight. He'd waited for the perfect time. This was it.

He glared at her, persuading her to agree by his intense gaze.
"His fate is in your hands, Meg."

Over and over the scene replayed in his mind. Each time, it seemed he became more of an observer, yet still in the middle of it. A new perspective seemed to come each time.

At first, he felt as he had that night—that he was justified in his actions. Because it was as if he was there again. His feelings were true to him and how he felt at the time. His conscience pricked him later and he'd apologized. But as the remembrances continued, it was like he was pulled away from himself, seeing Meghan for the first time—the devastation he'd caused her. One last time the scene played through his mind. This time, it was as though he hovered just above the scene. He heard a conversation. In his mind, or in his spirit? He didn't know.

"Son, don't do this. It will leave a scar on your conscience."

A second voice replied. "This is a trial for her. God will be pleased with her through this. And he will bring about a miracle for her."

"What about him? Is he lost to us now?" The first voice slowed, as if burdened by a great sadness.

Scott had never heard anything like this before. A sadness overtook him. His stomach churned to the point where he thought he might lose its contents. Were they talking about *him*? Who was he lost to?

"No, he'll come around. The Father is drawing him and Raphael is helping in this assignment."

"But his conscience is seared."

"A scar he'll have always. He will have to live with the deep pain he caused. But he can be redeemed. His heart is responding in a positive way."

Scott slipped from his chair onto the floor and wept. Someone really cared about him that much that they were afraid he'd condemned himself.

Great sorrow filled his soul. A scar on his heart. He could do nothing but weep.

⁓

Rose sat beside Scott on the floor. Something had certainly caused him grief. Her own tears were barely beginning to dry. She'd scarcely noticed Duncan as he crept from the office. When Scott slipped to the floor, her first thought was he'd passed out. When his weeping erupted, a great compassion overtook her. She couldn't help herself. She loved him. It was in her nature to help, especially him. Because she now realized she loved him with her whole heart and soul. She gathered him in her arms. Tears ran down her cheek.

She thought again of Rafe's words.

"Meghan Gallagher is right when she told you that God wants you to accept him in your heart. And if you forgive, your wrongs will be forgiven. Just as Jesus pardoned the woman caught in adultery in the Bible, he will absolve you, if you—"

"If I can forgive Mother and Jake."

Could she do it? The hurt had settled so deep in her heart. Jake might be easier to forgive than Mother. He'd hurt her physically and abused her emotionally, but she was grown when that happened. She'd given herself to him freely as part of her job.

Madam, on the other hand... could she absolve Madam?

How? What did it mean to forgive? Meghan didn't say she had to forget the wrong, just release the hurt and anger in her own heart.

Nearly impossible when she thought of... but she might be willing to try. Maybe Meghan could help her.

⁓

Trina's eyes widened when she opened the door a few inches.

"Jake, ya ain't welcome here no more. I want ya to leave."

He raised his hand to stroke her cheek, but she ducked away, leaving the door open. Silly girl didn't think to put her foot in it to keep him out. "Aw, Trina honey, you know how I feel about you."

He grabbed her and pulled her to him as he kicked the door shut with his foot. She pounded his chest with her fists. He grabbed her small hands and held both in one of his large ones. He'd been able to overpower her without striking her. With his free hand, he stroked her back. Trina could be a wildcat at times. He loved it. Rosie was that way, too. He smiled at the thought.

"Let me go! Get out of here!" Fear and rage warred in her milky gray-blue eyes. He let her go. Just to see what she'd do. She rubbed her wrists. He'd held her wrists as tight as he could.

He raised his hand again. She brought her arm up defensively.

Power surged through him. Smelling her fear, he drank it in like a thirsty man who'd had no water. He let out a long breath to calm himself before he lost control.

"Look, Trina, I don't want to hurt you. Let's settle down and have a nice talk."

"You don't talk."

"I swear, I won't do anything. I won't touch you until you want me to. I need your help."

She hesitated.

"That's better. Let's sit." He guided her to the bed by putting his hand in the small of her back. It made him feel powerful. A sign of possession.

"What do you want, Jake?"

"Like I said, I need your help. If you help me, I'll get you anything you want... that pearl necklace you've had your eyes on at the Pioneer Store." He leaned over and kissed her ear, then blew in it. She'd moaned with pleasure many times before when he'd done that. He stroked below her neck and felt her melt into him. She was his again.

"What do you want me to do?"

He turned her chin his way and kissed her, first gently, then with passion. She moaned. He knew how to give her what she wanted, just as she knew the same about him.

Pulling away a moment, while she was compliant, he stroked the nape of her neck. "Trina, my love, would you do me a couple of favors?"

She stroked his back. "Of course. Just name them."

"I need you to talk to a couple of women for me."

"Who?"

"First, Madam Margaret. I sent for her, but she won't see me now, and I have some important information. She'll want to know it. She might be so grateful she'd give you a silver dollar for your trouble."

"But I don't work for her."

"Well, I believe you could, if you wanted to. When you talk to her, she might offer you a good job at her saloon. I'll bet you'd get more there than here."

She twirled a stray lock of hair. "Who's the other lady?"

He kissed her ear. "The doctor's assistant. Say that a gentleman wants to meet her after she closes the doctor's office tomorrow night. But don't tell her it's me."

She placed a hand on his leg and stroked. It had been too long.

⁓

As Rose locked up for the night outside the office door, she turned and saw a young woman approach her. In the soft glow of a streetlight, it was hard to make out her features. As she drew near, Rose recognized Trina.

"Trina, how are you? Are you all right? You haven't been beaten again?" Rose turned to unlock the door but didn't. Perhaps she should hear what the young lady had to say first. Trina stopped a few feet away. When she spoke, her voice was soft.

"I—I'm fine, miss. Ye're the doctor's assistant? I remember ya taking care of me. Is yer name Rose?" The girl's voice trembled a bit.

"Yes, I'm Rose. Are you sure you're all right?" What was Trina doing here? Why had she come?

"I have a message for ya from a gentleman who wishes to meet ya right here tomorrow night when ya lock up." The statement sounded memorized.

"Who is it? Do I know him?"

"I can't say who he is, miss. But he has something he wants to tell ya."

Trina stood on one foot, then the other. Something was off about this whole thing, but Rose didn't know what. Did it have anything to do with Jake? Trina had most probably also been beaten by Jake. She shivered involuntarily.

"I—I can't meet him tomorrow night. And I'm not going to meet with a stranger unless it's in the office during the daylight hours. Please tell him that for me. You know—a girl can't be too careful."

Trina bowed her head. "Yes, I understand. I'll tell him, miss."

What was that all about? Rose shook her head, locked and jiggled the doorknob, to make sure it stayed locked, then walked home.

⟿

Jake waited in Trina's room for her return. He punched his fist against the flat of his hand. What was taking her so long? He needed to finalize his plan. Running over some of the details in his mind, he knew he had arranged for the buckboard to be put in place. Ropes—ready. The bandana would work well for a gag. He knew he'd have to take her forcibly, maybe even knock her out, but hoped it wouldn't come to that.

At the cabin, he'd already made sure everything was right where he wanted it. He'd even bought a new mattress to make it nicer for Rosie. The last time he was in Florence, he stocked up on all the essentials for Rosie to cook and bake for him.

All was in readiness for Rosie's arrival. He couldn't wait to take her for his very own.

⌒

The next evening, as Rose locked the office door, she felt someone come up behind her. Didn't Trina relay her answer to that man? She turned to face the mystery man. Something hard hit her head. A man's strong arms caught her. His breath smelled of whiskey and stale cigar.

"You're mine, Rosie O'Roarke. Do you hear? No one else can have you. Just me!"

Jake's gnarly voice. Oh no! She struggled to free herself but found he had one arm around her waist, the other over her mouth, partially covering her nose, making it hard to breathe. Even drunk, he had always been so much stronger than her. He removed his hand from her mouth just long enough to place another hard blow to the side of her head.

Stars blanketed her vision, her balance faltered. His arms gripped her like a vise. There was nothing she could do. She tried to scream, but only a small whimper came out.

"Scott! Help me!" She could barely even hear herself.

How could he hear her when he was already fast asleep? She had to try again. With all the strength she could muster, she screamed again. And earned another blow to the head.

He dragged her a short distance and threw her into the back of a buckboard. He'd been lying in wait for her. He'd planned this! If she had the strength, she'd punch him out.

"You're mine, Rosie O'Roarke, and we're gonna be together! Just you and me! And no one else around for miles and miles."

Who could help her? She would surely die at Jake's hands.

One last sharp blow to her head, added to several she'd already suffered, and everything went black.

Chapter Twenty-One

Scott thought he heard a noise outside.

"Rose? Is that you?"

Silence.

He rolled over and lit the lamp on the bedside table. All seemed quiet, but his gut churned. He reached for his crutch, grabbed the lantern, and hobbled into the office. He stopped. Listened again.

Nothing.

Then a sort of muffled cry.

"Rose! Is that you? Is everything all right?"

He clacked to the door and fiddled with the lock. When he opened the door, he noticed a buckboard nearby with...Rose! She lay in the back, unconscious—or dead.

Dead? Don't think that way!

"Rose! Can you hear me?" She didn't move.

Someone came up behind him.

"Doc, you ever get in my way again, you're a dead man!"

Something slammed into his head. He dropped the crutch and crumpled to the ground, landing on his broken leg. Immense pain shot through it. Barely conscious, he looked up into the face of Jake Thomas.

"You hear me, Doc?"

Scott struggled to a sitting position as Rose's tormenter leaned over him. His breath stank from alcohol and cigar.

"Jake Thomas. What do you think you are doing? Rose has made a better life for herself. Leave her alone."

"Nothing doing, Doc. She's mine. You'll never have her! Don't you think I haven't seen you two alone in the office together? I look in windows. You think you're alone. She moons over you! And you—how can you treat her as well as you do, when you know what she is?" Jake grabbed Scott by his shirt and pulled him halfway up, then shoved him down hard. Agony shot through his leg. He hoped he could still limp inside, and he would, as soon as he could find his crutch. It was just out of reach.

Thomas leaned over him again, swung his fisted hand landing another blow.

⌒

Something jarred Rose awake. Darkness surrounded her. Her head would surely explode from each jolt of the wagon. Where was she? She listened, hearing only the rattling of wagon wheels. Then she remembered. Jake had kidnapped her. She'd been closing the office. He'd struck her in the head—several times. She hoped she didn't have a concussion. She tried to move—but couldn't. He'd gussied her up like a pig for roasting over an open fire. She struggled against the ropes and the gag in her mouth. Jake had never been a slacker. He'd tied everything tight. It seemed he was taking no chances, giving her no opportunity to escape. At least for now. She'd have to keep on her toes. Be watchful.

The pain in her head caused her stomach to churn. Blood pounded through her. If she couldn't control her breathing, her chest would explode.

How much time had passed? Was it only minutes, or hours? She had no idea.

What would Scott think when she didn't show up for work? Would he know something happened to her? What about Meghan and Olivia? When she didn't come home, would they raise the alarm and start a search for her?

Of course they would. Meghan was her friend, and Olivia was quickly becoming one. Rose had only lived at the boardinghouse about three months, and even though Olivia knew she'd been Rosie, the woman had welcomed her with open arms.

Another bump jarred her, and she yelped.

"Awake, are ya, ma Rosie girl? Whoa there." Jake brought the buckboard to a stop. The springs under the seat squeaked, the wagon shifted. He must have jumped from the driver's seat. Dirt crunched under the weight of his footsteps as he came around and climbed into the back. He kneeled beside her. A whiff of the whiskey, the cigar, and his body odor gagged her. Ugh. She'd never really been attracted to him, had she? He was a job, a customer to satisfy. He'd paid good money for her services, and sometimes it wasn't too bad.

"Rosie, ma gal, we're out in the middle of nowhere, miles from New Boston. If I take the gag off, and loosen your ropes, will ya promise to behave like the lady y'all pretend to be?"

She nodded. Better to play like an opossum. Meghan had taught her that the opossum played dead to mislead its predator. She could pretend to be submissive, watch and wait for an opportunity to escape. Being tied and gagged meant no chance.

She would get away from this man. Somehow, some way, he'd let his guard down, and she'd escape. Even if it was the last thing she ever did.

Chapter Twenty-Two

Scott stood his crutch upright and pulled himself up. His head was splitting, but he had a hard head. He'd learned that during the tornado. He'd been knocked out then, too, but he didn't have a concussion then, or now.

It hurt powerfully, though. He hobbled toward the sheriff's office. No use looking for her. She was long gone. Not by choice, either. Her poor unconscious form in the back of the buckboard, Jake had bludgeoned her, too.

His leg throbbed, but he didn't think he'd injured it further. It had only been about four weeks since his accident. He remembered the agony of it. This wasn't nearly as bad. His leg pained him, but not as much as when he broke it.

When he reached the sheriff's office, he banged on the door. He peered through the window and watched as Sheriff Randall came to the door.

⁓

Rose woke with a start. Where was she?

The steady rhythm of the wagon as it made its way across the prairie had lulled her to sleep. Thankfully, Jake didn't sing in his off-key style. The night was dark. She had no idea where they were. Stretching felt good, yet she lacked the strength to raise herself up to look over the edge of the buckboard.

She had to bide her time. Watch for a change to escape. The only way to do that was to play along for a while—up to a certain point. Maybe get him to trust her.

"Jake, where are we? I'm hungry."

He half-turned his head. "There's hardtack in that canvas bag near your feet. We'll be home in a couple hours. You can rustle up really good grub then."

She let out a long breath. How would she escape this obsessed madman? Even her Scott at his worst was nothing like Jake. They weren't even in the same class.

Her Scott. He was becoming "her" Scott. The kiss they'd shared, the heart-to-heart talks. Once Meghan turned down his marriage proposal, he'd not courted anyone else. Hope birthed in her heart that Scott could love her, as she knew Duncan loved Meghan—even with their problems.

How could this turn out well? What would Scott do when he discovered her missing? Did he even know by this time?

On and on in the dark they drove. Rose lay quietly in the back of the buckboard. Her mind wouldn't rest, but she needed sleep, knowing she'd need all her wits about her to plan an escape.

She tried to remember everything Jake had previously told her about where he lived. Out in the country where no one could find him. No neighbors for miles around. Yet he was close enough to a town that he could get supplies.

But which town? New Boston? Florence? Wichita? She had to find out.

⁓

Scott waited for Sheriff Randall to open the door, then limped inside. "Rose Rhodes has been kidnapped!"

Randall gestured for him to sit across from the desk, then sat behind it. "Sit down before you fall down, Doc. Tell me what happened."

Scott plopped in the chair and rubbed his head. The last thing he wanted to do was sit, but if he hadn't, he probably would have fallen, like Randall said. "Jake Thomas came to my office and kidnapped Rose this evening."

"How long ago?"

"I'm not sure. It was dark already. Rose had closed the office and I'd gone to bed. I'm not sure how long ago it was. I heard something and went to investigate. Rose was unconscious in the back of a buckboard. As I went to see about her, Thomas confronted me. He punched me hard and knocked me out. When I came to, I headed right here."

"I didn't even know Thomas was back in town." Randall took off his gun belt and pulled out a box of bullets from desk drawer.

"Evidently, he came back to take her. He's out of his mind, I believe."

"What leads you to think this?" Randall began filling up the empty loops on his gun belt with bullets.

Scott swallowed. His own selfish attitude of Meghan came to mind. He pushed it aside for now. "Well, I recognize the signs of mental instability. He said that Rose belonged to him and only him. That's not a healthy state of mind."

"No, it's not." Randall finished the loops, then checked his six-shooter and filled it. "First thing in the morning, I'll get a posse together. But I need to tell you, there's only a slim chance we'll find her."

Scott stood and began to limp back and forth in front of Randall's desk. "Why don't we get a posse together *now*? Because if you don't, I'm going to find her myself."

"Now, don't go off half-cocked." Randall's neck stiffened. "We won't find her tonight. Only Indians track at night." He cleared his throat. "We'll go together—in the morning."

"I'm going to find her if it's the last thing I do." His crutch thumped against the floor.

"What about your patients?" He slid the box of bullets back into his desk drawer.

Scott stopped. "They're used to my 'fishing trips.' I'll leave 'em a note, but I'm going to do this." He pounded a fist on the desk.

⁓

Rose awakened again, her head throbbing. When had she fallen asleep? The last thing she remembered was the swaying of the buckboard. She must be exhausted to fall asleep in the middle of all this. Jake snored beside her. The mattress was new. He really had planned this.

The cabin was small, only a little larger than her room at the dance hall. The back wall had a plank on two barrels. She figured he used that as a countertop. To the right, another barrel. On the left, different rough-woven burlap sacks and boxes. The right wall held the bed tight to the corner.

The next thing she spotted was the door.

She crawled over Jake, careful to not wake him. She needed to explore...to discover whatever she could about her location. Her mouth was dry. The hope of a well outside drew her. *Was this what a thirsty horse drawn to water felt like?*

Could she manage to escape? She stepped outside without a sound. The sun was beginning to come up, the morning sun enveloping the cabin in a soft glow. That meant the cabin faced east.

To the left of the cabin was a little barn, then a chicken coop, and a corral. She turned to the right. Nothing but an outhouse. No real road or path. Only a couple of slightly worn wagon wheel tracks led out on-to the horizon.

She walked around to the back of the cabin. A small rise sloped about a hundred yards away or so. As she made her way toward it, the cabin door slammed.

"Rosie girl! Where are ya? Ya can't get away! There's nowhere to go!"

Jake was up and roaring. She turned back toward the cabin, determined to lead him on, even though it was deceptive. He needed to believe that she was all right with this new arrangement.

"I'm out back. I'm exploring." Her voice sounded loud. Out here in the country, where it was dead quiet, no breeze at dawn, sound carried.

"All right, then." His tone was calmer. "Come on back and I'll show you around."

When she reached the front, he grabbed her arm and pulled her inside.

"There's no need to be rough."

He released her arm with a shove, knocking her against the table in the center of the room. She put her hands out to steady herself. "Just want ya to know who's in charge."

She rubbed her arm where he'd grabbed her. "You don't have to tell me. I know."

"Fix me some breakfast."

"What do you have?"

He went over to a trunk next to the boxes and sacks and pulled out a skillet and fished out some tin plates, flatware, and a couple of mugs.

In the center of the room, a small table, with two chairs. He'd obviously thought ahead. Was this all because he'd planned to kidnap her and bring her here? He must have been devising this for quite some time. Her skin crawled. He set the items on the table and grabbed her arm again.

"I'll show you the chicken house."

She rubbed her arm again. How long could she pretend submission if every touch left her bruised?

Chapter Twenty-Three

Scott straightened the crutch and pulled himself up. Randall rose and came around the desk.

"Look, Doctor, I know you have feelings for this woman. But this is my job, not yours."

"Sheriff, I have to find her. It was my fault she was taken."

"Why's that?" Randall leaned against the desk.

"I tried to stop him ... but couldn't."

"Because Thomas beat you senseless. An injured man, at that."

"I still think ..."

"Look, Doc, you can't blame yourself for this."

"If only I'd not had this blasted leg ..."

"What would you have done? I think you'd have been hard pressed to overpower him—even with a good leg." Randall's gaze bored right through him. "Nope. You better stay here and let me do my job. I'll find Jake Thomas and bring him to jail. He'll do some pretty hard time for all he's done."

"Sheriff, I know this is your job, and I appreciate your concern ... but I have to do this myself. Besides, you have a town to protect—and you don't have any deputies right now."

The sheriff let out a long breath and put a hand on Scott's shoulder. "If you're determined to do this thing, be careful. You know Thomas is a dangerous man."

"I'll be careful."

"Where will you start?"

"I think I'll visit the dance hall where Rose used to work. Maybe the bartender heard Thomas say something about where he lives. Maybe he even boasted about taking up with Rose." Scott limped to the door.

Randall came from behind him and opened it. "That's a good idea. Then come see me if you find out anything."

"Do you have any other ideas?"

"I'll check the other saloons—maybe Thomas did some drinking at them, too. If he ever purchased or homesteaded his land, there'd be a record of it in the land office."

"That's a great idea, Randall."

"Maybe by morning we'll have something to go on."

"We?" Scott's heart pounded.

"I'm coming with you—at least for a day or so."

"Thanks, Sheriff."

"You're going to need someone to keep you out of trouble."

So long as Randall didn't keep him from finding his precious Rose.

⌒

"Jake, you don't have to be rough. I'm here, and you've got me. Where could I go?"

"Now, ye'er seein' things my way, Rosie girl. That's the way I like it. Let me show ya around." He took her elbow and guided her to the chicken house. Oh, how she hated his touch. Somehow she'd have to put up with it—at least for a while, until she could plan her escape.

"This is the most important building you need to know about for now. I gather eggs here every day I'm home. You have ta be careful not to let them chickens out. They'll run off, but there ain't nothin' out there for 'em. They'd just starve. Or get eaten by varmints. But that'll be yer job now. Have you ever gathered eggs before, Rosie girl?"

She cleared her throat. "Um, no. But you'll teach me, won't you?"

His eyes gleamed. The smile on his face was so sincere she almost felt guilty for deceiving him like this. But it was necessary, and would be, until she found a way to escape.

"Why, shore thing, girl! I'm happy you wanna learn. Does that mean you think you'll be happy here? That's what I want, Rosie girl. I want us to be happy."

She swallowed. "I—I'll try. That's all I can say right now. Why did you kidnap me? And knock me out." She rubbed the lump on her head. "You could have asked."

He stepped out of the chicken house and tugged her along with him. "Would you have come? Can you honestly tell me that you would have come if I'd asked all nice like? Because you wouldn't even meet with me last night. I had to find another way."

In the small barn, a lone milk cow stood in one of the two stalls. Jake's horse was in the other. He showed her where the baskets and buckets were kept so she could gather eggs herself. The baskets were kept on a low shelf, the buckets underneath.

"Oh, and you'll be milkin' the cow, too. Mornin' and evenin'. Do ya know how?"

"No."

He tugged on her hand, leading her to the cow. The animal turned her head, chewing her cud, her bulging eyes staring at her as if to say, "who are you?" Jake grabbed a metal pail from under the shelf, then lifted a small, three-legged stool from where it sat in the corner. He sat down close to the cow and stuck the pail underneath her.

"This is how ya do it, Rosie girl." He wrapped his hand around one of the cow's teats and pulled. Milk squirted into the pail. "Wanna try?"

Rose's stomach churned. She swallowed the bile rising in her throat. He wanted her to be a farm wife and slave to his every whim? She had to escape. Planning, watching, waiting for the perfect time. Because if she failed...

Scott hobbled into the Silver Spike just before closing. Things were quiet. The music had stopped, and the bartender faced the back mirror, washing up the used shot glasses. As the swinging doors clapped closed, the bartender looked up and smiled when he saw Scott.

"What'll you have?"

Scott limped up to the bar and leaned against it. "Nothing but information, thanks."

"I'll see what I can do. Whaddaya need?"

"Jake Thomas."

The bartender rolled his eyes. "A scoundrel, if you ask me. Mean when he's drunk. Why? What's he done now?"

"Did he ever say where he lives?"

"Not really."

"Was there any place he may have talked about?"

The bartender's brow furrowed. "Seems to me, he said something one time—quite a while back—about having a cabin out in the middle of the prairie. Said no one would ever find it—or him."

"So he never mentioned where that cabin might be?"

"I think he said north of here. But he never said how far."

Scott smiled. "Thanks a lot. It gives me a place to start."

North. That could mean Florence to the northeast, or Mennonite farm communities straight north. Or open prairie. There wasn't much of anything west of New Boston yet.

Maybe tomorrow's inquiry at the Santa Fe land office would turn up something. But if not, at least he and Randall could head north out of town. It was a place to start.

He'd find Rose. He had to.

Chapter Twenty-Four

Rose tripped over a shovel handle as Jake pulled her through the barn. "Jake, slow down. Please, can we just go back to the cabin? I haven't eaten since yesterday suppertime."

"Why shore thing, Rosie girl. We can go back, but if you're hungry, you'll have to fix something." He smacked his lips together. "All I want—is you."

The thought of his touch sent chills down her spine. She wanted to turn and run, but instead she girded her spirit. She must maintain her pretense until she could escape. So, she lowered her eyelashes then lifted them to gaze into his eyes. "Jake, would you do something for me?"

His eyes narrowed. His smile not reaching his eyes. "What do you want?"

"Would you spend time 'courtin' me? After all, that's what normal people do before they're married. We didn't get to have that. Could we now?"

He took a step back and looked at her, measuring her sincerity. She knew how his mind worked. As soon as he had shown her everything on his land, he planned to have his way with her.

His guffaw filled the barn, startling not only her, but both the cow and the horse. "Why, shore, Rosie girl. I'll court ya. If that's what you want. But if you hadn't noticed, there's just one bed. And you are my wife, Rosie." His tone changed, became harsh. He pinched her cheeks between his thumb and finger. "I'll take ya whenever I want ya. You're mine. You belong to me, and no one else. Ever."

How could he think she'd want to be with a such a cruel man? Stranger yet, how could he think her his wife if they'd never had a ceremony?

Stall him. "Couldn't we wait until after my... woman time? It just started. You won't want a baby right away, will you?" The very thought of carrying Jake's child turned her stomach.

As quickly as his harshness had come upon him, it left. He pulled her to him, and planted a long, sloppy kiss on her lips. Oh, how she wanted to wipe that off. Instead, she conjured up a sweet smile. His hands traveled up her back. He smashed his lips on hers again.

A loveless kiss. Meeting those man needs—that's all he'd ever wanted her for.

How could she escape this? Maybe when he was asleep. Or, if he got drunk enough, she could steal his horse. But how could she get back to New Boston from here when she didn't even know where *here* was?

She eased out of his arms. "Let's have something to drink. I'll bet you're thirsty. I know I am. Have you got any whiskey? I'd love a drink." She hated rambling when she got nervous.

He draped his arm around her shoulder, squeezed her tightly against him as they ambled back to the cabin. Halfway across the yard, he turned his head to nibble on her ear and kiss her neck.

When they reached the cabin, as gently as possible she slipped out of his hold and pushed him toward the table. He plopped into one of the two chairs, his eyes only half clear. She prayed it wouldn't take much to make him pass out.

"Where do you keep the whiskey?"

"Over there in the right cupboard. Shot glasses are there, too."

She set the bottle and glasses on the table.

His arm wrapped around her waist. He swung her around until she landed on his lap. She released a nervous giggle. "All in good time, Jake. But since you brought me here to live, I just want to get settled first. That's what a woman likes to do when she moves to a new place."

"Plenty of time for settling you in later."

Her stomach growled. If she fainted from hunger, would he just take her? She glanced at the bed. He'd spent money for a new mattress and a new brass headboard. The quilt clean and fluffy. Had someone given him advice? Maybe Trina. It seemed the girl went out of her way to please him. Why hadn't he just taken Trina instead of her?

She let out a long breath.

Could she survive the night? The next half hour?

Only if she retreated to that secret place in her mind, the one she'd created years ago during her dance hall days, would she find a small measure of help. Her imaginary lover met her there, the one who really cared, instead of the hot-blooded man who knocked on her bedroom door. She envisioned who he was, what he did for a living, how he looked, and his hair was always blonde like the sun.

When she met Doctor Scott Allison, a handsome man with a head-full of golden hair, she could hardly take her eyes off him. She'd followed Duncan Wilcox in after Meghan was shot by a stray bullet. She watched as he treated the woman she hoped would one day be her friend. While she'd taken an immediate shine to Scott, he'd become enamored with Meghan.

She'd been so disappointed. Yet how could a doctor, an educated man, ever fall for her—a dance hall girl?

That's when she knew she had to change her life. It took a month or so to work out the details, but when the tornado struck, it seemed right. With all the chaos in town, it could be days before anyone really missed Rosalie O'Roarke. Her transition to Rose Rhodes had been easier than she thought. And becoming Scott's assistant made it all perfect.

After Jake had beaten her, Scott's gentle and caring treatment touched her so deeply, but her heart would not cooperate with reason. Admiration had grown into attraction, and now her heart swelled with love.

She poured the amber liquid into both glasses and hoped Jake wouldn't notice when she pretended to drink. Twirling her finger around a strand of hair, she tilted her head and smiled.

Would she ever see Scott again?

⁓

Scott entered the Santa Fe land office near the newly opened train station. He couldn't believe how fast the station had grown. It had doubled, then tripled in size from a basic pine shack of six months ago. He was also amazed at how quickly Jackson had been promoted, overseeing the day-to-day operation. Just a few short months ago, he'd had been a porter. Then soon, he'd become ticket master and telegrapher—now station master. Having come up within the ranks, Jackson could easily perform any of the necessary jobs.

"What kin I do for ya, Doc Allison? Don't usual' see ya around here."

"I don't often come myself to send a telegram."

Jackson pulled out a sheet and readied his pen. "Who to today, Doc? Kansas City? Topeka?"

He shook his head. "Not sending one today." He glanced over to a large, thick book at Jackson's right side that read *Land Deeds*. "I need to look up a parcel of land."

"Are ya thinkin' of buyin'?" Jackson slid the book in front of him and opened it, his eyes sparkling. He looked Scott square in the eye. Six or seven years ago, the Negro wouldn't have dared it. The stationmaster was a former slave. It was wonderful to see how far he'd come when given opportunity.

He leaned against the window. "Actually, I want to know if you could look up a name for me."

Jackson narrowed his eyes a bit. "Why you wanna do dat?" Light dawned in his expression. "Oh, ya wanna be a neighbor? Folks always talking about ya goin' on yore fishin' trips. Ya wanna place where you can always go?"

"Could you look up any property belonging to Jake Thomas? And if he doesn't have a purchased tract, could you look on your homestead list?"

Jackson nodded, his beam revealed gleaming teeth. "Why sho', Doc. Jus' give me a couple minutes, will ya?"

Scott limped away from the counter and looked at the schedules on the wall. Three trains arrived and left every day now. Morning, afternoon, and evening. Astonishing how quickly the town grew.

"Doc, what was that name again?"

He turned back to face Jackson. "Jake Thomas. But I suppose, if he used a proper name, such as Jacob, it could be under that. I don't know if he had a middle name, or what it would be."

Jackson's eyes narrowed as he flipped pages back and forth in both the deed book and the homestead list.

"I don't see nothin' under any of dos names, Doc. Sorry. Maybe it's in another book. Depends where the land is. These only cover New Boston and for a few miles surroundin'. If he's closer to Florence or Emporia..."

"Thanks anyway, Jackson." Scott turned to go, then turned back. "Could you telegraph Florence for me?"

"Why, sho', Doc. Be glad to."

Scott placed a dime on the counter. "Will this cover it?"

Jackson picked up the coin and smiled. "Sho' does, Doc. I'll let ya know when I hear anythin'."

"Thanks, Jackson. It's very important."

Where did that scoundrel live?

Chapter Twenty-Five

"Hurry up, Rosie, I'm as hungry as a she-bear waitin' to gnaw a fresh kill."

"It will only take a few minutes." Rose dropped a dollop of lard into a hot skillet, then swished it around. One thing she was grateful for—that Madam had taught her to cook simple things—like scrambled eggs and bacon, saying she'd need to know someday. That was about the extent of her skills when she learned how to make breakfast. The housekeeper had also taught her how to put together a sandwich and make a simple stew.

She smiled to herself. Meghan was also just learning how to cook, but she'd used the word "culinary." Must be a fancy word for cooking.

Rose couldn't imagine what it would have been like to grow up having servants cook and clean for you all the time. When Madam's "business" grew from just her bedroom to take up the whole house, they'd hired a housekeeper, but Rose had been nearly a teenager when that happened. Especially in her younger days, when Madam stayed in bed until the afternoon, Rose had learned a few things about putting a simple meal together. Once they'd gotten a housekeeper, she learned more.

Jake's gravelly voice pulled her from her thoughts.

"Well, hurry it up, anyway. I'm starved." Jake came up behind her and put his arms around her waist. She tried hard not to stiffen or pull away, but she loathed his touch. Better get more used to it, at least for a while. To escape, she was going to have to endure not only this, but more. She'd been so exhausted the night before. Maybe he was, too. He hadn't forced himself upon her, and for that, she was grateful.

"You can sit down. I'll bring it over."

"Maybe I just want to be near you." He inhaled a deep breath. "Mmmm. I love your new smell. What is it?"

"It's called 'clean.'"

"You used to use rosewater. I loved the smell of rosewater on my Rosie girl."

She didn't reply but dropped some bacon slices on top of the melted lard, which caused splatter. Jumping back, she nearly knocked him over.

"Stupid!" His hand slammed into the side of her head. Stars danced across her eyes and blood flushed through her body. She needed to calm him down before he took another swipe at her.

"I—I'm sorry." She rubbed her head where he'd hit her. "Sit down—please. I'll bring these over. Bacon often splatters like that when first put in the pan."

His harsh gaze softened just a bit. He grunted and turned away, ambling to the chair. "It's just that you sometimes make me crazy, Rosie girl."

Rosie girl. That's all he'd ever called her. A thought came to her. Maybe she should begin using his favorite nickname she'd given him when they first met. Not much at first. As her plan to win his trust unfolded, she'd use it more often.

"I know, Jakey. But we have all the time in the world now, don't we?" The words practically squeezed her throat shut. She couldn't wait to get away from him.

"Aw, ya called me Jakey. I done right bringin' ya here." He came up behind her again. His lips brushed her hair on the back of her head. Strong arms gave her a short squeeze, and then he returned to the table.

She hoped deceiving him was the right thing to do. But what choice did she have? She'd been living lies so long, it came naturally to her. Would she ever be free?

⁓

The next morning, Scott knocked on Sheriff Randall's office door, then pounded when he didn't get an answer.

"Sheriff Randall! Open up! It's Doctor Allison."

From inside, a muffled "I'm comin'."

The door opened, and Randall stepped aside to allow Scott to hobble in.

Randall closed the door, then went to the small, potbellied stove in the corner, and took the coffeepot off the top. He opened the lid, then poured out the grounds in a nearby waste can. "It's pretty early. Did you find anything out?"

Scott limped over to the guest chair, his crutch clacking on the wooden floor. "Yes, I did. He's in the Florence area but doesn't have legal property or homestead in that area."

"I'll be right back. Want some coffee?"

"Sure."

Randall stepped outside the side door. Scott's good leg fidgeted while he waited. A minute later, the sheriff returned.

"Where'd you hear that Thomas is in Florence?" Randall started making coffee. "Do you like your coffee strong or weak?"

"Pretty strong. I went to the Silver Spike. The bartender had to think about it for a couple of minutes—but thought he remembered Thomas saying he lived out in the middle of nowhere—north of here." He shifted. "I got Jackson to telegraph Florence, figuring that's where he'd go. We just got an answer a few minutes ago. He's been seen recently in that area."

Randall set the coffeepot on top of the stove. "I have some leftover biscuits from yesterday. I can pack those, and we can be on our way after breakfast, if you'd like." He started a fire in the stove.

"Thanks, Sheriff." He kept looking at Randall's legs—how he was able to walk without a limp, without a crutch. Scott shook his head. He'd heard stories like this before from some of his patients. When something of your own doesn't work, you get a bit fixated on others' ability to do what you can't right now. All he could see was Randall walking around on two good legs, able to do whatever he wanted. Ride in the saddle all the way without an aching leg, pulling his own weight. Yes, he'd be all right, but complete healing was still weeks away.

The sheriff handed Scott a slice of buttered bread. "Here, this should tide us over until we get to Florence. This—and the biscuits. We can have lunch there. I'll pay. This is an official investigation."

"You don't have to pay for my lunch. I have cash." Scott took a bite and began chewing.

"Well, I figure you're going to need your money, Doc. I can take one day—today. We'll find out what we can, but you'll probably want to stay until you find her. If you find out where Thomas lives, I want you to telegraph me immediately. The Florence Hotel has a telegraph office. I'll come right back. Don't go after him by yourself. I'd stay with you now, but I don't have any competent deputies."

"I will be staying up to four days."

"Who will look after your patients?"

"No one. They'll have to take care of themselves." He took a nibble. "Besides, now that the gunfights are over, there's very seldom a serious injury or illness."

"I know. But still..."

"If it will make you feel better, I'll wire Abilene for another doctor."

"That does my heart good to hear. Now, let's eat and be on our way."

It couldn't be soon enough.

Chapter Twenty-Six

After breakfast, Rose followed Jake outside to look at his spread. Though she'd wandered around some, and he'd shown her the outbuildings when she was first brought here. This time, he showed her things about the barn, the chicken house, and the corral he hadn't gone over before.

"And back behind the chicken house is an area you can plant a garden come spring." She nodded. In her heart, knew she wouldn't be here then, but she didn't tell him that.

He led her to the barn. "When I'm not here, you'll be in charge of the cow. Use fresh hay, once you've mucked it out." He picked up a wooden pitchfork, then handed it to her. No metal in it at all. Was he afraid she'd use it on him? Even the "spikes" were rounded and made of wood. Obviously, he was taking no chances.

They moved from the barn to the chicken house. How much was there to know about chickens?

"Where are we, Jakey?" She used his favorite name again, hoping to soften him up.

He turned toward her, his eyes narrowed. "Now, what difference does that make to you, Rosie girl? You ain't gonna be goin' anywhere anytime time soon." His tone showed his suspicion. How long would it take to soften him? To get him to trust her? The thought of mucking out stalls, gathering eggs, and being a farm wife did not appeal to her.

"But, Jakey, I need more clothes than what I'm wearing. You took me without letting me pack a carpetbag." She put a hand on his shoulder, hoping he'd respond to a gentle touch.

"We'll go into town next week. Until then, just wash it out. I showed ya the tub yesterday."

"But—"

He turned away. Her hand fell from his shoulder, her arm limp at her side. He wouldn't be giving her any information today.

"Come with me. I've got more to show you."

There was more? Her thoughts wanted to carry her into a pig pen, even though Jake didn't have one. She needed to keep focused. Every little piece of information she could learn about him, about this life, would help her plan her escape. At least, she hoped so.

◆

Scott and Sheriff Randall finally left New Boston around eleven in the morning. After they'd ridden about an hour, Scott's leg began to throb, just from the gentle bouncing. Down the road some ways, he spotted some large rocks. Unusual for this part of Kansas. It would be a good place to stop.

"Sheriff, can we take a short break? I need to rest my leg."

Randall drew his horse to a stop. "Sure. I still don't know why you insist on this fool errand. Your leg is bound to hurt. Are you sure you're all right to continue? We can turn back."

Scott loosened the knots where they'd tied his broken leg to the stirrup straps. When he turned to set his crutch down, Randall had already dismounted and stood beside him. He gritted his teeth.

"I won't return to New Boston until I find her."

"Here, let me help you down. You don't need to set yourself back by reinjuring your leg."

Randall held the crutch while Scott lowered himself down onto his good leg.

The sheriff carried both canteens, and a small cloth bag, which Scott hoped held the biscuits left over from this morning's breakfast. Even though Randall had said they were leftover from yesterday, he'd gotten fresh ones this morning.

The thought of the hotel's leftover biscuits made his mouth water, even plain, without butter or jelly. How could he be hungry already? It seemed just a short while ago, he'd eaten breakfast. Then he realized—it was nearly noon when they finally trotted out of town. After a small meal, Randall had taken Scott back to the office to pack for his trip and leave a note to the townspeople. The sheriff had also reminded him to send a telegram to Abilene, for another doctor, which he did, though reluctantly.

He looked down at his pants. He hadn't wanted to ruin every pair of pants he owned by splitting up the side seams. He only had two pairs he'd allowed to be split. One pair he wore, one pair clean. A pair of scissors did the job on the set of trousers.

He had no idea how long he'd be gone. Secretly, he'd determined in his heart to be gone as look as it took. He'd do whatever was necessary, for as long as it took to get Rose back.

Again, he realized what a horrible thing he'd done to Meghan— just a couple months or so ago it was? Anxiety now reminded him of his desperation then. Goodness. How things had changed in that time. How he had changed in that time. He would never do such a thing again and wished he had never done it. The seemingly angelic conversation he'd overheard told him he would have a scar on his soul the rest of his life. Scars are permanent, but the pain lessens. In his case, his guilt.

Minutes passed by as the men snacked on biscuits and drank from their canteen.

"Are you ready?" The sheriff took the canteens to the horses and came back for Scott.

"Yes, I'm ready." He wasn't really, but push on he would. Rose needed him. He mustn't fail her.

⁂

A couple of hours later, Scott and Randall rode into Florence. Nothing had changed since he was last here on one of his "fishing" trips. Florence was little more than a hotel, train station/stage stop, general store, and livery stable. People from New Boston didn't come to Florence for any reason. Why would they when New Boston had everything they needed? That's why he liked it here. He got his privacy.

"Here are your room keys, gentlemen." The hotel clerk turned back to the slotted cabinet on the wall behind him and picked the keys for Rooms Seven and Nine. "They're both the same. Supper's at six. Corned beef and cabbage. Be prompt or you won't get any. We've got some leftover sandwiches from lunch—ham and cheese. Just go into the dining room and ask the waiter."

"Thank you." Randall took the key to Room Nine. "Excuse me, sir. Do you know the people hereabout?"

The clerk's eyes narrowed a bit as he saw the tin star. "Are you looking for somebody? Did they break the law?"

Scott picked up the key to Room Seven. "Yes. Do you know Jake Thomas?"

The man's eyes widened. Obviously, he recognized the name. "What's he done?"

"He kidnapped a woman."

The clerk raised an eyebrow. "Now, why would he go and do that? Must be a saloon girl. Them's the only kind he's interested in."

Scott leaned forward. "Not anymore. Now, will you just answer the question?"

"I answered it. Got any more?"

Randall broke in. "Do you know where Jake Thomas lives?"

The clerk put a finger to his chin. "Nope. Can't say that I do. I know he's not too far away—couldn't be—he comes in here so much."

Scott placed a dime on the counter. "Would this help you remember more?"

The clerk moved the coin back toward Scott. "I don't accept bribes. If I had something to say, I'd say it. I told ya what I know. Now, if you'll excuse me, I've got other duties to attend to. Hope you enjoy your stay." He turned back and began fiddling with some papers.

"Why don't you go upstairs, Doctor, and get settled? I'll bring up your valise and the sandwiches."

"Thanks, Sheriff."

It took about five minutes to climb the stairs. When he finally reached his room, he let out a long breath.

And prayed.

Maybe for the first time, he really prayed, whispering to the air. "God, help me find Rose."

Chapter Twenty-Seven

After supper, as Rose washed the dishes and cleaned up, her thoughts traveled to the rest of the evening. Her eyes lighted on his large barrel of whiskey in the left front corner of the cabin. He frequently dipped his metal cup into it during the day. Could he not get by without a drink? Might he be what Scott called an addict? He had told her one day about this newer term used for people dependent upon drugs. Perhaps Jake had an addiction, not to drugs, but to whiskey? It would explain why he'd get so violent at times. The whiskey controlled him.

"Rosie girl, ain't ya done yet? I need ya. Come 'ere, will ya?"

"Be there in a minute."

"Aw, you can finish that later, can't ya?"

She wiped her hands and swallowed, steeling herself for what was coming. How could she get out of it?

"Jakey, you remember when ya came to see me that one time during my woman time?"

His gaze narrowed.

"It wasn't so nice, was it?"

Still he said nothing.

Jake handed her a drink. "Here. Drink this."

"I'd rather not. I—I don't drink anymore."

"What? Are ya too good for me now?" He pulled her to the bed. "Gonna have to take you down a peg."

"Jakey, please. Don't rip my clothes. They're all I have." She swallowed. "Give me the drink."

He handed her another metal cup. She took a sip. As she lifted the cup to her lips, he began fumbling with the buttons on her blouse.

"Please wait. Aren't we courtin'?"

"You belong to me—and no one else. I'm the only one to have ya. You're mine."

He kissed her neck, running his hands down over her hips. She shivered, but not from pleasure.

"Wait, please—until I finish my drink. Let me get ready."

"Why sure, Rosie girl." A fiendish smile came to his lips.

"Now remember... it's my woman time. You know you don't like it."

That seemed to get through to him. He relaxed his fists. "If ya think this will stop me—later—you're wrong."

He stood nose-to-nose with her, his hot breath on her cheeks. "And if you get any ideas about escaping here... I'll kill that doctor."

She gasped.

"You know I'll do it. I'll leave ya here, sneak into New Boston and slit his throat."

༄

The next morning, she crawled out of bed over Jake as she had the first morning she'd awakened in this god-forsaken place. He'd gotten roaring drunk, but because she'd submitted to his every whim short of going all the way, he hadn't hit her. Thank goodness for that. She couldn't think straight when he whacked her.

Going about her morning ablutions, she scrubbed herself several times, as if she could be cleansed both outward and inside by the hard rubbing. She must survive this and escape. Somehow she needed to keep him from his murderous intent for Scott. Thank goodness for her woman time. She usually hated it but was thankful this time.

Was Jake awake? She glanced over. Gentle snoring answered her question.

She picked up the water bucket to refill it. The pump was located outside the back door. That's when she saw the rise again and wondered where they were. Most of this area of Kansas was very flat, with few small slopes in the terrain.

How could she get information from Jake about where they were?

As she made her way toward the chicken house to gather eggs, a thought came to her.

She remembered the story of Samson and Delilah. Reverend Street liked using that story to warn the audience about the women in the houses of ill repute. If she remembered right, Delilah wore Samson down by constantly asking him to trust her with his secret. What if she played Delilah to Jake's Samson? Maybe she could charm Jake into being comfortable enough to tell her where they were.

Hope flowed into her heart like Sand Creek's gentle current after a rainy day. What a deliciously wonderful way to get back at him!

More lies, though. Pretending. She hated it. Yet her whole life was a lie. Rose Rhodes didn't exist. Rosalie O'Roarke did. She was born to a fallen woman, and she'd lived as a soiled dove.

She had wanted to change. And she had. She'd discarded her old way of life like an old rag. Her life was decent and respectable. Now here was Jake, trying to pull her back into a lifestyle she'd already left.

Was that all she was good for? She didn't want to be a soiled dove. She'd changed her life and look where that had led. To a spread somewhere in Kansas with the man she hated most.

Despair sagged her shoulders.

Who could she turn to for help?

Meghan said she needed to trust God, that she needed a Savior. Would Jesus save her? How could he accept a fallen woman?

How could she get information from this man?

This man who held her captive.

Who threatened to kill the only man she'd ever loved.

⁓

Scott awoke the next morning to someone pounding on his door.

"Coming!" He groaned as he eased himself out of bed, then grabbed his crutch, the thumping noise of its tip against the wooden floor waking him the rest of the way as he hobbled to the door. He'd been exceptionally tired last night after dinner. The pain in his leg alternated between throbbing and aching most of the night—even with a pain powder. The ride to Florence had taken more out of him than he'd thought.

"It's Sheriff Randall."

"Be right there." He unlocked the door.

Randall entered. "Thought I'd give you a taste of your own medicine, Doc. I'll be on my way now. Telegraph me if you find out anything. I'll tell your patients you'll be back on Monday. You said four days total."

He closed the door behind the sheriff. "That's what I said, yes. Nonetheless, I'm going to stay here as long as it takes."

"I understand your need to find her. However, I want you to consider something. You're part of New Boston now, Doc. People depend on you to be there when they're sick or injured. I know this is hard for you to hear, but have you thought that maybe, after all this, she won't want to be found? That it's possible she'll go back to her old life and stay with Jake Thomas?"

Scott shook his head. "Impossible. I know Rose. You don't. She wanted out of that life, and she left it. She's made a new life for herself. I'm in love with her. I want to marry her."

Randall raised an eyebrow. "All right. I'll take your word for it. Be careful. You know he's a dangerous man. Again, telegraph me if you find out anything. Don't be a hero and try to rescue her yourself. You won't do either one of you any good."

He saluted with two-fingers. "Yes, sir. I'll keep that in mind."

Randall's stern gaze bore into him. "See that you do."

Chapter Twenty-Eight

Rose cracked eggs into the skillet. The sizzling seemed loud in the otherwise quiet room. She glanced over at the bed where Jake still slept. He moaned and rolled over, but he didn't awaken. Good—she didn't want him waking up just yet. She'd come up with an idea but needed more time to ponder how she would carry it out. She could be persistent, like Delilah was, but with Jake, she'd also need to be subtle. Again, the thought came to mind about using the nickname she'd given him. Jakey. It seemed to soften him. Might it erase those hard edges that sealed his lips?

Think about a plan to escape. Keep your mind on the goal—to return to New Boston and your new life... with Scott.

Scott. She'd been in love with him for months.

His heart had been drawn only to Meghan.

But not anymore. Scott had finally accepted that Meghan loved Duncan. He'd moved on.

After that, Rose had noticed that Scott didn't seem to think of her as just a former patient, or only as her assistant. Instead, he seemed to smile at her more often. Confide in her some. It all appeared to be part of how he looked at her in a new way. Could he ever love her?

Her mind wandered to last spring. He'd gently taken care of the injuries Jake had inflicted upon her. It was the first time any man had ever touched her tenderly or treated her with respect. That was when she first began to wonder if she was falling in love with him.

She bit her lip. Would she ever see Scott again? Could she keep Jake from killing him?

Jake snorted. She turned. His eyes smoldered with lust. Forcing a smile, she held out a dinner plate, though empty. "Breakfast is ready."

After the meal, he tugged her back to the bed and pushed a mug of whiskey in front of her face.

"Please, Jakey, remember?"

His eyes narrowed. "Rosie girl, I don't wanna hit ya. But ye're makin' it hard to control my temper. You're mine, remember?"

"I know. I also remember how disgusted you got..."

"All right. All right. But you can't use that excuse much longer than a few more days."

He pulled her dress off her shoulder and nibbled her neck. "I'm still gonna look, though."

She could put up with his pawing and nipping. For a few more days until she had a plan in mind to escape.

⸺

For two days, Scott had ridden the circumference of Florence, at least ten miles in every direction. Yesterday, he'd ridden the southern and western parts of the countryside. Today, because his leg ached, he'd only explored the eastern side. He'd been riding for hours, but the hotel clock read three in the afternoon when he hobbled into the dining room and sat at the usual table.

A waiter came, a fresh-faced young man in his late teens. "Sir, would you like something to drink before supper is brought out?"

Scott laid his crutch on the floor beside his chair. "Have you got coffee?"

"Yes, I'll bring some. Cream or sugar?"

"No, thank you. I like it black."

The waiter turned to leave, then turned back. "Sir, did I hear you're looking for Jake Thomas?"

Scott leaned forward in his chair. "Yes, I am. Do you know where he lives?"

"The last I heard, several months ago, was that he had a place about fifteen miles north of town, but it's off the main road, out in the middle of nowhere."

Had he found Rose? "Are you sure?"

"Last I heard." The waiter returned to the kitchen.

Scott's heart pounded. This was just the break he'd been waiting for. Now he could telegraph Sheriff Randall. Tomorrow morning he'd head north—and not stop until he'd searched every inch of that area. Until he found Rose.

Could she become 'his' Rose? She certainly meant more to him now than an employee or even a friend. She'd shared her problems with him...about Jake. About her mother. Being with her every day at work was like a fresh, blue-skied, sun shining day. Was he falling in love?

Being without her these last few days, he realized how much he missed her. He'd come to depend on her. She'd ingrained her way into his heart and filled it with her unique love and understanding in ways Meghan could never have done. Thank God, he was being given a second chance. He'd make the most of it. She had to live and be all right—so he could tell her how he felt about her.

⁓

Three days. Rose felt she'd been back in Hades for three days already. Or was it four? But not one day more. Today was the day she was going to do the final push to learn where she was. It had to be today, or she'd go out of her mind. Even though her monthly time had kept him from certain things, he'd stepped up other touches in other places. Evidently to anticipate his next time he'd have his way with her.

Getting Jake drunk would be the key. She'd observed several levels of drunkenness with him since she'd been held captive. He drank all day long yet didn't always appear drunk. Only that first night had he been so roaring drunk. But she'd been afraid to try anything and was out of sorts that night. So great was her fear of being beaten again. It was time to turn things around. To take advantage of her position with him.

"Rosie girl, come 'ere."

She'd just finished the supper dishes and walked toward him slowly, sashaying her hips the way she knew he liked.

"Aw, that's my girl."

As she reached him, he began pawing her and fumbling with her buttons. She allowed it, knowing that this would be the last time and he wouldn't be going much further than mauling. It was tonight or never. She'd flee in the morning, whichever direction she felt led to go.

"Jakey...Jakey..." She used his favorite name. She'd been calling him that since the second day, more often as each day passed. Tonight, she'd use it all the time.

Later that evening, she put his head in her lap and stroked his hair, slow and easy. He was already drunk and drowsy.

"Jakey..."

"You know how I love it when you call me that."

"Jakey, will ya take me ta town?" He liked it when she reverted to her former speech patterns. He'd struck her only once for using "uppity" language with him, saying he wanted things just the way they had been months ago.

"Tomorrow, darlin'. We'll go to town tomorrow. I need to check my mail. And you do need new clothes."

"Aw, thanks Jakey." She stroked his hair methodically. "Jakey...where's town? What town is it?"

"You don't need to know that. You have me to take care of ya."

She moved her hand from his hair and began fondling his rib cage. His chest expanded with air and released slowly. He trembled. Now was the time.

She cooed. "Jakey, Jakey. Where are we?"

He relaxed.

"What if somethin' happened to ya? What would I do? What if you needed somethin' I couldn't give ya?"

She had him, now.

⌒

Her caresses deepened, and he drew air into his lungs. Jake could hardly contain himself. She'd said her woman time was ending soon. He'd only wait one more day, then take her as his very own, then leave her here, sneak into New Boston, and cut that doc's throat. That way, she'd have no one to go back to.

"Rosie girl, give me a drink, will ya?"

"I'd rather give you something else." She leaned over and kissed him. Her full lips on his started a fire in him he couldn't put out.

"Jakey, will you tell me somethin'?"

Every time she used that name. Whenever she touched him, the fire in him raged. He could never get enough of her. The months he was without her were pure torture. But he'd used that time to obtain more cattle and sell them. There hadn't been time to do anything else. Not even be with her. But now, she was all his. He couldn't deny her anything. He'd done right bringing her here. He couldn't wait to take the rest of her, tomorrow night.

"What is it, Rosie girl?" He shifted his position, putting *her* head in *his* lap, and sighed.

"Where's here, Jakey?" Caressing her body caused a shiver of desire to go through him. Could he trust her? She hadn't tried to escape since he brought her here.

"Let's talk later. Kiss me, Rosie girl."

Chapter Twenty-Nine

The night wasn't going the way Rose had planned it. She'd asked several times, in that sweet, seductive tone he liked. Still he had yet to answer her question. He kept saying, "Later, Rosie" or "Do this, Rosie girl" or "Do that." He'd pass out before she could ask him again. If she could just catch him in that dreamy time between sleeping and waking, while giving him pleasure of some sort, maybe those precious words would slip out before he realized it. Thank goodness for her woman time. It had saved her. She didn't like to think about what he'd do to Scott. Sometimes he was all bluster. He didn't always do what he said he would do. She hoped that would be true this time. That he wouldn't leave her here, then go kill Scott.

Rubbing his chest slowly and methodically, she tried not to shudder—hating every bit of it.

She whispered in his ear. "Jakey...Jakey, can ya hear me?"

"Hmmmm. That feels good."

"Jakey, I'll go to town for supplies. Can you tell me how to get there?"

He put a hand behind her neck and drew her face down to his. His eyes were barely open. They were unfocused. Good. She could use that to her advantage.

"Jakey...did ya hear me?" She forced her voice to show a tenderness she didn't feel.

He pulled her down and smacked his lips against hers, keeping her for maybe a minute, before releasing her and taking in a long breath.

"Ya'd go to town for me, Rosie girl? And come back?"

She caressed his cheek. "Why, sure. Where else would I go? Jakey..."

He slowly inhaled and released another long lungful of air. "South fifteen miles to Florence."

Dare she trust him? Was he lying to her even now?

The cabin faced east. She'd find her way.

He dragged her down to him once more, fondling her in places she wished he wouldn't.

A memory came, unbidden... of her first time. Although this time she hadn't had to tolerate the worst of Jake's advances, it still reminded her of when she had. And that reminded her of the first time.

"Rosalie, now that you are a woman, it is time you learn the ways of men." Mother sat her down on her birthday. *"I have a very special birthday present for you tonight."*

Rosie's shoulders twitched. "What is it, Mother? I'm so excited! I'm fourteen today! All the girls have wished me a very happy birthday."

"Yes, they're being nice to you today, because they know what your present is."

"They do?" Rosie tingled all over. "Can you give me a hint?"

Mother smiled. "All in good time. But it will change your life. Tomorrow morning, we'll have another talk."

"But Mother, why do I have to wait until tomorrow morning?"

"Because, dear, you're going to experience something tonight that is wondrous, exciting, and... well, after tonight, you'll know what I mean."

Rosie hugged Mother. "Thank you, Mother."

Mother flashed a small smile. "Just make sure to look your absolute best this evening. I will say this. We're having a small party for you in the main room tonight. A young man is coming to meet you. It's his birthday, too."

"Oh. We're having a party with someone else?" Rosie wasn't sure how she felt about that. It was her birthday. She wasn't sure she wanted to share it.

"It will be all right, dear. His father's a good friend of mine. Both of us agreed that you two would enjoy meeting each other and celebrating your birthdays together in a special way. You'll both get a very special birthday present."

The next morning, she didn't want to get out of bed and hurt in places she'd never noticed before. Far from being wondrous and exciting, it had been hurtful and excruciating. Embarrassing and traumatic.

Mother came in and sat on the edge of the bed. "Rosalie, you must get up. I need to tell you some things."

"Why, Mother? Why did you do this? I thought you loved me! This is the worst thing you could have done to me!" She pulled the covers over her head.

Mother pulled the covers down and exposed her nakedness. Rosie quickly jerked them back up to her chin.

"Rosalie, this was a gift I gave to you, so you wouldn't have your innocence stolen. It was given freely, and not taken, as mine was."

"I didn't give it! You did!"

A thought struck her. What had driven Madam to say that? Had something happened in her mother's life when she was young?

⌒

Scott intended to search every inch of this territory north of Florence until he found Rose. And when he found her... he'd never let her go. Her past didn't matter—and he'd told her so on many occasions. His stomach churned. What had she been forced to do to survive? She had to still be alive—she had intelligence and perseverance.

He mounted his horse, Jovie, and headed north on the road out of Florence. Jovie was short for Jovial, a four-year-old gelding he'd received from—of all people—Wilcox's boss, McMasters—in lieu of payment for medical services for all his cowhands for a specified time. His cocoa-tinted coat with black mane and tail had caught his attention—a fine-looking mount. On closer inspection, he discovered Jovie also had a black spot in the middle of his forehead.

That somewhat unique feature always helped Scott identify him in a crowd of other horses.

He'd rested his leg last night, and so far, it wasn't giving him too much discomfort. A pain powder he'd taken at breakfast helped too.

When he'd ridden a few miles, a man driving a buckboard on the other side of the road drew near. Maybe he knew where Jake Thomas lived.

As they came close, Scott reined Jovie in. "Excuse me, sir. May I ask directions?"

"Whoa." The man brought the buckboard to a stop. "Where are you headed?"

"Do you know where Jake Thomas lives?" Scott cleared his throat. "I've got business with him."

At the mention of the name, the man flinched and flicked the reins.

"Wait! Can't you tell me anything?"

The buckboard sped away. Scott thought about going after him but wasn't sure what that would accomplish. Obviously, the man didn't want to talk about Jake Thomas. He pressed Jovie's sides to spur him to action.

A few minutes later, he spotted another man on horseback riding toward Florence. As he came closer, Scott recognized him. Rafe! He squinted. Why wasn't Rose with him? He was alone. Weren't angels supposed to rescue people? Although, Rafe had never said he was an angel.

When he reached Scott, Rafe turned his horse and rode beside him.

"Son, don't you think you might need a little direction?"

"Rafe! Where have you been?" His worry spilled out. "Why didn't you stop Rose from being kidnapped? How am I supposed to find her? Do you know where she is? Can you take me to her?" His voice pitched higher and louder with each question. Blood rushed through him.

The old man touched his shoulder. The storm within him stopped. Peace and warmth flooded his whole being. When Rafe lifted his hand, the heat remained.

"You'll have to ask the Almighty as to why Rose from was taken. Everything that happens, good or bad, he uses for his own purposes. He doesn't plan evil, men choose it. Sometimes God stops it, but many times, it's allowed to test the person whom will lose the most. You remember Joseph? Why did God allow the boy to be sold into slavery? Because fifteen years later, Joseph would save the world, by being second in command to Pharaoh. Don't you know your Bible, son?"

Scott coughed. "Apparently, not as well as I should. I'm sorry. I guess I'm more upset than I realized. I'm desperate to find Rose."

Rafe smiled. "Yes, you want a second chance at love. You truly love Rose, and you don't want to lose her."

The old man tugged in the reins, coming to a stop. Scott stopped, too. Rafe continued. "But what's most important is your heart. Keep searching, and don't waste this chance."

Scott swallowed. "I won't, sir. Believe me, I won't."

Rafe laid a hand on his shoulder. "Allow God to change your heart completely and become the man she already thinks you are. Be the man that even Meghan Gallagher can again respect.

"Remember what you heard earlier, son. Ask Jesus in your heart. Learn to know his ways. He can change your life. He is meek and lowly, yet he is the King of kings and Lord of lords. The next time he comes, he'll arrive in his full array of splendor."

Scott blinked. He was about to thank him, but Rafe and the horse were gone.

⁓

Rose climbed out of bed just as the sun was coming up over the horizon. Today she'd escape. Hopefully, Jake would sleep most of the morning. After cleaning herself up, she took several biscuits she'd made yesterday in preparation for the journey. She filled a canteen she'd found in the corner with Jake's saddlebags.

It was time to leave.

Taking one last look at Jake to make sure he was asleep, she crept out of the cabin and made her way to the barn. If caught, she could be hanged for a horse thief. Better that than to be Jake's slave until he tired of her. Her woman time had ended yesterday, but she told Jake she needed one more day just to be sure.

Jake's horse nickered as she entered the barn. Sal had grown somewhat accustomed to her as she'd done barn chores the last couple of days. She spoke quietly to the horse so as not to arouse it, or the cow—or even Jake.

"Hey Sal. It's all right. We're going to take a little ride, you and me. How would you like that?" She slung the canteen strap over her neck and put an arm through it to carry crosswise. The drawstrings of the bag of biscuits was long enough for her to do the same. Not wanting to take the time to saddle the horse, she slipped a halter over the mare's head as Jake had shown her. Well, today she wasn't moving Sal to clean the stall. Today she would mount her and leave this Jake-made prison.

The horse seemed to nod in agreement. She hoped that meant God would approve of what she was about to do—steal a man's horse. But she had to get away. And who knew? Maybe Jake had stolen Sal from her previous owner.

She led the horse out by hand, not wanting to create more work for herself than necessary. Her hooves barely made noise on the ground, moist from dew.

When they were about fifty feet from the house, she stooped to her knees, then sprang up and swung a leg over the bare back of the horse. After fixing her skirt a moment, she pressed Sal into a trot.

A distant shout from the direction of the cabin sent tremors through her body. Blood rushed through her.

No! He was awake!

Something whizzed by her ear! Was Jake shooting at her? She couldn't stop or even turn around to find out. She urged the horse into a gallop.

Another whistle by her ear. Another miss. Her heart raced as she leaned forward to the horse's mane to make herself a lesser target—something she'd heard in the dance hall from cowboys about how they escaped Indians in years past. Surely, Jake wouldn't risk a third shot. He might hit Sal. Then how would he get around?

A minute went by. No more shots. Rose exhaled. Drew in and let out another breath. Then a third. Finally, her breathing began to return to normal.

She couldn't afford to slow down until she found the main road. But even then, she'd have to keep going, but maybe at a trot, instead of a full gallop. Who knew if Jake had a neighbor close by who could lend him a horse? If there was a way to come after her, he'd find it.

Inhaling, then exhaling, Rose hugged Sal's mane and held on for dear life.

Chapter Thirty

Scott's leg began to pain him, even though he'd taken a powder at breakfast. He'd have to dismount and rest soon. At least the sun was at his side, so he could see up the road. Whoever came this way, he'd ask every one of them where Jake Thomas lived.

Someone would know.

A covered wagon came to the edge of the horizon. As it drew closer, he heard singing. It sounded like both adults and children. A family? Maybe they were coming to live in Florence or New Boston. If they weren't from here, they wouldn't know Jake Thomas, or where he lived.

He pulled on the reins just as the wagon also slowed, then stopped.

"Hello there. I'm Doctor Scott Allison from New Boston. How are you all doing today?"

The man of the family, who held the reins of the two oxen, answered. "We're fine. We hail from Indiana."

A buxom wife sat next to the man. Two children, a boy and a girl, peeked through the canvas opening from the back.

"How far is it to New Boston from here? We've been traveling for over a week now." The man extended his hand. "Sorry, where are my manners? I'm Cordell Worthington. This is my family. Nice to meet you, Doc."

Scott thought a moment. Travel in a covered wagon with a family was slow. It might take them another day or two to get to New Boston.

"Well, Florence is just down the road. Only an hour or so. You could rest there for the night, then make New Boston tomorrow."

"Thank you. We appreciate that." The man turned to someone in the back of the wagon. "Did ya hear that, Lucy? We'll be there tomorrow."

Turning back to Scott, he shifted on his seat for a better angle to face the front. "Say, do you know these parts?"

Scott tilted his head. "No, not really."

"That's too bad. A young lady seemed lost a little way back." He jerked his head to the left.

"What did she look like?" His breath caught. Could it be Rose?

"Pretty little thing. Looked like she hadn't changed clothes in days." The man shook his head.

"How far?" Scott nearly kicked Jovie's sides to get moving. But he wanted to hear the man out. It must be Rose.

"Oh, about five miles back."

"Thank you. I'll take care of her." Scott gave the man a two-fingered salute. "Stop by when you get settled in New Boston." He spurred Jovie into action.

He couldn't wait to see her.

༄

Rose was exhausted. She'd found the main road, and thought she'd turned south. But clouds had covered the sun and for a while, she lost her bearings. She rode up the road, then turned around. On her way back, she encountered a covered wagon and asked them if they knew which way Florence was.

"Well, I think that's the other direction from where you're going, missy. We're headed that way, if you want to come along." The man had kind eyes.

"No, thank you. I'll think I'll rest for a short while." Jake's horse needed rest, too. She'd ridden her at a hard gallop for a long time. Where could she find water for the mare?

She had no idea how much time had passed since she left Jake's cabin. Hopefully, he hadn't found a way to follow her.

⁓

At least an hour or so later—she wasn't sure how much time had passed, Rose sat at the side of the road, head down, eyes closed. She needed a short rest. Only a few more minutes. Sal stood a few feet away, munching on some prairie grass. She took a drink from her canteen and shook it. She'd drunk most of the water already. If only she were safe—with Scott.

"Rose!"

She jerked her head up. Scott?

The sun was so bright, she put her hand to her eyes to shield them.

It looked like ... Scott?

"Rose! Rose!"

She jumped up and ran toward him.

"Rose!"

His voice! It was Scott!

"Scott! Oh Scott! Thank God!"

He drew up next to her and slid off. Oh, she hoped he hadn't hurt his leg more. A momentary wince crossed his expression until ...

Their lips met. She put all her love into that kiss. When he pulled away, both gasped for breath. "Are you all right?"

"I can't believe you found me!" Her eyes misted. She sniffed, reached for her handkerchief in her sleeve, but her fingers came out empty. She'd lost it somewhere. He reached inside his pocket and gave her his.

"Thank you. I am all right."

"Are you sure?"

"He didn't hit me... much."

His loving gaze searched her face as he stroked a healing bruise on the side of her cheek.

"Did he hurt you in other ways?"

"No, thank God. My woman time kept worse things from happening. He pawed me a lot, but I'm all right. I truly am. I escaped this morning." She put a hand on his arm and met his steady gaze. She couldn't take her eyes off him.

"Rose, I—I'm so glad I found you! Are you sure you're all right?"

What a sight for her sore eyes he was. Tears ran down her cheeks. She dabbed them away, but love poured from his now-teary eyes, taking her breath away.

"Thank you so much, Scott." She looked down, then up, meeting his gaze.

A thought crossed her mind. "What's happened in town while I've been gone? Does everyone in town know about me? Who I am?"

Had her biggest fear come to pass? That the townspeople would learn her identity and force her to leave town.

He offered a gentle smile. "As far as I know, not many. I don't think the whole town knows yet. But they'll probably find out after we get back. Shall we get back to Florence now? I need to telegraph Sheriff Randall. Can you tell me where Jake Thomas lives?"

Rose pointed from the direction she'd come. "A long way back, I don't know exactly how far, there's a faint dirt path that will eventually lead to Jake's cabin. He's kept it real secret."

"It's good you escaped. You'll be able to bring charges against him. He'll go to jail for what he's done."

Her eyes widened. Her stomach wrenched. "I don't know... I'd be exposed."

Putting a hand on her back, he gently guided her to Jake's horse. "We'll talk about it later. Let's get you home."

He gave her a boost into the saddle, then mounted Jovie. She reached out her hand. He grasped and squeezed. They rode close together, their legs touching occasionally.

The warmth when they touched flooded her soul like a warm bath on a cold evening, comforting and peaceful.

She loved him. Now that she was with him again, she knew it. But did he love her? He had never said so.

If her worst fear came about, how could they ever be together? Her stomach roiled. Good thing she hadn't eaten much. She felt like retching. Had Jake spoiled her chance at happiness?

Chapter Thirty-One

That evening, when Rose opened the door to the boardinghouse, the first person she saw was Meghan. As their gazes met, her friend let out a screech, which brought Duncan charging from the drawing room. Olivia and the de Campos came running from the kitchen. Hannah bounded down the stairs. Bernie didn't seem to be home.

Scott came in behind her, his presence strengthening her as everyone crowded around her. He closed the door and took charge. "I know you all want to talk with Rose, but right now, she's exhausted. She's home safe, and you can talk to her tomorrow."

Meghan gathered her in her arms. "Rose, I'm so glad you're all right! I've been so worried."

She released Meghan, then turned to Olivia. The woman's motherly hug comforted in a way she hadn't expected. "Of course, you're weary, you poor dear." She clucked like a hen gathering a wayward chick. "Let's get you upstairs. My goodness, you look like you was rode hard and put up wet—as the cowpokes would say. We'll take good care of you. You just wait and see. Are you hungry? I'll bring you some leftover stew upstairs after you've had a bath." She paused a moment, only to talk to Luisa. "Luisa, could you get a bath ready for our precious Rose?"

Luisa nodded, and started upstairs. Carlos, age ten, and Maria, just seven, stared at her with their beautiful, big dark eyes. Maria curled a finger on her lips and looked up with a shy smile. She felt a bit awkward but gave them the best smile she could muster.

"Hello, Maria. Carlos." The boy's brow furrowed, but he said nothing.

It would be a while before the bath was ready. She needed to lie down and rest. Craved to be alone. To think about what she should do and what the consequences would be if she testified against Jake. Her whole sordid past would come to light. Could she bear it?

"I'd like to lie down until the bath is ready, if you don't mind?"

"I'll walk up with you." Meghan started toward the stairs, taking Rose's arm, but she hesitated.

"Good night, Rose." Scott's soft, soothing voice touched her in ways she couldn't even fathom right now.

Rose turned and hugged him tight at the waist before rising on her toes to kiss his cheek. "Thank you for rescuing me. I'll never forget that. We'll talk tomorrow."

His smile warmed the deepest places in her heart. "I'll check on you tomorrow. No need to come to the office—unless you want to. You've been through an ordeal." He kissed the top of her head and left.

Duncan came over. "Can I give you a hug, too, Rose?"

"Thank you, Duncan. It's good to be home." What a wonderfully kind and considerate man. No wonder Meghan loved him. She hoped they were working out their differences. That he was here tonight was a good sign. At least they were talking.

Meghan touched her elbow. "Are you ready?" Then, looking over her shoulder to Duncan, Meghan smiled. "I'll see you in a just a minute."

He smiled back. "I'll be waiting."

That definitely sounded like they were working things out.

Olivia returned to the kitchen, presumably to warm up the leftover stew. Rose was hungry enough to eat two large bowls, though one regular-sized bowl would usually satisfy her.

As they climbed the stairs, Meghan put her arm around Rose's shoulders. "I'm so glad you're home, and you're not—injured. But I suspect..."

"I don't want to talk about it now."

"I understand." Meghan gave her a grim smile. "You know I'm here whenever you might want to talk."

She managed a weak smile. "Yes. Thanks, Meghan. I appreciate you more than you know."

Once she got to her room, she closed and locked the door, then leaned back against it—and let out a long, slow breath. She just wanted to crawl in a hole and never come out.

She lay on her bed and waited until Luisa knocked on her door to tell her the bath was ready. All the scrubbing at Jake's hadn't helped her feel clean. Would a bath help?

Her thoughts turned back to Madam. Why had her mother forced her into that life? She remembered Madam's words: *Rosalie, because you're a madam's daughter, you will have no other choice in life. People will always think, like mother, like daughter.* She had a hard time accepting that. There must have been more to it than that. Maybe she should talk to Madam, if only to get that question answered.

A knock at the door drew her from her thoughts.

Oh no! Who could that be? Surely not Jake. Although she knew he could sneak past everyone.

"Bath ready, Miss Rose." Luisa's soft and pleasant voice came from beyond the door.

She let out a long breath. "Thank you. I'll be right there." Rose dragged her sore and weary body off her bed, gathered her soap, towel, and nightgown, and went to the bathroom to clean up and relax.

She'd lied and allowed certain things all in the name of escape. It made her feel dirty inside. Would she ever feel clean?

⁓

Jake rode into New Boston under cover of darkness. It had taken him all day to walk to his nearest neighbor hoping he'd be able to sneak into the barn and leave, unnoticed, with a horse. He'd done it, though. And no one had seen him.

How dare Rosie run off—on his horse! He'd spent a good deal of his ride into town thinking about how he would make her pay. It took several hours for the rage coursing through his body to ease.

He let out a deep breath as he headed toward Madam Margaret's Saloon and Dance Hall. It was time to get Rosie's mother involved. He needed the madam to help change Rosie's mind about coming back to the cabin with him. Madam needed to see that he was the man for Rosie. That only with him would her life be good.

For his part, no other woman satisfied him like Rosie girl. He was frustrated more than he could stand at not getting to have his way with her—all because of her "woman time" as she called it. But she was right. It was distasteful during that time.

Now that he'd cooled off some, his mind cleared enough to plan his next moves. He needed to check with his business partners to see when another roundup should be made. One of them would meet him later this evening at the Silver Spike. He was hoping to talk with Rosie's mother first.

He dismounted his new horse and tied it to the railing outside Madam Margaret's, then walked inside. He'd have to think of a clever name for it.

A middle-aged woman crooned a low song as she slowly came down the stairs from the upper floor. Jake didn't take much note of her. She wasn't real pretty, but that didn't seem to stop her from making a grand entrance. She certainly had the attention of the men who whistled at her. The song ended on a wistful note.

"Hey, Madam Margaret, give us an encore!"

Madam Margaret? Rosie's mother? This woman? He shook his head—she did look somewhat like his Rosie girl. Lots older. Nevertheless, he needed to talk to her. By this time, she'd reached the bottom of the steps. He moved boldly toward her.

"Madam, I'm Jake Thomas. I think you're going to want to talk to me."

She raised an eyebrow and raked her gaze over him. Younger women had done it, and he loved that feeling. But somehow when Madam did it...

"And why would I want to do that?"

"Because I want to talk about Rosie."

"Who's Rosie?"

He threw his head back and let out a harsh laugh.

"Okay, then you won't care to hear that I'm the one who's had her." He turned to leave.

"Well then, come upstairs with me." She looked over his shoulder. "Pete, could you get me a bottle and two glasses?" A few moments later, the bartender brought over a bottle. She nodded toward Jake. "Give *him* the two glasses."

Jake took them and followed her upstairs. He'd get her to see things his way.

Chapter Thirty-Two

"So, what do you know about my daughter?"

Once they'd gotten to Madam's room, she'd gone behind a privacy screen, taken off her dress, and put on a purple silk robe. She motioned for him to sit at the marble table in the middle of her swanky room. Red felt wallpaper hung on all four walls, making the space look dark and mysterious. Gold-painted molding edged the floor and what he'd heard called a chair railing. A huge crystal chandelier hung from the high ceiling. Having a ten-foot ceiling in an upstairs bedroom suite was very unusual. The large chandelier was also unusual in such a space. He'd heard about them in ballrooms. It had already been lit and provided ample light to the room. He let out a low whistle. Obviously, the madam was rich. He'd never seen anything like it before, although it reminded him of Rosie's less elaborate room at The Silver Spike. She'd used a lot of red in her room, too.

He sat as Madam opened the whiskey bottle. Top-notch brand. Very expensive. He was impressed. He never would have guessed. Rosie had never said much about her mother. Only that she hadn't talked to her in three years.

"Name's Thomas, Madam. Jake Thomas. Your daughter's the one for me. She's the one I want above all others. When I'm with her, life's good. If she's not with me, I miss her somethin' fierce."

"Have you been courtin' Rosie?"

He snorted, then let out another harsh laugh. "Ha! Court her?" He put his hand to his forehead. "No, Madam. I don't 'court' women. I take 'em."

She raised an eyebrow. "If I understand you right, you've already 'taken' my daughter. So, why are you here?"

He poured himself another drink. "Oh, I've had her, Madam. Many times. She's the one for me, as I said. But she escaped from me this last time."

Madam's neck stiffened. "Are you telling me that you took her by force? That's kidnapping. And against the law."

He downed his drink. The high-quality whiskey burned his throat and he loved it. He couldn't wait to feel its high-class effects.

"Yep."

She poured him another drink. "Why did you come? I want a straight answer."

He finished off the glass while thinking on how to answer. "I need your help to get her to come back to me."

"And why should I help you?"

"I already told ya. I want her all to myself."

Madam's gaze bored right through him, but it didn't unnerve him. Many women had tried to scare him that way. He stared right back, trusting Madam would wilt, just like other women had. He loved that feeling of power. She finally looked down, breaking contact.

"If I were to help you—and I'm not saying that I can—what's in it for me?"

He tossed the cork in the air a few inches, then caught it. "I want you to help me get her back. Ye're her ma. She'll listen to you." He put the cork down on the table and rubbed his chin. "What's in it for you? I'll offer you ten percent of my cattle business."

"You mean a percentage of your profits from rustling?"

He cleared his throat. Did she know he rustled cattle, or was this a lucky guess? "It's business, Madam."

She rose quickly and walked toward the door. "It's against the law, sir. I want nothing to do with outlaws. I run a clean establishment here. It's time for you to go."

"Fifteen percent." He rose slowly but didn't follow her to the door. "All you have to do is get her to come to you—back to this life. She thinks she's too good for me. But, she's not. She's just what I need."

He strolled to the door. "Think about it."

She said nothing but gestured with her wrinkled hand for him to leave.

He laid a hand on her arm. "I'll be back in a week."

～

The next morning, Scott unlocked the office door and limped to the back to put his white jacket on. He wondered if Rose would come in today. He had told her she could have the day off. She needed time to recuperate, but he desperately wanted to see her. Even if only for a few minutes. If she did come in, they might have an opportunity to talk a little bit. She'd been curiously reticent all the way home from Florence. He knew she'd been through a horrible ordeal, living in fear that Thomas would beat her if she didn't bow to his every whim. She'd said he couldn't have his way with her because of her woman time. But he suspected there was more to it than that. He wondered what.

When she'd told him what she'd done to escape, pride swelled his heart. He was thankful she'd made some good come from her captivity—her escape.

Concentrate on *her*—not on what happened. Ponder whether they could have a future life together.

What strength she'd had to muster up to deceive the man like that! Was she different now? How was she dealing with this? Was anyone helping her? Well, maybe Olivia, being a bit older, could help her, or Senora de Campos.

She'd tried so hard to change, not wanting anything to do with her old life. Not even wanting to talk to her mother, who'd just moved to New Boston and opened yet another dance hall.

If he ever got his hands on Jake... he almost certainly violate his Oath of Hippocrates. He wanted to strangle that man for kidnapping his precious Rose. God, help him release the rage.

Lord, help Rose to heal emotionally from being held captive and terrorized.

⁓

Two days later, a short knock on the door before it opened—that was their shared signal—told him she was here.

"Rose, you came in. Are you sure you are all right?" He hobbled over to meet her and closed the door after she entered.

She took off her cape and bonnet and hung them on the coatrack in the corner. "Yes, I'm fine." She turned to him and gave him a small smile. No, she wasn't quite all right, but she was a trouper. She'd come in, even though she probably needed more time to herself.

His crutches clacked on the floor as he limped back to the exam table. "The appointment book is pretty light today, not many patients to see." Looking up, he noticed dark circles under her eyes. Obviously, she hadn't slept well.

"How would you feel if we closed early, then go visit the sheriff? After I took you home the other night, he came to see me. He said we could come in today. I think he understands what you went through."

She looked at the floor a moment, then into his gaze. "I'm not going to make a statement."

"Why not? We have to put this man behind bars."

"I—I can't."

He guided her to the couch. She sat on one end, he at the other. "Why?"

"You know why. I'm scared, Scott. If I make a statement, and there's a trial... well... everyone will know who I am—my past. They'll run me out of town."

Scott scooted closer and reached out his hand. "I think they're better than that."

"No, that's one thing I've learned. People don't change their attitudes about women like me."

"But, Rose, they've already seen your change."

"They don't know it's Rosalie O'Roarke, dance hall girl. That I'm now Rose Rhodes, doctor's assistant."

He reached out and gently tucked her hand into his. "I know you're afraid of how they'll react. Shouldn't we give them the benefit of the doubt?"

She released a long breath. "What about you? Do you believe me?"

He squeezed her hand. "Of course I do. What's past is past, Rose Rhodes. You're very precious to me, you know."

She smiled. "Even more dear than Meghan?"

He rolled his eyes. "You know how I feel about you. I'm never going to live that down, am I?"

Her smile faded. "See? How easy it is to remember the bad? That's what the townspeople will remember."

He waved his hand. "Let's ponder the possibilities, shall we? If they do, we can go somewhere else. Where they don't know us, and we'll start over."

Her eyes widened. "You'd be willing to do that? For me? You love it here. So do I."

He let out a breath. "Yes, I like it here. But, if it would make you feel more comfortable to leave..."

"I don't want to go. I'm just saying I might be run out of town."

"If the townspeople tried to do that, they'd have to get past me first. I wouldn't let them. If they make life miserable for you here, let's move somewhere else."

She looked down. "Thank you... for your willingness to... leave. You're under no obligation, you know."

"Since we don't know what will happen, let's take it one step at a time, all right? We'll see the sheriff this afternoon after we close the office. Then we can go out to dinner at either the hotel, or the boardinghouse. I think Missus Baldwin always has extra."

Her lips curled up slightly into the smallest of smiles. He took that as a yes.

"All right. One step at a time."

He nodded. "That's all we can do."

Chapter Thirty-Three

The minutes ticked off to the time to close the medical office. Rose fumbled with the strings of the apron she wore to protect her dress. Finally, she got the knot untied and hung the apron on the wall peg next to Scott's jacket, grasping her hands together to calm the tremor.

"Scott, would you please see me home."

He turned toward from the medicine cabinet, where he'd placed the new medications. When her gaze met his, she quickly looked down.

He moved toward her quickly, despite his crutch. "Are you having second thoughts about giving your statement to the sheriff?"

"I never had any thoughts on it at all. That was your idea."

Balancing on the crutch, he put his free hand on her shoulder. "I know it's difficult, but I believe you need to see this through. You don't want him around to kidnap you again, do you? Or worse?"

She couldn't think straight. If she could only get her heart to stop pounding. If only Jake hadn't threatened to kill Scott. Besides her fear that the town would discover her identity, she couldn't help looking over her shoulder whenever she was on the street. And when she was with Scott, she had mixed feelings. Calm because she was with him yet fear for his safety. She hadn't told him of the threat yet. Maybe she should, but she just couldn't bring herself to do it.

Scott's gaze brought that blessed quietness. His sweet smile, sparkling blue eyes, and gentle manner—that seemed only for her—helped bring a tranquility to her soul.

He rubbed her shoulder. Her fears melted away with every knead of his thumb. If only Jake stayed away. She couldn't help thinking he was planning something again. When would he strike?

"Let's go. I wanna get this over with—and get Jake out of my life—for good."

∽

A few minutes later, they knocked on the sheriff's door. Scott released a long breath, his heart lighter. He hoped Rose would not change her mind. It was the first step in bringing Jake Thomas to justice. Sheriff Randall would have the testimony he needed to arrest Thomas and bring him to trial.

Randall opened the door and gestured for them to enter. "Glad you could make it." He closed the door behind them, then turned to Rose. "I'm glad you came, Miss Rose. And I'm very glad you're not too much the worse for wear."

His stomach churned. At least on the outside she wasn't, but he knew she was struggling emotionally with more than the relief she must feel after her escape. Dark clouds stormed in her eyes, as if a war was raged inside her, yet he couldn't comprehend what the fight was even about. He had an idea, but surely, she'd see everything would turn out all right in the end.

"Take a seat, will you, Doc, Miss Rose?"

As they sat on one side of the desk, Randall sat on the opposite side of his big desk and pulled out a clean sheet of paper and a pen, before uncapping the inkwell in front of him.

"Now, in your own words, Miss Rhodes, can you tell me what happened?"

"I was kidnapped just after I'd closed the office and locked the door. I think it was five nights ago." She pulled out her handkerchief and began twisting it.

"And did you see who it was that kidnapped you?"

"Not until later."

The sheriff leaned forward. "Tell me exactly what happened."

She took in a deep breath, then released it. "I didn't actually see him, but I recognized his voice. And his smell—of whiskey and cigar. He hit me a few times on the head. I was barely conscious. But I do remember what he said."

Randall's pen stopped its scratching on the paper. He looked up at Rose and offered a small smile. "What did he say, miss?"

Scott took her hand. "It's all right. You're safe now."

She looked toward the ceiling, then down, nibbling her bottom lip—something she always did when she was upset. "He said, 'You're mine, Rosie O'Roarke. Mine and no one else's.' It was him."

"What was your prior relationship with him? I know what it was—I just need an official statement of it."

"He—he was a customer, when I was a dance hall girl at the Silver Spike."

Scott glanced to Rose, then Randall. Rose's eyes shifted downward, then up to meet Randall's gaze. The sheriff's expression gave nothing away. Stoic, as usual. She probably expected him to condemn her.

"Was he a regular client?"

"Yes."

Randall softened his tone. "Did you ever lead him to believe he had exclusive use of your services?"

"Of course not. He knew that I saw other men. I think he became obsessed with me, that's all."

"Why do you think that?"

Rose shook her head. "I don't know. He's always been possessive. He'd pay extra to control my evening whenever he was in town... I can't imagine his way of thinking. If I could have figured him out, maybe I'd have been able to stop him. I just thought he was a brute."

165

"Let's go back to the night he kidnapped you. What happened after he took you to his place?"

⁓

Rose continued her story, but it was so hard. It was hard to tell him about the days at Jake's ranch, though the sheriff's patience helped. Her mouth was like she'd stuffed a ball of cotton in it. Blood rushed to her face as she flushed providing some of the details the sheriff asked about. Thankfully, Scott brought her a glass of water.

However, she did hold back the most intimate of details...of her woman time. She would just let the sheriff think Jake had raped her. He would have if not for her monthly.

She glanced over to Scott. His gaze seemed bleary, staring past the sheriff, not even looking at her. What was going through his mind? Would this statement change things between them? She had to share about caressing Jake. Of pretending to care to keep Scott safe, until she could escape.

If she did, wouldn't such actions make her look bad? Would anyone believe she was truly taken by force? Surely it would be best to just let the sheriff think Jake had forced himself on her.

Randall finished writing things down, then pushed the paper across the desk. "Would you look at this Miss Rose and see if I've got everything written down right?"

She quickly read through her statement. Thank goodness Meghan had taught her to read. She was so thankful for her friend. "It looks like you've put it down correctly. Thank you."

Randall dipped the pen in the inkwell, then extended it to her. "Would you please sign it where I've placed the X?"

"May I sign with my new name?"

"Is it legal?"

She shook her head. "Not yet."

"Sign with your legal name, then your new one next to it."

She let out a long breath, took the pen, and signed her name just right of the X, Rosalie O'Roarke/Rose Rhodes."

Scott scooted the paper and pen back across the desk to Randall. "Is that everything you need?"

Randall took another clean sheet from the drawer, then dipped the pen in ink. "Now I need your statement, Doc."

The sheriff raised his eyebrows, but his eyes had a twinkle in them. She got the feeling the Randall was enjoying this. And why shouldn't he enjoy his job? Scott liked being a doctor, and she certainly loved nursing. Her heart skipped a beat. When this was all over, would she be able to continue in her new profession? Would people find out?

Pushing aside the discouraging thought, she listened as Scott unfolded his story. She loved listening to his rich, confident voice she'd longed to hear when trapped at Jake's. She winced as he talked about the blows he'd sustained from Jake. Even injured, he'd come to her defense, and tried to stop the abduction.

How had she never thought to ask him about that night?

This had been a nightmare for both.

Yes, Jake needed to be arrested and put in prison for what he'd done, but it was going to cost her everything. Could she pay the price?

⁓

Scott walked Rose back to the boardinghouse and kissed her good night. His plan was to take her to dinner, but she'd wanted to go home and go to bed.

As he walked back to the office, he thought about her statement and his own at the sheriff's office.

He'd been so proud of her while she gave her statement. She'd endured so much. How clever of her to use a favorite nickname to hatch an escape plan. She sure had spunk, and far more courage than he thought she had.

And yet she'd willingly submitted to Jake's pawing to be able to give herself a chance to escape. Why hadn't she told the sheriff about that? And why didn't she tell him about her monthly woman time? Was she embarrassed? He didn't know.

What she'd done worked, but at what cost to her own soul? He hoped it wouldn't mark hers like his was—the scar he'd heard talked about by—the voices in his heart? Any deception she'd done helped her escape. Was there something she hadn't told him?

Chapter Thirty-Four

A few days later, on Saturday, Rose had just returned home from a short shopping trip to The Pioneer Store, when a voice called out to her from the boardinghouse's drawing room. As Rose entered, a flush of heat went through her. She couldn't bear to call her "Mother" or "Ma." The woman didn't deserve that title.

"Madam, what are you doing here?"

Madam Margaret rose and stepped toward her, then gestured for her to sit next to her on the couch. "I've come for a talk, that's all. It's time I told you some things."

Madam looked older. Gray streaked in several places throughout her upswept dark hair. The gaudy red brocade satin plunging V-neck dress with black lace trims around neckline, bodice, and sleeves hugged her plump figure in check. Although for a middle-aged woman, she still had a pretty good figure. How could she breathe? The dress was at least two sizes too small.

Rose looked around. On a Saturday afternoon, anyone could walk through the boardinghouse and spot them talking, but she certainly didn't want Madam in her private bedchamber. At present, no one was around. She let out a breath.

"Is this really necessary?" She realized her tone of voice was harsh, but she had little love for the woman who bore her.

"I'd rather we talk somewhere more private, some place like—your room. Can we do that?" Madam was several inches taller than her, and never missed an opportunity to look down her nose at her.

"What I have to say is for you alone. And believe me, you won't want anyone else to hear it." Madam shifted her posture, putting her hand on a hip. Several necklaces and bracelets jangled.

Rose let out a long breath. "All right. Follow me." What was so all-fired important that the madam had to speak to her in private? They climbed the stairs. When they reached her room, she gestured for her mother to enter.

She closed the door behind her. Madam sat on her bed. Rose sat in the chair from the desk, a few feet away. She plucked at her blue gingham sleeves with white cuff.

Madam took her gloves off and laid them in her lap. "What I have to say is not pleasant. It's not easy for me to tell you, and it won't be enjoyable for you to hear. But I won't lie. This is about your origin."

Rose's chin jutted out. "What do you mean? Are you talking about who my *father* was?" She'd never known. Madam had never told her. "Because I don't need or want to know. It doesn't matter. You forced me into a life I didn't want. You—my own *mother*!" She spat the word, it was that offensive.

Madam's chin rose. She swallowed, then looked down a moment. "You have no idea what you are talking about. There are many things you don't know. It is my purpose today, to tell you only of one thing. What you do with that information is up to you."

Rose jumped to her feet and headed toward the window. The sun shone in. It was a beautiful day outside. But the weather inside her small bedroom was stormy. "Why tell me anything at all? And why now? After all these years?"

Madam cleared her throat. "Because it's time you knew. I think you're old enough. Your appearance tells me you're thinking you might be better than anyone else. Or more than you are. I gave you the only life you could ever have. I did the best by you possible. You should be grateful that men love you."

"Love? No. That's not love. You made me a fourteen-year-old boy's birthday present! You think that's love? I didn't want that. I wasn't old enough. And, he was too young. But you forced him on me. How dare you?" A long, low growl escaped her lips as she plastered her face against the window. "Now get out. And don't come back. I don't ever want to see you again."

She heard Madam rise, but instead of leaving, her mother came up behind her. "No, I'm not leaving until I've said what I came to say. Once you've heard it, maybe we can talk more later. When you're ready to listen."

Rose turned her head toward Madam, hoping she saw her disdain. "Then say it."

Madam placed a hand on her shoulder. "Come and sit down. Let's talk this over calmly." She wrenched away from the madam's touch.

Despite her anger and need to lash out at the madam, she turned slowly and resumed her position in the chair a few feet from the bed. Her mother sat on the edge and picked up her gloves.

"Let me tell you a story."

"I don't have time for that. Doctor Allison is expecting me to come in soon."

"This won't take long. The story is short."

Rose folded her hands in her lap, but her toes tapped the floor. "All right, I'll listen."

"Rosie, dear, I know you must hate me. But there's so much you don't understand about *why* I am the way I am."

"Spare me, *Mo-ther*. You chose this life. I didn't. I want more than a brothel can give me. I want real love, not a physical imitation. I want what my friend Meghan has, a man to love me, who will marry me. I want a man who won't take advantage of me—or make me feel cheap."

"That kind of love doesn't exist, dear, except in fairy tales. I give them a year of happy marriage. Then that cowboy will come to me and ask for someone like you to give him pleasure."

"He's not that kind of man. And I'm not that kind of woman anymore. Now, get on with it, Madam. You said you had something to tell me."

Madam cleared her throat. "Yes. Remember now, I want to prepare you. It's very unpleasant, but I hope you'll be able to understand me a little better once you've heard."

"So you said."

Madam looked down a moment. When Rose caught her gaze, it was full of determination, with maybe a touch of vulnerability. "When I was fourteen, I was...assaulted." She drew in a long breath, then released it slow.

"You are the result."

A sledgehammer smashed Rose's heart. She swallowed, but words would not come. She'd always known Madam was young when she'd had her, but she hadn't heard this before. "Y-you w-were—ra—? And I..." Her heart fluttered, stomach sinking as if she'd swallowed a lead weight. "I don't understand. Why did I need to know this and why now?"

"For years you asked me about your father, and I would never tell you. The truth is, I didn't know him. Still don't know who he was." Madam stood. "Well, I've said what I came to say."

Rose stood and placed a hand on Madam's arm. "Don't go just yet. Please, tell me more. It's just—such a shock!"

Both resumed their seats. Rose put a hand to her forehead. This was too much. No wonder her mother had never spoken of her father. For as long as she could remember, she had asked her mother about why she didn't have a father. All Madam would say was that he was never going to be part of their lives.

"Nothing more to tell. It was traumatic. I don't remember much. I was young, too, you know. I was running an errand for Aunt Sally. You remember her. I told you she raised me. Well, she threw me out of the house when I asked for help."

"What can I say, Mother? I'm sorry." Feelings of tenderness for the madam she hadn't felt for years, since before her fourteenth birthday.

"I had to make a living for us. Since I was damaged goods, no decent man would marry me. I've tried to do the best I could for you.

Got the only job I could. You remember Fergie Saylor? She owned the house before me. Treated me with more kindness than Aunt Sally ever did. She didn't even throw us out after you were born."

"But why did you force me into the same thing?"

"I was preparing you. You were growing up, and I didn't want what happened to me to happen to *you*. I wanted—needed to control the situation. Men coming to call on me were already noticing you. They offered me a lot of money...so I figured for your first time...if it were someone your own age...it would be better than someone...older."

Rose pressed her hands to her ears, then dug the heels of her hands into her eyes. Her heart pulsed and pounded like waves crashing against a beach. Had Madam protected her by controlling her first encounter, or was it something else? What was the truth?

She fled to the window, trying to focus, but seeing nothing but darkness where only a moment ago was sunshine. She wondered whether the darkness came from her own soul.

"Why are you telling me this, now?"

"Because I see what you're trying to do. I hate to discourage you, but once people find out about you...well. I want you to know, you'll always have a place at Madam Margaret's. And I'll keep that nasty Jake Thomas away from you. I have men who work for me who take care of that sort of thing."

Rose couldn't think of a thing to say.

Madam continued.

"I admire your attempt to better yourself. Just don't be too disappointed if it doesn't work out. Come back to me, and I'll show you how to run the place. I'll teach you everything you need to know. You'll be well respected among the cowboys and rail workers. And you can have any man you want. Shoot, you can have the doctor, too!"

The hammer in Rose's brain was pounding double-quick time. The knowledge that she was not born of love, but lust, power, and corruption, was nearly too much to bear. The vilest of circumstances. How her skull hadn't yet cracked from the pressure, she didn't know.

Madam was raped. And at the same age Rose had first been forced on by the boy. Did Madam plan that so that her daughter wouldn't be assaulted by a stranger? The boy was a stranger, but he was her age. Madam had said so. If so, it was still very cruel. Against her will. Her innocent soul had been violated forever.

Somehow she would eventually come to accept this information about herself. She should to talk to Meghan but needed to catch her friend on a positive day. Even though they were talking again, Meghan and Duncan still hadn't ironed out all their differences yet.

This was a nightmare. She'd never considered how she was conceived before, always guessing it was youthful passion from her mother. How was she ever supposed to see herself in a positive way knowing she was the product of such an evil act? She'd tried so hard to put her old feelings of fatalism and inferiority behind her.

When she'd first seen Meghan on the street, the day her friend arrived, she knew that's what she wanted to be. A woman of esteem and wholesomeness. Someone people could look up to and admire. A lady. And she'd done it.

Now the fragile veil she'd put in place to change her life was ready to rip apart.

How could she ever continue her plan for her new life? She had so much to overcome. Could she do it?

Chapter Thirty-Five

Several days later, Rose scurried to the medical office trying to shield herself from the blustery weather. Already November. It hadn't snowed yet, and Rose hoped it wouldn't for weeks yet. Trudging through snow reminded her of the dirty slush in the Baltimore streets. Not her idea of a good time.

She couldn't decide what, if anything, to do with the information Madam had given her. The knowledge shook her to the core of her being. Everything she'd thought about who she was, who she wanted to be, was now colored by the fact that she'd been conceived by a revolting, unspeakable act.

Although she'd felt sympathy for Madam, it hadn't lasted long. How could this woman, who was her mother, ask—no, not ask, nearly demand of her—to forsake being Rose, and become Rosie again? How dare Madam suggest she join her in the brothel business!

After Madam left that terrible afternoon, she'd cried till the sun came up. The next day, her head pounded, and her sinuses were so clogged, she stayed in her room. Meghan and Olivia had urged her to eat something, but her imagination of a phantom man attacking Madam was all she could think of. She knew what it was like.

Even in the life, there were times when men forced themselves on her. Certainly, Jake was one of those. In that existence, she had no say in anything. She belonged to whoever employed her. Their customers also had a claim on her. Only one day off a week. And if she felt bad for any reason, unless she was contagious, she worked.

She'd hoped for so long to better herself. Kept looking for a chance to escape that dreary reality. When the opportunity presented itself, she took it. Now it seemed it was all about to fall apart on her.

When she reached the office, she found the door already unlocked. Scott was up and about. Hopefully, they'd have a busy day, with little, or no, time to talk. She wasn't in the mood to answer questions. How could she share Jake's threat of murder? If she could keep him safe by going to work for Madam Margaret, she'd do it. He'd be safe then.

It pained her to have to tell him what she was planning to do, but she had to do it sometime. She had to protect him any way possible.

She gave the soft knock they'd arranged, then opened the door. The twinkle in his eyes took her breath away, he was so handsome. He jumped up on the exam table. That stray lock of wheat-colored hair which always loosed itself when he moved suddenly, flopped across his forehead, making him appear much younger. He tossed the crutch aside.

"Did the doctor give you permission to do that?"

He chuckled. "Let's check the leg, shall we?"

She removed her cloak and wool bonnet and hung them on the coatrack, then moved to the back of the office and put on her white apron, tying the strings as she walked toward the exam table.

He swiveled to lift his injured leg onto the exam table. She placed one hand under his thigh and the other under his calf to help guide it.

"How does it feel?" She gently ran her hands from his ankle up to the knee on one side, feeling for any swelling and bumps indicating the bone had separated. He did the same with the other side. Her eyes fixed on his expression, detecting only a slight wince as they neared the point of break.

"Pretty good. I've been behaving myself since we got back, and I think it's about healed. It's been six weeks now. Hardly any pain. I've been able to put the crutch down for several hours at a time now."

"I thought you said it usually takes eight weeks."

He nodded. "Usually, it does, but I'm wondering—because of our 'friend' Rafe—if maybe something a little out of the ordinary happened. He's the one that set it, after all."

"That's what he said."

Scott slid off the table, putting his main weight on his good leg, and limped to the back of the office to put on his white doctor's coat.

"I think we're ready for business."

She smiled. "Yes, we are."

⁓

As Scott adjusted his coat, his gaze was drawn to the dark circles under Rose's eyes. How long since she'd slept? Was she still traumatized by her captivity? And the guilt over what she'd had to do to survive? Probably. He wished he could help her. Would talking help or hurt her?

They went about their various tasks. She took inventory of the supplies, spending longer than usual, it seemed. He poured alcohol into a tray and dipped his scalpels, scrapers, needles, syringes, and scissors. They worked in silence. Usually, she would talk about what was going on at the boardinghouse, what Luisa cooked, or something funny Mrs. Baldwin said. How could he get her to share with him what she was feeling?

He limped to where she stood at the supply shelves, placing an arm around her waist. She stiffened. Why? She'd never done that before.

"I'm worried about you, Rose. You've been so quiet since we returned."

She continued counting bandage rolls.

"Rose, honey, something is obviously wrong. Are you feeling ill?"

He reached around and gently took the clipboard from her, setting it down on the worktable, then turned her around to face him.

She bowed her head, continually rubbing her hands on her apron, as if trying to wipe dirt off her hands. He put two fingers under her chin and gently lifted it. Her face was wet with tears. He hadn't heard a whimper out of her. So brave, not wanting to show her grief, even with him.

He brushed away her tears with his thumbs, as she finally looked him in the eye. He bent down and brushed his lips against hers, then again. When he raised his head, she put a finger to touch the spot where their lips met. Did she feel the burning, too?

"Will you please tell me what the matter is?" He rubbed her shoulders, his thumbs kneading lazy circles just above her collarbone.

More tears spilled from her eyes. A sob escaped. He drew her to himself, hoping to afford her some comfort. Her shoulders shook, arms hanging limp at her sides, but no sound came from her lips.

"Let's sit down. I'll close the office and we'll talk. Please tell me what is happening." He put his arm around her waist and guided her to the couch, where she sat, then moved to the door and locked it.

He turned the sign over from "Open" to "Closed." Another couple of weeks and he wouldn't even be walking with a limp.

She pulled a handkerchief from her sleeve and dabbed her eyes, then blew her nose. She wouldn't meet his gaze—again. Why was she retreating within herself? Just a few weeks ago, she'd shared everything with him...about her mother...about Jake. Had her captivity changed her?

He sat next to her and put his arm around her shoulders. She leaned her head on his neck and let out a long breath.

"Rose, I want to help. I—I want you to know... that I love you."

She drew in another long breath and blew it out slowly.

"Scott, these past few months of working for you, have been the best of my life. And being loved by you is the most wonderful feeling I've ever had. But I'm sorry." Her voice was void of emotion, as if her spirit had died.

He drew back and tilted her chin toward him. "What do you mean?"

"That this has to end."

His neck stiffened. "What does?"

"I'm quitting, Scott. I—I'm going to work for Mother."

"What?" A log hit his chest. "What are you saying?"

She pulled away, turned her head. "Just that. I—I've reconsidered my new life. I—I don't belong here. I ain't no lady. I ain't never been and won't never be."

He reached for her, but she stood and moved to the exam table. No! This cannot be! "But Rose, honey... I love you. We can work something out."

She looked at the floor, crying those silent tears again, and her shoulders shook. Her hurt ran deep. Had his love not made a difference to her? Was she tossing him away like Meghan had? No. Rose wasn't like that. And yet...

"I—I love you, but I can't be with you." She patted her eyes with the tip of her handkerchief.

"Nonsense. We'll be married." This was ridiculous. He tilted his head to one side. "Why can't you be with me?"

"People will find out about me and ruin everything."

"I'm not understanding you. What happened? Let's get married—soon. Well, I'm asking. Will you marry me?"

Tears sprang to her eyes again. "I—I don't know. I want to say yes, but I don't know."

He limped over and grabbed her by the shoulders. Should he try to shake some sense into her? No. She'd had enough brutality. Besides, he wasn't that kind of guy. "What's happened? I'm not letting you out of this office until you tell me."

Her shoulders seemed to shrink. "I—I'm damaged merchandise. Not fit for marriage or family life."

He released her but reached for her hand. "You're the one I really love. I want to marry you, have children with you. You'll be such a beautiful mother."

"I—I can't." She sniffed.

"Why? Please tell me."

"If I tell you, you'll hate me."

"I could never hate you. I love you."

She took another long breath and drew out its release. "I—um—Madam was forced... when she was young. I—I'm the result."

Compassion flooded his being.

He pulled her to himself. Sobs racked her. They stayed that way until she fell asleep. Then he picked her up and laid her on his bed and closed the door. He dragged his feet back to his desk and buried his face in his hands. Poor Rose. Evidently, she thought this would make a difference to him. Maybe he should talk to someone about that. But who?

He thought of his minister, Reverend Street, then remembered that Meghan couldn't get a straight answer from him when she'd asked about an experience with God. After his own personal encounter with Rafe, he could understand why Reverend Street had no idea what Meghan had been talking about.

Folding his hands together, Scott bowed his head and whispered, so as not to disturb Rose. "Lord, how do I get through to Rose? I love her so much. I didn't know what love was until she came into my life. I'll do anything you say. Please, show me the way. Come into my heart and speak to me. Remove the scar..."

A silent sob shook him from the core of his being. Tears blinded him. As soon as one rolled down his cheek, many others came to take their place. But this time it was different than when Rafe had visited the office... when was that? Weeks ago. That time, he'd felt such conviction, such remorse. This time, he wasn't thinking of himself at all. He was thinking of Rose. Crying out to God on her behalf.

"Please God. Help me."

Peace engulfed his whole being. Love like he'd never felt before wrapped him, cocooned him like a warm blanket.

Son, welcome home. A voice inside his heart he'd never heard before. Was this God?

Chapter Thirty-Six

Rose awakened to darkness. Not a bit of light gave a hint to her surroundings. Scott's scent tickled her nose, and she felt a mattress beneath her. Scott's bed? Then she remembered. She'd finally given in to his pleas to share her pain. And yet there was still one secret she couldn't tell him. Not if she wanted him to survive until this was all over. Though she had expected rejection, he had gathered her into his arms, then cuddled her close, whispering words of love and acceptance into her weary soul.

She must have fallen asleep. Now she lay in his bed.

Alone.

Dread filled her heart at the thought of working for Madam, but she had no choice. Her biggest fear was that the town would find out that Rose Rhodes was really that soiled dove, Rosalie O'Roarke. But if Rosalie returned to the brothel, Rose wouldn't be exposed, and Scott's reputation wouldn't be at risk. Not only that, Jake would have no reason to harm him. However, if she married Scott, the town would eventually find out about her past. And, according to Madam, there would be no forgiveness.

Then there remained the problem of Jake. The sheriff had issued a warrant for his arrest, but he hadn't been seen anywhere near New Boston. He was a slippery one, though. It seemed like he had eyes and ears everywhere. For several years, lawmen had tried to catch him rustling cattle, but he'd always eluded capture. Now he'd added kidnapping to his list of crimes. What would he do next?

Kill her? Follow through on his threat to kill Scott because she'd escaped? She shivered at the thought. He'd probably slip out of town before anyone could arrest him.

Hopefully he would be brought to justice soon. Until then she would be safe at the brothel. Madam would see to that. She didn't really care to learn the business, yet if she lived there, she would need never worry about being abducted or beaten.

What might it be like to feel safe again?

⁓

The sun was just beginning to set as Jake sneaked to the back of the doctor's office and peered through a window. Nothing. The office was empty. He'd wait until it was completely dark to leave town, but he had one more stop to make after this one—Madam Margaret. It seemed she hadn't persuaded her daughter to join her yet. He'd seen Madam go to the boardinghouse, presumably to visit Rosie, but she'd left alone. And for a week now, Rosie continued to work for the doctor. He should have already slit the man's throat. He was hardly ever alone, though, and when he was, something else seemed more important.

That would change soon.

He had to make a back-up plan.

Snatching her again seemed the best choice. This time, he'd go west—and make sure she didn't get away. If he couldn't grab her... well, he'd make sure no one else would ever possess his Rosie—least of all that high and mighty doctor she had gone cow-eyed over. Doc couldn't have her if he was dead, now, could he?

Slinking along the shadows, he made his way to Madam Margaret's. He slipped into the alley and stopped at the back staircase he'd discovered the last time he'd been there. He glanced up to the door at the top—Madam's room. Did she know how easy it was to reach her?

Rose had been so upset. With love, Scott had coaxed her to share her true feelings and the dark secret of her origins. And he still loved her. She'd intended to quit and go back to her mother's brothel. Not that she wanted to. She might still have to—depending on what happened with Jake. He hadn't been caught yet, but if or when he was...

Was Scott here or had he gone to the restaurant for supper? Quietly turning the handle, she opened his bedroom door a crack and peeked into the main room. Scott looked terribly uncomfortable with his back hunched and his head lying on the desk. Eyes closed. Steady breathing. Now would be the perfect time to slip away... back to the boardinghouse. Time to pack. She'd not collected much in the way of clothes since changing her lifestyle. Only three dresses, plus what she wore for work, and a cloak. She'd left all her fancy silk and satin dresses behind when she left—swearing never to wear them again.

A harsh laugh rose in her throat, but she managed to clamp her lips closed before it could escape. She never would have believed in that just a few short months, she'd return to the life she'd vowed never to go back to. She tiptoed by the exam table, stopping long enough to gaze upon this man that she loved so dearly. Pain sliced her heart. How she wished they could marry, that things could be different. What a dear he was, still willing to marry her, a former dance hall girl. No... a soiled dove. How could he not understand the risk to his reputation? And she couldn't let Jake murder him in cold blood.

Closing the office door behind her, she walked out into the night. She headed toward the boardinghouse. It was still home, even if only for a short time.

Jake climbed the back stairs to Madam Margaret's private room. She'd be surprised to see him, but this way was better than trying to get past the muscleman. When he reached the top step, he peered through the window in the top of the door, taking in Madam's room from a different angle. Didn't look much different from this position. She was in there by herself, sitting at that fancy marble table. Good. He knocked on the door. Her startled expression gave him confidence. She took her time getting to the door, then opened it only a few inches—probably to see who was outside.

"Well? Aren't you going to invite me in, Madam Margaret?" He stepped forward, poking his foot in the open inches.

She seemed to consider the matter then she let out a long breath and opened the door.

"What do you want, *Mister* Thomas?"

"I came for yer answer to my proposition. Rosie is still working for the doctor, I see. Why ain't she workin' for you?" Killing was distasteful to him. Fighting, he liked that. Gave him a chance to prove his power. But if Rosie didn't come back to him soon ... well ... he'd do it. He'd kill to have Rosie back. That doctor deserved it.

Madam turned her back to him, walked over to the table, and sat down. She placed a cigarette in one of those long extender things he'd seen rich ladies use from time to time, then lit it, blowing out a long breath of smoke in his direction. If she thought that would put him off, she had another think coming.

"Mister Thomas, I'm not inclined to do business with you. You can have one drink. Then you leave. If you don't go, I'll send for Rufus." She looked him up and down. "He's about twice your size. I don't allow trouble in my dove house."

He strolled over and poured himself a drink, then sat down on the opposite side of the marble table. Same chair he'd sat in a week ago.

"I can make it worth yer while to go into business with me. All I want is Rosie."

Madam blew another round of smoke into the air. "Seems to me, she doesn't want anything to do with you." She poured herself a drink and took a sip. "I did some checking around town about you. You're not a nice man. I don't tolerate men beating up my gals. I heard tell, you laid into my daughter about six months ago. That, *sir*, is a deal breaker. I would never do business with you."

She stood. "Now, ya had your drink. Time to leave."

Jake downed the rest of the contents of his glass. "You'll be sorry. So will she."

Chapter Thirty-Seven

Jake punched one fist into the other as he rushed down the stairs. Blood roared through his ears. His vision narrowed and all he could see was what was right in front of him. But what he wanted to see was Rosie... to have his way with her for all the times he'd missed her. To take her and... He knew he should wait until he got her back to his cabin. First, he'd take her, then kill that "too good" doctor of hers, then strangle the snooty madam, who'd turned him down. He'd make them all pay!

Energy, like a fire, burned through him as he headed toward the Silver Spike. Sam should be working tonight—he could always get a bottle off him. After he downed a few, then he'd find Rosie. By the time he was done with her, that stupid doctor wouldn't want to even look at her. She'd never think of leaving of him again.

He couldn't wait to lash out.

Rose had just crossed the railroad tracks when someone who looked like Jake walked under a new gas-powered streetlight. Her breath caught. It *was* Jake. She hoped he hadn't seen her.

"Rosie girl! Rosie! Come 'ere!"

Oh no! He'd seen her. She gathered her skirts and ran down the boardwalk.

"Help! Someone help me!"

"Rosie girl! You're mine! No one else can have you!" His voice carried across the street. Anyone could hear him.

Where was he? She glanced over her shoulder. A few more strides and he'd catch her.

She screamed.

He caught her and whacked the side of her head.

She screamed again. "Someone! Please! Get the sheriff!"

He put his hand over her mouth and punched her in the stomach. Air whooshed from her lungs. She couldn't breathe. He pulled her back against him. Her back arched in an awkward position, forcing her neck to tilt. Something cold came under her chin. Jake's gun barrel.

Oh my God, is he going to shoot me?

His voice was a hoarse whisper. "You're coming with me, Rosie girl, and this time, you're not getting away! You're mine!"

She couldn't catch her breath. He pulled her head back by the hair and planted sloppy kisses all over her face, neck, ears. Then, he pulled her into an alley. Out of the corner of her eye, too late to move, she saw his flat hand come to meet the side of her head.

Not again!

He shoved her down, and threw himself on her. She tried to scream, but only a small whimper came out. She had to cry out, but who would hear her?

No, oh no! He was going to take her right here? His hands pulled at her dress and ripped it off her shoulders.

No God! No!

"Let her go, Jake Thomas!"

Thank God. Sheriff Randall.

Jake stood, pulling her up with him, and fastened his iron arm around her throat, and putting his gun to her chin again. He dragged her back to the street. With her head pulled back the way it was, she couldn't really tell where they were, but somehow she knew they'd gotten back to Main Street.

"Nope. I'm taking her, and you can't stop me!"

"You let her go or I'll shoot you where you stand."

Randall's voice resounded through the street. Music from within the Silver Spike and Madam Margaret's stopped. The swinging doors creaked as they flapped open and closed again and again. Had all the patrons had come out to watch?

Jake laughed. "You won't risk shootin' a woman. Just let me ride out of town with her. I'll never come back. Try and stop me and I'll kill her!"

A shot rang out. Jake crumpled, pulling her down with him. Was she shot? She didn't feel any pain. Was he? In an instant, Sheriff Randall was standing over her, pulling her out of Jake's grip. She turned to look. A hole right in the middle of his forehead.

Trembling uncontrollably, she wobbled to the boardwalk, pulling up her torn dress to above her bosom. The vision of Jake—his blank stare, the hole in his forehead—stayed with her. He was dead. Why didn't she feel relieved?

⌒

Scott awoke with a start. Was that a shot? Where? He rubbed his eyes and went to check on Rose. She wasn't there. Where was she?

Someone pounded on his door. He recognized the voice. Jackson. "Doc, ya gotta come! Quick! Sheriff needs ya!"

He rubbed the sleep from his eyes as he limped over to the door. He needed to splash water on his face, but there didn't seem to be time.

"Doc! That Jake Thomas fella's dead!"

"Could you do me a favor?"

"Why shore, Doc."

"There's water in that pitcher on the side counter. And towels on the shelf above it..." He couldn't suppress a yawn but covered his mouth. At least he was able to direct Jackson with a nod.

Jackson seemed to only take an instant to get things ready for him.

He sometimes forgot Jackson's past, as he'd risen through the ranks from porter to stationmaster.

"My ol'e massa allus needed a splash to get hisself fully awake. The ol'e missus wouldn't let me he'p her."

He wiped his face, tossing the towel on the exam table. He grabbed his bag. "What can you tell me, Jackson?"

"Well, seems like that Jake Thomas fella got hisself shot dead by the sheriff. And your gal, Rose, was in the middle of it."

Rose? Oh dear.

They exited the office. Scott didn't bother to lock the door.

༄

Rose couldn't get her breath. She couldn't stop shaking. Jake was dead! She kept thinking of what would have happened if the sheriff hadn't come. Memories of the other times Jake had forcibly had his way with her kept surfacing—mixed with the shooting. What if the sheriff had missed? She could have been killed!

"Rose! Rose! Are you all right?"

Scott drew her into his arms.

Sobs escaped her. Waves of emotion rippled through her... the shock of Jake's death... the security of Scott's embrace... the fact that she was alive... the trembling that wouldn't stop. That Scott would be safe.

"Shhhh. It's all right now." Scott drew back, and cupped her cheeks, wiping her tears with his thumbs.

"Doc, you may want to take her into Madam Margaret's. It's quieter there than the Silver Spike." Sheriff Randall's voice. "And maybe Madam's got a cloak or something..."

She shook her head. "N-No. J-Just take me h-home, Scott."

His eyes poured out their love and concern. "Madam Margaret's is closer. It's all right. I won't let anything happen to you. You're safe now."

"A-all right."

"I saw it! It was murder! Jake never had a chance!" One of the gamblers from the Silver Spike voiced his opinion.

Other voices joined in, some in agreement, some disagreeing. Scott began to lead her away, but she stopped, listening.

"Yeah, it was murder!"

"Was not! You know how Jake was. Always after his 'Rosie girl.' He had a gun."

"Do you think he found her?"

"Is that why he had the doctor's assistant with him?"

"What's her name, again?"

"Rose Rhodes."

"He was looking for Rosie O'Roarke."

"Not the same person."

"Their names are similar."

"Rosie was a dance hall girl. She's been gone for months."

"Yeah, well Miss Rhodes has only been here for a few months."

"Coincidence—don't ya think?"

The town was beginning to put things together. What would she do now?

⁓

Scott opened the front door to Madam Margaret's and ushered Rose in. He knew this might be difficult, but maybe, just maybe, God could use this to reconcile Rose with her mother. As he looked around, the patronage had pretty much cleared out. The hour was very late, the time most places like this began their closing routines of cleaning the bar and the tables, washing the glasses, mopping the floor, and taking the money drawer into the back.

A middle-aged woman stood at the bar. At the sound of the ruckus, she turned. Scott's breath hitched. Might he be looking at what Rose would look like in fifteen-to-twenty years? Rose looked so much like her. Gray streaks didn't mar the beauty of Madam Margaret's black hair. Her short, pudgy nose, thin lips, and pointy chin were just like Rose's. But the eyes were different. Rose's were like smooth, light cocoa. Madam's were dark like black coffee—and calculating.

Madam's eyes widened when she saw him with his arm around Rose. She practically ran over to her daughter—but didn't touch her. "Rosalie, are you all right?"

Scott looked at Rose. She didn't even acknowledge her mother's presence. He'd better take charge of this.

"Could we sit down? Do you have some medicinal whiskey here? And—a cloak?"

A harsh laugh escaped Madam. "Why, sure, Doc. Fact is, all our whiskey is used for 'medicinal' purposes." She turned to one of the girls. "Sally, could you get my cloak?" She nodded her head toward the pegs on the wall by the stairs.

Scott put his hand in the middle of Rose's back and guided her to the nearest empty table. He pulled out a chair and helped lower her into it. She looked straight ahead, not acknowledging where she was, whom she was with, or who else was in the room.

"She's had a shock, Madam. But I expect you've probably already heard."

"Yep, I heard. Glad the sheriff took care of that low-down trash of a man." She looked to Rose, then met his gaze. "That's the man who beat and kidnapped her, wasn't he?"

"Yes. That was Jake Thomas."

"He came to see me a few minutes ago. Wanted me to invest in the cattle rustling business, and help my poor Rosalie get under his control again. I turned him down."

At the words "my poor Rosalie," Rose slowly turned her head toward the madam, and glared. "When have you ever been concerned about me?" A particularly vicious tremor shook her, and she nearly fell off her chair.

Madam brought a bottle of whiskey and a glass, then poured a drink and handed it to Rose.

"You don't have to like me, girl, but I am your ma. Sometimes, you still gotta mind your ma. Drink this. You'll feel better." She put the cloak around Rose's shoulders.

Rose pushed the drink away and stood, grabbing the cloak tight around her. Though still shaky, she balanced herself and turned to him.

"Get me out of here, Scott. I never want to see this place again. Just take me home."

"Of course, my dear."

He glanced to the madam, who raised her eyebrows and backed away.

"Take good care of her, Doc. She's my baby girl, and whether she knows it or not... I do love her."

Rose stopped for a moment before moving forward.

Scott prayed under his breath, *Lord, help.*

Chapter Thirty-Eight

Rose awoke the next morning in her bed at the boardinghouse. She yawned and stretched but didn't get up. Scott had been so gentle and kind after that awful business last night. He'd put his arm around her and walked her home. She'd nestled her head in the nape of his neck and shut her eyes to the outside world, until they'd passed the downtown area.

A knock at the door grabbed her attention. "Rose, it's me. I've got a breakfast tray if you want it."

Meghan, the nurse—again.

"Come on in."

Meghan opened the door while one-handedly balancing the tray on one hip. After entering, she closed the door and set the tray on the desk.

"How are you feeling this morning? Are you hungry?"

Rose pushed back the covers, sat up, and stretched again. "I'm feeling quite well. Thank you. What's for breakfast?"

Meghan removed the dish towels from plates and bowls, putting the silverware in its proper place. "Luisa made her famous *huevos rancheros* again. It's her favorite way to serve eggs... with tomatoes, cheese, chorizo, and spices. This time, you've got toast, jam, and juice to go with it."

Rose threw off the covers and sat at the desk.

"Are you really all right? How horrible! You must have been terrified."

Rose took a drink of juice. "I was. I—I tried to avoid him. Will Sheriff Randall get in trouble for killing him? He shouldn't. He warned Jake what would happen." She took several bites of the egg dish.

Meghan absently twirled a lock of hair. "I don't know. There's talk going around town about it right now. The mayor and the town council aren't real pleased. Randall has worked hard to clean up the town, but sometimes the authorities think he shouldn't have to use force. Strange, especially when they know that sometimes that's the only way to stop more violence from occurring."

"The sheriff's doing what he thinks is best, isn't he?" Rose took a bite of toast.

Meghan nodded. "He always seems so friendly and helpful. I'm sure everything will be all right."

Rose scooped a bite of the huevos rancheros, thinking as she ate, how she would respond. The cheese and the chorizo melted together.

"How are you and Duncan getting along? Things seemed to be going well the night I got home."

Meghan sat on the bed. "We're doing better. I—I'm beginning to accept Duncan's call to ministry. I'm wondering how we'll manage financially. Most preachers don't make a lot of money."

"I'm sure it's difficult, but don't you believe your God will provide for you?" Rose cleared her throat. "Did Duncan tell you what happened at Scott's office a while back?"

"About Rafe? Yes. Even though I find it hard to believe. If you hadn't already told me both you and Scott had met Rafe, I'd have thought he was a figment of Duncan's imagination. But the Bible says, out of the mouth of two or three witnesses..."

"It was a very different experience. I'm not quite sure what to make of it." Rose looked past her friend to the far wall for a moment, then blinked herself back to the present and smiled at Meghan.

"Well, I think you know about my 'experience' with God. I've read in the Bible that your encounter with a possible angel is probably more common than my experience with the presence of God. But God knows each one of us, and he gives us something he knows we'll accept."

"Yes." Rose couldn't think anything more to say, so she took another bite of Luisa's fine cooking. They were both quiet a moment before Meghan spoke.

"Say Rose, when you're feeling more up to it, we need to talk about when you're going to come to the school and talk to the children."

Rose paused in her eating. "You're right. Can we talk about it next week?"

"And will you talk to Scott for me...and arrange for him to come the day after you? I—I may step out of the classroom that day—for a short while." Meghan fiddled with her handkerchief.

Rose swallowed the last bite, then shoved the tray to the back of the desk. "Meghan, are you still uncomfortable being around Scott? He's changed, you know."

"That's what you tell me." Meghan picked up the tray.

"Meghan..."

"Rose, I know you love him. I've forgiven him. But as I've told you before...forgiveness doesn't mean I forget what happened. It's going to be a long time before I'm comfortable around him again. Please relay my apologies to him, but I'm sure he understands...especially if he's changing as much as you say he is."

Meghan left.

Rose let out a long breath and decided to get dressed and meet the day. She'd given a lot of thought to her plans. How could she possibly go back to Madam Margaret's? Just being in there a few minutes last night showed her the impossibility of going back. She'd worked too hard to change. She'd never go back to that life. Ever.

∽

The next Saturday, an icy wind drove Rose and Meghan into the Pioneer Store. Both proprietors, Richard Decker and Mike Nieman looked up as they entered.

Mr. Decker stepped from behind the counter. "Can I help you find something?"

"Thank you, but no. I know where the material is." Rose gestured toward the back.

"If we can help you with anything, let us know." Mr. Nieman nodded, then scribbled something on a sheet of paper.

Rose needed material to make another dress. Meghan was shopping for food. Olivia had entrusted Meghan with certain items to be purchased at the store for the boardinghouse kitchen. It was part of the lessons Olivia was teaching Meghan on how to run a household—something Meghan freely admitted to knowing nothing about, but with her engagement to Duncan, she was becoming a quick study.

The door chime sounded as another customer entered. Rose turned her back to the wind as she fingered fabric bolts. Temperatures were dropping considerably as Thanksgiving approached. Olivia was planning a huge turkey dinner for all the boardinghouse residents, plus their friends who might not have a place to go.

President Lincoln, God rest his soul, had established a national holiday for Thanksgiving as the fourth Thursday of November. Rose had always looked forward to it, but Madam had loathed it, because business sloughed off that day. Married men usually spent the day with their families. Single men were often "adopted" by families. Only the rowdier of the single men wandered into the saloons and houses of pleasure.

Even Christmas had been just another day at Madam's brothels.

Only Rose's birthday had been a cause for celebration. Madam always got her one present... until her fourteenth birthday. That wasn't a present, more like a nightmare that haunted her every day. Until now. She loved Scott, and she knew he loved her, too. But could they have a future together? He said so, but she still wasn't sure.

Rose looked for Meghan, who was at the counter, handing Mr. Decker the list Olivia had given her. He turned away and started filling it, stepping behind the counter for some items.

Mr. Nieman came out from around the counter and walked toward her.

"Are you finding everything you need, Miss Rose?"

"Yes, thank you, Mister Nieman."

"Miss Rose, are you all right after your ordeal with that cattle rustler?"

She cleared her throat. "Yes. Thank you for asking."

Mr. Nieman stared her straight in the eye. He'd been to the Silver Spike when she was there.

"What I can't understand is why Jake Thomas singled *you* out. He kept going on and on about Rosalie O'Roarke." He shook his head. "I don't understand it."

Rose swallowed hard. "I—I'm sure I don't know." She hated lying, but still needed to protect herself.

He seemed to take a long look at her... his eyes giving her the once-over. "Although, you do resemble Rosalie quite a bit. Maybe Thomas saw that and that's why he went after you."

Rose let out a long breath she didn't realize she'd been holding. "Yes. You might be right." She grabbed a bolt of dark green wool. "I'd like five yards of this, please, with thread and buttons to match."

Mr. Nieman smiled. "Why sure. I'll measure this out right now."

She turned to the button display nearby, trying to catch her breath. Meghan came up beside her. "Are you all right? You look pale as a ghost." Her eyes streamed with compassion.

Rose exhaled. "I'm fine. I—I just... need to catch my breath."

"He said Rosalie. I hope he didn't recognize you."

"He didn't. Well, he didn't say he did." She fingered fabric and lace remnants from leftover bolts that might go with her choice of dark green wool. "He did tell me something useful. It made me feel a little better."

"What?"

"He said I resembled Rosalie, and maybe that was why Jake took me."

Meghan's eyes widened. "I don't know if that's good or bad."

"I believe, at least for now, it might be good. I can remain Rose. The town doesn't know."

"I hope so." Meghan turned back toward the counter but twisted her head to meet Rose's gaze. "For your sake."

Chapter Thirty-Nine

That night, Hannah Samuelson removed her apron at the Harvey House Restaurant in the railroad station and walked toward the Baldwin Boardinghouse. She seemed to spend most of her life at the restaurant, although she loved the friendship between the ladies at the boardinghouse. Women at the boardinghouse seemed to be the more permanent residents—living on the second floor. Because she was the newest female boarder, she didn't feel a close kinship to any of them yet—even though they'd welcomed her.

Meghan taught school, but she was engaged to the cowboy, Duncan Wilcox. Rose Rhodes worked hard for Doctor Allison, and her hours were unpredictable. The close friendship between Meghan and Rose made her feel a bit of an outsider. Olivia had Luisa de Campo to talk to. Carlos and Maria were charming children, but children couldn't be real friends to her.

Bernhard Warkentyne, the owner of the mill crossed the tracks as she approached. He didn't have much business yet, but he'd been visiting farmers as far as forty miles away—north of New Boston. His earlier attempt at establishing a mill had failed, but with talk of Wichita lobbying the Santa Fe Railroad to move the railhead, "Bernie," as she liked to call him in her private thoughts, had been trying to persuade many Mennonite farmers to move to the region.

If the railhead did move, New Boston wouldn't be left completely without some means of industry. The town could survive, and maybe even become a more decent place to live. Most of the saloons and dance halls would close. Hannah hoped that Wichita *would* take the railhead away, though she kept that opinion to herself. It wasn't a popular view. The only concern she had was whether the restaurant would close if the railhead moved. She supposed if the railhead changed, the restaurant would relocate...and she would move, too.

Bernie was such a handsome man, even though most women might think him a bit plain. Maybe he was a bit gangly, but Hannah didn't mind that. His eyes were a bit far apart and small for his face, but they were expressive whenever he spoke of the mill—his pride and joy.

"Bern—M-Mister Warkentyne!" He looked over at the sound of her voice and waved. He stopped and waited for her to cross the tracks.

"Miss Samuelson—how are you—fine evening?" He had such a smooth and pleasant voice. No wonder people listened to him. Young though he was, he carried an authority and held the respect of nearly everyone he met.

"I'm fine, Mister Warkentyne. I-It is a lovely evening, isn't it?"

"Are you—now—leaving Harvey House?" She knew he'd worked hard to lose his Old Country accent. It sounded like he'd made good progress.

"Y-Yes. What do you think Missus B-Baldwin will have for supper tonight?"

Bernie lived on the third floor. He'd lived there for the longest period of any other man. She talked with him at breakfasts and supper, with others were present. She'd gotten to know him quite well, even though it seemed they mostly spoke only of unimportant things. Sometimes, he'd talk of a detail about his hopes and dreams, or his past in Europe. Try as she might, she could barely remember what he said. She loved listening to the sound of his voice, looking at his hands, his shoulders. She'd have to pay more attention. On the other hand, he seemed to remember nearly everything she'd told him.

"Or do you think Luisa made her chicken en-chil..."

"Her enchiladas?"

"Yes. I never remember what those are called."

A stiff wind blew her bonnet off. Bernie raced down the street to fetch it while she drew her cloak around her tighter.

When he brought it back, he seemed almost like a puppy who'd gotten a trick right for the first time. His grin and wide-open eyes fascinated her. She must stop this. Obviously, he didn't think of her that way.

"Here, Miss Samuelson. Tie strings good and tight." If she didn't know better, she could have sworn he was shaking his finger at her. Almost a scolding. But there was no harshness in his tone. Only warmth. Though the night was cold, it touched her heart. If she wasn't careful, her feelings could turn to love. But, did he feel the same?

⁓

As Scott opened the office for the day, a memory came.

"Scotty boy, if you'll clean up your room now, I'll take you to the circus this afternoon. If you don't, you'll never go. Only if you're a good little boy will I reward you. But if you're bad, you'll be punished."

He'd always remembered Father as a kind man. Father had never hit him. He'd taught that physical violence was wrong.

Unbidden, another memory surfaced.

"Scotty, I told you to weed the garden for your mother. You didn't get it done soon enough. It was to be done by yesterday morning. You didn't finish it until last evening."

"But, Father, I worked as hard as I could to get it done. School ran late. Teacher kept all of us after class because one student acted up."

"Your fault, wasn't it?"
"No, Father. It wasn't me. I'd wouldn't do that."
"You know you're a worthless son! You never do anything right!"
He'd bowed his head in shame.

A tear ran down his cheek. He hadn't thought of that in a long time. Memories came unbidden, of times when Father had berated his performance or punished him for something he hadn't done. He'd escaped Father's harsh words when he went to medical school. Then he'd come here. Didn't go home for a visit. Mother wrote him letters begging him to come to Kansas City sometime. She missed him terribly. He wished to see her, too. But he didn't ever want to encounter Father again.

"You know you have to forgive him, don't you?" Rafe's gentle voice penetrated his thoughts.

His gaze swung toward the voice. Rafe stood near the door.

The older man moved toward him and put a hand on his shoulder.

"How can I? I'm just now remembering how cruel he was to me."

Heat radiated from Rafe's touch, like warm water seeping into his pores. Pain left. Peace entered. Love enveloped.

Rafe said nothing, but not only did the warmth continue to saturate Scott's body, it seemed his soul was being healed, too.

"Son, you're remembering so you can choose to let go of all the past. Everything."

Scott sucked in a long, deep breath and exhaled. His knees buckled from giddiness. The only thing he could figure out was that the warmth was causing some sort of weakness, yet it seemed more a heaviness. Rafe guided him to the couch.

He sank into the cushions and laid his head back. Memories of many times Father had called him "stupid, worthless, useless" came back to him.

Various memories came quickly. The one where he'd made his decision to become a doctor. When he'd treated his first patient, his little sister. He was twelve. Annie was eight. She'd always looked up to him.

Annie had fallen and scraped her knee.

"Scotty, can you fix me?" Her sobs pierced his young heart.

He helped her up.

"Of course. Let's go inside. I'll get you all cleaned up."

"It hurts." Tears streaked down her cheeks.

He put his arm around her little waist and helped her into the house. Mother was gone to one of her social gatherings that afternoon, leaving him in charge of his younger siblings still at home.

"I know it hurts, Annie B'nanny, but you'll be all right."

When they reached the kitchen, he pulled a chair from the table, and got her comfortable. Then he scrounged the house for a couple of clean towels, and one of his clean handkerchiefs.

Once he'd cleaned up her knee, she looked up him, smiling through her tears. "Scotty, you oughtta be a doctor someday. You're awfully nice. It hardly hurts at all anymore."

He returned her smile.

A hope was planted in his heart that day.

"That was a fateful day for you, wasn't it, son?" Rafe's eyes radiated God's love for him. Now that he'd experienced God's love, he recognized it when he saw it.

"Yes."

⁓

As Rose approached the office, something seemed to stop her. She peeked in the window. Rafe was there. Of course. He was guiding Scott over to the couch. Was Scott all right? His limp was still pronounced, but he looked different. Should she intrude? No. She continued to watch as Scott sank into the couch, allowing his head to rest on the back for a few moments.

When he lifted his head, his expression was one she'd never seen before. Maybe he'd tell her about it.

She blinked. Rafe was gone.

Her breath caught as she entered the office, Scott looked at her. His countenance of love and peace unnerved her yet made her hungry for it.

He scooted himself forward to stand.

"Hello, Rose. Rafe was just here."

She took off her cloak and hung it up. "I know. I—waited. It seemed like a private moment."

Scott smiled. "He was healing me of hurtful memories. God showed me I need to forgive my father."

She tilted her head to one side. "I thought you said your father was a wonderful man."

He walked to the back of the office and put on his physician's apron. He only had a slight limp now. She followed him and put on her apron.

"He was. But I'd forgotten he could be harsh, too."

"How do you mean?"

"He called me worthless, useless... a bad son."

Rose put a hand on his shoulder a moment. "I'm so sorry. That's terrible."

Scott smiled. "I remembered the day I decided to become a doctor. My little sister skinned her knee. She said I was so good at taking care of her knee I should become a doctor when I grew up. I think a seed was planted that day."

"That's wonderful." She readied an instrument tray. "Do you think you can?"

He turned toward her. "Can what?"

"Forgive your father. After all, no child should hear what he said to you."

He looked off toward the far wall. "I think so. It hurt, but it was a long time ago. Rose, I don't think I've told you this before. While you were missing, I gave my heart to Jesus. It's so different... kind of hard to explain. Something happened..." He patted his chest. "In here."

She nodded. Like with Meghan, God had become real to him. She longed for that, too. Could that ever happen for her?

Chapter Forty

Hannah tapped on Olivia's door. The older woman's eyes widened, but she stepped back and let Hannah in.

"Missus Baldwin, c-could I talk with you a moment?"

"Please, call me Olivia. I'd thought we'd gotten past the formalities. You know you're welcome to come and talk anytime, don't you? Goodness gracious, is everything all right?"

Olivia gestured for her to sit. She chose to sit in the chair by the desk.

"What did you want to talk about?" Olivia sat on her bed.

She fidgeted.

Olivia evidently couldn't take the silence. "You're from Ohio, aren't you? Is everything all right back home? I think you got a letter recently, didn't you?"

"Y-yes, I did."

"Would you like to talk about it?"

She looked down, then into Olivia's gaze. The woman's eyes seemed kind and understanding.

"You know, when Meghan has a problem, she just launches right into it. Why don't you try that?"

Hannah swallowed. "Thi—this is my first time away from home."

"Ah, you're homesick. Is that it? It's all right, you know. To be missing home. How old are you again? Seventeen?"

She nodded.

"You should still be in Ohio. What caused you to move here? Besides the Harvey House job?"

Hannah cleared her throat. This wasn't as easy as she'd thought it would be.

"I-I miss my friends more than anything. It's just Pa and Grammy back at home—except for my sister Elizabeth, who is two years younger than me. Grammy is still in good health. She and Elizabeth keep Pa's house for him since Ma died. I-I was just in the way."

Olivia's brow knitted. "Oh, I'm sorry you felt that way. Has anything happened since you've been here to make you feel unwelcome?"

Hannah jerked her chin. "No! It's not that... it's just..." She coughed.

"What is it, dearie?"

"It-it's just that—I-I don't really have a real friend here." There, she'd said it.

"What about the girls you work with? The other Harvey girls?"

"I'm not close with any of them. They all live on the same floor at the hotel. And they've all been together longer. Their friendships are established. I-I'm so out of place there... and here, too." She sniffed and bit her lower lip, but her eyes watered, so she closed them.

Olivia put a hand on her shoulder. "My goodness. I had no idea. I feel just terrible."

"It-it's not your fault. I... I see how you and Luisa talk all the time, and Meghan and Rose talk all the time..."

"And you're left out. Oh, I really am so sorry. I didn't realize we were shutting you out."

Tears rolled down her cheeks. "I-I don't mean to feel this way."

"Of course not." Olivia pulled her out of the chair and over to the bed. Hannah let the older woman guide her and sat quietly studying the palms of her hands while Olivia sat beside her. "I tell you what. Let's have a girls' night out next week. What do you think of that?"

Hannah tried to smile.

Olivia patted her knee. "Tell me more about life back in Ohio." She pulled out her handkerchief from her sleeve and blew her nose. Maybe things would be all right after all. Olivia was a kind woman and friendly, and easy to talk to, but enough older she couldn't be a good friend.

⁓

A week later, it was Thanksgiving Day. Luisa and Olivia had outdone themselves. Olivia always made too much food. Rose could hardly believe the boardinghouse wouldn't be full of guests. Many of the men went to Wichita for the day, as that town seemed to be growing by leaps and bounds. Like here just a few months ago. New Boston was still growing, but slower. New ranches were springing up south of Wichita that drew a lot of the cowboys from New Boston. She knew Mr. Warkentyne—Bernie to his friends—was trying to get more farmers to make their homes near New Boston, yet he'd only been slightly successful so far. They were settling north of New Boston. They'd already started their own local communities up there, although they were much smaller than New Boston. Some still came here for their larger supply shipments and anything they needed by rail. The less populated farm towns generally only had one small store, and maybe a stage stop. She'd heard Bernie talk about it a few times at dinner.

Olivia had pulled her aside after dinner in the drawing room a couple days ago. Meghan had gone out with Duncan for a walk. Luisa and her children were studying at the dining table, once the dishes were done. Bernie and Hannah were evidently still at work.

"Rose, could you do me a favor?"

"Certainly."

"Hannah and I had a little talk last week. She's been feeling homesick—and left out."

"What do you mean?"

"She feels like she's not making friends here."

She thought a moment. "I guess we're all pretty busy, aren't we?"

Olivia nodded. "Here's how she put it. 'You and Luisa talk all the time. Meghan and Rose talk all the time.' That's why she's feeling left out. I'm sharing this because we need to do a better job of befriending Hannah. I feel like I've failed her or something. This boardinghouse welcomes all who come to live here—no matter how long they stay. I'd like to think I've befriended them all, too."

"You certainly received me even before you knew who I was."

"I hope you'll always feel at home here, my dear."

"Thanks, Olivia. I appreciate you, your wisdom, your strength."

Meghan tapped her on the shoulder. "What are you thinking about?"

"Did you say something?"

"I said—did you get the napkins on the table? We're ready to bring the food out. Before it all gets cold in the kitchen." She giggled.

Rose smiled. "Sorry. I was remembering what Olivia said the other day."

Meghan nodded. "About Hannah."

"Yes."

Meghan tapped her cheek with her finger. "We really need to include her more, don't we?"

"Yes."

"Why don't we start after dinner?"

"What shall we do?" Rose tilted her head to one side.

"Well, it's not too cold. Maybe we can ask her to go for a walk with us?"

"I like that idea." Rose folded a napkin and placed it under the fork. "Where's Duncan today?"

"McMasters wanted all his cowhands at the ranch today. He's trying to keep them from leaving."

"I've heard a lot of them are already going. The Wichita cattleman are really lobbying the railroad hard, aren't they?"

"Well, I'm not privy to Mister Fagin's dealings, but he assured me that my job is safe. And that the Santa Fe Railroad will always have an office in New Boston."

"But he didn't say anything about the railhead leaving, did he?"

"No."

They walked to the kitchen, then brought out serving bowls filled with potatoes, green beans, corn, peas, and carrots. The turkey had been meticulously sliced by Bernie Warkentyne.

"I'll bring it to the table." Bernie picked up the platter as if it were as light as a baby's rattle, but Rose noted he carried it with both hands.

After everyone was seated, Olivia took her spoon and dinged her glass. "Thank you all for sharing Thanksgiving dinner today. It's the second one in this house, but last year it was really only my husband and I." She sniffed. "And even now we're not full up. But I appreciate all y'all bein' here."

Meghan smiled. "That's her southern' comin' out."

The women giggled. Bernie chuckled. Maria and Carlos merely smiled, but their faces glowed. They'd never had a Thanksgiving dinner like this one before. Luisa shared that their father too often frequented the saloons and dance halls while he was alive—even on holidays. Amazing to think it had only been a few months since the tornado. Life had changed a lot for most of the boardinghouse residents since then. Hers, too.

"All right, everyone." Olivia smiled. "Let's bow our heads and pray."

Rose looked down. She wasn't sure she could join in.

Olivia continued. "Heavenly Father, I thank thee for all whom thee bringest to this house. I pray blessings on our day. Thank thee for this bounty that we may partake of it. I thank thee for Luisa and her help in preparing this feast. I thank thee for all my boarders, those here, and those who are not present with us today. In thy name, Amen."

"Amen" came from various people around the table. Rose whispered it, just barely.

A knock at the door had everyone's heads turning. Olivia jumped up. "I'll get it."

She returned a few moments later—with Jackson, the Santa Fe Railroad station manager. Rose had always liked him and the way he talked. Wonderful to think that an ex-slave could be promoted based on his work merits alone.

"How y'all doin' dis fine Thanksgivin' Day?"

"Fine" and "Good to see you, Jackson," came from Hannah and Bernie. Rose wondered if there wouldn't be something between those two sometime in the future. After Olivia had talked to her about Hannah, she began to take notice of the girl more. She observed that often Hannah and Bernie talked at supper together. They'd sit next to each other or across the table. At least two to three times a week, they'd walk home from work together. Was something developing? If so, why was Hannah still feeling left out? A thought occurred to her. She'd want female friendship, too. Just like she'd wanted a real friend in Meghan.

"Olivia, why didn't you tell us he was coming?" Meghan showed mock irritation.

"Why, Miss Gallagher, I didn't know fer shore if I's able to come. Missus Baldwin done invite me a couple weeks ago. But ya'll know the railroad. Ya never know what's gonna happen wid it. Trains ain't runnin' durin' the day, dey'll start up agin tonight. So dat's why I'm here now."

Olivia ran to the kitchen for another place setting, while Bernie scooted over closer to Hannah to open a spot for Jackson. Rose smiled to herself. Did Bernie have a secret desire to get closer to Hannah?

Jackson sat down just as Olivia brought his plate, glass, silverware.

Rose looked at her dinner plate. It was beautiful. A cream-colored china with a gold rim and gold filigree with burgundy rectangles containing a unique design around some of the ornamentation. The rectangles were interspersed throughout at regular intervals. Olivia only brought out her best china on special occasions... like Meghan and Duncan's engagement. That was the only other instance she'd ever seen it.

Olivia clapped her hands again. "Now that we are *all* here, I'd like to pray the blessing again."

Rose bowed her head as Olivia prayed.

"Father in heaven, we again thank thee for your great blessings, mercy, and love. Bless us today as we observe thanks and bless this food. In thy name we pray, amen."

"Amen" from the people at the table. This time, Rose said it aloud, but under her breath.

Bernie took a slice of turkey from the platter with the serving fork and put it on Hannah's plate. Then he speared one for himself before attempting to pass the platter.

"Why don't we just have everyone pass their plates here, and we'll put a slice on it?" Olivia stood and reached a hand out to receive Jackson's plate. One by one, plates were passed until everyone had a slice of turkey.

The vegetable bowls were circulated next.

"Um, is there gravy?" Hannah's soft voice was nearly lost in the murmuring of conversation of others around the table, but since Rose was sitting across from her, she heard it.

"Is there gravy?" Rose made sure her voice carried.

Olivia's eyes opened wide as a full moon. "Oh, my goodness! Of course, there is! I can't believe I forgot that. Well, my mind is just so full of the goings on in town and around here that I just plain forgot." Rose smiled to herself. Olivia always talked more when she was flustered.

Luisa jumped. "I will get. *Señora* Baldwin, you sit."

Olivia gave Luisa an undetermined look. To Rose, it seemed Olivia was grateful, yet slightly annoyed. Rose figured it was Luisa's formal designation for her. She knew in private, Luisa always called Olivia by her first name. Maybe Olivia expected her to always call her that.

Luisa hustled into the kitchen.

Carlos' wide-eyed, lip-licking expression told Rose he couldn't wait for the gravy to come, either. Little Maria's chin dropped, but Rose saw her staring at the kitchen doorway.

A minute later, Luisa returned holding a bowl of steaming gravy, with ladle handle sticking out of it.

Luisa ladled some of the gravy on top of her children's turkey slices, then passed the bowl around the table.

Meghan started passing the potato dish, as it was next to her plate. Rose passed the cranberry sauce ... a delicacy, since cranberries weren't native to Kansas. Olivia had gone all out for this dinner. With everything that had happened, Rose felt kind of left out of the holiday preparations, yet she knew there was nothing she could have done about it. Why, just a few short weeks ago, Jake had held her captive in his cabin. She shivered at the thought.

"Are you cold?" Rose turned to see Meghan smiling warmly at her.

"No. I was just thinking how thankful I am ... that I'm here—safe and sound."

Meghan put her fork down and touched Rose's arm. "I'm thankful, too. I prayed for you every day you were gone. That God would do a miracle, that you would escape or be rescued ..." A tear formed in the corner of her eye. How dear she was.

Rose swallowed. "And he answered your prayers ... in ways you would never expect."

Meghan dabbed her eye with her napkin. "You escaped, and you were rescued. That's a double answer, if you ask me."

"Yes, I believe so." How Rose wanted to believe that God really answered prayer. As she thought about it, she realized, that in a way, he had. She wasn't quite ready to trust him with her whole life yet, but she began to understand what Meghan was talking about.

Carlos tapped Meghan on the arm. "Mi madre...My mother...*decir*...uh, says...it will...snow soon." He looked up expectantly. His eyes were round as marbles. "I say—right, Señorita Gallagher?"

"*Si*, Carlos. *Que ser correcto?* Did I get that right?" Meghan was trying to learn Spanish while teaching the children and their mother English. A daunting task, but she seemed up to it. She loved teaching as much as Rose loved helping people at Scott's office.

Luisa and Carlos smiled. Maria giggled. "Senorita, you, how you say, okay."

Meghan let out a breath. "I'm never sure. I was tempted to say 'is' twice, I think. It really is a challenge to learn another language. I applaud all your efforts."

All three of the de Campos nodded and resumed their eating.

Bernie took a drink of water, then turned to Jackson. "I hear rumors. Is true railhead going to move in spring? Really leave New Boston?" He'd come a long way with his English, but often left out words such as "the", "it, or "will" especially.

Jackson pointed to his mouth. He'd just shoveled in a large bite of turkey. Rose glanced around. All eyes at the table were on him. He swallowed, then took a drink of water.

"Well, it ain't set in stone yet."

Olivia joined in. "But surely, as a Santa Fe employee, you've been told what their plans are. After all, everyone who works for them will be at the mercy of their decision. Shoot—the whole town will be affected by what they do. Haven't they told you anything?"

Chapter Forty-One

Jackson looked around and fidgeted in his chair. Rose felt bad for him. "Sorry. Ah really don't know nothin'." He cleared his throat. "Y'all have ta talk to da bosses. Dey's de only ones knowin' anythin'."

From her right, Meghan tapped Rose's arm and nodded. Rose then turned to Olivia with a low voice. "Meghan says she'll talk to Mister Fagin and Mister Baker this next week."

Olivia flushed. "Jackson, I'm sorry. You're my honored guest. I didn't mean to make you feel uncomfortable." She looked down a moment, then up. "Goodness! Where are my manners? You are *all* my honored guests, even though all ya'll live here most of the time! Eat up, everyone! There's pumpkin pie and cinnamon spice cake for dessert."

Jackson's tense expression visibly relaxed. She let out a long breath.

The rest of the dinner went quite pleasantly. It was all so delicious, she ate too much. Even eating only a small portion of everything stuffed her. She turned to Meghan and looked across at Hannah. "Are you two up for a walk later?"

Hannah smiled. Meghan nodded. "After we help Luisa and Olivia with the cleanup?"

Rose smiled. It would be a fun time. Hannah was a sweet girl, if somewhat shy. She could understand that. Sometimes, around certain people, she felt the same way.

What was Scott doing today? He said he'd wanted to be alone. It seemed like he'd been alone a lot lately. What was he thinking?

Scott spent Thanksgiving Day with the sheriff. Neither had family around. Both Rose and Olivia had invited him to the boardinghouse for dinner, but since he learned Wilcox wasn't going to be there, he'd wanted to spare Meghan any further emotional pain.

He liked Randall. The sheriff had been uncommonly gracious and helpful with Rose. Randall had never said a word to anyone even though he knew about her past.

They'd eaten Thanksgiving dinner at the hotel—turkey and all the trimmings. Conversation had been pleasant—talking about holidays past. Nothing deep. Treasured memories of times with family. Randall was one of four brothers who'd grown up in Indiana. Since his eldest brother would inherit the family farm, and Stuart was brother number three—he needed to find something else to do to make a living. As a teenager, Randall had been a deputy in their small town near Fort Wayne. He'd been in the Indiana Legion during the war, charged with protecting the state. Why he hadn't been officially in the army, Scott hadn't asked. If Randall wanted him to know, he'd tell him sometime. It wasn't really any of his business.

As they paid their bill, Scott wanted to talk to him further, in a more private place.

"Say Randall, your place or mine? I'd like to talk to you about something."

Randall cocked his head to one side. "How about your place? I've still got some drunks in the cell. Sometimes when they wake up, they're angry. They can't appear in court until tomorrow—since it's a holiday."

"Sounds good."

They walked in silence for a few minutes, then Scott unlocked his office. Randall had been to the office numerous times and made himself at home on one end of the couch. Scott sat at the opposite end.

"Say, Doc. I notice you're walking quite well now. Not much of a limp at all."

Scott nodded. "I am doing well. Thanks for noticing."

"How long's it been—since you busted it?"

Scott thought a moment. "It's been about eight weeks, but I'm young. I heal quickly." His conscience pricked. He let out a long breath. "And—I think God may have speeded up the healing a bit."

"Really? God?"

This was not the direction he wanted this conversation to go. "Um—yeah. Say, Sheriff, can I ask you a question?"

Randall's brow furrowed. "Sure."

"What were you thinking when you pulled the trigger on Jake Thomas?"

Randall's neck stiffened, and his eyes darted around. "Why?"

He looked down a moment, then directly at the sheriff. Randall's gaze bore into him.

"Well, before you get all upset, I'm only asking as a doctor. How many men have you killed, Sheriff? In the line of duty, of course."

Randall relaxed a bit and he blew out a long breath. "Well, truth is, while I've had to shoot others, Thomas was the first one that died."

"How are you dealing with that?"

Randall stood and began to slowly pace back and forth across the room. "I've had nightmares nearly every night. It's been horrible. I can't hardly get any sleep."

"Why didn't you come talk to me about it?"

Randall lifted an eyebrow. "Really, Doc? What good would it have done? Especially that first week? Your attention was on Rose. I'm surprised no one brought charges of malpractice against you. Your mind wasn't on your work."

Scott nodded. "You're right. But, how are you doing now? Are you still having nightmares?" The fact that the sheriff was upset about the whole thing showed Scott that he wasn't used to showing brute force.

"Not too much anymore."

"Are you sure you're all right? I've been hearing rumors..."

Randall shot up. "What rumors? Am I being investigated? Why?"

Scott rose and put out his hands. "It's all right. Really. I just want to find out how you're doing."

Randall stood. "Am I going to get fired?" The sheriff's voice had an edge to it.

"No. Look, it's all right. Why are you so defensive?"

⁓

Hannah was very happy Rose and Meghan had asked her to take a walk with them. She hoped to get to know each one a little better, but suspected Olivia was behind this invitation. Even so, she was thankful for it.

As they put on their warm outer clothing, she realized this could well be a significant day for her. Making friends was important.

She had such hopes for her life... someday a husband and family. Maybe Grammy could be convinced to move here. She was in good enough health to stand the journey. There had been women on the train older than Grammy.

Hannah didn't hate Ohio, but her prospects weren't good there. Most of the young men in her hometown weren't interested in her. Because she was plain. When she looked in the mirror, she saw nothing of note. Weak chin, thin lips, average nose, eyes not big or small. Her hair was about the only thing she could say she liked about herself. It was a dark strawberry blonde. In the sun, it shone like gilded rays of sunshine. Indoors, it looked like a dark golden flame, red and gold mixed together. But it was straight as a stick. Curl never held longer than a few minutes. She'd tried everything...from secretly using heated rods a friend had lent her, to wetting her hair just before bed and tying it up in strips of cloth. In the morning, however, the curls, though beautiful, never stayed in longer than an hour or so. Very frustrating—in an age where curl was everything.

Hannah looked around. "Wh-where shall we walk?"

Rose pointed in front of her. "How about to Sand Creek? It might be higher because of last week's rain."

Meghan nodded. "I could you take you to 'Our Tree.'"

"*Our* tree?" What did that mean?

Rose giggled. "She means Duncan's tree. She's claimed it for herself now, too."

She shook her head in amazement. "Is that where you have 'church'?"

Meghan let out a breath. "Yes. Duncan started taking me there over the summer. He feels close to God there. Early next year, he'll be putting up a tent there...just under that tree. It's where he wants to start his own church."

"Really?" A third Protestant church! Maybe she'd try it. She didn't feel close to the people in the other tent churches. They were friendly enough yet didn't seem too interested in getting to know her more. They usually forgot she was even there.

"Are you reconciled to that, Meghan?" Rose's voice held concern. Why wouldn't Meghan want Duncan to start a church?

Meghan stopped. She and Rose stopped and turned toward their friend. "Hannah, I'm sorry. What you don't know is that I've had a hard time accepting that Duncan feels called to be a preacher."

She didn't know how to respond to that, so she remained quiet but tried smiling a small smile.

Rose put a hand on Meghan's arm. "Are you in agreement with it now?"

Meghan's smile didn't reach her eyes. Yet she could tell it was sincere. "Duncan and I spent some time apart a couple months ago." She caught Meghan's glance. "About the time you arrived, I think."

"I came in late September." She counted off the weeks on her fingers.

"I think you know Duncan was seriously wounded in August during the gunfights."

"I-I heard that. I'm so glad he's all right now. H-He is, isn't he?" She couldn't imagine how Meghan had dealt with such horrendous fear. To be in love, then to nearly lose him... She shook her head. It was beyond her.

"Yes, he's fine." Meghan's smile lit up her face. It reached her eyes this time, with something indistinguishable behind it.

"Meghan, why don't you tell Hannah a bit more about it." Rose started walking. She and Meghan followed.

"What would you like to know, Hannah?"

"H-How did you handle it? I can't imagine."

Meghan and Rose exchanged a look. A tear came to one of Meghan's eyes. "I learned to totally rely on God—for the first time in my life."

This intrigued her. "H-How do you mean?"

"I finally asked Jesus into my heart." As they walked along, Meghan would alternately look down at the brick walkway, or ahead. She supposed Meghan wanted to make sure she didn't trip.

"I don't understand. You went to church, but you hadn't really relied on God before?"

"No. I hadn't experienced him, either."

She tilted her head to one side. "G-God can be experienced?"

Meghan giggled. "That's how I first reacted. When Duncan asked me if I'd ever experienced God, I was as flabbergasted then as you are now. I didn't know what he was talking about."

"Th-That makes me feel better." She turned to Rose. "H-Have you experienced God, too?"

Rose blushed. What did that mean? Did her question offend her?

"I-I'm sorry. I didn't mean to offend you." Hannah swallowed.

Rose smiled a small smile. The sound Meghan released was a cross between an unladylike snort, and a strange laugh.

"Um, no, not in the way Meghan has."

Rose seemed uncomfortable talking about this. Hannah hated making her feel that way.

"Y-You don't have to answer. I-I'm just naturally curious." She cleared her throat. "We're still getting to know each other. Th-Thank you for asking me to go on this walk with you."

They reached Main Street. Looking around, they saw no one, not even a lone rider, buggy, or wagon out on the street. She supposed because it was a holiday, and everyone spent time inside with their families.

"It's all right. Meghan tells me I have probably encountered an angel."

Hannah must look like an idiot. Surely her eyes were popping from their sockets. Her mouth, as Grammy had said when she was younger, "would catch gnats" unless she closed it. "A-An angel? That's a-amazing!"

"His name is Rafe. If you saw him, you wouldn't think he was an angel..."

Her ears burned as she listened to Rose's accounts of encountering Rafe. A real, honest-to-goodness angel! Her mind was afire.

By the end of Rose's story, they'd returned to the boardinghouse. Home, at least for now.

Hannah hoped for something more. Her soul tingled with longing to know and feel the same thing. Would she ever?

Chapter Forty-Two

"I was ... upset ... to say the least." Randall's voice sounded tenuous. Not the confident, secure sheriff Scott was used to hearing. Randall twiddled his thumbs as he sat on one end of the couch. Scott had suggested they relax and talk calmly. The sun was already beginning to hang low in the sky. Within a couple hours, it would be nightfall.

"Of course, you were." Scott leaned toward him. "You have a conscience. I can't imagine. But it was in the line of duty."

The edges of Randall's lips curved up slightly. Maybe Scott's words were making a difference.

Randall stood and headed toward the door. "Thanks for asking me to spend Thanksgiving Day with you. Gotta get back to the jail now. I'm pretty sure those drunks will have come to. They'll need some grub—and some strong coffee."

Scott stood and walked Randall to the door. "You're welcome. And, you're all right. You're perfectly human."

Randall extended his hand. "Thanks, Doc."

"Hey, we're friends now, aren't we? Why don't you call me Scott?"

The sheriff nodded and smiled wider. "Then, call me Stuart or Stu."

"Stuart. I like that."

They shook on it, and Stuart left.

It was time to pay a call on Rose. He'd missed her today.

Rose removed her outer wrappings when the young women returned home from their walk.

Luisa and Olivia talked in the kitchen, their voices low and comfortable. Evidently the children had gone upstairs to their room. All three de Campos stayed in one room. Rose hoped that would change soon. Carlos was getting too old to be in a room with his mother and little sister.

Meghan and Hannah went up to their rooms.

She turned her head at the knock on the door. Was it a certain town doctor she'd come to love?

"I'll get it!" Her heart leaped when she peeked out the window and saw Scott. She quickly opened the door.

"May I come in?"

"Of course."

An indistinguishable, but fresh, aroma met her, like the crisp outdoors. The pine scent of the cologne he used after shaving. A pleasing, manly smell.

He took off his coat and hat and hung them on the coat rack, then turned, and drew her into an embrace, brushing his lips on hers. She could easily lose herself in his touch, his kiss. Her arms went around his neck—his around her waist, pulling her closer.

He deepened the kiss. When they came up for air, she cleared her throat and gestured to the parlor. "Shall we go in here?"

Nodding, he placed his hand in the small of her back. She loved it when he did that. Possessive, yet comforting. Protective, and reassuring. Safe. Loving. Just being in his presence had her head spinning.

"How's your day been?" He sat on one edge of the settee and patted the space beside him.

She sat next to him. The warmth emanating from him wrapped her like a quilt. He leaned over and again pressed his cold lips against her warm ones. But that was all right. Heat spread through her.

He stroked her cheek with the back of his fingers, moving to her shoulder, then trailing down her arm. "I missed you today."

"You could have eaten Thanksgiving dinner with us. I did invite you."

"I know. I had some business to take care of."

"Really? Were there patients? You should have let me know."

His eyes roamed around the room. "No, just dinner with the sheriff."

"A lot of people think he murdered Jake." She shifted toward him.

"He didn't—he feels terrible about it. He's had nightmares. His first kill in the line of duty."

Rose squeezed his arm. "Poor man. I can't say I'm too sorry Jake is dead, but I feel badly for Sheriff Randall."

Meghan appeared at the door. "Oh—I'm sorry! I'll talk to you later, Rose." She looked at Scott. Her expression neutral. "Doctor Allison." She turned and left.

"Miss Gallagher."

Rose sighed inwardly. They were back to formalities.

Would Meghan ever be able to feel comfortable around Scott again?

"Oh, how I wish Meghan would forgive me." Scott rubbed his hand along the back of his neck. "Maybe I should leave."

Rose put a hand on his arm. "Please don't. I missed you today."

"I make her very unhappy. She can't even be in the same room with me." When would Meghan ever be able to truly forgive him and tolerate his presence?

"I thought maybe..."

"I've asked God for forgiveness. He's given it. I know he has."

"I'll speak to her again about it."

"No. Let her be."

"Maybe she needs more time."

He sighed. "I suppose you're right." He stood. "Would you like to go for a walk with me?"

Rose giggled.

He cocked his head to one side. "What's so funny?"

"I just came from a walk—with Meghan and Hannah."

"Hannah Samuelson? You haven't mentioned her much."

"She just came to New Boston a couple months ago. She's a Harvey girl. Maybe you've seen her."

"What does she look like?"

"She's young-looking, with light red hair. Almost a golden blonde with flame in it."

He thought a moment. There had been a few times at the Harvey House when he'd seen a plain-looking young woman with strawberry blonde hair. Was that Hannah? "I think I've seen her."

He moved toward the door and began putting on his coat.

"You-you're not leaving already?"

"I don't want to spoil the rest of Meghan's day. It's better I go."

Rose's expression fell, and she let out a long breath. "I understand. You're such a wonderful man—to think of her comfort before your own desire."

"I didn't used to be that way—and that's why Meghan has trouble forgiving me."

"If she would only talk to you—see how you've changed."

"We can't force her to talk to me. She must want to. I'll be praying for her."

She rolled her eyes. "You do that."

"Rose, are you angry with God? Because he's done so much. And what about Rafe? You can't deny his existence."

She started to turn away, but he seized her arms and swung her around. She pulled away.

"I'm sorry, Rose. I didn't think—" He knew she hated being grabbed. Leftover trauma from Jake Thomas.

She held out her arms, and he walked into her embrace. "I'm sorry, Scott. I know you understand." He put a finger under her chin and brought it upward, then pressed his lips against hers. She released a soft moan, and he deepened the kiss. Finally, she broke it off and stepped out of his arms. He felt empty without her.

"My lovely Rose..." He stroked her cheek with the back of his fingers. She took his hand in hers and kissed the back of it. Her warm lips tickled his skin.

She released his hand. He kissed her again, then turned and put on his hat.

"Rose, please don't make me wait too long to marry you."

Chapter Forty-Three

The next few days flew by in a hurry. Rose worked in secret on all the Christmas presents she planned to give. She loved embroidering and planned to make handkerchiefs for every long-term boarder. Of course, she would also make nice ones for Meghan and Duncan, and a very special handkerchief for Scott.

The Saturday morning after Thanksgiving, there was an early knock on Rose's bedroom door. It had to be Meghan.

Rose put on her robe. "Come in. Meghan. You're up early."

Meghan entered and leaned against the desk. "I want to apologize about the other night. I guess I'm not used to seeing you two together—outside the medical office."

"It's all right. I understand. He hurt you."

Meghan looked down. "Even so..."

A moment went by. "Is there anything else the matter? Is it Duncan? I thought you were getting along well again."

Meghan glanced and smiled. "No, it's not Duncan. I just wanted to remind you that you're to share at school on Monday."

Rose thought a moment. "You're right! I'd forgotten. Thanks for reminding me."

"I hated to—you've had so much to deal with lately." Meghan pulled out the chair from the desk and sat.

"It has been difficult. There's a lot I can't talk about." She plopped on the bed and exhaled. "Thanks for caring."

"That's what friends are for, isn't it?" Meghan reached out and squeezed her arm a moment.

Rose smiled. "And I so appreciate your friendship. You know that, don't you?"

"I do. And whether you know it or not, I care for you, too. You helped me to be grateful for what I have—and—understand some things about men I didn't know before."

"Do you think you'll be able to be comfortable around Scott again soon? He really has changed, you know. I think he'd like you to see how much."

Meghan smiled. "I'm trying. I might step out of the room for a while when he comes... he is still coming, isn't he? I'll be just down the hall. It's nice of the Catholics to let us use their church for school until ours is built."

"Of course. He wouldn't miss it—unless he has an emergency."

"Thanks, Rose."

"You're welcome." She stood and went to the wardrobe and pulled out an everyday dress. "I guess it's almost time for breakfast, isn't it?"

Meghan put her hand on her abdomen. "My stomach growled. I didn't realize I was that hungry." She moved toward the door.

Rose giggled. "Me, too. Let's go see what Olivia and Luisa have cooked up for breakfast."

"I'll leave so you can get dressed."

"You don't have to."

Meghan thought a moment, then leaned against the door. "Okay. Can I ask you a question, then?"

"Of course."

"When you saw your mother—after Jake died—how did you feel?"

She removed her robe and slippers. "I was in shock. She pretended to care."

"Maybe she really does."

Rose stepped into her skirt, then buttoned her blouse. "Meghan, there are things you don't know about. Lots of things about me..."

Meghan stayed at the door. "It's all right. You don't have to tell me—if you don't want to."

She sat on the bed to put on her stockings. "I—I think I need to. But I need to prepare you. It's bad—possibly worse than you've ever heard."

Meghan's expression softened.

What a friend she was.

Rose said nothing until she finished putting on her stockings and boots. "You may want to sit again, Meghan. What I have to say is pretty ugly."

Meghan's expression was somber as she moved to the chair and sat quietly. "I'm listening."

∽

Hannah passed by Rose's room on her way downstairs. Even though the door was closed, she recognized Meghan's voice. They were talking low and serious, not lighthearted. As if something confidential was being shared. The intenseness in Rose's voice, the kindness she heard from Meghan's responses, even though she didn't understand the words—touched her heart. She stopped only a moment to listen, but still couldn't distinguish the words. It was wrong, but she was grasping for any crumb of knowledge that could help her get to know those two women a little better. They were more her age, although a couple of years older. Olivia and Luisa were at least ten years older.

Maybe someday she'd find a female friend to be able to share all her heart with. She'd had a good start with Meghan and Rose on Thanksgiving Day—yet longed for more.

She valued her budding friendship with Bernie. It could even turn to love, given enough time and encouragement. He seemed to like her as much as she liked him. She wasn't ready for marriage yet, she only wanted a friend. Bernie was a hardworking man. He'd established a new mill. Even though most of his customers lived an hour north of New Boston in little farming communities that didn't have their own mill, just a store and maybe a blacksmith. Bernie had talked about them enough that she almost had a picture in her mind of what they were like.

A sob escaped from inside the room. "Oh, you poor dear!" Meghan's cry from inside the room was muffled, but very distinguishable.

What did that mean? Feeling guilty, she rushed down the hall to the stairway, slowing down only after reaching the stairs. She didn't want to appear she was running from something. Even though she knew she shouldn't have been eavesdropping.

⌒

"Oh, you poor dear!" Meghan's sob touched Rose's heart. Her cherished friend felt her pain. Meghan took her handkerchief from her sleeve and dabbed her eyes.

Rose wiped her own tears away with her fingertips.

Meghan blew her nose. Her expression full of compassion. "When did you find this out?"

"Do you remember that day Madam came to see me? It was a Saturday, a week or so before Jake kidnapped me."

"Why did she wait all this time to tell you?"

Rose let out a long breath. "She said it was because I shouldn't try to be more than I was. That maybe I was 'uppity.' Meghan, do I look down on people, think I'm better than them?"

Meghan shook her head. "Not at all." She looked down, then up, meeting Rose's gaze. "So she didn't like that you had changed your life?"

"She tried to explain a lot of things—including why she'd forced me into that life. That's when she told me what happened to her.

I was so angry—and yet, in a way, I felt a bit sorry for her... that she'd had to endure that."

Meghan stood. "Do you have fresh water?"

"Not fresh, but it's on the dresser. Thanks so much for listening."

Meghan splashed and wiped her face. "Now I don't feel like I was just crying." She smiled. "And—you're welcome. You listened to me when I griped about Duncan."

"Are you two all right now?"

Meghan sighed. "Yes, I am reconciled to it. He will be an excellent preacher."

Rose smiled. "If he can remember to talk in full sentences."

Meghan giggled. "Um, yes. When he talks about God, he uses subjects. I noticed that, too. And you—you've grown so much, you talk like a lady, and not a dance hall girl."

Her heart warmed. "That's because of you."

Chapter Forty-Four

Monday morning, Rose went to the medical office early, to put on her nurse's apron, and gather a few supplies for the school demonstration. She wiped her hands on her apron. She'd never spoken in public before. Even though she knew some of the schoolchildren, her mouth had already gone dry. How would she ever get through a whole hour of class?

Meghan had explained how challenging the students could be, especially Greg Fagin and Jeremy Baker. They were the most intelligent. There were new children this term, too. She could only wonder what they'd be like.

She threw a stethoscope, a roll of bandages, a pair of scissors, and a sheet into a burlap sack and went to the door. Scott should probably be reminded where she was. She knocked on his bedroom door.

"Scott, are you awake?"

No sound. She knocked again, then opened the door. The room was empty.

Maybe he went for an early morning walk, now that he could get around without limping—too much.

Moving to the desk, she pulled out a sheet of paper and grabbed a pencil, then scribbled a note explaining where she was and what she'd taken for class. And reminded him it was his turn tomorrow.

Taking one last look around, she stepped out, locked the door to the medical office, and started out for the church.

It was only a few short blocks away.

Scott's proposal of marriage came to mind. Though she desperately wanted to marry him, it would be a disservice to him—because of her past. Even though time after time he'd said it didn't make a difference to him, she could hardly believe it.

The last thing he'd said on Thanksgiving Day was "Please don't make me wait too long." Did that mean he would move on—and not marry her?

Was she her own worst enemy?

There was still the matter of her real identity. What would the town do if they knew? Madam said they'd make her leave town. Why? All she'd ever wanted was to be respected and to be a lady. Was that too much to ask?

Then, there was Rafe. If he really was an angel, she should listen to what he'd said about forgiving her mother and turning her heart toward God. His visits always unnerved her. She wanted to believe, she really did. But the past was hard to put behind her.

She reached the church. Children played outside, wrapped up in their coats, scarves, and mittens. Proper attire for the morning chill.

Meghan stood in the doorway and caught her attention.

⁓

Scott returned from an early morning walk to find the office empty. Wasn't Rose supposed to be here to open the office? She was usually on time, or early. Where was she?

His leg bothered him some. He had begun walking to exercise and strengthen the leg but might have overdone it some this morning.

He hobbled around the office, finding the note on the desk.

Dear Scott,

I'm at the school today... telling them how wonderful it is to be your nurse. And remember, tomorrow, it's your turn to tell them how much you love being a doctor.

I'll be back as soon as I'm finished.

Love,
Rose

That's right. She'd told him over the weekend she'd be doing that presentation. She was also Meghan's messenger.

Even though he knew he'd been forgiven for what he'd done to Meghan, he still felt regret and sorrow. He realized his emotional scar would be something he'd have to live with his whole life. Maybe someday, it wouldn't hurt so much. Healing had begun in his heart, but as he remembered the "conversation" he'd heard from—was it really angels? They'd said he'd have a mark on his soul, but he was redeemable. He accepted that.

"God, thank you for forgiving me. Help Meghan to forgive me, too. And help my precious Rose forgive her mother and know you in her heart."

Soon Wilcox would be setting up a third tent church across Sand Creek. Maybe he'd take Rose there, after a few weeks. Rose said Wilcox planned to begin just after the New Year. He looked at the calendar. January first was a Sunday. He wondered if Wilcox would set up the tent then or wait a week. Maybe Rose could find out.

Rose stood to one side of the room. It was jammed full of fresh-faced students—about twenty in all, gazing at their teacher with wide eyes. Clearly, they all loved Meghan.

"And now, without further ado, here's my dear friend, Rose Rhodes, to speak to you about what it's like to be a nurse." Meghan stepped to one side as she gestured for Rose to move to the front of the class.

She cleared her throat as she moved in front of the students. There was Greg Fagin, in the back, scribbling on his tablet. What was he writing?

As she looked toward the front of the room, Chrissy Fagin locked eyes with her. At only six, Chrissy had a cherubic face and nature to match.

Her mouth went dry and she coughed. "Um, Meg—uh, Miss Gallagher, do you have a glass of water?"

Meghan smiled and nodded. "Certainly, Miss Rhodes." She went to the desk and poured water into a small glass, then handed it to her.

Even though she wanted to gulp it down and run—instead—she took a few sips, handed the glass to Meghan, then squared her shoulders.

"Thank you, Miss Gallagher, for inviting me here today. I know many of you already, because you've cut yourself and needed stitches, or become ill and needed Doctor Allison.

"I've only been a nurse for a few months, but I can tell you it has been the most rewarding time of my life. Here's what I do:

"I take inventory, and make sure we have plenty of supplies. Administering medication though, is sometimes a challenge—as some of you know. What's one way your mother helps you take your medicine that helps the bad taste?"

Liddie Sampson, Jewel Sampson's daughter, raised her hand. Rose didn't know Mrs. Sampson well, only that she was the culinary head at the hotel. Scott had told Rose about her.

"Yes, Liddie." Rose smiled. She knew what Liddie was going to say but wanted the girl to share it with the class.

"Ma puts some of the pain powder in juice."

"Does that work?"

Liddie ducked her chin a moment, then looked up. "Well, it makes the pain powder taste better—but makes the juice taste bad!"

Rose smiled. "Then it's a sort of compromise, isn't it? Yet you get the benefit of feeling better in the end, don't you? And isn't that what you want? To feel well?"

Liddie nodded. "Yeah."

Rose took a step to the side and held up a bandage roll. "Doctor Allison has also trained me in basic medical care, such as cleaning and stitching wounds. He even lets me do the final sutures of major surgery."

"Ooo." "Wow!" The reactions of the children as they looked at her with wide eyes and open mouths almost made her laugh. They were impressed. It made her feel more at ease.

The rest of the hour seemed to fly by. The children loved hearing their own heartbeats or those of friends when she let them use the stethoscope. They also had fun "bandaging" each other.

Before she knew it, Meghan had moved up beside her.

"Thank you, Miss Rhodes, for your remarkable presentation this morning. Let's thank her, shall we?"

The class erupted in applause. Meghan's arm went around her waist. The warmth of the ovation, coupled with the affection from her best friend, filled Rose's heart to overflowing.

"Thank you, Meghan. Uh, Miss Gallagher."

"Aw, it's all right, Miss Rhodes. Everybody knows you're best friends." Rose smiled at Susie Baker. Susie was Donald Baker's daughter, one of the two Santa Fe executives who had come to establish New Boston as a town and the railhead.

Meghan and Rose looked at each other and giggled.

"Yes, we are." They both said it at the same time. Thank heaven for Meghan. Her only real friend.

Later that evening, after the dishes were done, Hannah sought out Meghan in the parlor. She looked at her watch, pinned to her pinafore. Meghan's fiancé, Duncan, was due to arrive at any moment, but maybe she could ask her for a time to meet later. Rose had yet to return from the medical office.

When Hannah entered, Meghan was pouring a cup of tea.

"Can I speak with you a moment?"

Meghan smiled. "That's about all I have. Duncan should be coming any minute now. But sure."

She leaned on the end of the wingback chair. "I-I just w-wondered if we c-could maybe find a time where I might a-ask you a couple questions about something?"

Meghan nodded. "Sure. How about after Duncan leaves? Around nine or nine-thirty?"

She looked to the clock on the wall, just to make sure her watch was on time. It read eight o'clock. "That's fine. Thank you."

Would she be brave enough to talk to Meghan about what she'd overheard? Could Meghan ever be a real friend?

Chapter Forty-Five

"Let him rest there, Rose. He'll wake up in a few minutes. He should be fine to go home after an hour or so." Scott dipped his hands in the washbasin and reached for a towel. "I think we're done for the day." He glanced at the man who'd come in with an emergency cut. It was so deep, Scott had sedated him.

He walked around the table and put a hand on her shoulder. "Nice job, Miss Rhodes. I couldn't have done it without your help."

Her expression shone. How he loved seeing her smile. He'd like to put a smile on her face like that every day for the rest of her life—if it were possible.

At the coatrack, she exchanged her work apron for her cloak and hat. "Thank you, Doctor Allison."

He moved toward the door. "Um, Rose, could I speak to you a moment...before our patient wakes up?" He'd given him enough chloroform to keep him out an hour, and it had been only a little over half an hour.

She tilted her head to one side. "All right."

He gestured to the couch. "Could we sit a moment? We can still keep an eye on our patient."

She sat at one end of the couch, he at the other.

"Have you given any thought to what we talked about the night of Thanksgiving? You love me. I love you. There really isn't any reason we should wait a long time."

She looked down, then up into his gaze. Her beautiful cocoa-colored eyes misted over. The corners of her mouth drooped a bit.

"Scott, I do love you. There are a few things we need to talk about and some things I need to get settled in my mind and heart."

He thought a moment and looked around. "Oh! You'll want a house. Of course."

"Yes, we'll need that, but it's more than that. I need time to come to grips with everything that's happened."

The wind dropped out of his sails. He had hoped she'd made some progress on her emotions. Evidently not.

"I understand. I won't speak of it until you're ready. Let me know when you're ready to talk about it again."

She let out a long breath. "Thank you. I'm sorry. This is very difficult for me. I—I've talked with Meghan some, and it's helping, but I still..."

"Yes, I know. You need more time." He scooted over and took her hand. "That doesn't mean I'm going to stop kissing you, though."

He pulled her to him and firmly planted his lips on hers. She relaxed into his kiss and put her arms around his neck. His hands trailed up and down her back.

"Don't ever stop kissing me, Doctor Allison." She put a hand to her bottom lip and smiled.

"Never." He drew her into an embrace and ran his hands through her curls. He could have stayed there forever.

The groan from the exam table brought him back reality. Their patient was waking up.

༄

A knock on her bedroom door drew Hannah's attention out of the book she was reading. She rose.

"Hannah?"

It was Meghan. Could she talk about what she needed to? Or should she wait until she knew Meghan better?

"Come in. It's not locked." She never locked her door until she went to bed, because the boardinghouse was safe. Olivia screened her boarders carefully, and only the most reputable of men were allowed rooms on the third floor. They weren't allowed on the second floor, except certain times of the day. Any breach of trust and they were evicted.

Meghan closed the door.

She gestured for Meghan to sit. "Sit wherever you'd like."

"I'll take the bed."

She put her book down on the desk and sat at the other end of the bed. "Th-thank you. I-I just want to get to kn-know you better."

"What did you want to talk about?"

"How l-long have you been here in New Boston?" She wanted to get the conversation started. Small talk would help.

Meghan looked up a moment, figuring in her head. "Goodness! I've been here nine months now."

"H-how did you get to know people? I-I seem to be having a hard time."

Meghan's eyes softened. "I'm sorry. It's probably our fault for not including you in things. And I'm engaged now, still teaching school..."

She nodded. "You *are* busy. D-Do you mind if I ask h-how you got to know R-Rose so quickly? H-hasn't she only been here since June?"

A strange look passed over Meghan's expression. She didn't know the meaning. "Why yes, I guess it *has* only been six months." Meghan shook her head as if she could hardly believe it. Her gaze drifted around the room before settling on the window.

She waited. Meghan pulled herself out of her reverie. "I'm sorry. You asked me how I got to know people? May I ask you a question, before I answer?"

"Sure."

"Are you shy? Was it hard for you to make friends back home?"

Hannah swallowed, looking down. "Y-yes. I'm shy. And when I'm ner-nervous, as y-you can see, I st-st-stutter some."

"It's all right. We all have our challenges. It's how we meet them that makes the difference."

She looked up and met Meghan's gaze, and sensed acceptance, even caring.

Meghan stood and went toward the window. "I'm naturally outgoing, so it wasn't difficult for me to make friends with Olivia right away. We were both southern women and we had that understanding."

"What about Rose? How did you get to know her?"

Meghan turned toward her but waited a moment before answering. Was she uncomfortable? It almost seemed as if she squirmed a little. "After the tornado, Rose came to town and moved into the boardinghouse. I started getting to know her then. She worked with Doctor Allison as his nurse. I'm not comfortable around blood or injuries. And then Duncan was hurt in the tornado, and my attention was on him."

Hannah thought a moment. "So, you and R-Rose became close after you took care of Duncan."

"Yes."

"Then y-you got closer after he was shot?"

"Yes. That's how it was."

She picked at the edges of the quilting knots on her bedspread but said nothing.

Meghan seemed to sense her uneasiness and sat on the bed again. "Please don't feel nervous around me. I'm sorry if I make you uncomfortable."

"Y-you don't. I-it's me. I-I'm uncomfortable with my-myself right now."

Meghan's eyes filled with concern. "Why?"

"B-because I have something h-hard to a-ask you."

Meghan tilted her head to one side. "You can ask me anything."

Hannah swallowed. "I-I'm sorry. I overheard y-you and Rose the other day. I-I heard you say something like 'Oh, you poor dear!' I didn't mean to listen. I-I was passing by at j-just that time." She let out a long breath and expelled it. There. She'd said it. How would Meghan respond?

～

It was late when Rose finally finished up at the medical office. She was tired and hungry.

"Remember, you're going to school first thing in the morning. I'll meet you outside the church." Rose untied her apron strings.

Scott nodded. "I'll remember. Do you think Meghan will be there?"

"I'm hoping so. But if she's not, please don't hold it against her."

"I'm not angry with Meghan. Just sorry I treated her so horribly. I've apologized. What else can I do?" He smiled. "I guess I'll have to wait until God heals her heart." His beam always warmed her inside.

She said nothing but reached for her cloak. He helped put it over her shoulders. "Thanks, Scott."

His fingers trailed along her neck. A shiver went through her, a good shudder that woke a fire down deep in her heart.

He bent, and his lips met hers—warm, yet firm and soft at the same time. She'd been kissed by many men over the years, but none had meant anything. Scott's kiss meant everything. She loved him with all her heart and soul. Why couldn't she consent to marry him right this minute?

"You'll never marry! You might as well get that through your head, young lady!" "You're mine! All mine! You belong to me!" The voices of Madam and Jake haunted her.

Maybe someday she'd be free of them.

Until then, she couldn't hurt Scott by making him believe they could have a happy marriage.

Chapter Forty-Six

The next morning, Rose waited outside the Catholic church for Scott. She didn't know if Meghan would be here this morning. Her friend had given her the key to the church yesterday after lunch, in case she and Scott worked late—which they had.

She unlocked the padlock and restored the key to her reticule, then looked around. Still no sign of Meghan. Rose knew it would be difficult for her friend to be there, but she still hoped Meghan would come.

"Good morning, Rose." Scott's low tenor timbre voice greeted her from behind.

She turned. "Good morning, Doctor Allison."

"Are we being formal?" His smile warmed her heart.

She returned it. "I'm afraid we are—especially in front of the schoolchildren."

"Ah, I understand." He looked around. "Any sign of Meghan?"

"Not that I've seen. Let's go inside. It's cold, and we need to get the stove going so the children won't catch their death."

She led the way to one a large extra room in the church, and set about starting the fire in the stove as Meghan had shown her yesterday, then showed Scott where to stand until after she introduced him.

A few minutes later, the twenty or so students made their way into the room and sat at their desks.

Rose pulled at her watch pin, now fastened to the collar of her jacket. She wore a blouse, skirt, and short traveling jacket ensemble today, hoping it would make her feel more authoritative—especially if Meghan didn't arrive until after Scott was finished.

She picked up a ruler and rapped it against the desk. "Attention, please! May I have your attention?" The students' roar dulled into silence.

"Thank you. If you remember... yesterday, Miss Gallagher said Doctor Allison would join class. I shared what it's like to be a doctor's assistant and nurse. Today, you'll hear from the doctor himself. Sco—Doctor Allison, if you please?"

Scott moved from the side wall and took center stage.

She moved to the back of the class, to watch for Meghan. If only her friend would come.

⁓

"Hello, class. What would you like to know about being a doctor?" Scott thought it better to allow the children to ask questions. Frankly, he hadn't had time to prepare a formal presentation.

Greg Fagin raised his hand. "How much schooling did you have to take?"

"Well, many American doctors, especially here in the Midwest or farther west, apprentice under an established doctor. I was one of the lucky ones. I went to Yale University and got a medical degree. Just finished up a year ago, 1870."

"So you're a brand-new doctor, huh?" The boy seemed bright—not belligerent—just curious.

"I have a year of experience."

One of the girls spoke. "Could you tell us what it's like to be a doctor?" She must be new and hadn't been to the office. Her flaming red hair drew his attention. An anomaly here, for certain.

"That's why I came." Scott launched into his speech about helping others, bringing healing, and the warm feelings he received knowing he'd helped someone get well. That took nearly half the time allotted. That was fine with him. He enjoyed sharing his love of medicine.

"How do you figure out what's wrong with a person?" another little girl with blond pigtails asked. He didn't recognize her, either.

"Well, I have a stethoscope, which I believe Miss Rhodes brought to class yesterday. She told me you all really enjoyed listening to your heartbeat. That's one thing I do. I feel your forehead, don't I? I can tell if you have a fever. There are new instruments that are just now beginning to catch on. They're called thermometers. I'm planning to get one after the first of the year."

"What's a thur-mo-ter?" Jeremy Baker scratched his head.

Scott smiled. "It's a ther-mo-meter—a device that takes your body temperature. Medical science is beginning to do amazing things. We're studying the human body more so that we can properly diagnose when someone is ill."

Movement at the back of the room caught his eye. Meghan had slipped in and stood next to Rose. He saw them quietly gesturing to each other, whispering in each other's ears.

"Does anyone else have any questions?"

The class was quiet.

He picked up a bandage roll and stuck it in his pocket. "Miss Rose—would you do the honors of wrapping up?"

Rose began to move forward. "Of course, Doctor Allison."

He walked the few steps toward the back, hoping to get a word with Meghan, but she didn't give him the chance.

"Let's all thank Doctor Allison for his time this morning, shall we?" Meghan took firm control of her class as she moved forward and stood where he had just moments before. She looked around the classroom but wouldn't meet his gaze.

The class applauded.

"Thank you for having me."

He joined Rose at the back of the room.

Meghan turned to her desk and picked up a text. "Class—take out your readers and we'll start on page forty."

He wasn't going to get an opportunity to speak with Meghan.

⌒

As Hannah polished silverware at The Harvey House that morning, she thought back to Meghan's response the night before.

Meghan's eyes widened, her back stiffened. "You—heard me say that? What else did you hear?" Her voice was sharp.

She swallowed hard, but this didn't remove the lump in her throat. "N-nothing. I-I promise."

Meghan visibly relaxed and let out a long breath. "I'm sorry. I was startled. Please forgive me. I don't usually respond so harshly." She wiped a stray lock of hair away from her face. "It's just that Rose shared something deeply personal with me. What you heard was my shock." Meghan leaned forward. "Please forget all about it."

She looked down. "I-I'm sorry to have caused y-you distress. I w-won't say a thing to Rose about it."

Meghan smiled. "That's best. Truly it is. And I won't say anything about this, either." She laid a hand on Hannah's arm for a moment.

"I-I'm sorry I said anything at all."

"I'm not. I'm glad you confided in me." Meghan's voice soothed like cool rain on a hot summer day. She stood and moved to the door, then turned.

"It took a lot of courage for you to say what you did."

Blood rushed through her face. "Th-thank you for b-being so k-kind."

Meghan left. She sat thinking a long time before going to bed.

She hoped Meghan would continue to think kindly of her.

"Miss Samuelson?" Jewel Sampson's voice cut through her musing. The culinary head also oversaw the Harvey girls. Hannah liked Mrs. Sampson but was a bit afraid of her.

"Yes, M-Missus Sampson?"

"You've been polishing that knife for five minutes now." Mrs. Sampson's voice wasn't harsh, but firm.

"Oh, I'm s-sorry."

Mrs. Sampson walked close to her and lowered her voice. "Don't be nervous, Hannah. Just relax. Can't have you stuttering when you take customer orders now, can we?"

Hannah nodded, but didn't trust herself to say anything without a stutter.

"All right then. Just pay attention to your work." Mrs. Sampson tapped her cheek. "I've heard that if you think about what to say in your mind first, then say it—maybe you won't stutter so much." The older woman gave her a curt smile, then walked away.

Hannah exhaled. If it were only that easy. It never worked for her. She couldn't even remember when it had all started. It seemed she'd always talked this way.

Chapter Forty-Seven

"We need to get our Christmas decorations up." Olivia brought in a large platter of steaming roast beef. Just thinking about the tender, stringy meat left Rose's mouthwatering. She'd grown up thinking roast beef a delicacy.

Luisa brought in two bowls of vegetables. Rose loved watching the steam rise from the top and the aroma...

"Yes, we should." Meghan's smile always seemed to light up the room these days. Rose understood why. Since Meghan had made peace with Duncan's decision to be a minister, she'd become more engrossed in wedding plans. Rose overheard Olivia discussing with Meghan the importance of slow consideration, not just random choices in wedding plans. She was sure Meghan would choose Olivia as her matron of honor. If she asked, Rose would gladly serve as—what? A bridesmaid? Didn't that person have to be "pure?"

"What about—how you say—Christmas tree? No trees here." Carlos was learning but still didn't speak much more English than his mother.

"Si, *Feliz Navidad*—how you say—Merry Christmas? How long? When?" Little Maria was still trying to learn English, too. With Meghan's tutoring, they were improving but still had a long way to go.

Olivia and Luisa sat once they'd placed dinner on the table. They'd brought roast beef, potatoes and gravy, corn, peas, and green beans. It seemed that every dinner was a real banquet, and yet, as she remembered Thanksgiving dinner, just a week or so ago, she realized this humble meal paled in comparison to that plentiful feast. She smiled as she remembered Jackson's entrance. Would Olivia ask him to spend Christmas dinner here as well? She hoped so.

Olivia giggled at Maria's question. "Christmas is only three weeks away. Have you asked Santa Claus what you want him to bring you for Christmas—or as you say Feliz Navidad?"

Maria's countenance fell, and she stole a glance at Carlos. Rose looked to Luisa, but her face was bland, expressionless.

Finally, after a few awkward moments, Luisa spoke. "We do not have money—for *Papá Noel*—San-ta Clowse to visit us."

"But that's the point. Christmas is about giving *and* receiving to others. And for the children..." Rose watched Meghan take in Luisa's expression and stopped.

Olivia intervened in the awkward silence. "Shall we pray God's blessing upon our food? Rose, would you do the honors?"

She coughed. "Certainly." How was she going to do this? She tried to remember what others had prayed and hoped she could say something simple.

"Dear Heavenly Father—be here and everywhere adored. These morsels bless, and grant that we might feast in Paradise with thee. Amen." It wasn't a perfect remembrance of the prayer she'd once heard Meghan pray, but some of it was right.

"Amen." The chorus of voices around the table responded to her prayer.

"So—what about—Christmas tree?" Bernie passed a bowl of cooked carrots in browned butter to Rose.

"Who regularly checks in with the railroad executives?" Olivia passed the potatoes, then the gravy.

Bernie rose and held out his hand for Olivia's plate. Then he served everyone a hunk of roast beef as conversation continued.

"Wh-why do you ask?" Hannah took some green beans from a bowl and passed it on.

"Well, I figured whoever saw Mister Fagin or Mister Baker next, could ask them about importing Christmas trees. Surely they've thought of it." Olivia passed the butter.

Meghan spooned some peas onto her plate, then passed it on to Rose. "I'll ask them. Their wives usually drop by school once a week anyway, just to see how things are going and see if we need anything."

"That's a great idea, Meghan." Olivia cut a bite of beef.

"I'm happy to do it. If they're getting trees shipped in from the East, do we have any decorations?" Meghan poured herself some water from the pitcher in the center of the table.

"I think we might have a box in the cellar. Carlos, Maria, do you think you could help me look after dinner?" Olivia spooned some gravy over her beef, plus the potatoes.

"After dinner—there are—how you say—lessons." Luisa's firm voice intruded. Rose glanced over. The cook-housekeeper's expression was solemn, but not harsh. It seemed that Luisa merely wanted the regular routine to be followed.

"Well, perhaps on Saturday, then." Olivia's kind expression matched her tone.

Rose would have to think carefully what to get Carlos and Maria, and their mother. Besides the handkerchiefs she was embroidering, she felt maybe this Mexican family, who'd experienced the tragic loss of their husband and father during the tornado, needed extra kindness this Christmas.

Her best Christmas happened when she was twelve.

༄

"Mother look at the Christmas tree!" Rose clapped her hands together. "It's so pretty!" A gentleman caller had brought the twelve-foot tree the night before. She was beside herself with happiness. Mother's pleasure shone through her

eyes. Maybe this man would marry Mother. A rich man, his clothes were of the finest quality. He visited at least twice a week, once on Wednesday evening, then on Saturday afternoon. She'd overheard a conversation between Mother and the gentleman, who called himself Joseph once. They were in the parlor, and she wanted to hear what they said. She hid in the back hall just outside the parlor entrance.

"Margaret, you are so beautiful. I wish I could spend every waking moment with you."

Mother's voice quaked a little. "Joe, ya know I—wish the same."

"But we can't, can we?"

"It probably wouldn't be wise—for you."

"I love you, Margaret. What else is there?"

Mother took in a sharp breath. Rose put her hand over her mouth to keep from making her own reaction heard.

"There's your position, your family, your career. Your place in society would be destroyed."

"Oh posh! I could work all those things out. With you by my side, Margaret, I could accomplish anything."

"What about Rosalie? She's just a child. If you married me, she'd join us."

"You know how I feel about Rosie. She's a sweet girl—and she's going to be a real beauty. Just like her mother."

From her place outside the door, Rose's heart warmed even more toward the man she hoped would become her stepfather. She didn't know much about Joe—only that he was kind, he liked her, and he loved Mother. What else mattered? Why couldn't they be a family? Would Mother say something to offend him? She hoped not.

"You are so kind. I—I think I really love ya, too, Joseph. But you know..."

"Hush now."

She peeked around the doorway. Joseph put a finger on Mother's lips. Mother gently removed it, then moved in and kissed him. When their kiss deepened, as Rosie had seen many times before, she knew what came next.

It was time for her to stop watching. But she couldn't leave until she knew Mother's answer.

Joseph broke the kiss, then spoke again. "Let's just enjoy Christmas. Shall we give little Rosie the best Christmas of her life? And you too, Margaret. I want to give you the best Christmas of your life. Time enough after the New Year to make plans."

Rose peeked around the corner again. A tear rolled down Mother's cheek. "Yes. Let's do ... make this the best Christmas for all of us."

No other Christmas compared with that day. She longed for it every year, but it never happened. To be loved and to love. Would it ever happen for her?

Chapter Forty-Eight

Scott entered The Pioneer Store on Saturday, December tenth. He barely limped now, although his ankle was usually stiff first thing in the morning. September seemed so long ago. How his life had changed since then.

What could he get Rose that would prove his love for her and his intention to marry her? Nieman greeted him from behind the counter. Decker waved at him from the back of the store.

"Hello, Doctor Allison. What can we get you today?" Nieman gestured for Scott to join him at the counter.

Scott looked around, then strolled to the counter. No other customer was in the store at present. He wouldn't have to whisper, but he kept his voice low. "Well, you know Rose and I are courting. I've asked her to marry me, but I need something special to give her for Christmas. Something like ... a ring? Do you have any?"

Nieman reached underneath and pulled out a thick, heavy catalog. He plopped it on the counter, opened it, and flipped to a certain page. He pointed. "Have a look-see, Doc. Lots of different rings here. Take your pick. If I order it by next week, it will still come in time for Christmas."

Scott looked at the various rings. They were all very nice. He calculated his price, then looked at rings in his price range. His gaze focused on three of them, all different settings. They were diamond solitaire rings, but each was a different shape. The designs were square, star, and pear-shaped. He liked the star-shaped one the best and pointed. It was a little over his price range, but it would be worth it for Rose.

"I'd like to order this one."

Nieman turned the catalog around to face himself, then bent down and peered at the page. He grabbed his order pad and proceeded to write down the information.

"Okay, Doc. I'll get that order in first thing Monday morning. It should be here just before Christmas. If it comes in sooner, I'll let you know."

Scott reached into his pocket and drew out his wallet. He'd put a blank check in before coming.

"Just pay for it when you pick it up, Doc. I trust you. I know you're good for it." Nieman put the order book back under the counter.

"Thanks. I appreciate that."

"Anything else today?"

"No, I don't think so." Scott turned, and nearly ran into...

Meghan.

"Oh, pardon me!" She looked up, then saw it was him. "So sorry." She moved quickly to the back of the store where the fabric table was.

He followed her. "Please, Meghan. Will you just talk to me for a moment?"

She slowed on her way to the fabric table. Her shoulders slumped, as if she was resigned to the fact that she'd have to talk to him. She ran her hands over various fabrics but didn't make eye contact with him.

He came to the fabric table and stood a short distance away. "I know Rose has told you that I've changed my life, Meghan. I feel—I wish—I could make it up to you for how I treated you. Every time I see you, I'm reminded of how despicably I acted. If I could say I'm sorry every day for the rest of my life, it wouldn't be enough. I truly regret everything I did that day—with one exception. I really did do my best to save your cowboy. I'm glad he's all right now."

She turned toward him and finally met his gaze. Her expression softened. "I'm sorry, too, Scott. I held it against you, nursing my hurt. I've released it now. Both Rose and Duncan told me what happened in your office when Rafe came to visit—from their viewpoints." Her lips curled up slightly. "I'd like to hear your side of the story of that day... sometime. Maybe the four of us can get together and discuss spiritual matters in the future. You do know that Duncan is starting a new tent church on New Year's Day." She dipped her hand into her reticule and drew out a small card. "Here's an invitation. We'd love to have you and Rose come."

He smiled. "You know, I have become a new person now. I know what you were talking about. I've had more than one experience with God now, not just with Rafe."

Her smile was large and genuine. "That's wonderful. I'm very glad to hear it. Rose and I will figure something out about getting together." She turned her attention to the fabrics again.

"Can you keep a secret?"

She turned her head, her eyes wide. "Of course."

"I'm buying a ring for Rose for Christmas. I've asked her to marry me, you know."

"I suspected. She's not accepted it, though, has she?"

"Yes, and no. I think she's still trying to overcome her past."

Meghan nodded. "Yes, she is. There are things..."

"I know. She's told me. It doesn't make a difference."

"It does to her."

He let out a long breath. "Let's pray God heals her heart."

Meghan smiled again. "That's a wonderful idea." She put her hand on his arm a moment. "You're very good for her, you know. I pray daily that your love for her will help her move forward."

He put his hand over hers. "Thank you, Meghan. And—you've forgiven me?"

"Yes. I didn't feel it for a long time, but I do now. God showed me that my decision to forgive was more important than feeling it. He said the feelings would come. And, they are. Thank you for doing a great job with the schoolchildren the other day. I know they enjoyed it. You'll have to come again some time."

"I'd be honored. And thank you, Meghan. I hope we can be friends."

She nodded. "I think we can."

He turned and left. A heavy burden had lifted. Yet the pain of the wound would never leave him.

⌒

That evening, Rose was working on her embroidery when she heard a knock at her door. "Who is it?"

A muffled "Meghan." She opened the door.

"Goodness! Meghan, you look radiant! Come tell me all about it."

Her friend sat on the edge of the bed. "I finally talked to Scott today."

"Oh, I'm so glad! I told you, didn't I?"

Meghan rolled her eyes. "Yes, you did. He has changed. Much gentler in his way of speaking."

She smiled. "I agree. Of course, I am a bit prejudiced, you know."

Meghan chuckled. Rose joined her.

"It's been a while since I've heard you laugh." Meghan's giggle turned to a warm smile.

She grew serious. "I know. This fall has been so difficult."

"You've had a hard time. I can't imagine."

"Well, you had your own trying time, just before mine... with Duncan and all."

Meghan nodded. "That's true, in more ways than one." She thought a moment. "I invited Scott to our new tent church. I'm inviting you, too. I also told Scott you and I would figure out when the four of us could maybe plan a time to talk."

Rose tied off the threads and cut the ends. She was now finished with Olivia's handkerchief. Tomorrow, she'd start Luisa's. She'd already finished Carlos's and Maria's. She wanted to finish most of the others' as quickly as possible, so she could spend extra time on Meghan's and Scott's embroideries, since they were going to be more intricate. "That's a wonderful idea."

Meghan stood and went to the door. Her lips curled up in a tease. "And... I saw Scott shopping for your Christmas present."

"Oh you! You're teasing me."

Meghan giggled again. "You bet. See you in the morning."

She nodded and smirked. "Good night."

It was good to hear Meghan laugh again, too. There'd been nothing much to smile about for such a long time, Rose wondered when she would ever feel joy.

Chapter Forty-Nine

Time flew by. It was almost Christmas. Carlos and Maria had helped Olivia find her box of Christmas decorations. The railroad had imported nearly a thousand pine and fir trees. Olivia, Luisa, and the children picked out a Fraser fir and set about decorating it in the parlor. Bernie came home early that day to lift Maria up to put a tin star on top.

Almost immediately, both plain and elaborately wrapped presents of all shapes and sizes began to appear. Rose asked Olivia if she had any material scraps. Olivia had a whole box full of fabric remnants. Everyone who lived there could use these to wrap their gifts.

Rose smiled as she placed a few gifts under the tree. She would keep Scott's present to herself until Christmas Day. The rest she put under the tree as she finished them.

Hannah joined her. "It-It is a beautiful tree, isn't it?"

Rose turned. "It sure is. Did you have pretty Christmas trees in Ohio?"

Hannah smiled. "W-we did. Although not quite as grand as this one."

"Oh?"

"W-we usually tried to find and cut our own t-tree. It was s-something of a family tradition. My f-father and brothers would drag it into the house. M-Mother would complain about all the needles."

Rose's mind drifted back to that Christmas when she was twelve. What a lovely tree Joseph had given them. She shook her head to clear the memory. "And you had lovely decorations for it?"

"W-we made most of them ourselves. We'd wad fabric r-remnants into a ball shape, then tack it down with beads and shiny ribbons scraps. Ma would pop a kettle full of popcorn, and we'd string it."

As Hannah spoke of things she enjoyed, her stutter lessened. She'd have to consult Scott's medical manuals, but maybe there was something she could do to help the young woman speak better. It seemed Hannah stuttered more when she was nervous or uncomfortable around someone. The girl was certainly comfortable around Bernie, even though she'd stuttered a lot around him at first.

It was generally known that stuttering was probably more emotional in nature, and not caused by anything physical. Scott had one medical book on mental illness, but that was all. Not much was known.

"Wh-What are you thinking about?" Hannah's sweet voice interrupted her thoughts.

"Oh, I'm sorry. I was thinking about something. But I was listening. Christmas at your home sounded wonderful."

"They were." Hannah's lips came together in a line.

Olivia and Meghan joined them. Olivia clapped her hands together. "Meghan has some questions to ask you girls." Sly smiles and whimsical expressions passed between the two newcomers. What was happening?

Meghan gestured for them to sit. "I'm planning my wedding—as you all well know. Olivia has been a great help—of course—having been married before. I've asked her to be my matron-of-honor."

Both Rose and Hannah said "Oh!" at the same time. "That's wonderful!" "Congratulations, Olivia!"

Meghan held up her hand. "We haven't set a date yet, but it will probably be mid-June, not long after the school term is over."

"Wh-what did you want to ask us?" Hannah leaned forward. Rose hoped the girl wouldn't be disappointed. For that matter, Rose hoped *she* wouldn't be upset. Meghan was going to ask her to be a bridesmaid. Her stomach churned. She wasn't pure. Although knowing it didn't seem to make any difference to Meghan, Rose wasn't sure she could do it. But how to gracefully decline the invitation, should it be given? She didn't know.

As if Meghan read her mind... "Rose, would you please consent to be my bridesmaid?"

Rose smiled and nodded, not trusting herself to say anything. But Meghan wasn't finished.

"And, Hannah, would you register all the guests who attend our wedding? I'll have a lined book and a special pen and ink bottle for you."

Hannah smiled. "O-of course, I will. Th-thank you so much for considering me. I-I'm honored."

Olivia stood. "Now that's settled. Let's go make some cookies!"

Rose would talk to Meghan later.

How could she help her friend understand what stirred her up inside—just by asking a simple question?

⸻

Of course, Rose was chosen to be the bridesmaid. Hannah swallowed her pride and tried to not be jealous of Olivia and Rose. Again, she'd be left out of the most intimate of wedding plans. She let out a long breath as she trudged up the stairs to her room. It had been a long day at work. Well, every day was a long day.

Registering guests. Was that so important? She would stand there, smile sweetly, and remind people to sign the guest book. She'd done it before. Reality hit her full force. None of her so-called friends ever considered her close enough to include her in the bridal party. She'd never been a bridesmaid—and would probably never a bride. She knew she was too plain.

Bernie entered her thoughts. He'd be a good prospect for a husband, and she liked him a lot. Time would tell.

What would life be like as Bernie's bride? She couldn't imagine that much happiness.

⁓

Rose knocked on Meghan's door. "It's Rose."

"Come in."

Meghan smiled and patted the bed. On the bed were ladies' magazines, assorted sketches, fabric swatches, and various pieces of paper that looked like lists.

"Am I interrupting something?"

"No, just looking things over. I'd like you to look at these and tell me what you think." Meghan gestured to everything on the bed.

"My goodness. You're really planning a big to-do, aren't you?"

"It's a mixture of plain and fancy. If I were being married in St. Louis, I'd have an elaborate wedding. This may seem extravagant here but it would be considered simple in St. Louis."

Rose picked up a magazine and looked at the sketches of bridal gowns. So beautiful, yet she knew they were nothing she could ever afford. Meghan's father however, was quite well-to-do, and Meghan was his only child.

"Are you pleased that I asked you to be my bridesmaid?" Meghan's gaze held her in a penetrating, yet loving way.

She sat. "Yes, but..."

Meghan's lips tightened into a firm line.

"Is it because of what happened?"

Chapter Fifty

Tears clouded Rose's vision. Meghan pushed aside all the magazines, sketches, and lists, and scooted next to her. Some things fell off. She started to rise, but Meghan held her.

"Leave 'em. Please, tell me what you're thinking."

She sniffed. "I just can't—be your bridesmaid. The very word implies purity, and you know very well that I am not."

Her friend put her arm around her shoulders. "No, the word 'maid' means someone not wed. Don't put extra meanings on the word... please." Meghan gave her shoulders a squeeze. "And please—please, be my bridesmaid. I only have two close women friends here—Olivia and you."

She glanced at her friend. "What about Luisa?"

"I'm not close to her. She's harder to get to know. Olivia and her, however..." Meghan looked down.

"They seem to have an understanding with each other."

"Luisa is nice, and we've had a few good visits while in the kitchen. I'm trying to learn *el español*, and she's trying to learn English. We've had less talk about life and more about language usage and grammar." Meghan chuckled. "Carlos and Maria are delightful children though."

She nodded. "Are you *sure* you really want me to be your bridesmaid?"

Meghan rolled her eyes. "Of course, I do. I wouldn't have asked otherwise." She patted Rose's arm. "We're friends—and close ones at that. You asked for a friend, and by golly, you've got one. And this friend wants you to be her bridesmaid."

Rose looked down a moment, then met Meghan's gaze. No condemnation, no judgment, just pure affection and love from her friend. How did she deserve this? She thought back to the moment she'd asked Meghan to be her friend. Was that only six months ago? She still went by Rosie then.

Meghan leaned forward in her chair. "Why did you ask for me?"

She looked up at Meghan and smiled. "Don't you know?" The look on Meghan's face amused her. The girl really had no idea.

Meghan shook her head. "I can't imagine."

She let out a long breath. "I figure we're the same age, though we're totally different." She paused a moment. "I wish I could be like you. I wish I weren't ... what I am." She turned away. Her guilt and shame. She could hardly face this pure young woman, and yet, she needed Meghan to want to be her friend. Otherwise, she had no hope of changing her life—ever.

Meghan briefly touched her good shoulder—the arm Jake hadn't just about wrung off. "It's true, Rosie, we are the same age. But I still don't understand why you wanted me to take care of you, and why you wish to be like me. I'm not perfect."

She turned toward Meghan and wiped a tear. "But you're educated. People respect ya. Wherever ya go, even when ya walk down the street—decent people honor ya with a tip of the hat, a nod, or a smile. When I walk down the street—they turn their heads the other way or walk by me like I'm not even there. I guess what I'm asking ..."

Meghan's expression softened even more. "What would you like me to do?"

She looked down a moment, then straight into Meghan's gaze. "I'd like—if we could—to be friends."

Meghan's breath caught, her eyes widened. What would she say? Turn her down outright?

Rosie turned away a moment, then made eye contact again. Her lips tightened. Another tear rolled down her cheek.

"*I promise I'll keep it secret. I won't ruin your reputation. Won't tell no one of it. Could ya teach me to read and write—have manners—so I can be a lay—dee?*"

She'd certainly shocked Meghan that day, but the young tutor had accepted the offer and a new friendship was born. And her life had never been the same.

"Rose? Are you all right?"

She shook her head and focused her vision on Meghan. "Sorry. I was just thinking."

"You looked a thousand miles away."

She smiled. "No, only about six months. I was rememberin' when I asked ya to be ma friend." Very seldom did she ever revert to her old way of speaking, but she thought this an appropriate time, knowing Meghan would understand.

"You were so hurt. I felt so sorry for you."

"Thank you. You know, Meghan, you've had more to do with me changing my life than anyone, don't you?"

Tears came to Meghan's eyes. "I'm glad to have made a difference. You've helped me so much, too. I love you, Rose."

"And I love you."

Meghan gave her a hug. "Does that mean you'll be in my wedding party?"

She let out a long breath. "Yes, I'll be your bridesmaid."

"Thanks, Rose. You don't know how much that means to me."

No. Meghan didn't know what it meant to *her*.

⁓

Richard Decker entered Scott's office toward the end of the day, carrying a small package. Was that Rose's ring?

"Here it is, Doc. Just came in. I knew you didn't want to wait for it, and frankly, Mike and I are swamped with orders still being placed. You'd think people would realize it's only two days until Christmas."

"I'm glad I ordered early."

"Me, too. It's so busy... it's almost insane how much work we have to do."

"But I bet your sales are good."

Decker nodded, then turned toward the door. "Well, I'm on my lunch break. I just wanted to run this over."

"Oh wait." Scott went to the desk and pulled out his check. "How much was that again?" Decker gave him the figure, and he wrote it in. He handed the check to the storekeeper. "Here you go."

"Thanks, Doc. You can do business with us anytime." Decker smirked.

"Always do. You're the only mercantile in town."

"Thank goodness for that." Decker pocketed the check, then left.

Scott opened the box. The ring was stunning. Hopefully, Rose would realize how much he loved her when she saw this. Diamond rings were just beginning to become popular back East to celebrate an engagement. His cousin had given one to his fiancée a year or so ago. Reportedly, the woman fainted when she saw it.

Rose was made of stronger stuff. He couldn't wait to see her face.

⁓

Christmas Day started out slow for Rose. She relished lying in bed a little longer, even though she smelled Luisa's huevos rancheros and cinnamon rolls from downstairs. What a strange combination. Having Luisa help Olivia with the cooking certainly kept things interesting. Luisa was learning Olivia's way of cooking, but Luisa's Mexican dishes were also delicious and popular. There was a spicy smell to huevos rancheros, though. For those who didn't like them,

Olivia had made cinnamon rolls. She'd probably made regular eggs and bacon, as well.

The last few days had been long and trying. A little girl from a farm north of New Boston had been brought into the medical office a few days ago with a high fever. Scott had diagnosed it as the grippe. A couple of days later, her brother was brought in. The large Mennonite family lived about twenty miles north of New Boston. For them to make the trip twice in one week was a hardship—not only financially, she knew, but to be away from the constant chores of the farm. She only knew they were endless because they'd told her. At Jake's small farm, the work wasn't constant.

As she lay in bed, she thought about the time she'd have with Scott later today. He'd gotten her something special for Christmas. Meghan had hinted, but Rose had no idea what it could be.

She'd carefully wrapped the special handkerchief she'd embroidered for him, plus the cuff links she'd ordered from The Pioneer Store. She hoped he liked them. She couldn't wait to see the look on his face.

Chapter Fifty-One

A knock sounded at Hannah's door. She smelled breakfast and could hardly wait to get downstairs. But she'd caught her dress on the corner of the dresser and torn a small piece of lace off around the cuff. She'd just begun to repair it when someone knocked.

"Just a moment." She inserted the needle partially into the cuff and answered the door.

Bernie stood smiling.

"Merry Christmas, Hannah." He held out a small wrapped package.

"M-Mister Warkentyne!"

"Thought we—were—past—how you say—formal names."

"Formalities. Okay, then—Bernie. Y-You shouldn't have. I don't have your present ready yet. If you could wait downstairs for me for a few minutes, I-I'll be right down."

"No—I stand here—keep things—proper." His English was improving.

"S-Suit yourself." She pulled the needle out and reattached the lace by whipstitch, careful to blend the stitch in with the lace pattern wherever possible. Ma had taught her how to properly mend so it wouldn't show. She was grateful.

"So...what—is—*my* Christmas present, Hannah?"

She giggled. "Wouldn't you like to know? Y-You'll find out later...after dinner."

"Aw, come on. Can't you give me—hint? I'm ready to give my present. Don't want anyone know."

Bernie had come a long way in his learning of English. She's been helping him on those times they walked home from work together, and sometimes at meals. He didn't always get every word right, but he'd greatly improved.

"Wh-why not?" Very mysterious, and intriguing.

"Personal gift. Made it myself. Except hinge. Ordered that."

"Now you've r-really got me curious." She tied off the thread, then inspected her work by turning her wrist around and around.

He handed her the package. She turned it every which way but couldn't figure out what was in it.

"Open it." He laughed. "Women... how you—delay!"

"I-I like to savor the moment."

He grabbed the package and started to untie the ribbon, then handed it back to her. She opened it quickly.

She gasped. An intricately carved small box lay in the palm of her hand. A cardinal had been etched and painted in the cedar wood. He'd obviously spent a lot of time on this.

"B-Bernie, it-it's..."

"You are welcome. Less personal gift under tree. You open later." His smile lit up his whole face. He was so handsome.

"Thank you. But you shouldn't have."

"Maybe not. Hannah..." He paused a moment. "I have—feelings for you. I want—like —court you. If you—let me."

Her heart thumped a fast rat-tat-tat. He had feelings for her! Warmth flowed through her veins like hot tea.

"I-I give you my permission." Dare she hope he thought of her more than a friend? Wanting to court her certainly made it seem so. Or was it wishful thinking?

⌒

Scott tied a pretty forest green ribbon around his package. Decker had suggested wrapping it in bright green satin and had given him a fabric scrap. The trick was to keep all the edges of the scrap underneath the ribbon, which he'd crisscrossed around the ring box. He couldn't wait to see Rose's face when she saw it.

He'd wrapped a slightly less fancy package for her to open under the tree in front of everyone. As much as he loved the excitement of Christmas, he knew it would be better for Rose to give her the ring in private.

Her "under-the-tree" package was a brooch he'd bought a day or so after he'd ordered the ring. His family back in Kansas City only gave presents to his nieces and nephews. Since he wasn't going to be there, he'd sent money to his mother to spend on her grandchildren on his behalf.

A knock at the door pulled him from his thoughts. No more limp. It felt so good to walk normally. Only at night did his leg ache. Probably because he was tired and had been on his feet all day.

Stuart Randall peeked in. "Hey, Scott, are ya up? Merry Christmas!"

He waved Stuart in. "Merry Christmas! What's the weather like out there today? Any chance of snow?"

Stuart closed the door behind him and moved toward the couch. "Nah. It's kinda cold and cloudy but no snow. Doesn't have that feel."

He humphed. "Children will be unhappy about that."

"They certainly will. What was Christmas like at your home?"

Scott cocked his head to one side. "Well, since there were a bunch of us kids, we all clamored for attention once we got downstairs. 'Did Santa Claus come?' 'Where is he?' 'Is he still here?' That sort of thing. Mother and Father just stood at the Christmas tree and pointed to the floor. When we saw our presents, we scrambled to get the best spot next to our folks. It was chaotic."

Stuart snorted. "What do you mean by that?"

He chuckled. "Our parents were very methodical in handing out presents. We children always hoped ours would be the first one given. You can imagine, then, how the six of us, varying ages, tried to maneuver for places so we could sit on the floor right in front of our parents. It was a free-for-all." Scott shook his head but smiled at the memory.

"We didn't really have much of a Christmas when I grew up. It was just another day."

He frowned. "I'm sorry to hear that."

Stuart shook his head in dismissal. "It's all right. I've come to appreciate the holiday as an adult." He cleared his throat. "Are you ready to go? I've heard Missus Baldwin and that Mexican cook of hers are preparing a feast."

He nodded. "They sure are. Have you been formally introduced to Olivia Baldwin?"

"I think we met once, but I don't remember exactly when or what the circumstances were."

"She's a true southern woman, but she's also a bit of a spitfire."

"Really? How so?"

Scott laughed. "You should have seen her earlier this year when Meghan Gallagher got grazed by a stray bullet. She barged in here and tried to take charge. Pretty near bowled Miss Gallagher over in her intense enthusiasm."

"You mean she tried to take charge?"

"Not exactly, but when she gets nervous, she talks more than a hen in a chicken house. One can hardly get a word in."

Stuart nodded, one side of his lips curled up.

He snickered. "I declare. Are you thinking of courting her?"

The smile grew larger. "Maybe."

He laughed and punched Stuart's shoulder. "I wish you luck then, Sheriff."

༄

The dinner table was all set. Everyone had arrived. What a grand feast it was, too. Rose hadn't seen the likes of this before... a huge roasted turkey with cooked sausages all around, boiled herb potatoes, potato balls, creamed corn, lima beans, cranberry sauce, and stewed tomatoes. For drinks, glasses of cold water kept outside for a couple of hours in the shade. Tea would be served later. Rose sipped the coolness and let it slide down her throat. The colder the better, in her opinion.

She sat between Duncan and Scott on one side of the table, with Meghan on the other side of Duncan. Sheriff Randall, Hannah, Bernie, and Jackson sat on the other side. She was happy to see Jackson back at the dinner table. He didn't have family here. It was kind of Olivia to invite him to both Thanksgiving and Christmas dinners. Glancing to Hannah's left, Rose smiled as Sheriff Randall couldn't seem to take his eyes off Olivia. Was he attracted to her? Olivia deserved to be happy, but she hadn't even been widowed quite a year yet.

At the end to Hannah's left, were Olivia and Maria. The little girl had taken a liking to Meghan, who sat just to the girl's right. Carlos sat next to Luisa at the other end of the table.

Olivia rose and gave the blessing, and then food was passed. For a moment, Rose wondered who would get the honor of carving the turkey.

Sheriff Randall leaned over Hannah and addressed Bernie. "I wouldn't mind helping. It's been a while, but I could help—once you started it."

Bernie smiled. "I'd be glad to share carving duties with you, Sheriff." He stood and carved a few slices, then handed the knife over to Randall, who cut several more, at least enough for each person at the table to have one slice. Except for Maria, who shared a slice with Olivia.

Jackson cleared his throat and took a drink of water. He pulled at the bow tie around the collar of his shirt. Usually, he was dressed in an open-collared shirt, with snappy navy-blue Santa Fe vest or jacket, depending on whether it was summer or now, winter. He looked uncomfortable and seemed unusually quiet.

Conversation buzzed around her like a swarm of gnats.

Rose wondered what was wrong. "Jackson, are you feeling all right?"

His head jerked up as he met her gaze.

"Yes, Miss Rose. I's all right. I's just un-comfor'able." He took another sip of water.

"Are you sure? You could take off your tie and unbutton your collar." Scott set his glass down after taking a sip.

"That ain't gonna help, Doc. I's just tol' somethin' hard yesterday, and the town ain't gonna like it. No sir, dey ain't gonna like it one bit."

Scott picked up his knife and fork. "Then the rumors are true—aren't they? The railhead is moving to Wichita. When?"

Around the table, conversation stopped. Rose glanced around. All eyes were on Jackson. Poor man. How horrible to be put in this position of being the bearer of bad tidings. Especially on Christmas Day.

Jackson coughed. "Come spring."

Meghan inhaled sharply.

She could have heard a napkin drop from the table. Everyone was quiet for a moment—then all spoke at once. Goodness, how she felt sorry for Jackson. He couldn't change the decision. Finally, Sheriff Randall stood and dinged the side of his glass with his knife.

"May I have your attention, please."

All talk stopped.

"You all know Jackson is not an executive, correct? He doesn't have any more information than what's been told him."

Meghan leaned forward. "They didn't even tell *me,* yet."

"Please, Jackson, is there anything you can tell us?" Duncan's voice was tender and kind. A soft, understanding expression showed the cowboy's compassion for the station manager's dilemma.

Jackson took another sip of water and cleared his throat. "Well, they done tol' me that come spring, railhead's movin' ta Wichita.

Dey got better position than us... more people, more water, land. More of everythin'. And dey dat much closer to Texas than us."

"That's ridiculous!" Olivia practically snorted. "What are we gonna do now? They're leaving us high and dry. Santa Fe started this town. We're here because they made promises."

"It will be all right. You'll see." Bernie's gaze flitted from one person to another around the table.

"Mama—that mean we—leave?" Little Maria, bless her heart. She was wide-eyed. Her lips turned downward.

Bernie stood then. "Listen, folks. I—wanted—wait until things—finalized. Letters I've written to people—my faith—who look for new start. New Boston won't die. Industry, business—change, but we stay and make good of it."

He must be nervous. His English became more broken like when she'd first talked to him. Was that only three months ago? He'd worked hard on his English and was learning quickly. She suspected Hannah was responsible for that.

Olivia put her fork down and leaned back in her chair. "But what will the town do? Who are these people you've written to? What is your faith? I thought you were Christian."

Bernie sat and continued passing food along while cutting up his turkey. "Mennonite. I wrote people—in Germany and Russia. Months ago. When I—first—came. Thought farmers and cattlemen—share land."

Duncan cleared his throat. "That doesn't usually work out too well, in my experience. It's usually one or the other."

"Haven't heard back. Takes long to reach Russia from here. More months till I hear if anyone comes." He stopped and took a sip of water. "They—many—will come. You—see. Farming begin—when ranch ends. Friends live north. Support New Boston—come for supplies often. Not many stores yet."

"I hope you're right." Scott forked in a small piece of potato ball.

"It—be all right. Trust me. And God. This—best solution. God work all out."

Rose wasn't sure what she thought about that. The tension coming from Scott next to her on one side was nothing compared to the frustration radiating from Duncan on the other.

What would happen? Would New Boston survive?

Chapter Fifty-Two

"There's to be a town meetin' after the New Year." Jackson put his coat on. "Doc, you gonna be there, won't ya? Ye're an influence in town. Calm da people's fears."

"Of course I'll be there. I wouldn't miss it."

Scott closed the door as Jackson left.

Just when the town was getting its bearings after the gunfights, now the railhead was moving. Would New Boston survive? He hoped so. Time to think more about this later. It was Christmas Day, and he needed to give Rose her present.

He turned to her. "Are you ready for your Christmas gift?"

She smiled. Warmth traveled from his spine down to his toes. "Let's go into the parlor."

"Meghan and Duncan are in there." Evidently, Rose wanted as much as he did to be alone together. The boardinghouse wasn't that large, as he was finding out. In the summer, there'd been lots of places to go... take a walk, sit on one of the porches. But now it was winter... he couldn't give Rose her engagement ring on a walk or on the porch.

"I don't think they'll mind." He dug his hand in his pocket and felt the small package. "In fact, I think they'll be very pleased."

Her eyes grew wide, then narrowed. "What are you up to, Doctor Allison?" She only used that tone of voice when playful—or mildly suspicious.

"Oh, something special." His face stretched with his grin. He could hardly wait to see her reaction.

"All right. Let's go." She led the way to the parlor, where Meghan and Duncan sat on the settee. Rose sat in one of the wingback chairs.

He cleared his throat and stood behind the chair a moment. "It's entirely appropriate that you two are here to witness this moment." He moved around to the front of the chair and knelt in front of Rose, turning his head to talk with Meghan and Duncan. When he turned back, Rose's eyes were as large as some of the eggs he got in payment. Her lovely mouth opened slightly, and she licked her lips.

He grabbed the small package in his pocket and brought it out. "Rose, my love, merry Christmas."

Rose gasped as she took Scott's gift in her hands and fumbled with the ribbon.

"Ooh! I wonder what it is! I'll bet I know." Meghan's expression was wide and smiling. Duncan grinned, too. Whatever this was, they seemed to know about it, and approved. What was it? Everyone had already opened all their packages under the tree. Scott had given her a beautiful brooch... a green background cameo with an antique finished filigree around the edges.

Finally, she unwrapped a little box. Her heart fluttered as she pulled the top off.

It took her breath away.

A star-shaped diamond solitaire ring sparkled in the light, creating red, blue, green, and gold off the different facets.

"Rose, I am now officially asking you—in front of witnesses. Will you do me the tremendous honor of becoming my precious wife? I love you more than I ever thought possible."

Her eyes misted, her vision blurred. A tear ran down her cheek. How could she possibly say no? She loved him so much. There had to be a way to make this happen. He'd spent his hard-earned cash, which she knew wasn't abundant, on this ring and the brooch. She knew he'd also sent money to his mother to spend on his nieces and nephews since he wouldn't be there for Christmas. He must have been saving up a couple of months for this.

She met his gaze. Love poured from his eyes straight down into her heart. How she loved him!

"Yes. Of course I'll marry you." She fell out of the chair and into his arms. He was soft and warm, and fit her so perfectly. She always marveled at that.

Meghan and Duncan clapped softly behind her.

"Congratulations! I'm so happy for you!" Meghan's sweet voice called from behind her.

She drew away from Scott a moment, giving him a sweet smile, trying to convey she'd be back in his arms in a moment. She stood and met Meghan's hug.

A strong hand grasped her shoulder. Must be Duncan. "Congratulations, Rose. You deserve to be as happy as I am!"

She turned and hugged him, too.

"Here, now! Wait a minute! She's my lady!" Scott came to claim her and put his arm around her waist.

"Well, put it on!" Meghan's cheer could not be denied.

Scott gently pulled the ring out of the velvet sleeve, then slipped it on her finger.

It was breathtaking. Never had she owned such a beautiful ring. She'd had lots of gaudy, cheap costume jewelry rings, but never the real thing. Its simple beauty touched her heart. A thin gold band—a wedding band underneath, the star would help anchor the diamond to the wedding ring. Now she could hardly wait.

But she'd have to. Nothing was resolved. She let out a deep breath.

"Thank you, Scott. I love you so much. I don't deserve you. I don't deserve..." She pulled her handkerchief from her sleeve and dabbed her eyes.

From a distance, it seemed, she felt, rather than heard Meghan and Duncan slip out of the parlor, leaving her alone with Scott.

Scott pulled her into his embrace.

Her tears flowed unchecked. She didn't deserve to feel this happy.

⁓

New Year's Day 1872 began quietly at the boardinghouse. Hannah was glad, because she'd had a sore throat for two days. The restaurant had remained open until just after midnight to celebrate the new year. She'd been working extra hours in addition to her own, because several of the girls either were out sick or hadn't returned from their Christmas break.

When she got home the night before, she threw off her coat and jumped into bed without even changing into her bedclothes. She was that tired.

Even though she smelled breakfast being prepared downstairs, she couldn't bear to get out of bed. Every time she moved, a chill enveloped her. She must change into her nightgown. Yet she couldn't muster up the strength to do it.

She fell back to sleep wondering when she'd feel well enough to change clothes.

⁓

"Anyone seen Hannah this morning?" Olivia placed a platter of scrambled eggs on the dining table. Rose's stomach growled. She hoped no one heard.

"I haven't seen her." Bernie sounded worried. "Should someone check? Make sure she—all right?"

"I go." Luisa laid a platter of bacon on the table. "Need wake *los ninos.*"

Rose had thought about responding, but she was hungry, and needed to keep up her strength. More patients kept coming to the office. Scott planned to add on when spring came... so he could call it a clinic. That way, he didn't have to give up his own bedroom when a more serious patient needed more time to recover.

Luisa dashed into the dining room. "Olivia, Rose, come—*por favor*. Hannah sick. Meghan, too."

Meghan was sick too? Oh no! Scott said the grippe could be fatal sometimes. Meghan couldn't be seriously ill. She had such a wonderful future.

Rose stood. "I'll check on Meghan and be right over to see Hannah."

Bernie stood, too.

No thought was given to breakfast now.

⁓

Hannah felt something cool on her forehead. She shivered. Chill after chill, like an icy breeze that never let up. Yet when she felt her own forehead, it was hot.

"It's all right, dearie. You'll be fine. Just rest." Olivia's sweet southern drawl penetrated her semi-sleep.

"Olivia, what time is it?" Hannah tried to rise, but weakness overtook her.

"Don't worry about that. You just rest." Olivia pressed a hand to Hannah's shoulder.

She didn't have the strength to fight.

"Next time you wake up, we'll change you into your nightie, but now it's more important to keep you warm."

She dreamed of Grammy... the most loving person she'd ever met. The sweet older woman had taken good care of Hannah whenever her parents were needed elsewhere.

"Hannah, dear," Grammy would always say, putting her arm around Hannah's shoulders and giving her a hug. "Everything will be all right. Just trust in the Lord, and he will make your path straight."

Her life hadn't been horrible in Ohio, but she'd wanted more. And she'd gotten more here, as a Harvey girl.

Another chill enveloped her—even in her dreams. She heard a moan from far away.

Was it her own?

Rose laid a fresh towel next to Meghan's bed. She was tossing and turning. How had she caught the grippe? Was it from the students at school? Rose turned and dipped a fresh washcloth in the water basin, on the desk near Meghan's bed, and wrung it out.

"Rose."

Meghan's eyes were open and looking at her.

"How are you feeling?"

"What's going on? I tried getting out of bed this morning, but I'm just too tired."

Rose cleared her throat. "I think you've caught the grippe. Do you have any chills? Or nausea?"

"No, I'm just incredibly tired, and my throat is sore."

"You may still be coming down with it."

"Oh no. Today we start our new church."

"Well, Duncan will have to do that by himself. I'm sure he's quite capable. He's been having his own church by himself for quite a while, hasn't he?"

"Yes, but..."

"I know you want to be with him, but you need to take care of yourself first. Last summer, and even into the fall, you took care of him. You stayed with me when Jake beat me last spring. Now it's time for you to take care of yourself, and let me help."

Meghan's smile was weak. Rose dabbed her forehead with the damp washcloth and pushed her hair off her cheeks.

"You've talked about the grippe the last week or so. It's bad, isn't it? A lot of people are getting it?"

Rose pulled the chair next to the bed and sat. "Some cases are worse than others."

"I've had a sore throat since yesterday, but I thought it would go away if I went to bed early. That's why I sent Duncan back to the ranch before midnight."

"Sore throat is one of the first symptoms, but it's the same for the common cold, too." She stood. "You get some rest now. I'll check on you later. Hannah came down with it, too."

"Oh, poor girl. I'm sorry about that."

"She's young and strong, like you are. I'm sure you'll both be fine very soon."

"Thanks, Rose."

She smiled. "Finally returning the favor." She squeezed Meghan's shoulder and went to check on Hannah.

⁓

Olivia rose from the chair next to Hannah's bed when Rose entered.

Hannah mumbled a moment, then spoke clearly. "Grammy? Are you there?"

Olivia shook her head, motioning Rose close, and whispered. "She's dreaming, I think."

"Not delirious?"

"She doesn't seem to be. When she's awake, she's perfectly alert, though a bit slow of thought."

"Everyone's thinking is affected by illness." Rose went to the bed, leaned over, and checked Hannah's glands. They were swollen. Putting the back of her hand on Hannah's forehead, she felt the heat. Just then, Hannah shivered. Of course, chills too. The cough would come later.

Rose lightly shook Hannah's shoulder. "Hannah, can you wake up for me?"

The girl opened her eyes and blinked a few times. "Rose? What time is it?" Hannah rubbed her eyes, then looked past Rose to Olivia.

"Olivia?" Hannah's brow furrowed. "What's going on?"

Chapter Fifty-Three

The girl tried to rise, and quickly sank back into the bed.

Rose smiled her comforting smile. "You have the grippe. But you should be fine in about a week. We'll take good care of you. Do you think you can sit up long enough for Olivia and I to help you change into your nightgown? Let me help you a bit, so you don't get dizzy."

Hannah rose onto an elbow, and then Olivia and Rose helped her up the rest of the way. A shiver racked the girl when they removed her blouse. She'd been sweating, which was a good sign, but she needed clean undergarments.

Olivia said, "Where are your intimates?"

Hannah nodded toward her dresser. "In the top drawer. Thanks for helping me. I was so tired last night I just flopped into bed when I got home."

"That's what friends are for."

"Thank you."

They said little as they helped Hannah into clean undergarments and nightgown and bed jacket. They also removed her hairpins, combed out her hair, and put on a bed cap to keep her head warm.

Once Hannah was resettled in bed, Olivia left to go make broth and check on Meghan. Rose sat in the chair.

"Rose—are you excited about marrying the doctor?"

Where did that come from? She smiled. "Of course I am."

"When? Have you set a date yet?"

"No. But we probably won't marry until after Meghan and Duncan."

"Why don't you have a double wedding? I've heard of that happening sometimes. Or you could get married before."

"I don't want to take away from Meghan's special day. That wouldn't be fair after all she and Duncan have been through." She let out a breath. Marry before her friend? She'd never thought of that. There was no reason she had to wait, though... except in her own heart.

She looked down and fingered the ring Scott had given her for Christmas. Such an extravagance. But she loved it, for it symbolized his love and devotion to her. And his intent to marry.

A hush controlled the room. She looked over. Good. Hannah had fallen asleep. That was best. She slipped out of the room, still thinking about how unworthy of Scott's love she was.

⁓

By midafternoon the next day, Scott ran a hand through his hair and let out a deep breath. Six new cases of the grippe. At this rate, he'd never get any sleep. A knock on the door assured him he wouldn't get any now, either.

Rose entered. He moved toward her and took her in his arms, only kissing her lightly. "I don't want you to get the grippe."

She looked up at him. So trusting and beautiful. He couldn't take his eyes off her. His gaze lowered to her lips, then back to her eyes. She rose on her tiptoes and kissed him... a long, thorough kiss that made him want to stay in that moment forever. He pulled her closer and let his passion carry him away... only a moment. When she stepped out of his arms, he felt empty. Someday soon, he would never let her leave his embrace.

"I won't, silly." That playful smile of hers. The way her lips curled up and her top teeth gently touched her bottom lip.

He helped her with her coat. "How are Hannah and Meghan?" He had real concerns about Hannah.

"Hannah can't sit up very long, but she is taking broth. She hasn't thrown up yet. Unfortunately, Meghan is. Hopefully, she'll be better by tomorrow. Her cowboy has already been to visit, with Olivia present, of course. Bernie is helping Olivia a bit with Hannah... when Luisa or I can go in with him. He seems to really like her. I hadn't noticed before."

"I'll check on them tonight, with you, of course."

"There's no need for you to come. You have so many other patients. I'm doing fine with them on my own."

He stroked her cheek with the back of his fingers. "I know. You're very competent. Humor me, will you? I like to pretend I'm a doctor." She smiled and pushed her cheek closer.

"How many new patients today?"

"Six."

"How many total?"

"A dozen, and that includes Meghan and Hannah."

"You're concerned about an epidemic, aren't you?"

"If we keep getting this many new patients every day, we'll have to do something drastic."

"What would we do?"

"Well, we'll have to gather all the sick patients in one place, to keep them isolated from the healthy."

"Where in town could we do that? There's no place big enough. How many are we talking about?"

"A hundred or so, possibly."

"Oh no!"

"It's possible. If we can keep this outbreak from becoming more serious by separating the sick, it will keep more people healthy. I think either the hotel or the boardinghouse would be a good place."

"The boardinghouse isn't that big."

"Olivia has a few empty rooms now, doesn't she?"

"But she couldn't possibly handle that many. Not only that, but the de Campo children live there. So far, they're all right, but how long will they remain healthy if we move more sick people near them? I don't like that idea at all."

"I'll speak to the hotel manager. Maybe the ballroom could be used. We can pray against an epidemic, although it's close to that now."

"Yes. Praying it stops."

"Rose—how are *you*?"

She looked at him with questions in her eyes. "I'm fine."

"I mean, how are you really?"

Her eyes narrowed a bit. "I'm all right. Really, I am. With all that's going on right now, I haven't had time to think about myself. I believe you, Scott, when you say that we can be happy. I believe in God. I'm trying to forgive. I don't know...I just..."

"It's all right. Forget I asked. God is helping you. It's all right if it takes a little time. I'm patient."

"And for that, my dear Doctor Allison, I'm so thankful. I love you."

A knock at the door kept him from kissing her soundly again.

⁓

The chills had stopped, finally, but now a cough had set in. Hannah couldn't stop coughing. Lying flat in the bed, which had felt so good earlier in the week—now brought on a coughing spell. Her head pounded after a while. She couldn't sleep. Earlier in the week, that's all she did. How was she to rest and get well if she couldn't sleep?

Yet every day, most days, she would feel a little better than the day before. If it weren't for the cough, she'd feel fine.

Bernie had been so attentive. She hated that he saw her like this. But his gentle strength and encouraging words were like a healing balm.

A knock at the door had her pulling her covers up farther, just in case it was Bernie.

"Come—in." She coughed.

Olivia entered with a pitcher, a teapot, a bowl of something steaming, and condiments. "How are you feeling?"

She coughed and cleared her throat, which led to more coughing as her throat went dry. She nodded weakly and tried to smile. Sometimes she could hardly catch her breath.

Olivia set the tray down on the desk, then helped her sit up against the edge of the bed. She hated eating in bed. Maybe tomorrow she would be able to sit at the desk. Being in bed all the time was making her hips and shoulders ache. Her stomach and chest were already sore from all the coughing, her voice raspy.

"You don't have to talk. I hope you can eat this. It's vegetable chicken soup—mostly broth, but there's a little chicken in there, some carrots, celery, and a few peas. Nothing heavy."

She took a drink from the glass Olivia offered, then handed it back.

"Is there any way I could sleep this way, propped up? When I lie down, I cough. Are there extra pillows I could use so I could lean over to the side a bit?"

Olivia smiled. "Let's see what we can figure out. As soon as you finish your lunch." She set the tray over Hannah's lap, then turned to leave.

"How's Meghan?"

Olivia's lips tightened into a fine line. "Not as well off as you, but I think she'll be fine in a couple days. She cast up her contents. You didn't. That made her a bit weak, but she hasn't coughed yet. The grippe seems to be hitting everyone differently."

"Everyone? Are there a lot of people sick?"

Olivia let out a long breath. "Yes, not quite enough to call it an epidemic yet, but Doctor Allison is concerned. If he does declare an epidemic, everyone ill will be moved to one central location. So—you'd better get well quick." Olivia smiled and left.

She looked at the soup and her stomach growled. Her appetite had been somewhat affected during the chills and fever, but now she was a bit hungry. The soup smelled good. Hopefully, it wouldn't get stuck in her throat.

She'd do anything not to cough. It exhausted her and wouldn't let her rest. She'd never had the grippe like this before, to where she couldn't lie down. It was hard to sleep. She wasn't used to sleeping in anything but a flat position.

Olivia stuck her head back in the door. "I'll be back in a few minutes, and we'll set you up with some extra pillows."

"Thanks Olivia. I'm sorry to be such a bother."

Olivia smiled. "It's no trouble—you're a friend. I take care of my friends."

A friend? Really?

Chapter Fifty-Four

Two days later, Rose watched the snow fall from the office window. It was beautiful but wouldn't help people recover from the grippe. At least there were no more new cases—not that they'd heard of. The Mennonite farmers who lived north of New Boston seemed to be all right now. Scott hadn't had to call it an epidemic and take those drastic measures, but the new year was certainly not starting out well.

The Santa Fe executives had called a public meeting tonight to explain why they were moving the railhead. People murmured about it everywhere she went. The meeting would be held in the hotel, in the very ballroom where Scott would have created a makeshift hospital.

A knock at the door brought her attention back to the matters at hand.

"Meghan! Are you all right? What are you doing out of bed?"

Her friend coughed and practically fell onto the couch after she trudged in. Rose got her a drink of water quick. Meghan drank it down as if she had just been in the desert on a hot day.

"Hannah's worse. She can't sleep and started throwing up now."

"Oh dear. Why didn't Olivia come?"

"I'm feeling much better, and I needed to get out."

"You shouldn't be out in this snow and cold."

"Someone had to tell you we need more cough medicine and anything you have. Poor Hannah is beside herself in discomfort.

I wasn't quite that bad off. Yes, I threw up a day, but then I started to get better—except for my cough. But even that's much improved."

Meghan took another drink of water and lounged, pulling her coat tighter around her.

Rose turned to Scott.

He shook his head. "We're completely out of cough medicine. So many have needed it."

"Could we make our own?"

He thought a moment, putting a knuckle to his lips. "It's possible."

Oh, how she wanted to take that knuckle... and kiss... no, how she wanted to move the knuckle and press her lips to his and keep them there until she couldn't breathe. Stop it. This was not the time... or the place.

"Yes, we can do this. Rose, get the medicinal whiskey, and let's take Meghan home." He quickly wrote a note and fastened it to a nail at the window frame. Anyone coming for help would see it and know they'd gone to the boardinghouse. She hoped Meghan hadn't caught her death with a relapse.

⌒

Hannah sprawled, leaning to the left over a mountain of pillows, and yet she was still so very uncomfortable. So very tired, yet she couldn't sleep. Every minute or so, her throat tickled, making coughing unbearable. Clearing her throat did nothing. She must cough. Nearly impossible to stop once started. Surely, her insides would spill out. Or gag until she couldn't breathe. Olivia and Luisa took turns bringing broth and hot tea to her three to four times a day. Or more? Time dragged on and she had no idea what day it was. She couldn't think straight.

In the evening, Rose would sometimes sit with her and read. Or Bernie.

Bernie. God bless Bernie. How precious he was. She wished he didn't have to see her in this hateful condition. But his expression was always kind, even worried. Was she that ill? He was so attentive, and last weekend, he sat and read to her. From different books. He would read from the Bible, then from Mark Twain or something else.

He'd always press his lips to her forehead before he left, then kiss the back of her hand. No one had ever kissed the back of her hand back home. As she thought of it, a shiver went through her that nothing to do with the grippe. His stubble tickled her skin and he never failed to smile. Even though she felt like she'd been run over by a horse or mule.

She closed her eyes and prayed. And coughed. *Please, Lord, take this cough away and allow me to sleep.*

Her thoughts drifted from time to time. And the horrible tickle in her throat would start up again. She'd cough. Uncontrollable and unstoppable.

What day was it? It had to be a week into the new year. How long had she been ill? Since New Year's Day. She remembered that.

If this coughing was a sign that she was getting better, she'd gladly trade and go back to the chills. Yet, she hated that, too—never being warm enough.

Lord, when would this end?

Then, a terrible thought. Would she die? She was too young. And yet children died every day from all sorts of things. So did young women.

She would fight this—and do whatever it took to get well.

⁓

Scott walked south on Main Street, behind Rose and Meghan, letting them take his buggy. Meghan should have had more sense than to get out in this, though he understood her need to get out of the boardinghouse after being ill. He hoped she didn't suffer a relapse because of this foolishness. *God, help her.*

While walking, he mentally put together a recipe for a concoction that included a dram of medicinal whiskey, spices, and honey or molasses, combined with either lemon or apple cider vinegar. Maybe he'd make a couple of different types. He'd also make some nonalcoholic medicine, too... just in case more children became ill. The stronger stuff would be for the worst cases. He suspected Hannah would be borderline. He'd see how a non-alcoholic potion worked first. But she needed sleep, and her cough wasn't allowing her to get any. Which probably meant the other women on her floor weren't getting much either. And, whoever might be on the floor above her.

Although he hadn't had to call for the drastic measures of an epidemic, thank God, there might still be a few new cases. He prayed they would not be severe.

Chapter Fifty-Five

Hannah coughed and coughed. It wouldn't stop until she gagged. Then blessed relief for a couple of minutes. She'd almost fall asleep in that short time. Before it started all over again.

She'd resigned herself to try to be content with dozing, sipping water whenever she could. But if the water went down wrong, she would choke and that was worse.

A knock on the door drew her from her thoughts. Rose and Doctor Allison entered her room. She instinctively pulled her sheets up to her chin.

"How are you feeling?" Doctor Allison took out his stethoscope and put the ends in his ears, then gently pushed her covers down a few inches. "May I have a listen?"

All she could do was cough.

He smiled. "I'll take your pulse instead." He reached for her wrist and pressed his fingers over it and squeezed gently. "Let's get some of this freshly-made cough remedy in you. I made it myself—well, with the help of Rose and Olivia." His expression showed he cared. "I'm so sorry you have to go through this."

She coughed in response, then swallowed a drink of water. "Thank you, Doctor."

He poured some of his concoction into a glass and handed it to her.

It was sour and sweet at the same time. And strong. Her throat burned as it went down. Almost immediately, she coughed and felt even more tired, if that were possible.

She closed her eyes, not being able to keep them open. It seemed that finally, she was drifting off to sleep. In the background she heard voices.

"When she wakes up, have her drink another dose just like this one."

"Thank you, Scott." Rose's sweet voice.

"Will she be all right now?" Olivia's drawl was the last thing she heard.

⌒

Later that evening, Scott, Rose, Olivia, and Bernie Warkentyne left the boardinghouse to attend the Santa Fe meeting.

They rode in two buggies. Scott drove Rose in his buggy, and Olivia and Warkentyne rode together in Olivia's buggy.

They entered the hotel. Small groups of people made their way to the ballroom or stood off to the side. They seemed to be waiting for something—or someone. Scott didn't know what. He only knew he wanted to get good seats toward the front, preferring to be closer to whatever was going to happen.

As they walked into the elegant ballroom, Scott couldn't help himself. He stared, even though he was somewhat used to elegance. In Kansas City, he'd been to several ballrooms and elegant dining and living rooms. One fancy hotel had sponsored a dance for young women "coming out." Although his family was probably classified as "lower elite," they were still invited to all the major, and many minor, social affairs of "the season." Mother had explained to him that young women of good families needed this special introduction to society to find young men of quality, such as himself. He'd always felt a little shy around girls he didn't know very well. But he'd conquered his shyness and felt comfortable and confident around young women now. Being a doctor meant he had to overcome any sort of lack of self-confidence. And he'd done it while in medical college.

His thoughts turned to Rose. She was a great complement to him. Smart, beautiful, compassionate, and caring—a quick learner, teachable, and strong. He loved her so much. He'd seen her transform her appearance to the degree that even some of those closest to her didn't recognize her. He thought that odd at first. People usually only looked at the surface, not beneath it. So far, she'd gotten away with her new identity. But for how long?

Determined to see her through anything, Scott decided then and there that he would do whatever it took to get Rose established in her new identity. If the town found out, he'd support her right to change. And if anyone insulted her... well... they'd have to deal with him. Rose deserved her second chance after all she'd been through.

He looked around the spacious ballroom. At the far end, a couple of hundred chairs had been set up theater style, in front of a small stage and podium. Three chairs were placed at one end of the small stage, to the right of whoever the speaker would be. Scott figured those two chairs were for the two Santa Fe Railroad executives, Fagin and Baker. But who would sit in the third?

Fagin walked up to him. "Doctor Allison. I'm glad to see you here. How are the townspeople doing? I heard you didn't declare an epidemic. I'm happy about that. I was afraid people would panic. That would have been disastrous."

"I'm thankful, too. We only have a few bad cases requiring special medication." He leaned in toward Fagin. "Is it true you are announcing the railhead move tonight? Won't that be a cause for concern?"

Fagin put his index finger on his lips. "We don't want to cause undue alarm ahead of time. The rumors are already spreading, and we can't stop them. I'm just hoping people won't create a riot."

"Why would they do that?"

"You'll see. I'm asking you, Doctor Allison, to help me and Mister Baker keep order. You're a respected man in the community, and we'll need the voice of calm and reason. I expect you to be that voice." Fagin's gaze was strong and steady.

"I'll do my best. But, where's Sheriff Randall?"

"He got called away an hour ago. Sent his regrets."

Fagin moved to the platform and motioned for Scott to join him. As expected, Baker sat in the other seat beside Fagin. Scott tried unsuccessfully to hide his height as he mounted the small platform and sat in the vacant chair indicated by Baker.

The executive stepped to the podium and clapped his hands.

"Attention! May I please have your attention?" Fagin's voice boomed and almost echoed across the room. The murmuring began to wane as most of the chairs were filled once people sat down.

He glanced at Rose, sitting in the front row of the audience. Since he couldn't sit with her, at least he could see her. She smiled at him. It sent a warm river all through him.

Finally, the noise quieted.

"Friends and fellow citizens of New Boston. In case you don't know me, my name is Bernard S. Fagin. I'm the Executive in Charge of the Santa Fe Railroad Kansas Expansion Project."

"Yeah, we know who ya are!" someone shouted from the audience. "Get on with it!" "We have questions!" others yelled out. Scott didn't envy Fagin.

The executive raised his hands.

"I want to tell you that we will always be committed to the survival of New Boston. That is the most important thing you need to understand about this announcement. We established this town and we will not abandon you. I'm speaking on behalf of all the board of directors when I say that there will always be an office of the Santa Fe Railroad here in New Boston."

Murmurs of approval went through the crowd.

"Even so, we are moving the railhead to Wichita in the spring."

Shouts took the place of the murmurs. "What have they got that we don't have?" "Why? You are abandoning us!" "You just said you wouldn't leave us!" "What does all this mean?"

He shook his head. Baker rose and stood next to Fagin. Meghan had told him a number of months ago that Baker was always a calming influence after Fagin made startling statements or proclamations.

Baker leaned over and whispered something in Fagin's ear. Fagin turned and sat in one of the three chairs. Baker then raised his hands to get their attention.

"We will answer every one of your questions. We're sorry we need to do this. It's a matter of economics. Wichita already has more population. They're also twenty-five miles closer to Texas. They have the Arkansas River, and a couple tributaries."

Yelling from the crowd started up again. Scott felt sorry for beleaguered Baker—worried they'd ask him to speak. What could he say?

Scott knew Warkentyne had a plan if the railroad left. He'd announced it at Christmas dinner. He hadn't heard anymore.

That still didn't tell him what he should say if they asked him to speak. Baker went on.

"Did you hear what Mister Fagin said? The Santa Fe Railroad will never abandon New Boston. There will always be an office here. Yes, the railhead is moving to Wichita, but there are plans to bring other avenues of prosperity to New Boston. We'll hear those ideas in a few minutes. But first, I'd like you to hear from one of your own."

His throat constricted. Uh-oh. Baker turned to him. He swallowed.

"Doctor Scott Allison. Would you come and address the town?" Scott swallowed again as his throat went dry.

Chapter Fifty-Six

Scott stood and walked toward Baker. "Listen to the wisdom of our town doctor." Mr. Baker introduced him.

Rose's heart thumped. Blood rushed through her. Dear Scott. He hadn't said anything about addressing the gathering. She turned to Olivia and Bernie. Their eyes were as wide as she figured hers were.

"What's he going to say?" Olivia whispered.

Rose shrugged, speaking softly. "I don't know."

Bernie smiled and spoke in low tones. "I hope he calls on me to share my plan."

She smiled and turned her attention to the man she loved.

Scott raised his hands and clapped for attention.

"Friends, I don't have a prepared speech. But I want to encourage you to listen to what the executives are really saying. Yes, the railhead is moving. Many of a certain sort of business will probably move with them."

"You're right about that!" someone guffawed behind her.

"Good riddance to them, too!" A woman's voice. Rose turned but couldn't tell who had said it. Must be someone people would consider "decent." How would they consider *her* if they knew who she was? It was a question she could never answer, yet in a way, she wanted to know. Wasn't this her sticking point in everything? This masquerade as a respectable woman, knowing she wasn't? Would marriage to Scott be enough to make her honorable? How could she know?

Scott's "doctor voice" continued. "Citizens of New Boston, we will survive. I know the mayor and city council are working hard to plan our future. Let's give them a chance." Rose loved his soothing tones. "Maybe you can have a positive say in what happens. If we all come together for the common good, we can move this town forward."

He paused a moment, as if listening to something, or a memory came to mind. "I know this change may be difficult. Many of us will wonder whether we should stay here or move to Wichita. Someone we know has a plan. He's been working on it for quite some time. I'm throwing my support behind him. You probably know who I'm talking about."

Scott turned to Fagin, who nodded. Looking directly at her...no...he was trying to make eye contact with Bernie. She turned. Bernie's eyes glistened, and he gave a slight nod.

"I'd like to formally introduce Bernhard Warkentyne to you all. He owns the mill."

Mutters went through the crowd. "He's a miller. How can he have a plan to save the town?" "A farmer?" "What will happen to the ranches?" "Yeah, if there aren't ranches..."

Scott clapped for attention again. "Please, listen to his plan. I believe it's the way we should go. We should support his ideas all the way."

Bernie stepped onto the small stage. Scott shook his hand, then turned and sat down. All three chairs on stage now had occupants.

Rose turned to look. Rail workers, cowboys, and dance hall gals stood and walked out.

What now?

Scott couldn't see Warketyne's face from his view, the back of the stage, next to Fagin and Baker. He let out a long breath. Had he done what God wanted? He hoped so.

Warkentyne ran a hand through his hair and cleared his throat. He spoke slowly, with deliberation.

"Friends—you know me. Thank you, Doctor Allison, for asking me—to—share my plan..."

Warkentyne turned and smiled, then turned to face the considerably smaller crowd.

"Neighbors, I own the mill. Many farmers live north of New Boston. I think you know this. I am Mennonite. I've written my homeland in Russia. In Germany, too. I ask people to come. I receive letters back. They—are coming."

Muttering went through the small gathering that was left. He caught Rose's gaze. Heat flushed through him. He dipped his chin to acknowledge her and couldn't help sending her a grin.

Warkentyne's voice carried. He was easy to listen to—a natural leader. No wonder his people followed him.

"Many write back. They tell me—they want to settle here—in a new land where tsar—won't rule them."

Scott turned toward the railroad executives. Fagin was stoic, but Baker smiled. Maybe they really did care about the town, but of course, money talks, and in this case, money from Wichita.

"My mill is first to come here. More blacksmiths will follow farmers. They build homes. Will need supplies, tools, and plows. They need oxen, milk cows, pigs, and chickens. Will bring seed for crops... wheat—maybe corn."

More murmuring through the crowd. It sounded like people were beginning to approve.

"Other business—factories—can start. More products made from scratch. We make our own—tools, clothes, food, anything."

Warkentyne looked down, then up at the remaining audience. "We trust God. He will provide for us—just like Israelites in wilderness. Is my plan. Thank you."

"But how do we know they'll really come?" "When will they get here?" "Will they be here by spring when the railroad moves?" He didn't recognize the voices.

Warkentyne lifted his hands to try to get their attention. The group quieted down.

"Please, I explain." Warkentyne took a deep breath and let it out. "People suffer—how you say—per-se-cu-tion—many years. I come first. See if this *gud* place to live." He glanced around. "I know I stay here. Yes, hard times. I tried to build mill early last year. It did not work. No farmers. Ranches north from here left to build Wichita. Land opened for farms."

Whispers went through the crowd.

"Farmers now build towns. But come here—to New Boston for important supplies—because of train."

"Yeah! That's why we got sick!" "They brought the grippe with 'em!" "Yeah! My whole family was ill!" "They aren't helping us!" "Yeah, let 'em stay where they are!"

Warkentyne held up his hands.

Scott had heard enough. The miller needed help. He stood and stepped to Warkentyne's side, clapping for attention.

"Stop it—all of you!" Scott clapped again. He turned to Warkentyne, speaking so that only the miller could hear. "Why don't you have a seat? I'll take it from here."

The group calmed. Scott looked each one in the eye. Most of the ones left were merchants, a few ranchers who decided to stay and listen, a few rail workers, probably middle management, Jackson, the station manager, and their workers, the blacksmith, those from the bakery, Decker and Nieman—owners of the Pioneer Store, the two ministers from the tent churches plus the Catholic priest, and his beloved Rose and Mrs. Baldwin. In all, only about twenty.

What could he possibly say in addition to what had already been said that would calm the fears of the townspeople?

Chapter Fifty-Seven

"Hannah, are you awake?" Bernie's gentle voice infiltrated her rest. She opened her eyes a crack, then all the way.

"How did the meeting go?" She sat up a bit straighter. The stack of pillows Olivia had brought made such a difference. That—and Dr. Allison's cough remedy. She suspected there was alcohol in it—she'd fallen asleep so fast. Almost immediately after she'd finished drinking it.

"Fine, just fine. How are you feeling?" Bernie pulled up the chair.

"A little better. I got some sleep."

"Gud. So glad!" Bernie's gaze seemed to pierce right through her, and yet it was gentle and kind. The little lines around his eyes when he smiled were endearing. What was she thinking? He was only a friend. He did ask to court her, though.

"You were going to tell me about the meeting."

"Yes. Hard sometimes, but gud in end."

"What happened?"

"Railroad announce railhead moving. You know this."

"Yes."

"Doctor get up and said town be good. He ask me to speak—about plan to bring Mennonite farmers."

"What did people think about that?"

"Afraid farmers bring grippe—then Doctor calm them."

"Will the farmers come, Bernie?"

He placed his hand on her arm a moment. "Yes, I already hear from some. They come—on their way—or come soon."

She let out a deep breath and smiled. "What will happen to the Harvey House?"

"Should be all right. Hotel guests and new people want gud place to eat."

She yawned. He stood to leave.

"I go and let you sleep more." He turned toward the door.

"Bernie."

He turned his head back to look over his shoulder.

"Thanks for telling me."

"You are welcome." He was so handsome. Dare she believe that they might have a future together? Sometime?

❦

Tulips and daffodils bloomed in late March as the longer days and warmer weather brought a peaceful period to New Boston. Rose always loved the spring flowers. She loved the scent of lilacs and magnolias, although there weren't many in Kansas. She remembered them from back East. She loved inhaling the sweet fragrant smell when the star-shaped magnolia blossoms flowered before turning to leaves. If it were possible, lilacs smelled even sweeter.

Hannah had recovered and seemed to have a new enthusiasm for life. She'd noticed this before, but the Mennonite miller, Bernie Warkentyne seemed to have taken a shine to Hannah. They seemed closer. Rose was glad, because try as they might, Hannah never did quite fit into the women's relationships at the boardinghouse. But she'd seen Hannah and Bernie together numerous times. The combination sounded good together. Like Meghan and Duncan, Scott and Rose.

One Saturday morning, after she and Meghan had finished their advanced mathematics lesson, they decided to go to the Pioneer Store and look at dress patterns for Meghan's wedding dress. Before the gunfights last summer, Meghan and Duncan had barely decided to marry. Meghan's father had given her an ultimatum to work for a year before she married anyone. Rose thought that strange, but Meghan had told her privately she was thankful her father had cared so much for her so much to insist she grow up more before marrying anyone. She'd admitted to acting childish and it took moving away from St. Louis to help her mature. Meghan's father was a gentle man. Rose wished he'd been *her* father, too.

She'd met both Meghan's and Duncan's fathers when they visited New Boston after Duncan was shot. Duncan's father cared—but seemed a bit more distracted. Meghan said he was the owner of a large brokerage house in New York. Rose didn't know what that was, but evidently it took a lot of his time.

As they neared the Pioneer Store, Rose couldn't help feeling excited for her friend, yet anxious about her own possible marriage to Scott. Meghan talked on about something, but she was so deep in thought, she missed the last sentence.

"Well?"

"What? I'm sorry, what did you say?"

"I said, what do you think about Venetian lace?"

Rose shook her head to clear it. "Oh, yes. Let's look for that, as well as Chantilly."

"What were you thinking about?" Meghan held the door open. Rose passed by and entered the store.

"Oh, nothing."

"Yes, you were. You were thinking about Scott—and your own wedding."

Rose's eyes widened. "How'd you know that?"

"I'm a woman in love. I can see that we're in the same condition."

She giggled. Meghan joined her.

They made their way to the back of the store to the fabric and notions area. They found a shelf with lace samples draped over the edge. Rolls were above the samples.

Meghan chose a roll of Venetian lace from the shelf and unrolled it a couple of rounds. It was about five inches wide, with swirls, curves, and netting between. Pure white.

"It's beautiful, Meghan." Rose fingered it a moment.

Meghan ran her fingers over it. "I like it. It will be beautiful as a bodice or starched for a collar. I want to see what Olivia thinks. After all, she's making the dress."

Rose swallowed. She wouldn't be wearing a beautiful dress like Meghan's. Maybe she'd wear the first decent dress she ever bought—the one with olive piping and small flowers. It still looked new. They hadn't set a date yet, but she knew Scott wanted to get married as soon as possible.

She still had to face her greatest fear. All she wanted to do was run from it. No, that wasn't true. She just wanted to live without fear of being discovered. But the only way to do that was to tell the town. Yet she couldn't bring herself to do it publicly. Only a few knew her real identity. She hadn't even told Hannah or Bernie yet.

An idea came. What if she told them first? She could gauge their reaction. Something to think about. Would she have the courage?

∽

Scott decided he would ask Rose that evening to set a date for their wedding. They should get married before Meghan and that cowb— Duncan. He was so used to referring to Wilcox as "Cowboy" or "that cowboy" it was hard to change. Wilcox had forgiven him for blackmailing Meghan. He'd been so gracious about it.

He looked at the calendar, knowing Meghan and Duncan weren't going to marry until June. It was nearly April already. Maybe in a month? May was a beautiful time of year here. Warm and pleasant without the heat of summer.

Yes, for certain. The month of May for marriage to his precious Rose. He hoped she would agree.

Chapter Fifty-Eight

That evening, when he called for her, Rose fingered her diamond ring and thought about what life with Scott might be like.

"Let's take a walk, shall we?"

"Certainly." She grabbed her shawl and slipped her hand beneath his elbow as they walked down First Street.

"Rose, I think we need to set a date."

She stopped. Breathing was hard.

"Why should we wait? You love me. I love you. Let's marry before Meghan and Duncan."

"But, Scott—"

"If you're still afraid of what the town will think, don't worry. You don't ever have to tell them if you don't want to. Let everyone continue to think that you are the beautiful, charming, loving, kind, and considerate Rose Rhodes. Rosalie O'Roarke is gone. She left after the tornado."

She inhaled deeply and let her breath out slowly. She would love nothing more than to do that, but if someone recognized her...?

He stroked her cheek with the back of his hand. "What do you think about Saturday, May fourth or the eleventh, for our wedding? That's five or six weeks from now, a month or more before Meghan and Duncan's wedding."

Rose swallowed. Could this really be happening? In five weeks, or six, she would be married? Dare she agree?

He pulled her to him and lowered his lips to hers. His touch lit a fire within her. She returned his kiss with all the love she held inside. He groaned and pulled her tighter, his hand running up and down her back. His other hand curled around the back of her head, holding it in place. She wrapped her hand around his neck and stroked through his hair, so soft, yet with a bit of pine oil scent.

Finally, he pulled back. She hadn't wanted the kiss to end, but he was an honorable man and had never tried to go too far with her. The respect he showed her caused her heart to nearly burst with love. No one had ever treated her like that before.

Yes, they should marry quickly.

"How about May fourth? It doesn't give us much time, but we don't need a fancy wedding, do we?" She looked into his eyes, searching.

"Marvelous! That will give my family time to make plans to attend. My mother may be slightly disappointed she won't have longer to plan, but she'll understand there's nothing to delay our wedding."

He kissed her again, then picked her up and twirled her around.

"Scott! Put me down, you silly!"

"Rose—you've made me the happiest man alive!"

He gently lowered her until her feet barely touched the sidewalk, holding her tight against him.

"Shall we go tell the rest of them at the boardinghouse?" Scott set her all the way down, but still held her. Safe in his arms. No wonder she loved him. He respected her. She'd never been so secure and protected in a man's arms. If no one learned her secret.

⁓

Rose couldn't remember when she'd felt so hopeful. As she and Scott entered the parlor, Hannah, who lounged on the couch, looked up.

"Good evening, Hannah." Scott sat in a wingback.

"Good evening, Doctor."

"Hello, Hannah." Rose smiled at Hannah, who returned it. "Is everyone around? We'd like to talk to them."

"Meghan and Mister Wilcox aren't back yet from their dinner out. Olivia and Luisa are in the kitchen. I can go get them, if you'd like."

"That's all right, I'll go." Rose turned to the kitchen, leaving Scott with Hannah.

A minute later, she returned with Olivia and Luisa just behind her. Just then, the front door opened, and Meghan and Duncan entered the parlor.

"Good. You're all here." Scott gestured for them to sit, while he stood and joined her at the doorway to the dining room.

"Bernie's not." Hannah evidently couldn't resist.

"You can tell him, then." She broadened her beam to encourage Hannah.

"Well, what is it?" Meghan stood in the doorway.

"We've set a date for our wedding." Scott couldn't wait.

"Oooo!" "When?" "Congratulations!" "I want to hear everything!"

Rose looked around. Hannah smiled. Meghan and Olivia practically shrieked with excitement. Luisa grinned and wished them well.

Scott gently prodded her.

"We've set the date for May fourth."

"That's before ours! Wonderful!" Meghan quickly moved to hug her.

"We didn't want to take away anything from your wedding. You'd have gotten married before now, except for your father's..."

"Other things were also considered." Duncan tilted his chin down.

"We're so very happy for you!" Olivia's gentle Virginia drawl was so pleasing to listen to. "You'll have the reception here, of course, won't you? Where will you be married? Who's going to perform the ceremony?"

Soft laughter erupted from both her and Meghan at the same time. Olivia always talked too much when she was nervous or excited.

"We'll be attending to those details in the coming days. Of course, we're going to need help from all of you." Scott put his arm around her shoulders and drew her close to his side.

How would all this work out? She didn't know, but hoped for the best.

Chapter Fifty-Nine

A week later, Rose and Scott were in the office. They'd made headway in the wedding arrangements. Rose couldn't remember a happier time. She hadn't told Madam but figured her mother probably knew anyway. It seemed like every patient wished them well, and the Pioneer Store owners, Misters Nieman and Decker, bent over backward to help her with wedding plans.

Only four weeks to go now. In just a month, she would be Mrs. Scott Allison. Duncan would perform the wedding ceremony. Amazing the change in relationship. Not quite friends but moving closer. No competition over the same woman anymore.

Scott had asked his older brother, Ned, to be best man. He would make the journey from Kansas City a few days before the wedding. Most of Scott's family would be attending, although Rose was certain he hadn't told them about her past.

Of course, she'd asked Meghan to be her maid-of-honor. There would be no other attendants. Both she and Scott wanted a smaller wedding.

Olivia would prepare the wedding reception and dinner at the boardinghouse. It wouldn't be a large affair. The only people they invited were their closest friends. Meghan was busy planning her own wedding but promised to help Rose with her plans. They talked about it in the parlor one Saturday morning.

"Rose, you simply must have a new dress."

"Why? It's not like I'm pure."

Meghan placed her hand on Rose's arm. "Because it's your wedding. It's special. What's your favorite color?"

Rose thought a moment. "Red."

Meghan giggled. "*You* can't have a red dress, but I can." She tilted her head to one side. "You could have a rose-colored dress, a mauve. That would be beautiful on you. It would be in the same color family as my dress, which won't be red, but maybe a burgundy or maroon. Or an ivory-cream dress."

"That's a great idea. I like the idea of a mauve dress. I can't begin to thank you for your friendship. You mean so much to me."

"You've taught me so much about the world, Rose. About people. I love you like a sister. I never had one."

"Neither did I."

Meghan reached over and hugged her. She'd never felt so loved before.

Scott had already made plans to add a second floor on to the office. It probably wouldn't be complete in time for the wedding, but mostly. Work had begun on expanding the office outward, to make a larger room for a small ward, when patients needed more attentive care. They'd noticed the need for this during the almost-epidemic.

She'd come to the office early this morning, to get things ready for the day. Scott was over at the hotel for breakfast when she heard a knock on the door.

She took a step back. Rafe.

"Wh-What are doing here? Scott's at breakfast."

He seemed to almost glide into the room. Different than the impression he was an old, grizzled cowboy when she'd first met him.

"Rosalie, God wants you to know that he loves you, and he's so proud of you changing your life. I've told you this before. Anytime you need him, he'll be there for you. Just call his name."

Tears came. "I've felt a lot of love in the last few days. Was that God?"

He smiled and a wave of something washed over her. Tangible, yet invisible. Almost like a blanket had been thrown over her shoulders. Warmth spread all through her.

"Reach out to him, Rose. You were born Rosalie. Now, you are Rose. A sweet fragrance—a beautiful blossom. When you reach out to God, he will heal your heart. You'll feel clean. Do you want that?"

She couldn't stop the tears running down her cheeks. "Yes."

Rafe drew closer and hugged her.

A dam burst inside her. From a distance, it seemed, she heard wailing like she'd never heard before. Anguish and sorrow poured from the deepest part of her. The part that had toughened her for survival. She realized she was the one weeping.

He guided her to the couch. Time stopped. After what seemed like hours, the tears began to let up. She took out her handkerchief and blew into it. Rafe handed her another one.

"Rose, do you believe that Jesus loves and wants you?"

She swallowed. "Does he really want me?"

"Yes, he does. He wants you to know he loves you so much Rose. Trust him. With life, there will be challenges ahead, but with Christ within you, you can face anything. God can be the strength of your heart and your life, if you'll only ask him."

"All right."

"Then ask. I'm your witness. I stand in the presence of God and I confirm your desire and his to enter your heart."

She prayed for the first time. Rafe touched her shoulder, and peace flooded her entire being. She'd never felt this way before. Not only peace...but...clean. For the first time since she was fourteen, she was unsoiled.

When she looked up to thank Rafe, he was gone.

Chapter Sixty

A few days later, a man in overalls burst through the medical office door. He didn't even knock. Scott was cleaning some instruments, glad he didn't drop any.

"Help, Doc! The train derailed!"

"Where? I didn't hear anything." Scott grabbed his bag and began shoving bandage rolls and medicines in it, then grabbed his coat.

"'Bout five miles... out of town... Brakes failed... engine ran off... cars followed..."

"Do Fagin and Baker know?"

"Went there first."

"All right. If you see the Santa Fe executives again, tell them we'll be there as soon as possible. Round up every wagon, buckboard, and buggy you can. Tell Fagin to meet me here immediately."

The man let out a breath. "You got it, Doc. Thanks." The man left.

He turned to Rose. "It looks like we'll be busy for quite a while."

She smiled. He loved how the corners of her mouth turned up. How her smile lit up her whole face. He stroked her cheek, wanting to kiss her in the worst way. But this wasn't the time.

"Yes, we will." She filled an extra pack with all kinds of supplies and extra instruments. "Should we stop by the boardinghouse and see if Olivia can help? Even if it's just to give us some food? Maybe she has extra blankets, too. It's cold out." It was mid-April, but a cold day.

He closed the temporary office door behind them and locked it. "That's a great idea."

Fagin raced up to them. "Hi, Doc. Glad I caught you!" He tried to catch his breath. "I wanted to let you know, I'm taking care of things." He bent over a moment, then raised himself up, having his breathing under better control. "I'm guessing you wanted to let me know what all needed to be done?"

"I did."

"We're trained in emergency disasters, Doc." A trace of a smile passed through his lips, genuine, not condescending. "I've sent Donald Baker ahead to all the saloons. He's recruiting men to help with heavy lifting. The women are invited to come help you—if they've a mind to."

"Thanks. That puts my mind at ease. And—could someone from the hotel bring blankets, sheets, and pillows?"

"I'll see to it." Fagin turned, then twisted his head. "See you out there, Doc." He nodded to Rose. "Miss Rose." He dashed away.

"Are you ready?"

She swallowed, then set her jaw.

"Yes."

⁓

When they reached the derailment site, Rose choked from escaping steam, smoke from the engine, and the stench of blood. The terrible cries of injured people and animals tugged at her heart as nothing ever had before. She'd never seen anything so devastating. Not even the seemingly never-ending gunfights compared to this.

The engine resembled an accordion—the back half wrinkled on top of the front. How could a heavy engine have gotten like that? Flames shot up into the air from fires started when logs fell out of the stove in the engine. Had the engineers made it out safely?

Railroad cars were crushed or severely damaged. They draped unceremoniously half on, half off the tracks. A few had completely fallen off the rail bed and lay on their sides, or upside down.

Track was twisted. As cars had been forced into each other, and the engine had fallen forward, pieces of rail had bent and bowed under the pressure.

"Move that beam!" "Lead those steers away from the tracks!" "Find a heavy blanket and put out that fire over there!" "Those of you who aren't too injured, help those who are get away from the train!" "Over here! A man has lost his arm!" "We need help! A woman is trapped!"

Scurrying men raced to assist those in need.

Mr. Fagin had arrived before them. "This way, Doc! We're putting the injured beyond the caboose." They'd stopped off at the boardinghouse, where Olivia made several sandwiches for them and filled a picnic basket with canned fruits and vegetables, biscuits, and salted meat. Everything they'd need for a day or two out at the wreck site.

"I'll bring more out as soon as Luisa and I get them made. Oh, this is just awful. What a calamity! How can the town recover? First the railhead moves, and now this. What are we supposed to do now?" Olivia talked continually again. Bless her heart.

Rose slid her hand in the crook of Scott's arm. The uneven ground made walking difficult.

They found the injured. A few dance hall girls helped people get settled on a blanket. One of them turned as she and Scott approached.

"There, ya see? Here they come now!" Nettie from the Silver Spike. Rose was glad to see her helping. Although the girl had been a trial at times... a light sleeper, yet she'd treated Rose better than many others.

The injured who were able to sit up did so.

Where to begin? As if in answer to her question, Scott raised his voice so all around him could hear.

"Everyone, please! May I have your attention?" As heads turned his way, people stopped to listen. He clapped his hands together.

"Thank you. We'll be treating the injuries according to severity. If you're bleeding, we'll examine you first. If you're helping someone who is unconscious, we'll get to you next. Broken bones are third. More minor injuries will be treated after that."

She let out a breath.

It was going to be a long day.

⁓

As the sun began to slip beyond the horizon, the temperature dropped further. Scott's fingers were so cold, he could barely feel the tips.

He'd set a dozen broken bones, operated on several cases of internal injuries, and bandaged more people than he wanted to think about. Rose had been at his side the entire time. They worked so well together. She expertly finished the stitching of the less serious wounds and completed closing surgical incisions.

She had to be exhausted, but she never complained.

One of the dance hall girls came over and whispered in her ear, then left. Her eyes grew wide, with panic.

"Rose, what's wrong?"

She stood. "I have to..." She looked like an animal caught in a trap. He'd seen that look too many times in the past few months... and when he thought he'd never see it again...

"Tell me what's wrong. Please." He put his hands on her shoulders.

She pulled away and started running down the tracks toward Florence, not New Boston. Since they'd just finished with the last patient needing special care, he was about to clean up. But Rose needed him.

What had that dance hall girl said to set her into such a panic?

⁓

"Rosie, so this is where ya've been hiding. In plain sight of all of us. Everyone knows who ya are. After all, Jake took ya twice. Did ya really think you could just change how you look and no one'd figure it out?"

She could hardly breathe. The world closed in on her. She had to get away. She'd just run and run—until she couldn't run anymore. Where—she didn't know. She needed to run. Scott must think she'd lost her mind.

Nettie said several people had recognized her. She couldn't go back to face the town.

Her worst fear had come upon her.

"Wait! Rose! Stop! Let's talk about this. Tell me what happened."

The last thing she wanted to do was stop. She wanted to flee until she hit San Francisco. Then realized that would take too long.

Maybe go to Denver, where no one knew her. Somewhere she could start over—once again.

Chapter Sixty-One

"Please, Rose!" Scott yelled at the top of his lungs. Everyone could hear him plead with her.

She'd gotten about a hundred yards away before she finally stopped.

Defeat and discouragement threatened to choke the life from her. Her eyes filled with tears, which overflowed.

She'd felt so clean—was it only a couple of weeks ago? When God...

They were now far enough away from the derailment that no one would hear them. Ashamed, she looked down at her dirty hands, then wiped them on her apron. And kept rubbing. She felt so filthy. As if being around all the devastation today had caused everything she'd ever gone through to come back and haunt her.

The pain of the first time when she was fourteen. The erosion of her soul over the years thereafter. Especially the deception with Jake to escape. How could she ever hope to change her life? She'd tried so hard. Look where it had gotten her.

People had respected her as they did Meghan. She'd wanted that with all her heart and soul. To be esteemed as a person, not an object of pleasure. To be loved by a wonderful man. At least she had that now. Scott, even with his past wrong, loved her. And she loved him.

And God...

What would happen now? Everyone knew who she was and what she'd been. Would they throw her out of town, like Madam said they would?

"Rose, dear, what's the matter? Please tell me." Scott gently took the hand Rose kept wiping on her dress. *God, please help me.* She pulled it away.

Tears ran down her cheeks. He put his arm around her shoulders and drew her to him. She sobbed.

She fingered the ring on her left finger and tugged on it. *No. Don't do this, Rose.* He placed his hand on top of hers.

"Leave it on, please."

Her shoulders shook. "I—can't."

"Yes, you can."

She finally met his gaze. Oh, the agony in her eyes. How could he soothe it? What could he say? Any joy she'd exhibited lately seemed to be slipping away.

"Please tell me what that woman said." He fumbled one-handed with his handkerchief and dabbed her cheeks.

"She-she said everyone knows who I am... and that the whole town recognized me. Because J-Jake took me twice."

Scott gave her arm a squeeze, then removed his arm from around her but held her hand. "Do you believe her?"

"She said..."

"Let's go find out, shall we? Most of the town is there. We need to go back anyway. There will be more injured found by that time. They'll wonder why we ran off."

"I—I don't know if I can face them."

"Of course you can. You're a strong woman, Rose. I love you with all my heart. I'll be right by your side."

"You probably haven't even told your family about me... my past."

"Yes, I have."

She turned to face him, eyes and mouth wide open. "Y-you did?"

He couldn't help smiling. "I wouldn't keep something like that from my family. They needed to know who you were before they can know who you are now."

"But what about your mother? Wasn't she angry?"

"A little at first. She thought I was marrying a soiled dove. I explained how you never wanted that life." No response.

He squeezed her hand. "She understood and had compassion for you. As you know, most of my family is coming to the wedding."

Still, she said nothing.

"Mother can't wait to meet you." He looked over, but she wouldn't meet his gaze. "Come on, let's go see what they say."

⁓

A fresh round of tears and weeping hit Rose. She couldn't stop. Scott was the most wonderful man she'd ever met. Everything she had ever dreamed or hoped for in a husband. And his family accepted her! Even her past.

Rose, don't be afraid. You have new life. My life within you. Trust me.
That was the first she'd ever heard God's voice inside her.

They headed back to the disaster.

She hoped more misfortune wasn't ahead for her.

As they reached the derailment, more people were brought to them, and they continued to treat the injured, until they ran out of supplies. They'd need to go back to town to replenish.

Mr. Fagin came up to her and Scott. "Thanks, Doctor Allison, for all your hard work today. And you too, Miss Rose." He leaned in and spoke softly. "Miss Rose, I want you to know that Nettie's whispers are just that. Gossip. We know how hard you've worked."

She took a deep breath, then let it out. "Mister Fagin, what Nettie said is—true."

"Most of us have known it all along, but we didn't want to embarrass you. We all wondered why Jake took you. Why *you*? It had to be because you were Rosalie O'Roarke. But you were trying so hard to be respectable. We just let you do it."

Her eyes misted up—again.

Mr. Fagin turned to the crowd of those gathering around them.

"Hey, everyone! Our Rosalie has come back to us! She wants to be called Rose now. Is that all right with you?"

Rose put a hand over her mouth, trying to hold back her emotion. She could hardly see through the tears. What would the people say? How would they react? She was about to find out.

Mr. Baker came up and shook her hand. "Miss Rhodes, we all need the grace of God. I don't judge your past. You've worked hard to become a new person. We know about the madam, too. It doesn't matter to us."

Tears ran down her cheeks. She couldn't stop them.

Olivia came and hugged her. When did she get here? "Dearie, you know how I feel about you. You are such a precious member of our boardinghouse. We're going to miss you when you marry our handsome doctor."

Michael Nieman and Richard Decker of the Pioneer Store walked up. Both shook her hand, then Mr. Decker spoke.

"Why do you think we've been working so hard with you to help you plan your wedding? We're proud of you, and we were honored you came to us for your wedding needs."

Mr. Decker glanced over to Mr. Nieman, who nodded. "We want you to have an ivory wedding gown—as our gift to you."

Her breath caught. "Oh no! That's too generous! I can't accept that!"

Scott put his arm around her shoulder. "Of course, you can, dear. It's a gift."

"But, I'm not—"

Mr. Nieman added, "We want you to have the cream-colored. You'll look so pretty in it. We figured you'd be more comfortable with that color. Come by after things settle down here a bit. We'll show it to you."

She took her handkerchief from her sleeve and blew her nose. Scott took his arm from around her shoulders, turned to her and wiped her tears with his thumbs. Yet she couldn't stop crying for more than a moment.

The mayor and members of the town council stepped near. Each one graciously received her. It was overwhelming.

They welcomed her as if she had just stepped off the train. What a miracle! Truly God had done this.

Chapter Sixty-Two

Scott couldn't have been happier with the outcome from the town after they admitted they'd known since Jake kidnapped her that she was Rosalie O'Roarke.

The derailment had caused delay in the shipping of materials. The rail itself was gnarled beyond repair. The railroad executives had their blacksmiths working hard on it, but it wasn't the same. Not all the dents could be removed. New rail had to be ordered from the East. This disaster was costing the railroad money. They couldn't afford the expensive rail from Wales for repair.

A knock on the door revealed Jackson. "Hey, Doc, got a telegram for ya."

"Thanks, Jackson."

"Ya ain't gonna like it."

Scott held the envelope in his hand, then removed the message inside and read it.

RAIL SERVICE TO NEW BOSTON SUSPENDED FOR THREE WEEKS. STOP. WE STILL WANT TO ATTEND WEDDING. STOP. PLEASE ADVISE. STOP. NED

Scott pulled out a dime and handed it to Jackson. "You're right. I don't like it."

"Whatcha gonna do, den, Doc?"

"I don't know. Rose and I will have to discuss this."

"Say, Doc. Y'all tell Rosie I say she always been a Rose to me."

Scott smiled. "Thanks, Jackson. I know she'll appreciate hearing that."

He knew his brother wouldn't be able to get off work again for at least two months. That would put their wedding in July at the earliest.

They'd both been anticipating getting married soon. And even though it would be a small wedding, he still wanted his family to be there.

How would Rose take this latest development?

༄

Rose had invited Meghan to go with her to the Pioneer Store, to see the gown the partners were offering her, and to pick out something for Meghan to wear at the wedding. At the same time, Meghan would be picking out the dress Rose would wear as bridesmaid for the June wedding.

It was already late April. Her heart hitched. In just two weeks...she'd be Mrs. Scott Allison. She could hardly wait.

"Is Rose here? I need to talk to her. It's important." Scott sounded upset.

She turned. "I'm back here."

He joined them. "Meghan, can I borrow my fiancée for a minute?"

Meghan smiled and moved away.

"Rose, I have some bad news." The corners of his mouth curled down. "I'm sorry."

"What happened?"

"My family can't make the wedding."

"What are you saying?"

"Let's postpone until July or late June."

"Oh no! Why?"

"With the derailment, and the railhead move, things are delayed. Even our office project is behind. I want my family here. It's only a couple months. We'll be busy with preparations anyway." He trailed the back of his fingers down her cheek. "And you've Meghan to help... be her bridesmaid."

She gripped a support beam nearby. "Oh Scott. This is just terrible."

"It doesn't have to be. We'll have more time... it might be a blessing in the end."

Yes, it could be. Meghan should be married before her. She and Duncan had waited longer to fulfill the terms of her father's ultimatum.

He moved to her side, putting his arm around her shoulders. "Have you talked with your mother yet?"

"No."

"You're still having trouble forgiving her?"

"Yes, but I am trying."

"Remember, it's a decision. You don't even have to tell her if you don't want to. Just make that choice in your heart. God will know it." He gently turned her to face him. "He will heal your heart."

She hadn't told him all that had happened that day of Rafe's last visit. She'd only told him she'd prayed for the first time. He'd been so happy for her he jabbered on about reading the Bible, and other things she wasn't quite ready to hear. She had started reading the Bible. Meghan had suggested starting with the gospel of John. She loved getting to know her savior through the words of the apostle. There were lots of things she hadn't thought of before and didn't understand. That God himself had become human. She loved verse twelve of the first chapter of John. "But to as many as received him, to them gave he power to become the sons of God, even to them that believe on his name..." She believed in Jesus now. She'd heard his voice in her spirit just a couple of weeks ago. He'd made her feel untainted, loved, and accepted for the first time since she was fourteen.

"Scott, will you pray with me that I can do this?" But with her limited knowledge of God, would the almighty hear that prayer?

༄

The morning of June fifteenth, the day of Meghan's wedding, was perfect. Rose couldn't be happier for her friend. She stepped into the Kelly green satin dress with taffeta over the bodice, and in layers over the skirt part. Lace at the sweetheart neckline with layered taffeta sleeves with lace at the ends completed the dress. This was Meghan's day. Olivia's dress was similar, but a darker green. She wasn't sure about the color at first, but found it worked well with her light complexion, even though her hair was dark. She felt Irish in this dress, but knew it was purely coincidental. Meghan loved the color, and since she was the bride...

The ceremony would take place under Duncan's tree. The tent he used for church gatherings was pitched a short distance away. Both fathers had arrived a couple of days ago. Everyone seemed to get along so well. Rose remembered that they'd met before—last September after Duncan was shot. He had totally recovered, she was thankful.

His preaching was so different than anything she'd ever heard in either of the other two tent churches. He spoke of loving God with all your heart, mind, soul, and strength. God was someone you could know personally. Someone to be experienced, not a faraway, ethereal God who didn't care, but who loved and was interested in everything concerning her. She'd learned a lot in the last six months since he'd started that church. She and Scott attended nearly every Sunday.

She hadn't sought out Madam to tell her she'd forgiven her. In her heart, she'd accepted the sacrifice Jesus did for her. Both Duncan and Meghan had said the important thing was to make the decision to forgive Madam. To release Madam, not from guilt, but for her own heart. The decision didn't vindicate her mother, it allowed Rose to move forward. She'd made progress but wasn't quite ready to make that decision.

Meghan said she didn't have to feel it. How could she decide to do something she didn't feel right about?

She looked toward the tree. Duncan stood there in a handsome black suit and burgundy string tie. His boss, Mr. McMasters, stood next to him as best man. Duncan's father stood next to Mr. McMasters as groomsman. The preacher was someone Duncan said helped him come to the Lord in Kentucky. He'd arrived by train two days ago.

Rose had heard about Duncan's brother drowning when they were children. In fact, Duncan had shared that one Sunday morning. About his guilt, and how he'd finally been healed of it—and how he had reconciled with his father. Duncan had to forgive himself.

It had made a huge impression on Rose and started her own healing process. Maybe she could forgive Madam.

The music started. She waited until Olivia was standing near the preacher, before she began her slow walk toward the tree.

Chapter Sixty-Three

From where she sat, Hannah could see everything. Two sections of benches were set under a lovely shade tree she'd heard called Duncan's Tree. Each section had about ten benches. A fiddler from the hotel played a lovely, but noble tune. Everyone turned their heads.

First Olivia, then Rose strolled with slow, deliberate steps toward the tree, where the preacher, Duncan, Mr. McMasters, and a man who was obviously Duncan's father stood. Once there, Rose turned and faced where she'd come from.

The fiddler changed the tune. Everyone stood and turned to face the bride.

Meghan was stunning in her beautiful white gown with Venetian lace, her hand under her father's elbow. It seemed Meghan glowed with a joy that Hannah knew nothing of. She didn't know what it was like to be *in* love. Not yet. Although she could see possibilities with Bernie. They needed to know each other much better first.

Her breath caught as Meghan passed by. The details of her gown were spectacular... the lace, the satin, the taffeta. Sequins were sown over tiny gauze florets on the bodice. She hadn't noticed those before. Maybe they were a last-minute addition.

The music stopped, and everyone sat.

The preacher opened the little book he held.

"Dearly beloved, we are gathered here today in the sight of God and the presence of these witnesses, to join together Meghan Elizabeth Gallagher and Duncan Clarke Wilcox, in holy matrimony, which is an honorable estate, instituted by God. It is not to be entered into unadvisedly, but reverently, discreetly, and in the fear of God. Into this holy estate these two persons come now to be joined."

She smiled, so glad for Meghan.

⁓

Rose couldn't stop smiling. Such a happy day. Even though her own wedding was postponed for another three weeks, she was very happy for Meghan.

The preacher turned his gaze to Meghan's father. "Who gives this woman to this man?"

"I do." He gently uncrooked his arm from Meghan's hand, then placed her hand in Duncan's and turned away.

A moment later, the preacher continued. "Duncan Clarke Wilcox, will you take Meghan Elizabeth Gallagher to be your wife, to live together in holy marriage? Will you love her, comfort her, honor and keep her, in sickness and in health, and forsaking all others, be faithful to her as long as you both shall live?"

"I do."

A tear ran down Rose's cheek. She wiped it away. The look on Meghan's face was pure peace and delight—at the same time. Amazing.

"Meghan Elizabeth Gallagher, will you take Duncan Clarke Wilcox to be your husband, to live together in holy marriage? Will you love him, comfort him, honor and keep him, in sickness and in health, and forsaking all others, be faithful to him as long as you both shall live?"

Meghan smiled a moment. "I do."

Then came the vows.

"I, Duncan, take you, Meghan, to be my wife—according to God's holy will. I will love you...and share my life with you...In sickness and in health...In poverty and in prosperity...In conflict and in harmony...As long as we both shall live."

Full sentences—subjects and verbs. How far Duncan had come! It was Meghan's turn.

Soon, it would be *her* chance to say these vows. As she heard everything today, she absorbed the declarations of love, the promise of fidelity and faithfulness until death. The words struck her hard. No one had ever said those to her, not even in a general sense.

"I, Meghan, take you, Duncan, to be my husband...according to God's holy will. I will love you...and share my life with you...In sickness and in health...In poverty and in prosperity...In conflict and in harmony...As long as we both shall live."

As long as we both shall live. She and Scott would be standing here in only three weeks, saying these same words.

Waves of gentle love washed over her. She sensed God's presence. A tear ran down her cheek. Love for Madam that she hadn't felt in years flushed through her. Anger and bitterness left. Yes, Madam had done wrong, but she could release her now. The memories of betrayal were still there, yet Rose felt she could let go of the pain now.

God, help me to do this.

Another tear furrowed its way down.

She didn't bother to wipe it.

⁓

Scott stood at the back of the group of about forty to fifty attendees, watching the wedding. Meghan and Duncan were very gracious to invite him. Meghan and he were friends again. God had changed his heart, and hers, too. He was thankful. Chuckling to himself, he remembered something Meghan had said all those months ago about the right woman being under his nose.

Rose was the right woman for him. He couldn't wait until their own wedding. Three weeks from now.

⌒

"I now pronounce you—man and wife." The preacher turned to Duncan. "You may kiss the bride."

Rose let out a long breath. Meghan was now Mrs. Duncan Wilcox. She'd been smiling so much surely her jaw would crack, she was so happy for Meghan. Only nine short months ago, it hadn't looked like this wedding would ever occur.

She thought of her own part in that. Scott needed someone to correct him. What he'd done to Meghan was wrong. It took Meghan a while, but she'd forgiven Scott and their friendship was restored. Could she have that with Madam?

"Ladies and gentlemen, may I present to you, Mister and Missus Duncan Wilcox."

The fiddler struck up the familiar tune. Meghan and Duncan hurried down the center and took up places at the back—out in the open near the pitched tent. The tent had been put up in case of rain, and for church tomorrow, but the mild day was perfect.

Rose took the proffered arm of Duncan's father as they proceeded down the aisle amid claps and cheers for Meghan and Duncan. What a wonderful wedding.

She found Meghan hugging Olivia, who didn't seem to want to release their friend. A bit of jealousy flushed through her—but only for a moment. Olivia had been Meghan's first friend here, just as Meghan was *her* first real friend.

Later, after everyone had hugged the bride and shaken the hand of the groom, Rose climbed into Scott's buggy to head for the boardinghouse and the reception Olivia and Luisa were holding for the wedding party and honored guests. She didn't know how everyone was going to fit in the dining room and parlor. Olivia said at least thirty-to-forty people were expected... the railroad executives, a few ranch hands, families of some of the schoolchildren, and people from their church.

"I don't know where we'll fit them all." Olivia had scratched her head earlier. "But we'll find a way. Goodness, maybe I should take out all the furniture and let people stand and eat. No, that's not right. People can't eat dinner standing up. It's not proper."

Rose giggled. "Well, people could sit in the parlor. Could we get some trays, maybe from the hotel?"

Olivia looked at her like she'd sprouted a whiskey bottle from the top of her head.

⁓

It had all worked out somehow. Some people came and went quickly, without eating, especially those with small children. By the time dinner was ready, the dining room and parlor were still full of people, but everyone at least had a place to sit. Some had their plates on their laps, but Olivia had made easy-to-eat foods that could be scooped with a spoon or speared with a fork. No knives were needed. That helped.

"Rose, would you take a walk with me?" Scott had never left her side all afternoon. They'd not had a private moment except the buggy ride from the wedding to the boardinghouse.

"Of course."

They walked toward town once they got to Main Street.

Scott was quiet. She'd tried to gauge his mood, but he was quite adept at masking his feelings when he wanted to.

When they reached Madam Margaret's he stopped.

"Why did you bring me here?" She could hardly catch her breath for panic.

"We won't stay—not if you don't want to." His eyes shone with love, his voice tender and kind.

Now was the time. "No, it's all right. I—I need to do this."

They stepped inside to the smells of various tobaccos, to strong odors of whiskey and other liquors. After today, she would never set foot in here again—unless her mother asked for her. But now, she wanted to do this, seeing how reconciliation could heal. She needed healing. So did Mother. She hadn't called Madam that for years. Maybe she could now.

She felt so clean, released from a prison of shame and guilt, yet knowing without God in her life, she could never hope to be redeemed.

Redemption was a word she never understood before. Because of God's grace, she'd been saved, not only from her numerous sins, but from Jake's clutches—twice.

Twice God had redeemed her and set her free. Duncan preached that whom Jesus sets free—they're free! Not a captive to their old way of life. A prisoner no more. Made clean by believing in Christ. Invisible shackles fell off. Could she fly? She could—almost.

God had brought her and Scott together. They'd survived his broken leg, her captivity, her worst fear, and they'd come through "as silver." That's what Duncan had preached about last Sunday.

Scott put his hand on her back and gently guided her forward. "Is Madam Margaret here?"

One of the girls pointed upstairs.

Scott kissed her cheek. "I'll be right here when you come down."

"Won't you come with me?" How could she do this alone?

"I have every confidence in you."

She grabbed the banister and mounted the stairs.

At the end of the hallway, she knocked. A door opened.

"Hello, Mother."

THE END

Acknowledgements

Book number two! I can hardly believe it! And yet, I'm living it. So much has happened since *Meghan's Choice* was released last year. I can only hope that wonderful things are ahead for this story.

Rose's story was more difficult to tell because of her past. She gets a bombshell from her mother about her origins. That's a story very close to home to me. Only Rose took the news a lot worse than I did.

There are some true events and name borrowing for this story. The railhead did move from Newton, Kansas to Wichita in 1872. And I named the sheriff after a wonderful actor of the past who played the sheriff in television's "Laramie," Stuart Randall. In 2017, I had the flu twice. Hannah and Meghan both shared my bouts of flu.

As always, I thank my friends and crit partners Jeannine Brummett and Justina Luther who helped with this project.

I thank each of you readers, and I am thankful to *all* my friends and relatives, both the "ones I grew up with" and my "biologicals." I love you *all*. Whether you're a new or old friend, know that I appreciate you.

My agent, Cyle Young, who opened up a great door for me this year to become managing editor at Almost an Author.com, and Jim Hart, I'm thankful for this chance for publication. And Elizabeth Kim, who is indispensable in the book publishing process, walking and talking me through it all. Thank you.

DiAnn Mills and Sandra Byrd, my two CWG mentors, I wouldn't be here without you. Thank you for sharing your knowledge of writing and helping me in so many ways.

And last, but *most importantly*, my precious, fabulous, extremely wonderful husband, Kirby. He is such a support to me, in so many ways, I can't begin to say thank you and I love you so much.

About The Author

Donna L.H. Smith was born and raised in Kansas, but now lives in Lancaster County, Pennsylvania. She and her husband Kirby have been married thirty years.

Donna was born again in 1970, when God showed her He could be known by heart. She was raised in the church, but really had no idea she could have a personal relationship with Christ. A young man once asked her if she'd ever experienced God. She didn't have an answer to that. It wasn't long before God revealed Himself through His presence. She relays that experience in *Meghan's Choice*.

She has a B.S. in Telecommunications and an M.A. in Mass Communications. Her love affair with writing started in college in a scriptwriting class and continued, on and off, through different kinds of writing including educational media, marketing/public relations and both print and broadcast journalism.

Currently she serves as Managing Editor for an award-winning website for writers called Almost an Author (www.almostanauthor.com). She teaches workshops on writing at conferences and loves to encourage new writers of all ages.

Professionally speaking, she's worked at numerous jobs over the years, from secretarial to balloon decorating. She established an online homemade organic chocolate truffle business from her home for seven years. Her interests include music, drama, classic TV and movies. At her local church, she serves on ministry team and as a greeter. In 2019, she hopes to establish weekend retreats to help bring inner healing to people that especially suffer from rejection issues, something she knows a lot about.

Her vision for writing: To write compelling stories that change peoples' lives and point them to Christ.

You can visit her at: http://donnalhsmith.com. Find her on:

Facebook: Donna L.H. Smith—Stories Are My Passion.

Twitter: @donnalhsmith

LinkedIN: Donna L.H. Smith.

Email: dlhswriter@windstream.net Sign up for her newsletter at the email address.

If you've read her books, please consider leaving a review. Authors need to know how their readers feel.

Don't miss the other books in the Known by Heart series!

Meghan's Choice: An unusual ultimatum. A young woman's bold journey. Two handsome men. An amazing God. That's *Meghan's Choice.*

Meghan Gallagher complies with her father's demand that she work on her own for a year by choosing to tutor eight children in a wild Kansas railroad town. But she had no idea just how wild it was until she was hit by a stray bullet and rescued by a local dance hall girl. In short order, she meets a dark, handsome cowboy and a wholesome, attractive doctor who both vie for her heart. As things heat up around town, Meghan's love life catches fire as well. Is she scandalous to allow both men to court her at the same time? And—how close a relationship with God does Meghan want? Will she draw near?

Pre-publication, *Meghan's Choice* was named a semi-finalist in the 2014 Operation First Novel by Jerry B. Jenkins and an honorable mention for the Golden Leaf Award in 2015. Published, it was a 2018 Selah Finalist in the Western category and 2018 Will Rogers Medallion Finalist.

Hannah's Hope: Hannah is working as a Harvey Girl at the local restaurant when she meets Bernie Warkentyne, who is struggling to build a mill and attract additional Russian Mennonite farmers to the area in the wake of the railhead moving to Wichita. With good news springing up all over, it looks like the town of New Boston is finally settling down when a swarm of locusts descends, eating everything in its path. As the town works together rebuild, Harvey House Restaurant prepares to close its doors, and Hannah will need to find some other means to support herself. Will Bernie's offer of marriage be the way out for her?

If you liked this book, you might also
like these other Hartline books:

Kacy Barnett-Gramckow's *The Blessing:* May Somerville has suffered a year worthy of the Bible's Job, and the man who unknowingly prompted all her troubles has fallen in love with her. Isolated in Colorado's rugged mountains, her beloved family shattered by tragedy and loss, May questions her Creator amid her struggles to survive. Beset by unexpected storms, both physical and spiritual, May seeks blessings—reasons for hope as she works to restore her family. Separated from May by unforeseen circumstances and the expectations of others, Alex Whittier is determined to reverse injustices suffered by the Somervilles. But is it too late to redeem himself for the sake of the courageous young woman he's been unable to forget?

Patricia Riddle-Gaddis's *Escape to the Biltmore:* It's 1895. Beautiful Dr. Anna St. James has won the battle to earn the M.D. after her name when her father dies, suddenly throwing her into great debt. After moving to a shabby boarding house on the Lower East Side of New York, Anna receives a marriage proposal that would cancel her father's debt but would chain her to a man she neither loves nor trusts. Desperate to escape, she applies for a position at a TB clinic in Asheville, North Carolina, close to the home of her friend, Daphne Vanderbilt, who invites her to spend Christmas celebrations at Biltmore Estate. On her journey Anna meets the handsome Dr. Richard Wellington. She is captivated by the dashing British physician, but she soon becomes convinced that he is like every other male physician at a time when the American Medical

Association does not admit female doctors into its membership. Can they put aside their differences and allow their love to flourish?

Kay Moser's *Christine's Promise:* When the novella opens, Christine Boyd is the envy of all the ladies in Riverford, Texas, in 1885. She is, after all, the daughter of a revered Confederate general and the wife of wealthy banker, Richard Boyd. Beautiful, wealthy, elegant—she exhibits the exquisite manners she was taught in antebellum Charleston. She is the perfect southern lady. Or is she? The truth is that Christine's genteel outward demeanor hides a revolutionary spirit. When she was ten years old and fleeing Union-invaded Charleston, she made a radical promise to God. She plans to keep that promise. Tradition-bound Riverford, Texas, will never be the same.

Made in the USA
Middletown, DE
03 December 2018